"Barbara Metzger knows how to mix a dash of the ridiculous with her tried-and-true romantic instincts."
—*Romantic Times* (Top Pick, 4½ stars)

Raves for Barbara Metzger's romances

"Funny and touching . . . delicious, delightful!"
—Edith Layton

"A doyen of humorous Regency-era romance writing. . . . Metzger's gift for recreating the flavor and ambience of the period shines here, and the antics of her dirty-dish villains, near villains, and starry-eyed lovers are certain to entertain."
—*Publishers Weekly* (starred review)

"The complexities of both story and character contribute much to its richness. Like life, this book is much more exciting when the layers are peeled back and savored."
—*Affaire de Coeur*

"A true tour de force. . . . Only an author with Metzger's deft skill could successfully mix a Regency tale of death, ruined reputations, and scandal with humor for a fine and ultimately satisfying broth. . . . A very satisfying read."
—The Best Reviews

"[She] brings the Regency era vividly to life with deft humor, sparkling dialogue, and witty descriptions."
—Romance Reviews Today

"Metzger has penned another winning Regency tale. Filled with her hallmark humor, distinctive wit, and entertaining style, this is one romance that will not fail to enchant."
—*Booklist* (starred review)

"Delightful [and] fun."
—Under the Covers

SIGNET ECLIPSE

Published by New American Library, a division of
Penguin Group (USA) Inc., 375 Hudson Street,
New York, New York 10014, USA
Penguin Group (Canada), 90 Eglinton Avenue East, Suite 700, Toronto,
Ontario M4P 2Y3, Canada (a division of Pearson Penguin Canada Inc.)
Penguin Books Ltd., 80 Strand, London WC2R 0RL, England
Penguin Ireland, 25 St. Stephen's Green, Dublin 2,
Ireland (a division of Penguin Books Ltd.)
Penguin Group (Australia), 250 Camberwell Road, Camberwell, Victoria 3124,
Australia (a division of Pearson Australia Group Pty. Ltd.)
Penguin Books India Pvt. Ltd., 11 Community Centre, Panchsheel Park,
New Delhi - 110 017, India
Penguin Group (NZ), cnr Airborne and Rosedale Roads, Albany,
Auckland 1310, New Zealand (a division of Pearson New Zealand Ltd.)
Penguin Books (South Africa) (Pty.) Ltd., 24 Sturdee Avenue,
Rosebank, Johannesburg 2196, South Africa

Penguin Books Ltd., Registered Offices:
80 Strand, London WC2R 0RL, England

First published by Signet Eclipse, an imprint of New American Library,
a division of Penguin Group (USA) Inc.

First Printing, June 2006
10   9   8   7   6   5   4   3   2

Also by Barbara Metzger

Jack of Clubs
Ace of Hearts
The Duel
A Perfect Gentleman
Wedded Bliss

M

Queen of Diamonds

BARBARA METZGER

A SIGNET ECLIPSE BOOK

To the Yankees, for the good times
through the bad times

CHAPTER ONE

1800

"**M**ama!"

The gunshot woke Lady Charlotte Endicott from her nap in Nanny's arms. Now Nanny was shrieking and Mama was reaching across the carriage for Lottie. Another shot rang out, and loud, angry voices. The horses were galloping faster than Lottie had ever gone. Papa would be angry. He was an earl and everyone listened to his orders.

The coach was rocking, and then sliding, falling, tumbling, crashing down a steep cliff.

So much noise, then silence.

Lottie crawled from the debris, clutching her doll, unaware of the blood on her pinafore or the cuts on her face. Nanny's black boots stuck out from under the roof of the broken carriage. One of the horses was standing, blowing. The others were tangled and still, but Lottie would not look at them.

Mama never answered her calls.

Then a man came scrambling down the cliff from where the road was. He was the new groom, not Neddy, who'd promised to help Lottie name the pony that would be waiting for her at home at Carde Hall. Neddy'd been too sick to leave Kingston upon Hull with them after Grandfather Ambeaux's funeral.

This man was using bad words. His leg was bleeding, too, and he was limping. He looked around, then looked up and back, as if he was listening for the baggage coach that was following them. Then he saw Lottie.

"Bloody hell. The brat."

Lottie backed away, but stumbled over one of the broken wheels. The man grabbed her by the back of her gown and picked her up, doll and all.

"Do you know my name?"

Lottie nodded. "Dennis Godfrey. Nanny told me. I'm not s'posed to stare at your gold tooth."

"Damn and blast." He set her down and took a pistol from his belt. "I'm going to hang for this day's work anyway. Might as well make it harder for your papa to find me." The pistol was empty, though. While he reloaded, Dennis Godfrey stared at the child, thinking. "A'course, your papa might pay a king's ransom to get you back. They say Carde's got it. And he mightn't be so quick to send the sheriff or the militia after me, iffen your life depends on it." He tucked the gun back in his belt and squatted on his heels in front of Lottie, letting out a groan from the pain in his injured leg. He ripped the kerchief off his neck to wrap around the bullet wound. While he tied a knot he said, "Today must be your lucky day, little lady. Uncle Dennis is going to take you with me."

He was a servant, not a relative. Lottie shook her head. "No, I wait here for Papa."

Godfrey slapped her.

No one had ever struck Lady Charlotte Endicott in all of her three years. The shock and pain on top of everything else was too much. Lottie forgot to be brave, the way Papa had taught her. She was just a little girl, a baby, almost, and she wanted her mother. She wanted to go home.

She started to sob.

Dennis Godfrey grabbed her shoulders and shook her. "None of that, now. You're coming with me and that's the end of it, you hear? You play your cards right—the Earl of Carde, eh?—and you'll be snug as a bug as soon's I get my blunt. One sound out of you, though, one word to anyone, and you'll never see your family again. I'll hide you so far away no one will find you. Do you understand?"

He was still shaking her, but Lottie managed to say, "My brothers'll find me." Her adored older brothers always found her when they played hide-and-go-seek.

"You carry on, or you talk to anyone, or you tell my name or yours, and I'll find your precious brothers and shoot them dead!" He gave her a last, harder shake. "Like shooting rabbits. And I'll string them out for the vermin to find. Rats and crows and worms and—"

Lottie went limp in his arms.

"Good. Less bother this way." Dennis Godfrey rolled Lady Charlotte in his frieze coat, tossed her over the back of the one standing horse, and fled before anyone knew of that day's awful disaster.

To ensure the brat's silence, Godfrey added laudanum to his threats. He got the bottle from the same filthy-handed leech who dug the coach driver's pistol ball from Godfrey's leg a day later. The small-town sawbones, who acted as barber, undertaker. and veterinarian, also traded a sturdy mare and saddle for the highbred carriage horse, no questions asked.

The cutthroat turned kidnapper, who acted as groom, hired bully, and occasional highwayman, rode on toward London after sending a message back to Kingston upon Hull. Dennis Godfrey took byways and back roads when he could, traveling by night when the moon lit the way, giving no answers to anyone foolish enough to inquire about his haste or his burden.

Lottie woke up in a dark, dusty, stale-smelling room. Her whimper earned her a glare and a raised hand from the bad man whose name she was not supposed to say. She cringed back against the thin mattress on the floor, hurt, hungry, nearly paralyzed with fear. He threw her a piece of hard bread and a chunk of cheese, and pointed toward a chipped bowl in the nearby corner.

"You know how to use that, brat? If you don't, too bad. I'm not changing no nappies."

Of course Lottie knew how to use a chamber pot. She wasn't a baby. But neither had she ever used a dirty one. Or eaten with dirty hands. Nanny would be angry, but Nanny was not here. The bad man was, and another, smaller man he called Eyes. Lottie could understand why, because the stranger's eyes stuck out, like a frog's. She ate the bread and listened.

"I say we're going to get rich," Dennis Godfrey was saying from the bed, where he had his bandaged leg stretched out in front of him and a whiskey bottle at his side. "And get even. That damned fool driver paid for shooting me, he did, and now Phelan Sloane will pay. He never said the driver was armed, or so loyal."

"But why should he pay for the girl when she's nobbut his dead cousin's brat?"

"Because he'll hang next to me if I get caught. He hired me to stop the coach, didn't he? That makes him guilty as sin in anyone's book. It wasn't my fault the driver wouldn't turn back. Sloane will pay enough to let me leave the country and live in style somewheres. I already told him what bank to send the money to, else I send a letter to Bow Street."

"The earl's got deeper pockets."

"And more influence. Let Sloane deal with him. I don't care where the money comes from, just that it's waiting in that bank in London. I'd wager Carde'll be on his way north before he could get my message anyway. Sloane won't say anything about me to him. How can he, without confessing? Soon's the earl gets back to Town I'll send a regular ransom note." He laughed, raising the whiskey bottle to his lips. "I'll collect from both the toffs and they'll never be the wiser."

He looked toward Lottie's corner. "I might just have to send his lordship one of the brat's fingers to prove I've got her, iffen she gives me any trouble."

Lottie popped her thumb in her mouth.

"I've just got to figure what to do with the chit meantime."

"I say dump her in the Thames. You can cut off some of her curls first to wrap in the ransom note, to show you've got her. They'll recognize that fresh-cream color sooner than they'd know a finger. You'll have your money by the time anyone finds the body. And I'll have my cut. That way we won't have to worry about her naming names or nothing."

Godfrey took another swig. "I never killed no little girl. You?"

Ize, Ezra Iscoll, was more merchant than murderer, although he kept a knife handy. He generally sold used goods, of honest acquirement or otherwise; decidedly dishonest information regarding easy targets for cutpurses and burglars; and security, in the form of the secret spare rooms beneath his dingy shop in London's underworld.

Now he shook his head, looking more like a carp chasing
a fly than a frog. "She don't look so good now anyway.
What if she comes over sick?"

"She won't. Not if she knows what's good for her."

Lottie kept sucking her thumb, her eyes almost as wide as
Ize's.

Godfrey told his ally, "You go find Molly, tell her I need
her, but nothing else, just in case. She'll come. True-blue,
my sister."

"But your sister Molly's an old maid and a seamstress.
She don't know nothing about babies."

"She's got to know more'n we do. 'Sides, she ain't that
old," her brother loyally protested, "and if this deal turns
into the gold mine I figure it for, she can buy herself a store
instead of mending costumes at the theater. Maybe she can
buy herself a husband."

Ize's eyes popped a little more at the idea of plump,
pockmarked Molly with a dowry. His own promised cut of
this hugger-mugger wasn't all that big, not in light of the
danger of crossing an aristo. Ize did not fancy spending the
rest of his life in Botany Bay—if he had any life left after
the Earl of Carde was through with him—if Dennis Godfrey
got caught. He'd feel better with the infant elsewhere than
on his own premises. He'd feel better if he'd never met Dennis Godfrey, his sister, or a stolen, wellborn babe. Still, there
was the money, and there was Molly.

There was no use sending her a note, even without the
danger of its falling into the wrong hands, because Molly
could not read. Dennis Godfrey could not go because his leg

was paining him, so Ize took a hackney coach to the theater where Molly worked.

"What, are you dicked in the nob, thinking I could leave my job before the performance? What if that cow who plays Juliet splits her seams again?"

But Ize whispered about a fortune, and a foundling. He had decided not to mention the Earl of Carde, in case Molly's tender sensibilities were stirred, or her greed. Who knew if she'd rather sell information or the infant back to the nobleman? Dennis Godfrey trusted Molly. Ize trusted no one.

"A baby?"

Ize clapped his hand over her mouth. "You coming or not? If your brother's scheme works, you won't be worrying over no lousy post that pays tuppence."

Molly packed her few belongings, and a few lengths of material that belonged to the theater, and left with her brother's pop-eyed partner.

When they reached Ize's place of business, an abandoned-seeming storefront with one peeling door and one grimy window, down a garbage-strewn alley, Molly had second thoughts. Ize had her satchel, though, and pushed her through the opening. He led her through a midden heap of merchandise no one would ever buy, then toward a secret door and down a hidden staircase.

Her brother, Dennis, was asleep, or in a stupor, on the bed, with blood seeping through the bandage on his leg and an empty bottle beside him. Molly'd seen worse. She clucked her tongue and followed Ize's gesture toward an even darker corner of the cell-like room. She took up the single candle and stepped closer to the filthy bedding on the floor there.

"Lord above, there really is a child," she said, slowly

lowering herself to a corner of the mattress. She peeled back her brother's mud-stained coat. "And a pretty little thing at that, unless I miss my guess, under all that muck." She brushed back snarled curls that must have been a rare pale blond color, and looked into eyes the color of summer skies, despite tear-reddened rims. "A regular beauty, I swear. Won't you break the gentlemen's hearts in a few years?"

Lottie kept sucking her thumb.

"Who are you, then, lovey?"

Lottie stayed mum.

"I'm Molly, I am, what's come to keep you company. What's your name?"

Lottie looked over to the bad man on the bed. He looked to be sleeping, but she could not be certain. Give her name? She'd sooner give up her doll, and the promised pony at home.

"What's the matter, lovey, cat got your tongue?"

Lottie looked around for the cat.

Molly tugged the little girl's fingers out of her mouth. "Didn't anyone tell you you'd ruin your teeth that way? Come on, now, ducks. You've got to know your own name."

Of course Lottie knew her name. She was Lady Charlotte Elizabeth Endicott—and she would never tell anyone. She could never tell, not if she wanted to go home, not if she wanted to keep her brothers from being hurt.

"You can talk, can't you?" Molly asked.

Lottie nodded.

"Well, that's a start, anyway." Molly took a handkerchief from her sleeve, spit on it, and started to wipe Lottie's face.

Lottie jerked back, clutching her doll tighter.

"You're a shy one, all right. Or maybe you're not used to such common ways," Molly said after getting a better look at the child's clothes. They were in tatters and covered with stains, but no one could recognize fine fabrics and careful stitching better than Molly Godfrey. She sucked in a breath and glanced at her sleeping brother, then at Ize, who was paring his nails with a deadly-looking knife. "What the devil have those two gallows baits gone and done now?" she muttered. This was no street urchin. Even the doll wore richer apparel than any London orphan.

"Maybe your doll has a name."

No one said Lottie could not say Dolly's name, but maybe she better not. Maybe she better not speak at all, to anyone, until Papa came to get her.

"Well, let's try this, lovey." Molly stood and made a curtsy. "Molly Godfrey at your service, milady."

Lottie had been taught her manners, especially toward servants. And Molly was being nice, and knew her title. Maybe she would take Lottie home if she knew the rest of her name. Looking first toward the bed, then at the man they called Eyes, Lottie stood and made her best curtsy, just like Mama had shown her. She held out the doll and whispered, "Queen." The queen had given her the doll, so that was no lie. And everyone knew the queen's name was Charlotte, just like hers.

"Well, aren't you the proper little lady? I would have called you Princess, but Queenie it is. Now, Your Highness, let's see what's to do. I was right, and more's the pity, for there's nothing good can come from setting a peacock in the pigeon coop."

Molly's brother would not hear of returning the child from wherever he'd found her—he refused to say where or how, or why he was shot. He waited until Ize left the room to fetch another bottle of Blue Ruin before telling her, "The less you know, the better. All you've got to remember is how much blunt we stand to make. I've got one toff by the privates, and another by the throat. They'll pay, and keep paying. Even giving Ize his percent, or what he thinks is his cut, we're set for life, Sis. Just like Ma said, I'm taking care of you."

"Our mother also said you'd come to a bad end."

"Then I'll die a rich man. And they can't hang me if they can't find me. Soon as the gents start making deposits to the bank, I can ship out to the colonies. You can keep collecting and sending me my share, or come join me. One of the gulls don't know it, but he's going to support us for the rest of his life."

"And me, too," Ize put in, coming back and passing the bottle over after taking a drink.

Molly purposely wiped the bottle before having a sip. She handed it to her brother and asked, "But what about the girl?"

Dennis shrugged. "She knows too much. After I'm gone and you're on your way, then maybe they can have her back. Until then, you always wanted a family of your own, didn't you?"

Molly choked on her next swallow. "I'm to keep her?"

Ize took the bottle back. "It's that or the Thames."

The little girl was huddled under the coat again, rocking. "You wouldn't!"

Dennis made a gesture of slicing his own throat. "If it's her or us . . ."

So Molly took the child she called Queenie and left London that very day. She had what money her brother could spare, a trunk of secondhand clothes, boots, and hairbrushes from Ize's shop, and the name of the London bank where deposits were going to be made twice a year. Forever.

No slaving all hours under dreadful conditions for ungrateful actresses who were no better than they ought to be.

No wondering where her next meal was coming from if the manager found a seamstress who was faster or cheaper. No eating and sleeping and sewing all alone, without even a cat for company. Now Molly would have someone to care for, someone she wanted to sew pretty dresses for, someone who needed her.

Molly had an old friend who had left London years ago to set up as a milliner in Manchester. That's where she decided to go, to start her new life. She'd be a soldier's widow. With so many women in that same situation, no one would think twice about a mother and her fatherless child. Ize supplied a gold wedding ring.

The dead soldier would have been from a decent family, they decided, leaving her with a handsome jointure, enough to purchase a little house, with a garden for Queenie to play in.

The world had never looked rosier for Molly. Even the knowledge that her brother had committed a heinous offense—and that by taking the child away, she was most likely just as guilty in the eyes of the courts—could not dampen her enthusiasm. Molly was finally getting her chance for a better life. If worse came to worst, she could always flee the country, too, or marry Ize.

As for Lottie, no one asked her, and she did not say anything. She was so disappointed in Molly, she barely spoke for the entire journey. She did eat, though, and let Molly bathe her and dress her and comb the knots out of her curls . . . and kiss her good night.

They went, and Dennis Godfrey stayed hidden away, drunk and in pain, except to check the bank for his first extortion deposit and Carde House in Grosvenor Square for the earl's return.

The blackmail money came from the madman who had

hired Dennis Godfrey, but the earl did not come back. They carried Lord Carde home to his country place, instead, where he died of the fevers brought on by his search for his baby daughter, and grief from burying his beloved young second wife.

The earl's heirs or his executors would have paid a ransom to get the girl back, but it was too late. Dennis Godfrey died of his own wound turning putrid before he could book passage out of England.

Ize came to Manchester to find Molly and tell her the news. He felt his third share was not enough—he was actually getting a quarter, by his lying, cheating, dead friend's arrangement—and wanted half. Molly refused. Her brother's third would go to Queenie, for her future.

Ize did not argue, not when he thought he still had a chance of getting it all by marrying Molly.

Give up her new wealth and freedom? Make some denizen of the underworld who looked like he crawled out from under a rock, and who lived in a cave, Queenie's father? Never!

Ize thought about taking the brat—or her body, which could tell no tales to the courts—back to London for the reward. But Ize couldn't figure a way to collect the brass without naming Molly, who'd pin the whole thing on him in return. So he'd have to kill her, too, which did not appeal to him. Besides, they still had silence money from the man who'd hired Dennis Godfrey. That was as good as a pension from a rich uncle, except only Molly could withdraw it, now that her brother had stuck his spoon in the wall.

In case Molly heard about the reward and thought of giving the chit back to her family, cutting him out and handing him to the magistrate, Ize reminded Molly of her own culpability. She would not survive the prison hulks, he warned, being handed from the guards to the ship's crew to the convicts until she died.

Give up Queenie? The child was everything Molly was not: beautiful and bright, innocent and untouched. She was well behaved, too, as if she feared losing yet another home, another loving mother. Molly went to church every day to thank the Almighty for the angel he'd blessed her with. Give up that precious gift? Never!

Besides, she did not know anything about any dead earl or how high was the reward for some missing child's return. How could she, so far from London, when she could not read the newspapers or the broadsheets?

Other than her one friend, the milliner, Molly kept to herself in a tidy cottage outside Manchester. The air was cleaner there, and the neighbors minded their own business. She did occasional piecework sewing for her friend to keep her hand in, but mostly devoted herself to bringing up Queenie as a proper lady. She even hired an Irishwoman to come in by day to cook and clean—like regular gentry. She found a retired Oxford dean to educate Queenie, a portrait painter to give her drawing lessons, and the church organist to teach her music. With the learning of a lady and the dowry of a rich man's daughter, Queenie would not have to toil for a living, or sell her body just to eat. She could marry a decent, respectable gentleman with a profitable business or a bit of land. Perhaps she might even land a bloke with a title. Molly had dreams for the little girl she had taken to Manchester, and taken to her heart.

They traveled to London occasionally, to meet up with Ize and collect the money their new patron kept putting in the bank. *Mrs. Molly Dennis* was the name on the account, and Mrs. Molly Dennis grew into a respectable widow with a pretty, well-mannered daughter who was too delicate to attend the village school and too reserved to play with the local children.

And Lottie? With the resilience of a child, and no other choice, she grew into Queenie, a quiet sort of girl with a loving mother and a dead hero father. She had a tutor and a kitten and all the fancy frocks a little girl could want. She loved to sew and draw and dress her dolls and listen to her mother's stories of all the plays Molly had seen. In time Queenie forgot about having brothers or a grand house in London or a title before her name. The crashing coach and the bad man were too awful to remember, so she did not. But sometimes, even years later, she would wake up in the middle of the night, trembling, holding on to her pillow to keep from falling, and crying out: "Mama!"

CHAPTER TWO

1813

When a female reaches a certain age—that is, when a
girl approaches womanhood—she begins to wonder
about her future. Sixteen was a time for daydreams and
knights on white chargers, air castles and coy glances at the
boy next door. At that age, some of the village girls were already wedded or promised. Others who were not needed at
home to tend farms or younger siblings had left to take positions in the mills or gone into service. Daughters of the
wealthy landowners and manufacturers were planning their
come-out balls. Young ladies of the aristocracy were prepar-
ing for their court presentations. And Queenie was . . . asking questions.

Where was she to find the perfect match? How did her
parents meet? How did they know they were in love?

The older Queenie grew, the harder the questions were to
answer. What had seemed so simple to Molly thirteen years
earlier now seemed impossible. She'd dreamed of raising

her precious girl as a lady, then seeing her wedded to a fine gentleman. But how? Queenie Dennis was neither fish nor fowl, having the airs and the education of a wellborn female but with no connections, no known lineage, no history. Molly could not hide her own coarse accent that labeled her lower class, but the boys who worked the mines or the mills or the farms were not good enough for Her Highness, as the would-be wooers called Queenie when they were denied an introduction to the young beauty.

Sons of the gentry saw the diamond in their midst, shining with a handsome dowry. But their sires would ask more questions than a courting shopkeeper or a solicitor would. Their mothers would want to know the family tree, not just the bloom on one branch. Who were Queenie's people? Where did the dowry come from if Molly's husband was a common soldier?

Oh, how fast they would run if Molly told them her girl was rich with extortion money from a madman who had committed a crime. But what could she tell a prospective suitor? And what could she tell Queenie about her past . . . or her future?

The filthy little waif of thirteen years ago had surpassed even Molly's prejudiced estimation of her coming beauty. She was growing into a stunning female, with long, wavy hair like white gold and eyes of vivid blue. Her complexion was flawless and her figure was willowy, with enough curves to be womanly instead of girlish. Queenie took after her handsome father, plump, plain, brown-eyed Molly claimed when the girl asked, not her own side of the family.

Now, though, Molly's greatest fear—after Queenie's discovering the truth about her parentage and hating Molly for it—was that her baby would attract the wrong kind of attention from the wrong kind of man, one with no intentions

of offering an honorable proposal. So they never attended
the local assemblies, the potluck suppers, or the country
fairs. They never congregated in the churchyard after Sunday services, never breakfasted at the coffeehouse or dined
at the nearby inn.

Molly kept Queenie close to home, where she seemed
content with her lessons and her books and her sewing.
Queenie had an eye for fashion and a knack for design that
Molly encouraged, since it kept the girl busy. Let the towns-
folk think Molly was above herself. Let them think quiet
Queenie was a snob. Let the future take care of itself. Molly
was not ready to part with her greatest joy yet anyway.
Queenie was too young, too sheltered, too naive. Husband
hunting could wait.

The disease growing inside Molly's chest could not.
Then Queenie was too busy caring for her mother to worry
about beaux and betrothals. Now it was Queenie's turn to
nurse Molly, to comfort her and tell her tales and ease her
fears . . . and listen to her confessions of old sins.

She had done it all for love, Molly whispered through
dry, cracked lips. She had done everything for love of her
brother, and love for Queenie.

Through her tears, Queenie forgave her mother without
question. Of course she had questions aplenty, but she could
not press a woman struggling for every breath. And Molly
would have revealed all of her sins, for hopes of heaven, but
it was too late. Between the pain, the laudanum, and the
struggle to focus her fading eyesight on Queenie, the prettiest sight this side of paradise, Molly could only gasp, "I was
never married."

Then Queenie was alone. Her tutor had retired to his
niece's a year ago, and her drawing master had found a
wealthy patron in Bath for his portraits and his more personal

services. Molly's milliner friend had emigrated to Canada years ago. The taciturn Irish housekeeper went home at night.

Queenie tore the house apart looking for marriage lines, an inscribed Bible, a love letter, anything. Surely Molly had been delirious when she'd uttered those fatal words. But Queenie found nothing. Molly never had learned to read, despite Queenie's encouragement, so why should she have written proof of what might never have existed?

So Queenie was alone with her grief. And she was a bastard.

She did not even know who her father might have been. An army hero who had left England not knowing his beloved was with child? Or was Lieutenant Dennis a figment of Molly's imagination and her desire for respectability? Molly's brother might have known, but he was long dead. A sad end to a bad seed, Molly had always said, and a name never to be spoken. Which left Ize.

Lord, please do not let the toad be my father, Queenie prayed as she penned a letter to Molly's old—what? Friend? Associate? Lover? Heaven forfend. He'd want to know about Molly's passing, either way, and perhaps come in time for the funeral.

He did not, and few others attended the brief graveside service.

Afterward, while Queenie dyed some more of her gowns black, diluted with tears, she tried not to despair about her future. How could she hope to wed now? She understood and appreciated Molly's lies, to keep the stigma of illegitimacy from her daughter, but a prospective husband would have to know. He would have the *right* to know, and the right to reject a bride whose mother was no better than she ought to be and whose father was sewn from whole cloth. Of

course a man who loved her enough would not care, not in
the Minerva Press novels, anyway. Even that paragon of
love and loyalty would want to know where her dowry came
from. If not the dead soldier, then where?

Besides, what Queenie knew about men would fit in her
thimble. According to Molly, they were a lying lot, their
skulls filled with base lust instead of brains. They sought a
maiden's virtue, or her money. And husbands could control
every facet of a wife's life, from where she lived to what she
wore to how he spent her dowry.

So Queenie decided not to marry. She was almost nineteen now and had run Molly's little household for the past
two years of her mother's illness. She owned the cottage,
she had her dowry, and she could support herself as a seamstress.

Then she had to face the truth. Molly had not gone to
London to the bank for those two years and the money on
hand was running out. And no one in Manchester would
give Queenie any work. She was too standoffish, the established dressmakers felt. What she was, was still too uncertain around strangers. She did not know how to speak up
forcefully to sell her skills or show her potential. To the
modistes, she was too untried, too unknown, too young, too
peculiar. Even her name, *Queenie,* set her apart. The area
was full of Janes and Marys and Elizabeths. Whoever heard
of a Queenie, setting herself above the common folk?
They'd heard how she felt herself too good for the local
lads. She would be too uppity for their merchant-class customers.

And that left Ize.

Ezra Iscoll had improved his life over the years, running
a better class of fencing operation in a better neighborhood.
He even shaved, most days, before opening the shop doors.

He'd believed Molly when she'd said she'd feel better next month, next January, next spring. Then again, he'd believed she'd marry him one day. The bitch had lied, and Ize was losing his store. He did not want to return to the slums, so now Ize needed Queenie to get to the London bank, and he needed to know what she knew.

"All she said was that she was never married," Queenie told him over ale and sandwiches. She knew better than to offer the ugly little man tea and cakes. He might have shaved, but he had not plucked the hairs from his nose or his ears.

He twisted the black ribbon he'd tied on his sleeve as a token of mourning. "That's all right, then."

"No, it is not all right, not by half. I have to know who my father was, and why my parents never wed."

"What for? It won't change nothing. The past is past. Old Molly took her secrets to the grave, just as she ought. It's the money she couldn't carry with her, thanks be. Now it's our blunt, yours and mine."

The last thing Queenie wanted was to go into partnership with the greedy, goggle-eyed gremlin. Nor could she like the way he licked his thick lips when he looked at her, as if he was getting ideas about getting his hands on her dowry, now that she was fully grown and without Molly's militant protection.

"Where did the money come from if not my father's family?" she asked, hoping for information that could end their relation once and for all. She could go to Molly's benefactor herself if she knew a name.

Ize licked his lips again. He had not come so far in the fencing business without learning to drive a hard bargain. "I'll tell you if you come to London. I know Molly left a will, so that ought to convince the bank to hand over her accounts. I get my half"—no more thirds or less, not from a slip of a girl he could strangle with one hand, were he a violent man—"and you get some facts no one told you." Of course they would be the facts Ize wanted the girl to know. There was no way he was going to tell her about Carde or the reward. That would be signing his own arrest warrant. Miss Prunes and Prisms would rat on him quicker than she could say "Lady Charlotte Endicott." And the blackmail money would disappear, too.

Queenie was tempted. She wanted the information Ize was dangling in front of her like a carrot to a donkey. And there was nothing to keep her in Manchester. In London she could start her own business, not dependent on Ize or that troublesome bank account.

"I'll think about it."

"What's to think on? We could share a coach back to Town tomorrow."

Hours alone with Ize? Nights on the road? That was enough to convince Queenie to wait. "I have too much to do here, papers to sign and such. I have to pick a headstone for the grave, talk to the solicitor, make arrangements for the house. I will let you know if I am coming. Or I will send to you from Mrs. Pettigrew's." She named Molly's London friend.

"See that you do. And bring a copy of that will. Else I'll come back here to fetch you myself."

They both knew that was both a threat and a promise. Queenie knew she would never be rid of the man until she settled the bank thing once and for all, and she would never find out her heritage any way else, either.

The solicitor was not quite as easy to convince that selling the house and moving to London was in Queenie's best interests, or in keeping with Molly's last wishes. The solicitor disapproved of women handling money in the first place. The younger the woman, the less capable was she of managing her funds, in the second place. Thirdly, Miss Dennis needed a man to guide her before she fell into the wrong company, was swindled of her inheritance, or met a fate worse than death in the evil streets of the metropolis. The solicitor's nephew, now, was a likely lad with a mind to enter politics. With the proper wife and a bit of financial backing . . .

Queenie had a copy of Molly's will. The house and her dowry were Queenie's outright, for being such a loving, dutiful daughter. No court had yet declared her in need of a trustee, so the solicitor really had no choice but to accede to her wishes. She collected her gratifyingly generous dowry, sold the cottage and its furnishings, and left half the income, after the housekeeper's pension, with the solicitor to invest until she needed the money for her new business.

A female in business? Mrs. Dennis had not seen her daughter educated like a lady just to go into trade. The lawyer threw his hands in the air. Impossible!

Possible, and not his decision to make. For such a soft-spoken female, Queenie was learning to have a will of steel. She left for London within the month.

Not that it was any of the solicitor's affair, but Queenie did have a plan, and a place from which to carry it out. She actually knew someone in London, or near enough in Kensington to make no nevermind. Valerie Pettigrew had been a minor actress many, many years earlier, when she and Molly, as wardrobe mistress, had become friends. Valerie left the theater to become the mistress of a rich man, a lord willing to support her and the daughter they created. Unfortunately, although he loved Valerie and the child, he was married to the mother of his heir. Hellen—with two *l*s, after

the baron, Elliot, and because Valerie never could spell—
was a few years younger than Queenie. Queenie and Molly
stayed in the tiny spare bedroom in the Pettigrews' row
house when they came to London. Mrs. Pettigrew invited
Queenie to visit after Molly's sad passing.

Queenie accepted. She rode the mail coach, white-faced,
frozen in terror. She told herself she was not frightened of
the speed or the mostly male passengers or at being alone.
She told herself she was merely scared of the future. She
was lying to herself.

Mrs. Pettigrew was delighted to see her, especially when
Queenie made arrangements to rent the small bedchamber.
The aging baron seldom came to Town anymore, since he
was gout-ridden and afraid of suffering an apoplexy in his
inamorata's arms. His wife and son would kill him. His in-
frequent visits meant less frequent visits to Ize, to trade the
diamond bracelets and ruby pendants he brought, in exchange for money for coal and clothes and food.

Hellen was thrilled to have such an elegant, fashionable
friend staying with them. Her mother was too fat and indo-
lent to stroll in the park or attend the plays or visit the
shops—places where Hellen might meet men. Surely Queenie would want to view all the single gentlemen—and the
sights, of course.

First, Queenie had to speak with Ize.

First, Ize dragged her to the bank. Then he cursed, tore
down a broadsheet posted beside the bank's door, and, with
a foul look at a Robin Redbreast from Bow Street who was
studying the patrons inside the bank, dragged Queenie
away.

"Bloody hell, they must have caught Godfrey's pigeon.
He's the only one who would have told them about the account. Godfrey didn't, by Satan, 'cause dead men can't talk,

and Molly sure as hell wouldn't, not when she lived off the take for all those years. Damnation!"

Queenie was gasping for breath by the time Ize slowed down when they reached Green Park. He was so angry he did not notice when she pulled the poster from his hand and sank onto a bench.

Queenie gasped again. She was looking at a picture of a young woman who might have been her sister. *Blue eyes,* the notice said, *pale blond hair. Eighteen years of age.*

"Why, that might have been me!"

"Well, it ain't," Ize said, trying to grab the reward notice back from her. Queenie held on and read further.

"Gracious, look at the money being offered for information or her return. 'Lady Charlotte Endicott, once known as Lottie, is being desperately sought by her brother, the Earl of Carde. She has been missing since she was three years of age . . . lost in a carriage accident.'" Images of a falling coach and screams and blood flashed through Queenie's mind. "I remember. . . ."

"You remember what Dennis Godfrey told you. You ain't her, and that's that."

"Of course not. How could I be the legitimate daughter of an earl when Molly was my—Molly was my mother, wasn't she?"

Ize took a knife out of his boot, then looked around to see who was watching them. He tossed the knife from hand to hand, as if undecided what to do with it. He finally chose to scrape the dirt from under his fingernails.

"'Bout time you learned the truth, I'd say, iffen only to keep you from bumbling your way into jail."

Queenie's face paled even further. "Jail?"

"Righto. Jail, or transportation. Maybe hanging. They'd

hang me first, which is why you ain't going to say nothing to nobody, no matter the reward. You hear?"

"Nothing about what? Do you mean I am actually connected to this lady?"

"Connected, but not on the right side of the blanket, so to speak. Molly never wanted you to know—she loved you that much, and she were ashamed."

"I was her brother's by-blow?" Queenie guessed. At least that rogue was dead.

Ize made a sound that might have been a laugh. "As if that no-account would have taken in a bastard of his. He'd of left his own get to starve in the gutter. But he did have big plans."

"For the earl's daughter?"

"She were already dead. He bungled the job and kilt the countess, the driver, and the nursemaid, too. He was going to hang for sure, except the bloke what hired him was just as guilty. That's who was paying us off all these years. But before then old Godfrey had the knacky notion to hand back the dead heiress for the ransom."

"But she was dead. You just said so."

Ize spit on the ground. "But a hundred orphans were just begging for a home. He picked a pretty one, one that looked like the little lady. Blond hair, blue eyes. Close enough from a distance. They would of paid, too, but the old earl died, and then Godfrey. And then Molly went and fell in love with you and wouldn't hear of handing you over, specially knowing they wouldn't keep no foundling. Asides, she was already guilty of aiding and abetting her brother. And taking the blackmail money. She would of been convicted without a trial, mucking about with an earl."

Queenie set aside Molly's guilt or innocence. "Then I am an orphan?"

"Twice, now that Molly's gone."

So Queenie was not even her mother's daughter. She had no parents, no one at all. Her name was not *Dennis*. Neither was Molly's, it appeared. She must have taken her brother's first name, when Dennis Godfrey became a fugitive. Heaven knew where the *Queenie* came from. She supposed she had to be grateful to the wretched man for taking her from the orphanage. Foundlings had a poor survival rate in such institutions, living amid filth and poverty and disease, with no chance to improve their lot. Still, he was guilty of so many heinous crimes she was glad he was dead.

She looked back at the poster. "Someone should tell the current earl and his brother. You see, it says information may be brought to Bow Street."

"Someone should tell 'em what? That you've been living off their money for sixteen years? That you were meant to be the decoy? That your own mother was a blackmailer and your uncle was the murderer? Or maybe you'll tell them that I helped, that I knew about the crimes all these years, too?"

"No, I wouldn't."

He tossed the knife, with the point landing a scant inch from her shoe. "Damned right, you wouldn't. I hear about you going near the earl or to Bow Street and you won't have to worry about going to jail."

"I just thought they should know their sister was dead, that they should stop looking. They can bury their memories once and for all, instead of wondering forever." As she would be forever wondering about her own background.

"Pshaw. Who cares about them? They've got their fortune. And we're not getting any more unless we can think of a way of getting into the bank without being noticed." He eyed her blond hair under the black bonnet. "Maybe a veil."

Queenie did not think that would work. If the earl had

men watching the bank, surely they had notified the tellers. Besides, she and Ize did not know what name Molly had used on her account. *Molly Dennis,* as she was known in Manchester? *Molly Godfrey,* which was her true name? Furthermore, although Molly's will clearly stated that all of her estate and property was bequeathed to her daughter, Queenie had no way of proving that she was, indeed, Molly's child. Now she understood why she had found no baptismal records, no proof of her parentage.

"The money is not ours," she said.

Ize pulled his knife from the ground and wiped it on his trousers. "Then maybe I better have a share of that dowry Molly set aside for you. You think on it, missy. How you'd be nothing without my help."

Queenie was a nobody; she was not nothing. "That money is mine, to start a business. Our business, on the other hand, is finished. I will not speak your name, and hope you never speak mine again. Good day, Ize."

She went back to the Pettigrews.

Valerie Pettigrew knew all about the Carde story, the sadness of the old earl's passing and the tragedy of his young wife's death, both made worse by the disappearance of their baby daughter. There were rewards posted all over Town, Mrs. Pettigrew recalled, but the little girl was never returned. She knew the new tales about Captain Jack Endicott coming home from the war, setting up a gambling den to find young women of the appropriate age—and those who might know about his half sister. He was hiring the prettiest ones, and treating them well, by all reports.

"The Red and the Black, he calls his club, because he won't let any blondes deal or go with the men, in honor of little Charlotte," the older woman said, wiping a tear from her eye.

*   *   *

Queenie thought the tear might have been from the touching story of a brave young hero giving up his standing as a gentleman in society to go into a shady business, out of an oath sworn when he was a boy. On the other hand, Valerie Pettigrew might be weeping because, without her baron's patronage, she could not visit the latest fashionable spot among the demimondaines.

Queenie could. Leaving Hellen behind, to her friend's disappointment, Queenie took a hackney coach into Mayfair. The driver knew the address readily enough, having taken many a hopeful woman to the club. He agreed to wait for her for an extra coin, trying to stare behind the veil she wore, dubious of her black mourning outfit. "You got to have red hair or raven, miss. And be ready to smile at the gentlemen," he offered his polite and generous fare. "Good luck."

Queenie did not have good luck. She was last on line, it seemed, to speak to the man in charge of interviews. She did, however, get a good look at a portrait of the missing child's mother, a woman who looked enough like herself to make Queenie wish for the impossible. How sweet and ladylike, how perfect in her pearls, with a lovely house behind her. How Queenie could picture herself there, a cherished daughter. How foolish!

She lowered her veil and studied the other women who were waiting to be called to the desk at the front of the long, narrow receiving room. Most had either red or black hair as the driver had warned, and were dressed in flamboyant, low-cut style, defining their attributes and their ambitions. A few blondes, artificially yellow or otherwise, were there seeking a different position from hostess in the gambling casino. One woman, dressed in somber clothes, even had a child with her. Queenie could not imagine what that female was seeking here, but the woman was kind enough to speak to her before taking her turn at the front of the room.

"You need to know that your brothers are Alex and Jack. They'll ask about your pony's name and your doll's," she whispered, leaving the sleeping child on the bench when she walked toward the desk.

Queenie had heard from Mrs. Pettigrew about Alex, or Ace, as he was nicknamed, the current Earl of Carde, and Captain Jack Endicott, of course, the proprietor of the club. Neither name resonated in her mind. She thought she might have known a boy named Andy or Endy at the orphanage, and surely there would have been a Jack or a John.

She never had a pony. Molly wanted her to learn to ride, like a lady, but Queenie was afraid of horses, so never had. As for Dolly, she had disintegrated ages ago, and Queenie supposed half the girls in England named their toys Dolly.

Then the man at the desk half fell off his chair. He declared interviews over for the day and rushed through the rear door, where Queenie could see a dark-haired man with a crooked nose sitting behind another desk.

Queenie left.

She tried again the next week, after a fruitless sennight of seeking a position with an established modiste in London. No one wanted her dress designs or her sewing skills, except for positions that paid little for long hours in deplorable conditions.

This time she thought she spotted Ize near the club, but what business could he have there? She was unlucky again, for the interviewing office was closing for the day. A more forceful woman might have insisted that her information was important, that Captain Endicott would be relieved to hear her, but she supposed every one of the claimants to the heiress's place said the same thing. She raised her veil to stare at the portrait again before going.

A few days later, Mrs. Pettigrew looked up from her morning chocolate and her newspaper and said, "Now, isn't that strange? We were just talking about that Cap'n Jack and his club, and now they had a fire there last night. No one was hurt, thank goodness. They think it might have been a disgruntled gambler who set it on purpose."

Queenie thought it was Ize, giving warning to her or to Captain Endicott. Gracious, now she was bringing more trouble to that poor family, when she wanted only to give them an end to their search and sorrow. She thought about sending a letter, but she felt that would be cruel, her not being there to answer their questions, not taking responsibility for her unwitting complicity in their grief.

She tried to call at the gaming parlor one more time, dressed in one of her colored gowns, with a veiled pink bonnet instead of the mourning black, in case Ize was watching. She paused outside the door to read a new broadsheet that was posted there, one Ize had not managed to tear down. This time the reward for information was higher, and more detailed. Now they were looking for a young woman of about nineteen, once known as Lady Charlotte Endicott, or Lottie, now possibly identified as Queenie.

Great heavens, they were looking for her, naming her by name. Only that was not her name, nor was *Charlotte* or *Lottie*. She was nobody, a criminal through no fault of her own. She owed the Endicott family a debt beyond measure, but how could she hope to repay it from jail, if Ize did not kill her first should he suspect her intentions? Or he could cause more trouble at The Red and the Black, or Carde House in Grosvenor Square. She had the hackney coachman drive her past that mansion while she debated what to do. The elegant town house was under renovation, and did not look the least familiar to her. How could it, when she was naught but an orphan?

The Pettigrews were bound to see the new reward notice—and Valerie was constantly in need of money. Then, too, some of the dressmakers where Queenie had applied for a position were bound to recall her distinctive name. She would be hunted down, turned in, arrested, if Ize did not get to her first.

She had to leave. To go—where? She had funds, and she had ambitions. The war was over, and France was once again becoming the fashion capital of Europe. The dressmakers there were couturiers, not seamstresses and modistes who copied images from illustrations in magazines. Men were the designers in France, setting the styles for women everywhere. Queenie decided she would apprentice herself to one or another. Her French was impeccable, by her tutor's standards, and she knew her looks were attractive, if her skills and her bank notes could not win her a position. She would study hard and become a designer of distinction, an arbiter of English elegance, a businesswoman with a future. She might not have a name to call her own—she would find another, in France—but she would be somebody. And then she would begin to repay her debt of conscience to Lord Carde and his brother, Jack . . . and Lady Charlotte.

CHAPTER THREE

1816

Harlan Harkness, Lord Harking, hated London. Oh, the viscount liked the camaraderie of the clubs, the lectures at the Agricultural Society, the bookshops, and Tattersalls. Harry, as he was universally called, appreciated having his tailor, his boot maker, and his hatter all close by, and all knowing his preferences. What he disliked was the dirt and the smell, the crowds and the crime. And the matchmaking mamas.

The whole society business irritated Harry: the wearing of uncomfortable formal dress to make uncomfortable conversations with young females who would be more comfortable in the schoolroom—while their Machiavellian, maneuvering mothers tried to snabble every available bachelor.

What was wrong with a chap of twenty-and-nine staying unwed? Harry had plenty of time to create an heir, and if he did not, his cousin would make an admirable viscount.

Leonard already had two sons, and a shrewish wife. Besides, Harry was no prize on the matrimonial market that he could see. His face would not frighten dogs or small children, but he was no Adonis. His hair was an ordinary brown, his eyes were an ordinary brown, and his cheeks took on a silly schoolboy blush in the cold, the heat, and ballrooms. His physique was nothing out of the ordinary for a big man who worked along with his tenant farmers. He was not slim and graceful like the Town tulips—not when he had to help repair bridges and fix roofs after storms. In fact, he was clumsy on the dance floor, clumsier at light flirtation, and an outright clod when it came to courtship—to which it had not yet come, thank goodness. His fortune was not even large enough to raise eyebrows, or expectations, although Harking Hall was a handsome pile, if he had to say so himself. The hall was attractively set amid parks and profitable farmland, with a racing stable, an oval course, and paddocks, all in sight. He loved the place. He wished he were there now.

The London ladies did not care about fancy horses or fertile farms or fine old architecture. They cared about filling their dance cards, getting fitted for their fancy clothes, being seen at the right parties, catching the best "parti." The most advantageous match, the highest title and deepest pockets, seemed to matter more to the misses than affection, respect, or mutual interests.

They sure as the devil could not be interested in a plain country lumpkin like him. Yet they were setting out lures everywhere he went. Hell, they were digging mantraps for Harry, in Town less than a week.

He was staying at the Grand Hotel, rebuilt after the fire, where he at least could see Green Park from his suite's windows, imagining himself back in Lincolnshire. Invitations somehow found their way to him, for everything from Venetian breakfasts—after noon—to waltzing parties. Ha! Were the wallflowers so desperate they were willing to sacrifice their toes for his minor viscountcy? Then there were the invites to six dinners, routs, debutante balls, and theater parties—each and every night, even now in late winter before the height of the Season, with half of society at their country homes, where Harry longed to be.

Harry thought that might be what he most disliked about London and the *ton,* the mad rush to fill every hour with the pursuit of pleasure. What was wrong with sitting by one's own fireside with a good book and a good dog after a day of satisfying accomplishment? Harry found plenty of pleasures in his life without having to leave his home or shave twice a day.

As bad as the women were, the men were worse.

Harry enjoyed a fine wine, but not waking up wishing he were dead. He played a decent hand of whist, but was not about to gamble away what he'd worked so hard to restore and preserve. As for women, he was no monk, but neither was Harry a libertine, needing a woman, a different woman, every night, like so many of the Town bucks. He regretted that females had so few choices in life that so many had to sell their bodies, but he did not like buying a woman's favors. He liked the occasional tumble, with the kind of willing woman one could bed without having to wed—or pay.

Most of all he despised the morals of the beau monde, which were anything but beautiful. Adultery was rampant, and no one seemed to care.

So-called gentlemen tossed their marriage vows aside like so many flower petals at the wedding. The ladies were supposed to wait until they had presented their husbands with an heir before taking a lover, but who could trust an unwritten social rule when a holy sacrament was without value? No one seemed to honor his or her word.

Harry intended to, when the time came, and he intended to marry a woman with the same scruples. The thought of Harking Hall going to some other man's by-blow had kept him from looking for a bride, as he feared he would never find that rare virtuous female.

Maybe he was a prude, a prig, and a Puritan, as his brother-in-law called him. But Harry liked his life, and saw nothing wrong with taking pleasure in his accomplishments, instead of merely accomplishing pleasure.

He'd come by that sense of responsibility and hard work the hard way, haphazardly raised by parents who were precisely what he least admired. His father was a dissipated debauchee, paying his estate no attention except for what he could sell off to finance his gambling and his expensive ladybirds. Lady Harking was the scandal of local society, flaunting her young lovers at the neighbors' dinner parties in revenge, Harry supposed. By the time the former viscount succumbed to the pox and his wife drowned off a boat in Italy with some mad poet, Harking Hall was dilapidated and deep in debt, and Harry's sister's dowry was long gone.

Harry'd spent the last nine years making repairs: to the tenants' farms, the ancestral home, the Harkness family name, and the family coffers. He'd even managed to repay the money he'd had to borrow so his sister could wed respectably, her dowry restored.

Respectable, hell! Olivia's head had been turned by a handsome baronet, when a fine and fashionable London gentleman had paid her attention at the local assembly. Harry should have made her wait. He should have investigated Sir John Martin's background. He should have taken a horsewhip to the dastard. But Olivia was his only sister, edging toward spinsterhood, and Harry could not afford a London Season for her. She was older than Harry, and he thought she was wiser. Ha!

So here he was in London, choking on the air and dodging hopeful hostesses, chasing a drunkard, a gambler, and a womanizer just like his father had been, only this one happened to be his brother-in-law.

Good riddance, he'd thought, when Martin had left Harking Hall in the middle of the night. Olivia would be far better off without the muckworm, who had a mistress in the village, an ongoing affair with the vicar's cousin, and a room at the inn—Easy Ellie's room—when he was too foxed to ride home. Olivia had her son and her daughter and the management of Harry's home. She would not miss the pitying looks from the neighbors or the shouting and the tears, or the bruises she tried to hide. Neither would Harry.

Harry's niece and nephew would be better off without seeing their father stagger home, stinking of cheap wine and cheaper perfume, his clothes awry.

And Harry would have been a great deal better off if he had not had to keep paying his brother-in-law's debts. He had not wanted another blot on the family name, though, the scandal of having his sister's husband hauled off to debtors' prison.

Now he would not mind seeing the maggot hauled off to Hades. In fact, he'd drive him there himself, if he could find the shabster.

Martin had ridden off in the dark after a Valentine's Day celebration at Harking Hall, the first grand party the hall had seen in ages, now that Harry was in funds. Olivia had worn the Harkness diamonds.

Martin had worn out two horses—Harry's best carriage pair—getting away with the family jewels.

The Harkness diamonds had been in the family since the day some fool trumpeter had shouted, "Hark, the king" at just the right moment (or so the family legend went), saving the ruler's life from an assassin's arrow and thereby earning a title and a reward. The diamonds were meant for Harry's wife, which he did not have, and Harry's son, which he did not have, and hopes of perpetuity, which Harry did have.

No one stole from Harlan Harkness, Lord Harking. Not his money, not his good name, not his heritage. And not his heirlooms.

The coach and Harry's horses had been headed to London. Harry followed, sure he could find the rotter before Martin sold the gems and gambled the money away. Now he was not so sure. He'd asked at the gentlemen's clubs, even visited scores of unsavory gaming dens, without unearthing a clue to Martin's whereabouts, or his diamonds. He did not want to go to Bow Street, to air his family's dirty linen in public, but thought he might have to before too much time elapsed. First, he had one more place to try.

An old schoolmate of his, Harry'd heard, had opened a gambling casino, shocking the polite world but making a success of it, titillating the *ton* with the search for his missing sister. "Mad Jack" Endicott was just the scamp to thumb his nose at social conventions. Besides, he was a war hero and the brother of an earl, to boot. He could get away with much and still be accepted.

The Red and the Black was supposed to be an elegant gaming parlor, with lush appointments and luscious beauties dealing at the tables. Harry did not suppose Sir John Martin was spending his time—and Harry's money—in such expensive surroundings. What he was hoping was that Jack Endicott, now that he had dealings with London's underworld, dabbling in the demimonde, would know where a man went to sell stolen jewels, where a man hid out from his family.

Harry pulled his knit muffler up against the cold and walked to The Red and the Black. The city fops would have dragged out their horses and drivers for the brisk jaunt. Of course their cheeks would not have turned rosy, their hair would not be windblown, and their boots would not be dusty. What did Harry care? He was here to find a loose screw, not a lady wife.

Unsurprisingly for midmorning, the club's black door marked GUESTS was locked and no one answered his rap. The red door's sign said INTERVIEWS, but the long office was nearly empty except for two women and a clerkish-looking younger fellow. Despite Harry's intentions and his supposed disinterest, he hurriedly straightened his neckcloth and tried to brush back his hair when he entered the door and saw the women. Trust Mad Jack Endicott to attract the most beautiful ladybirds in London.

The smaller woman was a rounded dumpling of a brunette who flashed him a saucy smile while her friend spoke to the clerk. It was the friend who stole Harry's breath away. No, that was the fast walk and the cold. No bird of paradise was going to distract him from his mission, attract him to indiscretion. But, Lord, the black-clad female was stunning. The color of her clothes might be somber, but the cut was anything but, delineating her tall, slim figure under a velvet cape. The velvet did not look half as soft as her skin, either. He could not see her eyes, but he could glimpse a halo of shiny ebony curls under a scrap of ruffled black lace, with a plumed black feather held with a bright blue ribbon. Style, grace, and beauty all in one woman—and didn't she just know it? Hell, the woman had a dog that matched.

Harry admired the dog, too.

A long-legged black poodle, closely cropped in raven curls, had a blue collar fixed around his neck. He stood calmly, after giving Harry an inquisitive, intelligent look and one wag of a powder puff tail. The woman ignored the new arrival altogether, leaning toward the young man, concentrating on what the bespectacled secretary was telling her.

Harry took a seat on a hard bench, waiting his turn and enjoying the view of her animated profile and admirable bosom. No, he told himself, that was rude, and would give the wrong impression, besides. He was here for information, not a liaison with a dealer in a gaming parlor.

So he stood and turned his back, and studied the portrait on the wall and read about the reward for Jack Endicott's missing sister. Now, there was a true lady, Harry could not help thinking, looking at the angelic blue eyes in the painting, the serene smile, the erect posture, the composed features. Surely Lady Charlotte—or her mother or her cousin, whoever was used as a model for the missing child, now grown—would not be cursing, and not in French.

"Sacre bleu," he heard, his lips turning up at this latest affectation among London's highfliers.

Queenie had not meant to curse, especially not when there was a gentleman in the room. She had noticed the new arrival, of course. How could she not, when his entry pushed a cold draft into the nearly empty reception office? Then, too, his size was impressive and so were his hearty good looks, slightly disordered by the weather and his errand. Here was no London fribble, come to gamble away his fortune in the daylight hours or still castaway from the night before.

She turned her back on him, trying to ignore Hellen's

forward smile to the gentleman. She could not bother with the stranger's reasons for coming to The Red and the Black in the morning, not when her own were so important, and not when her hopes, her plans, and her dreams were being disordered.

Besides, she was more used to the French volatility than the somber British stoicism. So she cursed, then blushed and held her fingers to her mouth. Botheration. Now the young man in charge of this office thought she was no better than a strumpet, and heaven knew what the well-formed gentleman thought.

Nothing had gone right since her return from France, after all her grand efforts and preparations. For that matter, nothing had gone quite as she had hoped in Paris, either. Her expectations might have been too high, or her desperation too low.

Oh, with a bit of diligence and a new identity she had found a position with a well-regarded couturier, Monsieur Guatheme, who dressed royalty and wealthy women, the new aristocracy of France. Impressed by her drawings and her eagerness to learn, he was willing to let Queenie study in his studio and sewing room. After seeing what she could do taking charge of the chaos of his creative muse, the dressmaking maestro was willing to let her manage his day-to-day business while he made love to his beautiful clients. What he was not willing to do was pay Queenie. Monsieur expected her to study for free, or repay him for his lessons in a coin she refused to spend.

No one else was willing to take on an unknown apprentice, though, a woman without references other than her original designs and her soft-spoken manner. So Queenie had accepted Monsieur's offer and learned at his side. She also learned to carry a needle and scissors on a ribbon at her own side. She increased her vocabulary with French expressions for castration, having one's jewels sewn to one's jowls, and impotency due to darning needle.

Her old tutor would have been aghast. Molly would have been proud.

Queenie found her backbone, and she found a dog, on the advice of the protective, moralistic concierge she was lucky, and well funded enough, to find. Queenie knew nothing about dogs—she was learning about men and her chosen profession and that was quite enough—but her landlady had a cousin who had maintained kennels for fleeing noblemen. The returning survivors of the wars and the terrors could never know how many animals had been bred in their absence, or how many they now owned. Now Queenie owned a noble beast.

She called him Parfait because he was perfect. Polite and well trained, the large black poodle seldom left her side. He listened to her plans without criticism, her doubts with a perked ear, and her fears with a gentle lick on her cheek or hand. Truly he was the perfect companion, a better, more understanding friend than she had ever known. Once he understood who fed him, and to whom he owed freedom from a small cage and a crowded dog run, he gave her his allegiance and his protection. Anyone could approach him or his mistress, but let a man come between them, and the elegant, athletic, carefully bred, and refined dog reverted to his wolf ancestors.

Monsieur laughed, and left Queenie alone. The needle-woman's competency was more important than a quick tumble, and the poodle was bigger than even Monsieur's amour propre.

Queenie was content to study from Monsieur's master seamstresses, handling fabrics Molly could never have dreamed of, learning new methods and new confidence in her own sense of style. She was growing, getting ready to become her own person, not a pawn in some evil scheme, not someone's adopted waif, nor someone else's victim. When she had absorbed everything she could, then she would go home to start a new life. Such were Queenie's plans.

Until Monsieur started dressing his clients in her designs.

Oh, the cursing, the tears, and the hair pulling. Monsieur was distraught. How could such an accident have happened? How could one of his assistant's paltry fashions grace his most eminent patron?

How? Because he had stolen it from her portfolio, along with three others that appeared, under his name, in the latest fashion journal.

Ah, the scissor snipping, the fang flashing, the promise of lawsuits. Queenie was determined.

At last the Frenchman conceded. He paid her, not what the designs were worth, but enough to reimburse her apprenticeship. And he had the fashion journal print her new name, under his, of course, but for all to see. Winning was, perhaps, the greatest lesson that Queenie learned in France. Certainly it was the most satisfying.

Now she could return to England. Of course Queenie Dennis could not go back. Nor was that the name on the fashion plates in the five copies of *Le Grand Ensemble* she carefully packed. Instead she was now Madame Denise, dress designer. She took that name not for the villain Dennis Godfrey, who had wrought so much tragedy, but out of memory of Molly, who had taken her brother's name out of love, and taken Queenie to her heart. The *madame* was for maturity and credibility.

Because she was indebted to the house of Carde, and because she was part of their sorrow, she took *Lescartes* as her surname. Her fate was going to lie in the cards, one way or another.

Before she arrived in France, Queenie had cropped her long silver blond waves. Without the heavy weight, her hair took a natural curl, making her look like an old-master cherub until she dyed it black. A bit of kohl on her brows and lashes, a bit of powder and rouge, a sultry beauty mark near her lip, and she looked like a very wayward angel, indeed. Molly might not have recognized her, but the gentlemen certainly did.

And Queenie learned another lesson about power.

Without a quake or a tremble, Queenie and Parfait approached the same London bank where her mother's ill-found wealth rested. She established her bona fides with Monsieur's deposit, and sent for the remainder of her funds from Manchester, to the gratification of the clerk who assisted her, while assessing her response to his amorous innuendos.

Queenie's response was to ignore the man altogether. She gestured toward the slightly yellowed poster on the wall near his desk. "I see that they have not found the poor missing heiress."

The clerk puffed out his chest, without taking his eyes from Queenie's. "No, but we are diligent in our efforts. No one comes in here without being scrutinized."

So she had noticed. She stood, said, *"Merci,"* called her dog to heel, and left, past a soldier in a faded uniform who was acting as guard.

She found a tiny shop on Morningside Drive, with a front showroom and two smaller rooms behind that would be perfect for a working area and a fitting space. The narrow building even had an apartment above with two tiny bed-chambers and a sitting room. Best of all, it had a small rear yard for Parfait.

With new calling cards in her hand, Queenie approached the editors at the leading women's journals. The fashion plates shown in *Ackerman's, La Belle Assemblée,* and *The Ladies' Monthly Museum* were how London ladies selected their styles to be made up by modistes in their choices of fabrics and colors. Queenie aimed to have Madame Denise's name in those magazines, too, so the patrons would come directly to her.

The editors, all men, were not interested, although they did evince an interest in the ebony-curled dasher with her matching dog. Madame Denise was a young woman, albeit a gorgeous French widow dressed in the height of fashion. And she did have her name linked to the eminent Monsieur Guatheme's . . . but so did every other beautiful woman in Paris, it seemed. They turned her away, with regrets.

A new journal was making its debut, though. *A Lady's World* was the product of a young couple eager to make their own fortunes in the new economy after the wars, when the burgeoning merchant class had money to spend. The wives and daughters of the bankers and manufacturers might not be true ladies, but they could act and dress like the aristoc-racy if someone helped. The Milstroms were ready, and they were ready to take on an unknown designer who shared their enthusiasm.

Queenie sold them the very same fashion plates from the Paris journal, with a few alterations, and signed a contract for future dress designs. Now she knew she could support herself. The income was not enough for her needs, of course, but the rest would come when she developed a clien-tele and a cachet.

They would come in time, Queenie believed, her confidence restored by her early success.

She was not quite confident enough to approach the Earl of Carde or his brother, Captain Endicott, yet, however. She was determined to make restitution, or give them satisfaction, at least an end to their search. First, though, she had to know the current state of their affairs—and her own. Perhaps the earl's family had given up seeking Lady Charlotte, or they might have settled on a plausible imposter, or they might have warrants out for the arrest of one Queenie Dennis.

For all she knew, they might have caught and hung Ize by now, which would not have cost her a single tear unless he blamed her for the blackmail and the rest.

After discarding alternatives, she sent a note to Hellen Pettigrew. Other than Parfait, who did not count, Hellen was Queenie's best friend in all of England, her only friend. Hellen's mother, Valerie, was too driven by her own desires and the need for money to confide in. Then, too, she was a rich man's mistress, so her scruples were suspect from the start.

Queenie had to trust someone, but she still asked Hellen to meet her in the park, not giving her direction.

"What, did you think I would peach on you?" the other girl asked in indignation, after exclaiming at the changes in her friend as they took seats on a secluded bench.

Queenie had brought sticky buns to share, knowing Hellen's appetite and tastes. She held one out, and simply said, "The reward was high."

Through a mouthful of crumbs, Hellen sputtered, "I would never turn you in for the money! And Mama is in funds. The baron sent her a ruby pendant for Christmas, and a gold necklace for me. The money from their sale will hold us a good while." She fed a corner of her bun to the dog. "Besides, we never did know the connection between you and the reward notices for the Carde heiress. And even if we did, we had no idea where you had gone. You would not tell us, remember?"

Queenie ignored the unspoken resentment. She had fled to protect herself and her friends. "I will tell you if you swear not to repeat a word to anyone. Truly, my life might depend on your silence."

Hellen leaned forward, ignoring the dog, who was sniffing at her gloves. "I'll swear on my hopes of heaven"— which were growing dimmer by the day—"not to utter your name, but only if you tell me the truth."

So Queenie did, to her relief at explaining herself to someone, and to Hellen's amazement.

"You mean you were always meant to be Lady Charlotte, but now you do not intend to be?"

"Of course not."

Hellen shook her head and sighed. "I suppose not, with your hair dyed black. But you could do it, play the lady, live in a grand house with servants, never have to work a day in your life."

"I like my work. Besides, I am *not* Lady Charlotte Endicott. I am an orphan."

"But they do not have to know that, only that you came to Molly at the right time, from the wrong hands. They could not prove otherwise."

"And I could not prove the reverse. But I know. I will not torture that poor family with another false hope or another pretender."

"Well, I do not hear that they are suffering. It is not as if they are pining away for grief over a child they have not seen in over a decade and have little enough reason to believe is alive. Both brothers are doing well for themselves, according to the gossip columns. Captain Jack has a new wife and a ward, they say, and the earl is filling his nursery."

"I am glad for them both." And Queenie was, feeling an odd sense of kinship with the gentlemen. Besides, if they were content with their lots, perhaps they would view her confession more complacently. "What about Ize?" she asked now. "Has he been causing you trouble?"

Hellen took another bun from the sack. "He comes around every once in a while. Mama does not like him calling at our rooms, for the neighbors' sake. She merely says we have not heard from you and sends him on his way."

"Good. He is evil."

"He seems to give Mama fair value for her jewels, although he no longer has a shop."

"Perhaps so, but he is a dangerous man." Queenie had not fully mentioned Ize's part in the crimes, only that he was implicated and angry. "That is why I could not give you my address, so you cannot tell him."

Hellen was confused, a not unusual circumstance. "But if you are setting up shop as Madame Denise, you will have to give out your business cards."

"But Ize does not know that Madame Denise Lescartes and Queenie Dennis are one and the same. He must not know."

"I know that."

"Which is why we must not meet again."

"Pooh, he would not know you from the prince's latest mistress. I swear I barely did—you are so changed. Of course once you talked and I saw your eyes, I knew who you were, but I was looking to meet you anyway, wasn't I? If you speak French and keep your eyes half closed in that sultry manner, Ize will never recognize you for shy little

Queenie. Besides, what could be more natural than I would befriend a newcomer to Town, who is going to dress me in style?"

"I am?"

"Of course. You would not leave me out of the most exciting adventure of my lifetime, would you?"

"Now that you mention it, I was hoping you might agree to be my shop manager."

Hellen's round face fell. So did the bun from her fingers, to Parfait's delight. "A clerk in a shop? I was hoping to be a courtesan."

Hellen, it seemed, had plans for her own future.

CHAPTER FOUR

Now Queenie dropped her roll from numb fingers. She'd have to give Parfait less for his dinner. She'd give Hellen a good shake if they were not in the park. "You wish to become a . . . a . . ."

"A highly paid mistress to a wealthy gentleman. It is good enough for my mother," Hellen said in her own defense. "And it is not as if any handsome swell is going to come along and offer for the baron's by-blow, you know. My father is too afraid of his wife to settle an annuity on me or anything. So what choices do I have? Sewing for some toff's wife, or being his pampered pet?"

She looked at Parfait, with his leather collar to match Queenie's bonnet's ribbon, his sleek, well-fed, well-groomed appearance and relaxed manner. "I choose the life of luxury."

"But it is not always that way, surely you know. You have seen the women begging in the street, raddled, pox-ridden hags or emaciated girls with starving infants at their breasts. You could not want that!"

"Of course not. Only fools end in the gutters, wigeons who value themselves too cheaply or who accept the wrong protector. I am too smart for that, and too pretty not to be a success. And while I have seen the street-corner whores, I have also seen my mother and her friends. They have houses and maids and carriages of their own. The cleverest have savings and the others have their jewels for when their gentlemen tire of them. All they have to do is look pretty and entertain their polite friends. Champagne and a few cuddles, then bonbons and bank deposits. A girl could do far worse."

"But what of the gentlemen's other families?"

"What, should I pity those cold women who do not please their husbands enough to keep them home? Or should I be jealous? Who is to say their lords care for them more than for their paramours? Those marriages were business transactions, the same as a rich cull keeping a mistress."

"But it is wrong!"

"It would be worse to make Mama support me forever. The baron is not all that generous, and his health not assured. I need to contribute."

By bartering her body? Queenie could not look at her friend.

Hellen brushed crumbs off her gloves. "I do not intend to sell myself for a groat for a grope in the doorway, you know. You'll help me look expensive, won't you?"

Queenie would do anything to save Hellen from the life of a Covent Garden convenient. "But when my business is a success I can—"

"You can dress me in the height of fashion and send the bills to my gentleman."

Queenie shook her head. "No, I cannot do it."

"*You* do not have to do it. You have talent and an education, a profession you enjoy, and the manners of a lady. I have nothing but my face and figure. But I do like the gentlemen."

Queenie realized that her friend liked *all* the gentlemen. She had to pinch Hellen's elbow to stop her from batting her eyelashes at the serious young man who was conducting the interviews at The Red and the Black. Then she had to kick her ankle to keep Hellen from speaking to the handsome newcomer. She had not wanted to take Hellen along with her to the club at all, but Hellen was not to be denied her look at an earl's brother. Besides, how better to survey possible protectors than as a dealer at the gaming parlor?

Not only was The Red and the Black not hiring, but it was no longer a casino.

Queenie glanced back to see if the gentleman had heard her latest muttered imprecation. All she could see was the back of his coat, however, a garment she recognized instantly as of fine fabric and impeccable tailoring. His manners were also excellent, she noted as he pretended to study the portrait on the wall.

She turned back and in her French accent apologized again to . . . "I am sorry, monsieur, I missed your name in my haste."

The young man bowed slightly in return for her politeness, from where he still stood behind his desk. He adjusted his glasses, then consulted her card, having also missed her name in his mooncalf admiration for her looks. "Browne, Madame Lescartes, John George Browne, at your service. Soon to be headmaster of the Ambeaux Silver School for Females."

Now Hellen swore. "A blasted school? Why would anyone turn a successful gaming parlor into a dreary institution?"

Mr. John George Browne forced his eyes from Queenie and addressed the younger woman. "The captain felt he could do more for unfortunate young females by educating them than by offering a temporary position on their way down the primrose path."

Since that was precisely the direction Hellen was headed, with or without this plaguey club or its prosy schoolteacher, she turned her back on him and took Queenie's arm. "We might as well leave, then."

Queenie was not ready, wanting to hear more about the new venture and the earl's younger brother. "That is quite noble of Captain Endicott." And quite unlike his raffish reputation.

In light of her interest, Mr. Browne's face took on an earnest glow. This was, after all, now his own life's work. "Actually, the captain's wife was a schoolmistress before coming to London," he confided, since such was public knowledge anyway. "She did not approve of the connection to a gambling establishment. Captain Endicott had acquired a ward, you see, the granddaughter to a lord. The Red and the Black was deemed no place to rear a wellborn miss."

Queenie agreed. A gentlemen's wagering den was no place for a lady, or a decent female of any class. Her opinion of Captain Jack Endicott rose a notch. "So now the place shall become a school? But can that provide an income?"

"Oh, Miss Silver, that would be Mrs. Captain Endicott now, came into a bit of the ready. And the captain's brother is a great believer in schooling for the underprivileged, so there is a handsome endowment. The institution is to be called the Ambeaux Silver School in recognition of Miss Silver's father, a noted scholar, and for Captain Jack's stepmother, the mother of the poor little girl who was lost." His eyes strayed to the rear of the room, and the portrait.

Which gave Queenie the opportunity to ask more questions. "How lovely to commemorate such memories, but have they given up hopes for finding the young lady, then?"

"Not at all," Mr. Browne replied. "That is why someone is here at all times, despite the club being shut for the past months and work on the renovations for the classrooms not yet begun. There is also a man on the earl's payroll at Bow Street, ready to receive any clues. They thought they had a name for a likely lead, but the young woman never showed her face, despite the raised reward moneys."

Hellen had taken to fidgeting with her bonnet strings, anxious to leave this unpromising place, but Queenie would not budge. "Tell me, Mr. Browne, are you in position to hire staff for the new school?"

The young man puffed himself up with pride. "Indeed. The captain and his lady have entrusted me with interviewing candidates for the posts, as well as establishing curricula and class schedules."

"Those are great responsibilities. The family must have great confidence in your abilities."

Mr. John George Browne's chest swelled further at the lovely lady's interest and discernment. Few women, especially such paragons as Madame Lescartes, gave him a second glance. Which was why, perhaps, he expounded on his own background and blessings. "I am by way of being a protégé of Lord Carde's, the captain's brother, of course. My family does a small service for his lordship, keeping charge of Mr. Sloane, Lady Carde's brother, who caused the whole mingle-mangle of the missing girl in the first place, no matter how they tried to keep that bit quiet. He is dicked in the nob."

At Queenie's questioning look, he tapped his temple. "Touched, you know. But the family would not want him in a Bedlam, for the world to see and belittle. So my parents keep him at their inn outside of Town, making certain he cannot cause any more trouble or scandal. My brothers watch over him, although my sister mostly keeps him company. In addition to his generous fees, the earl sent me to university, and then recommended me to Captain Endicott for this post. His lordship feels I can go far, with experience and the proper backing."

"I am sure you shall, Mr. Browne."

Hellen stepped closer. The sandy-haired, bespectacled bloke was a man of means and potential? A family business, an earl's favor? She flashed him a wide smile, making sure to show her dimples. "You must be a very intelligent man, Mr. Browne."

Browne blushed red. "I, ah, hope I do not disappoint the earl, miss."

"Pettigrew, Miss Hellen Pettigrew, with two *l*s."

Queenie interrupted before Hellen could give the poor man her address, or another pat on his now trembling hand. "But are you succeeding in your quest, Mr. Browne? Have you filled the school's roster of instructors?"

Now Browne had to tear his eyes from the two dimples to look at Madame Lescartes. "Nearly so, except for a few places, since the school cannot open until reconstruction is complete."

"You shall need a competent sewing instructor if you hope to improve the girls' lots in life. Such knowledge will give your students opportunities for honest, gainful employment."

"Yes, teaching practical skills is to be part of their education."

"Then I shall apply for the position."

Hellen stopped smiling. "I thought you were set on designing your gowns and making your mark in the world of fashion, Que—ouch. That is, queer start, if you ask me."

Queenie raised her chin. "I can do both. And I can further the school's efforts by hiring its graduates. That must be the captain's intentions, to see his pupils settled in worthwhile careers."

Mr. Browne looked from one to the other of the women, bewildered at this latest turn. Were the females dealers, doxies, or do-gooders? He had no idea.

"Do not concern yourself, sir. I shall take up my proposition with Captain Endicott himself," Queenie insisted. "If you would inform him that I wish to confer on a matter concerning the advancement of education?"

Browne shook his head, wishing he truly could hand this confusion over to his employer. "I am afraid Captain Endicott is not conducting interviews. Nor Mrs. Captain Endicott, either, for that matter. They are not here."

"Then I shall call at Carde House. I believe that was where the captain's wife and his ward were residing."

"They are not there, either, nor the earl and his lady. They're all in Northamphire for Lady Carde's lying-in, and bride visits. They won't return until the school is ready to open, perhaps in late spring when the roads improve."

"Satan's smallclothes," Queenie cursed, not bothering with the French or keeping her voice lowered.

This time Harry could not ignore the heartfelt expletive. Nor the fact that the female might be in trouble. Besides, she was taking too long. He had business to conduct, a bastard to confront, and politeness extended only so far. The lady in black was beautiful, and her dog well behaved, but still, she was in The Red and the Black, which meant she was not entitled to all the niceties of a ballroom.

Still, he was a gentleman, so Harry stepped closer to the front of the room and asked, "Pardon, miss, is there some difficulty?"

Difficulty? The casino was closed, her dreaded confrontation with the Carde family was delayed yet again, and her best friend was bent on a life of sin. Where was the difficulty for the broad gentleman in his casual yet expensive attire? "Nothing that could concern you, sir," she said a bit abruptly, despite his courtesy. She was angry at the situation, this stranger for witnessing it, and the fact that she felt too weak to leave the office. All her energy and efforts had gone into meeting Captain Jack Endicott today, here, at last. Now she had no strength to face the same prospect at a later date.

"Come, Hellen," she said, disguising her relief that her knees had not yet buckled beneath her; they had been knocking together so hard. "Let us sit here and discuss our next move."

Hellen sank onto the hard wooden bench beside her, as despondent as Queenie was drained. "Well, at least you are not going to become a schoolmarm any time soon."

A teacher? Harry could not imagine a female less like the image in his mind of a schoolmistress. The raven-curled fancy piece had no pinched face, no scraped-back hair, no shapeless, colorless gown hiding whatever feminine attributes she possessed. Even if she had been garbed in a sack, her eyes when she looked at him would have given her away. A Siren's eyes, they were, calling a man to drown in their blue, blue depths. They were more intense, more vivid even than the lady's in the portrait, perhaps enhanced by the artful use of cosmetics Harry thought he could detect. No, this gorgeous female was no elevated governess.

And she was no business of his.

Harry stepped closer toward the desk and held out his

hand to the younger man, who was still staring after the woman as if she had stolen his heart or his wits, the poor blighter.

"I am Harking, a friend of Jack Endicott's," Harry said. "I have come to speak to Jack on a personal matter."

The man took his hand, but also bowed, recognizing quality, if not Harry's specific title. "I regret the captain is out of Town, my lord."

"Then perhaps one of his minions might speak with me on a delicate topic?"

"I am sorry, but no one else is here. The club is closed. As I was telling the ladies, The Red and the Black is about to be turned into a school."

Jack Endicott running a school? The devil-may-care cub had barely managed to stay in school on his own account, from what Harry recalled. Tugging his knit muffler around his neck again, Harry said, "It seems I have wasted my morning, then."

The younger man, at least seven years Harry's junior, seemed to be sincere in his attempt to help a friend of his employer, especially one who must appear fresh from the country. "Perhaps I can be of assistance? I am familiar with London, if not the intricacies of a roulette wheel."

Harry had to try something. He lowered his voice, although the women were holding a private discussion on one of the benches. "I am in Town looking for a certain man. I was hoping Jack might know of him or his whereabouts. His name is Sir John Martin, and I have reason to believe he is a gambler and a wastrel." He held his hand up to forestall the other man's protests. "Not that I am implying that Captain Endicott's former clientele was such a gathering of loose fish, but that Jack might have known about his ilk."

Mr. Browne straightened a stack of papers on his desk

while he considered. "The captain knew everyone. His business was to know who could pay and who was punting on tick, of course. That was how he became such a success, besides his head for odds. But that was before I got here. Mr. Bonner, who managed the club, has left, and Snake, that is, the doorkeeper, has gone north with the family. I am sorry, my lord. I know nothing of your Sir John Martin."

"I thank you anyway." Harry nodded and turned to go.

"But if it is a Town buck you are looking for," Browne called after him as Harry made his way past the women toward the door, "you might try the Cyprian's Ball tomorrow night. Every rake and would-be womanizer will be there, with Town so thin of other entertainment. If your, ah, friend is not in the petticoat line, he might still attend for the deep wagering. It is by subscription, so you do not need an invite. Anyone with the price of admission is welcome."

Harry did not want anything to do with the infamous gatherings that turned into orgies, where men selected their latest paramours or passing fancies. Lewd and licentious, the Cyprian's Balls represented the very worst London had to offer. The thought of attending one left a rancid taste in Harry's mouth.

Not so Hellen, whose mood improved almost as quickly as her smile flashed when she heard Harry was a lord. "Did you hear that, Que—Cousin? There is going to be another ball of the demimonde. Let's go!"

Queenie felt as if she'd swallowed the same bitter lemon as Lord Harking. "Are you insane? Those affairs are dangerous and depraved."

"Pooh, they are not all that bad. A girl can avoid any unsavory characters, and she can always say no to an unwelcome offer, can't she? Mostly it will be the perfect chance to be seen and meet gentlemen."

"You know no one to make introductions."

Hellen laughed. "Half the guests wear masks, silly. This is not the queen's drawing room. The whole point is to encounter strangers."

John George Browne had come away from his desk to escort Lord Harking to the door. "The affairs are not all that bad, at least in the early hours. Dancing, wine, good food, pretty girls."

"Are you going, then, man?" Harry asked in a harsh tone. "Since you appear to think such entertainment is attractive."

"No, I cannot afford to keep a—" Browne looked toward the women. "That is, I am a schoolmaster now. I cannot think my patrons would approve."

"Your mother would not approve," Queenie whispered to Hellen.

"Pooh, that is how she met my father. And besides, it is the perfect place for you to show off your dress designs and help your name become known. If you wish your business to be a success, you have to advertise it. You could wait years selling drawings before you came to the notice of so many fashionables in one night."

"The Fashionable Impures."

"Who are more likely to pay their bills on time than your society ladies, who believe they are doing you the favor by patronizing your establishment. And it is the brightest comet in the sky that catches the eye, not the cold, distant stars. You can only be talked about by dressing women who are talked about, you know."

Hellen was right.

Browne was telling Harry, "The ball is your best bet to find your man. You could search London for weeks before finding so many here-and-there-ians gathered under one roof. And respectable gentlemen, also," he added at Harry's continued scowl.

Browne was right.

Damn! Harry thought.

Diable! Queenie thought.

Sensing his mistress's distress, Parfait whined, which dragged Harry's thoughts from the sordid soiree back to the birds of paradise on the bench. Schoolmistresses, ha! They had their heads together, most likely discussing their outfits for the coming revelry. All such women cared about was clothes—and money.

His money. Lud, they would be lining up to put their hands in his pockets—or elsewhere. The highfliers could be worse than the matchmaking mamas because they were more desperate—and more obvious in their intentions. They had fewer years to assure their futures, for time did not sit gently on a whore's shoulders. Gently bred females at least still had their pedigrees and their dowries when the next year's debutantes made their curtsies. The barques of frailty had nothing but their beauty.

While young ladies gave the appearance of ignoring the purpose of their Seasons, the light-skirts flaunted their ambitions. That was what a Cyprian's Ball was about. Harry guessed he would be too busy fending off prospective Paphians to even locate Martin in the smoke and the crowds and the hidden corners. He would be fleeing instead of hunting, unless, of course, he had protection from the ravening pack. With a gun—no, with a woman on his arm, he ought to be safe. . . .

"We cannot go without an escort," Queenie was saying. "It is simply too dangerous for two inexperienced women. You know that when men overindulge, manners lapse. And not all who attend these affairs are gentlemen anyway, or ones who will listen to a woman's wishes when in their cups. I shall not go without a gentleman's protection unless I can take my dog. It would not be safe."

"You cannot take Parfait!"

Parfait heard his name and looked at Hellen. Hellen looked at Lord Harking. Harry looked at Queenie. Queenie looked at the floor. Mr. Browne looked at all of them and decided he might bend his own rules a bit. "What say we all go?"

CHAPTER FIVE

B rowne made the introductions. "Madame Denise Lescartes is a dress designer," he concluded.

And Harry was a Hottentot. But the female would serve his purposes more than adequately. Who would suppose he'd look at another female with such a beauty on his arm? In fact, Harry was savoring the notion of his bastard of a brother-in-law seeing him with the false French femme. Let Martin call Harry a prig and a prude. Let him turn green with envy—before Harry turned his flesh black-and-blue.

While Harry was pondering mayhem and making an impression, Queenie was also considering her choices. Yes, she decided, this gentleman was sturdy enough and somber enough to take his duties as escort seriously. Heaven knew he was large enough, with well-formed muscles and the occasional unmannered look to his brown eyes, like now, to discourage any other man's unwanted attentions. Moreover, he had none of those broken veins in his nose that betokened a tippler, nor pouches under his eyes from late nights. His complexion was healthy, his step assured.

Harking would do, Queenie decided, if she had to do this dreadful thing. There was something solid and trustworthy about him. Perhaps it was the humble knit muffler, or the boyish blush to his cheeks as he bowed over her hand.

"Will you and Miss, ah, Pettigrew do me the honor of accompanying me and Browne, madam? I am looking for my brother-in-law and the more eyes, the better."

The brother-in-law was a likely excuse, Queenie thought, somehow charmed that Harking would not want to admit seeking a mistress. But he had included Hellen and Mr. Browne in his invitation, taking charge in a masterful way that pleased her, despite herself. Now she would not have to be afraid of being in his company in private, or letting Hellen go off on her own.

"We would be honored," she answered for both of them. "I am hoping to advertise my new dress designs. The more people who see them, the better," she echoed.

The gowns were a likely excuse, Harry thought, a shade offended that Madame Denise Lescartes felt she needed a flimsy reason to act as his companion for the night. A female in her situation should have leaped at the chance, even if he was not as rich as Croesus or as romantic as a Romeo. Miss Pettigrew was bouncing on the bench in her excitement, and Browne was grinning. Madame Lescartes was frowning.

The dog growled. Harry stepped back, realizing he had been about to kiss Madame Lescartes's hand to seal their agreement before she could change her mind. He hadn't felt any ring under her glove, which somehow helped him ignore her recalcitrance. "Then we shall provide assistance to each other," he said, sounding too stiff to his own ears, which he feared were turning red. He added, "And perhaps we might have a pleasant evening while doing so."

Miss Pettigrew laughed and clapped her hands together.

"Of course we shall have a lovely time. Why would we not?"

Perhaps because Queenie feared Harking thought he was hiring a mistress, and he believed her a whore. She could read it in his open countenance, and how fast he had dropped her hand, as if he might be contaminated by her presence. The handsome hypocrite was going to a Cyprian's dance, all the while making alibis for being there, Queenie fumed. He might make alibis. He would not mistake her intentions. She raised her chin.

"Yes, we shall have a good evening. One evening."

Harry could not misinterpret her meaning. She was refusing his offer of carte blanche before he even thought of making it; she was that sure of herself and her appeal. What, were his pockets not deep enough? His manners not polished finely enough? Or did he simply not match her deuced dog?

The female could look as high as she wished for a protector, Harry admitted. Most men would be panting over the possibility of acquiring her services for a night, a week, a month, however long it took to satisfy their curiosity and carnal urges. But Harry was not most men, even if his breath was coming a bit fast at the thought of taking Madame Lescartes to the ball—and then home. To discover her secrets under the elegant clothes she wore, to feel those tight curls, and the tighter ones elsewhere, to feel that satiny skin next to— "One evening," Harry said with a gasp.

Perhaps the gentleman was not as prosperous as he looked, Queenie guessed, if he supposed her company came with too high a price for his purse. Many a nob visited the finest tailors and haberdashers without having a feather to fly with. How unfortunate if Harking was like so many others, punting on tick and putting a price on everything, even a night's companionship. Queenie did not know how she could tell him that she would not accept a shilling, not even the cost of her admission to the ball.

On the other hand, maybe he was becoming nervous, afraid of his wife's hearing about his illicit outing.

"If your family might be upset to read your name in the scandal sheets, perhaps we ought to reconsider. I understand reporters and gossip columnists regularly attend such functions." Queenie was counting on it, to get her name known.

"No, no one will care," he said. "And one appearance at a risqué ball would be a minor blot on the family escutcheons after—that is, shall Monsieur Lescartes be calling me out in the morning?"

What, was he a coward, besides clutch-fisted? Queenie shook her head, disappointed in her chosen chevalier. If he was frightened of some nonexistent Frenchman, how could he keep her safe from the rakes and reprobates at the party? "Monsieur Lescartes is not a consideration."

Whatever that noncommittal statement meant, Harry was relieved anyway. The idea of some man having this woman, possessing her, was enough to chill his bones, despite the muffler. Not that he wished to possess her, of course. He'd simply been without a woman too long, that was it. And his body was reacting like any red-blooded male to the sight — and was that a lilac scent?—of a seductive woman. "Yes, well, I shall be returning to Lincolnshire soon," he said, reminding himself. "Directly after the ball, I hope."

She nodded as graciously as a duchess. "So we understand each other."

"Of course. A pleasant evening in the public eye. Nothing more."

She held her hand out—to pick up Parfait's lead. "Nothing more."

*   *   *

She did not like him, Harry realized. So much was obvious by Madame Lescartes's curt farewell, and her reluctance to give her address. How did she think he was to fetch her to the ball? And what was she afraid of, that he would linger upon her doorstep like some lovesick swain, keeping away wealthier patrons? He had already told her he was leaving London shortly.

The sooner he left, the better, Harry told himself, if the opinion of a doxy mattered to him. He had spent enough of his life trying to establish a good reputation among his neighbors without beginning to worry how he appeared in a wanton's eyes.

They were magnificent eyes, though, a blue a poet could spend a lifetime trying to describe without finding the right phrase. No words could describe the life burning there, the intelligence, the—

The devil take it! Madame Lescartes was a loose London lady, nothing more. After a quick glance at the card she handed him, Harry vowed not to think about her again until the evening he had to pick her up for the ball. He had too much to do, anyway, visiting some of the lesser gaming dens, a few less reputable jewelers. Time was passing and heaven knew where Martin was selling the Harking diamonds.

He'd think about recovering his heirlooms, not whether it was proper for him to send flowers ahead of the ball. Or if he should carry with him the sapphire pendant he'd purchased, or send it the morning afterward in payment. And if there was time for him to have a dancing lesson.

No! He would not spend a second or a shilling trying to impress his hired companion. Of course he spent ages at the livery stable, selecting the proper coach and ensuring it was clean and polished. And he did survey the wares of every jeweler he visited before settling on the sapphire necklace, although the color was not nearly right for the woman's eyes. And he did let the hotel's assigned servant look over his wardrobe.

Lord Harking's appearance was a reflection on his skill, the fussy valet insisted, on the hotel, the viscount's own stature in society, and his respect for the lady.

Harry did not respect the woman; that was the problem. She was a means to finding his brother-in-law, Harry told himself, the same as little Miss Pettifog, or whatever the other gal's name was. Madame Lescartes was a link to Martin, nothing else. If he happened to find the dirty dish before the ball, Harry decided, he would cancel his arrangement with Madame Lescartes and send the pendant.

Right after he slit his throat.

The valet did not permit him to get near the razor. Or a comb or a mirror or the evening dress he had hastily packed before leaving Lincolnshire. Did he truly possess so many neckcloths that the valet could discard a score before declaring the final strangulating knot a masterpiece? And when had Harry bought a satin waistcoat with that narrow blue stripe? Lud, he had not been babbling in his bath about blue eyes, had he?

No, the gentleman's gentleman must have noticed the sapphire pendant in the velvet box. Why else would he be winking and smirking? Harry had not noticed the man had a twitch.

Finally, after what seemed like a week, Harry was ready. And pleased with his appearance when the valet finally let him look in the mirror. Madame Denise Lescartes might not like him, might not consider him fit to become her prospective protector, but he was not going to embarrass her, either. Not that he cared, of course.

Oh, dear, he did not like her. Queenie could tell by how Lord Harking did not linger after learning her address. This was a business arrangement for him, not a friendship. So how was she supposed to spend an already fraught evening with a disapproving gentleman? With steel in her spine and a—notepad?—in her reticule. His toplofty lordship's opinion did not matter; the well-dressed women's names did.

Besides, she was too busy to fret over one large gentleman's opinion. Her ensemble had to be perfect, as did Hellen's. Furnishing her shop and finding fabrics for her creations could wait.

They agreed that Hellen should dress and stay overnight at Queenie's rooms above the store. Valerie Pettigrew's rest would not be disturbed that way. And Queenie would not have to travel in a carriage alone with a strange man.

He did not appear dangerous. But Queenie was anxious anyway. Anxious? Her fingers might have been icicles and her toes frozen to the floor. Despite her hard-won poise and professed confidence, Queenie was terrified. All those people, all looking at her. Then again, what if no one looked at her? All her efforts would be wasted. Perhaps her work would be for naught anyway. She was too pale to do her clothes justice, too worn-out from long nights of sewing, the longer nights she spent awake and worrying. She was too thin, too bony. He would be ashamed, not that Lord Harking wanted her anyway, of course. Perhaps she should cancel.

Hellen would clobber her.

The momentous night finally arrived. As did Harking, with Browne getting out of the coach behind him.

Harry was struck dumb. She really was a dressmaker. The tiny shop was fairly empty, but the sign outside read MADAME DENISE DESIGNS, and had a whimsical painting of the poodle Parfait wearing a bonnet. The front window held a mannequin wearing a black gown. Harry's quick glance could not tell him if the style was in fashion—a longer look could not have told him, truth be told—but she really was a dressmaker!

Hope-born images of a gentlewoman fallen on hard times flashed through his mind, only to fade. No true lady attended the Cyprian's Ball. And no female with such a face and figure ever fell on hard enough times to ply a needle.

Still, Harry's dismay at the night dissipated. The lady was not necessarily for sale to the highest bidder; her gowns were! What a lovely evening it was going to be.

Queenie was staring out the door, at the magnificent coach waiting for some royal personage to board it, with four liveried servants to assist. Then she took another look at Lord Harking in the lamplight. He was dressed to the nines in midnight blue and pristine white, with no hint of the casual countryman about him. He was no less handsome in her eyes, but far more assured in his dark formal evening wear, as if he knew he belonged in London, as if its history ran through his blood, which it likely did. He really was a lord.

She must have spoken the thought aloud, for he said, "An unillustrious minor viscount. What, did you doubt I truly held a title?"

"Men are not always what they appear. I had only Mr. Browne's courtesy to you as evidence. I suppose some women might have rushed home to consult their *Debrett's Peerage* book."

"But you did not." That was a statement, not a question.

Then, because he truly was curious, Harry asked, "Does it make a difference?" He could not ask if she would like him better if he had a higher title.

"No, of course not." Except now her knees were locked in place and she would never be able to walk out of the shop to the coach.

While she stood staring at her toes, Harry belatedly handed over a box, a larger one than the jeweler's velvet case that was in his pocket. This box came from a florist, who might have been a diamond merchant, too, for the price he charged. Of course, when one went searching for the rarest of that new breed of orchid he'd heard of, one with vivid blue in the throat of the blossom, one had to pay. "You do not have to carry it, of course. I was not certain about your gown's color."

Queenie was already pinning the flower to her reticule, to carry with her or dangle from her arm. "It is perfect."

So was her gown, Harry thought, now that he could think after the first heart-stopping look at his evening's companion. Her gown was black again. Lud, do not let her be in mourning for the absent Monsieur Lescartes, he prayed, with her heart in the grave with him. But this ensemble was no widow's weeds, not the silk underdress or the gossamer lace that covered her arms but left half her admirable bosom bare. No, here was a celebration of life and love—or lovemaking, at any rate. Tiny blue flowers were embroidered at the hem, as if she walked through a meadow, and a circlet of silk forget-me-nots crowned her black curls. As if any man could ever forget this woman.

Harry might forget his name, and the direction to his hotel, but this night, this female, would stay in his mind's eye forever. Dash it, how was he to find a respectable bride when the time came?

He thought of offering the sapphire pendant, since her throat was bare. Most of the other women would be dripping in jewels tonight, he knew, but Madame Lescartes was correct. Her satin skin was adornment enough, letting nothing take a man's eyes away from the gown or the woman who wore it.

Then she turned to bid the dog farewell. Harry's eyes nearly crossed. There was almost no back to the back of her gown, almost to her waist. Which meant she wore no stays, no corset, no shift, nothing to keep a man's hand—once he tore his glove off with his teeth—from touching tender flesh. Great gods, how was he to get through the night and still call himself a gentleman? By fixing his gaze on the birthmark beside her lip, he decided. Not her full, rosy lips, which appeared eminently kissable, and not her blue, blue eyes, which made a man think of heaven. Not her creamy bosom, for certain, and not her soft black curls, which would look magnificent against a white silk pillowcase.

He looked at Hellen instead. The other woman was pirouetting in front of Browne, exclaiming over her own bouquet, which Harry had bought as an afterthought. She wore pink sarcenet and looked as sweet, and as tempting, as a raspberry tart. Browne was practically drooling and his spectacles were befogged, making Harry wonder if he looked like such a mooncalf himself.

Surely Madame Lescartes was a genius, he decided, to garb the younger woman so seductively, while retaining a hint of innocence, to say nothing of the engineering marvel of her own gown.

"You are bound to be a success with designs such as these," he said, knowing his words were inadequate, but heartfelt nevertheless.

His compliment meant the world to Queenie, for it was

not directed to her looks, for which she could take no credit, but toward her own efforts, her own imagination. She gave him a smile so bright it rivaled his missing diamonds.

Ah, the show. The drama, the well-rehearsed actors, the splendid scenery, the bright costumes, the scintillating dialogue. Drury Lane had nothing on the Assembly of Eros.

This early in the evening, few of the revelers were deep in their cups or sequestered in dark corners. Most of the guests were still looking for a partner for a country dance, a card game, or a cuddle. So all eyes were on the entrance when Harry and his party entered, still arguing over Harry's earlier purchase of the four tickets. The chatter abated; the movement stilled. Even the smoke cleared, it seemed.

Viscount Harking had never been seen in such surroundings. Hardnose Harking at the Cyprian's Ball? Hell must have frozen over. Very few of the women were acquainted with him—a situation they instantly decided to rectify. His companion was a total unknown—a she-devil in ice skates, obviously, to get him there.

Ah, she was French! That explained the style, the glitter, the à-la-modality of Harking's *chérie amour*. It did not explain Harking. Who knew the blockish rustic had it in him, the sly dog?

The other men would have taken his place here or in Hades gladly. The deuce take them, they would have suffered fire and cold for eternity—their souls were already likely consigned to the netherworld—for one night with Harking's incognita.

Regrettably, the men recognized possession when they saw it, and knew they had less chance than the proverbial snowball. If the viscount held his paramour any closer, he would be sharing her gown.

And what a gown! If the women could not pry an introduction to Harking, at least they could discover the name of the woman's mantua-maker. Whispers were soon making the rounds of the female's name, and her profession.

A waste, the men derided. With that face, that figure, Madame Denise Lescartes was meant for one career. Unfortunately, Harking had already claimed her time. She clung to him, and smiled slightly—but only for him.

Harry felt her hand shaking where it rested on his arm. To his surprise, and the burgeoning of his protective instincts, the elegant, worldly Madame Lescartes was nervous, uncertain, atremble at the attention they were drawing. He drew her nearer and placed his arm over her shoulder. He whispered close to her ear, "You are the most beautiful, intelligent woman in the room, and I am the luckiest of men."

And here he always thought empty flattery was beyond him.

It was. He spoke the truth.

CHAPTER SIX

Queenie laughed, a gentle, rippling sound like angels singing.

Lord Higgentham spilled his drink, Earl Mainwaring stepped on his partner's foot, and Harry felt ten feet tall.

"I mean it," he said.

Queenie knew he did. That was why she was smiling.

For a moment, amid the crowds and the jostling, the noise and the confusing swirl of movement, she had forgotten who she was. The stares and the strangers terrified Queenie Dennis, the shy, cowering waif who hid behind Molly's skirts. The leering men and the jealous-eyed women frightened the timid creature who lost herself in books and lessons, rather than playing with other children.

But she was Madame Denise Lescartes, not the girl she used to be. Oh, no, not by half.

Lord Harking's approval made her remember. His large, warm presence made her safe. She had nothing to fear from the envious glares from the women, the amorous ogles from the men, not while he was at her side, tall and broad and strong. His look of favor—and respect—gave Queenie back her confidence. Here was a decent man who did not have designs on her virtue, just her company for one paltry party. According to Molly, and Queenie's own experience in Paris, all men had lewd and licentious thoughts, but Lord Harking would never act upon his. His eyes might stray to her lips or her bosom, but he was a gentleman. Her own gallant knight for the night.

She laughed out loud. "And I am the most fortunate of women."

He waved his free hand toward the crowd, the boldest pushing forward, hoping for an introduction. "They are impressed, as I am."

Despite his words, one last shiver rippled through her. "They are staring and shoving, like pigs at a trough."

"I thought gaining their attention was the point. You have succeeded admirably. Would you rather dance, though, than speak with them?"

Her gown was meant to swirl. She should dance, Queenie knew, to show off the artful construction, the perfect drape, the daring back, but she was not proficient at the steps, having had few opportunities to practice—and hated being looked at as if she were on exhibit at a museum. Standing in one place, however, left her open to the crowds. "Perhaps we should stroll about instead, to look for your brother-in-law."

What brother-in-law? Harry had eyes for no one but her. He had even forgotten that he was a poor dancer himself, in his eagerness to hold her closer. With pride and a rein on his passion, he might have floated through the dance. Instead he fell down to earth with a thud. "Oh, Martin. Of course."

Harry did not like the knowing look behind Browne's spectacles, so he cleared his throat and told them all: "He is a fair-haired chap, about thirty-and-five, with pale blue eyes and a slightly hooked nose."

Which might describe a quarter of the gentlemen present.

"Does he possess nothing distinctive?" Queenie wanted to know, happy to have something to consider other than why Lord Harking made her feel so comfortable.

"My family diamonds, but I doubt he is carrying them, deuce take the rum touch. But no, he is of average height and build. His ears stick out a bit, but he keeps his hair long and his shirt collars high to cover them. He dresses in the current fashion, with unpaid tailors' bills to prove it, so I suppose he will be wearing a dark coat and white linen like every other man here."

So Harry and Queenie walked about the rooms, with Hellen and Browne behind them. For now, Hellen was content to gather admiring glances. When she could get away from Queenie's careful chaperonage, she would gather information. She knew a few of the women present through her mother's circles, so finding out a gentleman's prospects and proclivities would be a moment's work. With Queenie fashioning her wardrobe, Hellen could afford to bide her time, basking in Mr. Browne's sweet regard.

They edged the dance floor, with Harry trying to avoid any of his acquaintances so he could avoid having to make introductions. When he could not, he was abrupt, if not downright rude.

"No, you may not call on Madame Lescartes," he told Lord Vanderquist, "unless you are purchasing a gown for your daughter." Who was not the angry female at Lord Vanderquist's side, although they were of the same age.

"No," he told Sir Maxim, "the lady does not give private showings. Her designs are written about in the fashion journals. You can read, can you not? Or is your vision so poor that you truly need that silly quizzing glass you have stuck in your eye?"

"No, Madame does not need a ride home," he snarled at Mr. Carpenter. "But your wife might, from whichever party she attends."

He kept his arm on her shoulder, a grim look to his mouth, and less than an inch between them. No one could mistake his warning. The lady was not for sale. She was not that kind of woman, despite dressing like that, looking like that, being in this place. And if she were that kind of female, then she was Harking's. Possession mattered in a world where a man might diddle his friend's wife, but he would not hunt on another man's preserves—or steal his mistress.

Harry intended to enforce that unwritten codicil to the code of honor, even if the circumstances were not entirely appropriate. After all, Madame Lescartes was not his mistress and was never going to be. Why, he might not even see her after tonight.

He stumbled, and had to apologize for nearly knocking his companion off her feet . . . the way the notion of never seeing her again had knocked him to flinders. "Sorry. I was, uh, thinking I saw my brother-in-law ahead."

He was thinking that he had not brought a gift to the gathering only for another man to unwrap the treasure. He was thinking that French modiste or bachelor fare, she was a woman of uncommon distinction—and he wanted her as he had never wanted another female in all his living days. Chances were, he'd want her with his dying breath, too.

Which made him no better than all the other cads who were undressing her —what there was of her dress—with their eyes even as she walked at his side. He was no better than his profligate papa, no better than his sister's hedonistic husband.

No! He'd spent his adult life trying to be better than them, to be an honorable, estimable gentleman. He was not about to give up believing in his own decency. Or acting on his beliefs. Even if it killed him.

"Sorry," he apologized again, this time for stepping away from Madame Lescartes so fast she almost lost her balance again. He stayed close enough that no one could come between them, but not close enough to breathe her scent or hear the *whish* of her skirt or look down at the vee between her perfect, milky—

"I need something to drink. I think the refreshments room should be close by. Shall we see what they have to offer?"

Supper was not being served yet, but they found a footman ladling out a potent punch, and another with a tray of filled champagne glasses. After sampling the first and toasting the success of Madame Lescartes's new enterprise—Hellen raised her glass to her own venture—with the second, they stood chatting, avoiding any more introductions—or, for Harry, unwelcome thoughts. They could not stand in a quiet corner all night, however, despite both Harry's and Queenie's wishes, so continued their walk.

They found the room set aside for cards, and a few darkened chambers set aside for other purposes, empty this early, thank goodness. They found glass doors leading to a poorly lit terrace, and a young gentleman casting up his accounts over the balcony, even this early.

They did not find Sir John Martin.

They found Ize instead.

That is, Ize found Hellen when they returned to the ballroom. Cleaned, shaved, except for the hair in his ears and nose, and dressed in only slightly used finery, Ize had come to survey his customers in their milieu—and reclaim a ruby brooch that had somehow left his possession without payment. Hence the young gentleman clutching his stomach on the balcony.

Satisfied with the evening's work, Ize set his mind to pleasure, and spotted Hellen Pettigrew across the crowded dance floor in company with a toff, his fancy piece, and a flat. Thinking there might be profit in the newcomers, Ize waved across the room at Hellen, then headed in her direction.

Queenie turned her back to the room and pretended to adjust the ribbon threaded through Hellen's hair. "Oh, no. He'll be sure to recognize me next to you. We have to leave," Queenie whispered to Hellen.

"Leave? Now?" Hellen's voice was shrill enough that Harry took a step closer to the women, fists clenched against any threat.

"He'll only be more curious if we leave suddenly," Hellen whispered, watching Ize dodge around cavorting couples on his way to their position. "And he might follow. But if you go off with his lordship, Ize will think nothing of it, especially if you laugh and flirt with your handsome, well-heeled escort. Hurry, go be gay and silly and carefree. Ize will never suspect who you are because Queenie would never act like that. She would be quiet and quaking."

Which was precisely what Queenie was: struck dumb and deathly afraid.

She told herself to breathe, and then she told herself to be brave. She was not going to let her fears overtake her, not now when she had come so far. Straightening, she turned to Lord Harking and gave him a dazzling smile. "Perhaps we should have that dance after all, my lord. I swear the music is making my feet restless, and . . . and I am eager to see how such a fine figure of a man performs on the dance floor."

Floor, figure, eager? Before Harry could recover from the bewitching smile and the bewildering words, Madame Lescartes placed her arm on his, her chest nearly rubbing against his—damn the stupid striped waistcoat—and laughed that rippling laugh, only louder.

Before they left to take their places in the country dance, she turned to John George Browne. Harry might be wrong, but he could have sworn he saw a long sewing needle suddenly in her hand, then lost in the folds of Browne's neckcloth.

"You shall look after my friend," Queenie whispered, still wearing that wide smile. "Or answer to me."

Browne swallowed hard and nodded. "Won't let her out of my sight."

"Or mine. She stays in public, away from dark corners."

Browne gulped. "That, too, I swear."

Harry glanced back as he and Madame Lescartes walked away. "What was all that about?"

She patted his cheek. The gentleman on her other side in the set they joined sighed.

She laughed again as she curtsied to Harry, then the men at the other corners. "I was just reminding Mr. Browne that Hellen is young and innocent."

Hellen was no younger than half the women here, in Harry's estimation, and about as innocent as a fox with feathers in its mouth. Since he was currently circling a tittering blonde, he took the chance to look across the room. Miss Pettigrew was conversing with the strange, short man who had waved at them, while Browne looked on and scowled.

"Who is that man?" Harry asked Madame Lescartes when the steps of the dance brought them together again.

"What man?" she asked with a titter that matched the blonde's, and grated on Harry's nerves.

"The small, older man with protuberant eyes that you are avoiding."

Queenie silently cursed the viscount's perspicacity. Lord Harking's watchful escort had been a blessing, easing her fears. Now she wished he would mind his own business, and his feet. "Ouch."

"Sorry. I forgot which way I was supposed to leap. He is looking at us now."

Queenie missed her own step.

"Ouch." Harry was almost glad to take the next woman's hand as they changed partners.

When they briefly met again as the dance progressed, Harry asked, "But who is he? Why did you not stay to greet him?"

Queenie ground her teeth, still smiling, though. When she skipped off to twirl around the opposite gentleman in the set—Harry tried not to squash the feet of a tiny, big-bosomed brunette—she called back, "He is no one I wish to know."

Which was far more honest than her merriment.

Finally, a few more bruised feet later, the dance came to a thankful end. Instead of returning to Hellen and Browne, though, where Ize still stood, Queenie tossed her head and laughed. "Oh, I do hope the next dance is a waltz!"

"You do? That is, I hope you feel the same way afterward." As they waited through the interval still on the dance floor, far from their companions, Harry could not let the matter drop. Like a dog with a bone, he noted, "You did not wish to speak to the man, yet you left your friend with him."

"I left her with Mr. Browne."

Harry raised his eyebrows.

Now Queenie laughed without artifice. "Do you really think to intimidate me with your toplofty ways? Remember, I saw you turn scarlet when you trod on the hem of that girl's gown."

"She need not have burst into tears."

"Oh, she only wished you to offer to purchase her a new one. That one was barely torn."

"Instead you offered to create a frock just for her."

"She was holding up the rest of the set."

"You were being kind."

Queenie blushed at the compliment. "It will be good for business. She will tell her friends, who will patronize my shop. As long as you do not ruin any more gowns this evening, I can stand the expense."

They both laughed, feeling comfortable with each other once more. Harry took two glasses of wine from a passing waiter and handed her one, raising his own to her. "Because you really are kind. You never once criticized my dancing, and I have seen how protective you are of Miss Pettigrew."

Since Queenie could not, politely, comment on his dancing, she said, "Hellen is . . . young."

"Surely she is only a year or two younger than you."

"We have lived different lives, and I feel ages older. I want to help Hellen make the best choices for herself."

Harry knew nothing about Madame Denise Lescartes's life, but everyone knew that Miss Pettigrew was the natural child of a lord and his longtime mistress. From the looks of the chit, she was bound to follow in her mother's footsteps. "I should think Miss Pettigrew's path has been long determined."

Queenie frowned. "People can change. Or do you believe that our lives are set forever at the moment of our birth?"

In a way, Harry believed precisely that. He was born to

be a viscount, with the privileges and responsibilities such a position entailed. He had no choice, no more than Hellen Pettigrew had chosen to be a baron's bastard daughter. They were what they were. On the other hand, he had spent his life trying to break his parents' mold. And what of the supposed Frenchwoman? Her accent varied from colloquial French to carefully educated English. Her manners and bearing were those of a lady, but she was going into trade, with pride. She was friends with a demimondaine, yet obviously disapproved of that life for herself and for Hellen. She dressed to stir a man's senses, yet spoke of becoming a schoolteacher.

Who was she, and what was her background? Harry wondered. What class had she sprung from, and was she following her natural-born destiny . . . or forging a new path of her own? Harry would love to know what lay behind the shadows in her blue eyes, and what brought the smile to her rosy lips. He could never ask. He knew without trying that such personal questions would be as offensive to the woman as physical overtures. And intimacy, of any kind, was not part of their agreement.

"This is far too serious a discussion for such a night," he said. "Come, *chérie,* let us leave philosophy to the old men while we enjoy ourselves. Tomorrow you shall have to sew that little wigeon a new gown, and I shall have to look elsewhere for my brother-in-law. Tonight there is music and champagne and love in the air. Temporary infatuation, at any rate, if at a price. But I see that Hellen and Browne are taking the floor, so perhaps they will make choices of their own."

The orchestra struck up a waltz, Harry took Madame Lescartes in his arms, and they danced.

Or they floated. Harry forgot his questions. Queenie forgot Ize. They both forgot they were not very good dancers.

Tonight they were.

Harry had never enjoyed a dance more. Queenie had never felt so at home in a man's arms.

The doyennes of Almack's had never seen the waltz conducted this way. At the Cyprian's Ball, partners held each other far closer than permitted in the sacred halls of polite society. Their hands wandered places the lady patronesses preferred not to name. Eyes were joined, as well as thighs, and sighs.

The way Harry and Queenie danced was like making love to music.

"Smitten," the wiser women at the ball said to each other, shaking their heads. A clever girl kept her heart out of the business.

"Smitten," the men cursed. Now they had no chance.

CHAPTER SEVEN

B reathless, Queenie declared she needed to repair to the
ladies' withdrawing room. What she needed was to re-
order her thoughts. She had never felt like a wanton before.
She certainly had never acted like one! But that dance . . .

Perhaps it was the champagne. Or the music, the night,
the wearing of a gown meant for seduction. Or the man.
Heavens, never let her be so taken with a gentleman that she
forgot her principles more than she already had!

As it was, she was more forward than Hellen, letting a
man hold her so closely and moving closer herself. Had she
actually let her fingers roam to Lord Harking's neck instead
of sitting demurely on his shoulder? Had she truly pressed
against him in a turn to feel the solid muscle of his chest? At
least she had not touched his hair, brushing back a fallen
lock. Nor had she squeezed his shoulder to make certain his
coat was not padded. But she had wanted to. Gracious, what
must his lordship think of her? Queenie was all too afraid
she knew. This was the Cyprian's Ball, after all.

She was grateful to him, Queenie told herself. That was

why she had permitted—and taken—such liberties. Lord
Harking had rescued her from Ize and he had stopped asking questions she did not want to answer. Besides, he was a
very attractive gentleman, just the right size and breadth.
And he was well-mannered, unlike many of the crude, boor-
ish men she saw on the sidelines or overheard making sly innuendos. Because of them, Lord Harking would not permit
her to walk unattended to the rooms set aside for the women
to refresh themselves. Too many loose fish, he'd declared,
signaling for Browne and Hellen to join them in the corridor.

Queenie stepped inside the retiring room in relief. She
needed to think about what had happened, why she'd let
sudden, strange new feelings overcome her logic.

She had no opportunity to think, though, amid the chirp-
ing ladybirds who filled the room. They were trilling about
this lord, that gentleman, which officer, what merchant had
the most money and—with a laugh—the mightiest sword.

Queenie could not pretend to misunderstand. She
blushed, to the other women's hilarity. She was not the only
one who'd had too much champagne, too much of the potent
punch. Poor Lord Harking would blush, too, Queenie
thought, to hear his manly attributes so debated.

Thankfully Queenie herself, or Madame Denise
Lescartes, soon became the topic of the conversation, she
and her gowns. *Non,* she chose not to speak of France, but
oui, she could create an original design for one woman, and
oui, she could copy a favorite style for another. A costume
for a masquerade? An outfit to visit one's lover's unknowing sister? *Certainement.* But Queenie could also advise as
to the best colors, the most flattering styles. Without looking
directly at any of the women, she hinted how she could en-

hance a long neck or hide an unsightly bulge. Her designs were meant to flatter, not merely follow the latest trends.

She handed out the card for her store and warned that her prices were high, which made her all the more appealing to the avid listeners.

A true lady never discussed finances. These women discussed little else but money and the means to it. They appreciated another businesswoman and swore to start patronizing the Morningside shop as soon as they found someone to pay the bills, or pawned another bit of jewelry.

Queenie would have enough cash to purchase French fabrics and hire expert seamstresses. Soon she could start repaying Jack Endicott and Lord Carde. She handed out more calling cards.

Hellen was adding a bit more rouge to her cheeks and complaining that she had not met nearly enough gentlemen to make any kind of choice.

"Be happy you have a good man like Mr. Browne at your side," Queenie told her. "Many of the so-called gentlemen I have seen tonight are not fit to wipe your shoes."

"What, are my slippers scuffed?" Hellen raised her hems to look. Then she tugged down the neckline of her gown. "So they won't notice my feet."

Queenie pulled up the bodice before Hellen could ruin the gown. She was disgusted, at the younger girl and at herself. They should never have come to this ball, business or not. The lax morals were as contagious as the influenza. And almost as deadly.

Harry stayed near the room set aside for the ladies. He would gladly have gone out with Browne to find a privy, but he could not like leaving the women unattended. Some of the men were beyond pleasantly inebriated and could not be trusted. Others were stone-cold sober and could not be trusted.

At first he felt awkward, leaning against the wall in the corridor, sipping another glass of punch and attracting knowing looks from the chaps who passed by on the way to the cardroom. They must all think he was a fool, so besotted by the Frenchwoman's beauty that he could not let her out of his sight for more than a minute. What else could they think after that public display of passion during the waltz? He did not suppose anyone would interpret that heated dance as being due to the temperature in the room. And no one would believe that he was now shielding his dance partner from the worst of the libertines. They would assume he was guarding his bit of muslin from other lust-filled men like him.

Harry wondered what had come over him, to behave so far beyond the lines of proper behavior that he himself had drawn. The answer, of course, was Madame Lescartes, Denise, although that name did not seem to suit her. But she, with her mix of sophistication and staunch morality, did fascinate him. Her looks could turn any man into a rutting goat, he supposed, but there was far more to the female than physical beauty. She could put a needle to Browne's throat one minute and dance like a Gypsy maid the next. She could blush at an overheard warm remark, yet melt in his arms. No wonder his head was spinning.

He turned to admire some ugly paintings on the wall rather than suffer any more ridicule from London's rakehells and roués. But then someone patted his shoulder and said, "Lucky dog."

Another called out, "Good show, man."

And a third gent, high in the government, said, "I wish you put that much passion in your parliamentary speeches."

Harry turned from the cat scratch still life on the wall.
Gentlemen were winking at him, whistling, looking wist-
fully at the door that held his dance partner. They were not
poking fun at him, he realized. They were congratulating
him. They were jealous of him, old Hardnose Harking. He
was not the bumbling country bumpkin anymore in their
eyes, or the stiff, cold chap who so obviously disapproved of
them and their ways. He was not even the schoolboy some
of them remembered, trying to be better than the other lads.
Now he was one of them, the most envied member of their
feckless fraternity.

Harry should have been repulsed, but he was so pleased
he started whistling himself. Lud, the star of the night was
his, if only for the night, which no one had to know. He'd
found the diamond they were all looking for. He'd captured
the prize. He was Viscount Victorious, king of the courtesans' ball.

He was drunk.

He set his glass down on a side table.

The next gentleman to wander past was actually an old
friend of Harry's, Lord Camden, heir to a dukedom. Cam
was a tulip, but a fine horseman.

"A card game, Harry?" he asked. "We are looking for a
fourth."

"No, thank you." Harry tipped his head toward the door,
where high-pitched laughter and giggles could be heard.
Trying to sound nonchalant, and not like the proudest peacock in the room, he added, "I am waiting for my partner."

"Can't blame you," the other man said, having seen the
waltz. They both smiled, with nothing more needing to be
said.

After asking where Harry was staying and how long he
might be in London, Camden started down the hall.

Harry stopped him. "I say, Cam, you haven't seen my brother-in-law by any chance, have you?"

"What, Martin slipped his lead again?"

Harry resented the notion that he was his in-law's keeper, although that was what he had been, paying the dastard's bills, including the mortgage on Martin's own run-down estate. He was feeding and housing the man's family, as Cam well knew, as well as paying for the children's education. Yes, Harry had been insisting the wastrel stay in the country rather than pursue his more expensive pastimes in Town, but that was to avoid more scandal and more debts, not because Harry liked having the mongrel on a short chain. "I have a message for him, that's all."

"From your tone of voice I can imagine the nature of your message, and why Sir John Martin is playing least in sight." Camden chuckled. "Of course a lecture from you would be the pot calling the kettle black, would it not?" He gestured toward the door behind Harry.

Feeling his blasted cheeks grow warm, Harry frowned. "I resent being painted with the same brush as that boil on society's backside. I am not in debt to my ears or drunk half my days. Nor am I a married man."

"No, and Martin could never afford such a fancy piece."

Camden ought to consider himself lucky. He was smaller and lighter than Harry, without the viscount's muscles. Cam would be flat on the carpet, spilling his claret on his sky-blue jacket and butterfly-embroidered waistcoat, if Harry were a truly violent man. He did not practice fisticuffs as a sport, though, and he did not believe in striking his friends. At least not in public. Harry appeased his anger by saying, "You will speak of the lady with respect or meet me at dawn."

"Oho, so the mighty have fallen at last!"

Harry was sure his cheeks were bright red, but at least the lamplight was dim in the hallway. "No such thing. I just met the young woman."

"Time enough to lose your heart, I'd say, if you are ready to defend her honor with swords or pistols."

"No, fists are good enough for the likes of you."

"My apologies, then, to you and the young, ah, lady. I like my pretty phiz well enough the way it is. But think what you are about, old man. You cannot marry the chit, of course. A viscount and a . . ." He hesitated, wary of both Harry's scowl and his broad shoulders.

"A dressmaker."

Cam nodded. "Of course. A dressmaker. I heard someone mention that but thought he was jesting. Won't the gabble-grinders adore the tale? I can see the cartoons, Lord Harking being fitted by a female!"

Harry groaned. He had not thought his presence at the ball would be noted or commented upon in the scandal sheets. What if one reached Lincolnshire and his neighbors, or his sister? He groaned again.

"What, did you think no one would notice the monkish lord and his modiste mistress?"

"She is not my mistress, deuce take it."

"More's the pity. But you always were a slowtop."

"I told you, she is a respectable female."

"Well, you still cannot wed her, and you look as if you'll die if you don't bed her. So what does that say about her?" Lord Camden adjusted the diamond in his high neckcloth a fraction of an inch. "You cannot go around challenging every man in London to a duel, you know."

Harry knew it, and knew he'd like to choke his friend with that same blasted piece of snowy linen for speaking the truth.

"Of course," Cam was going on, "it makes you interesting for once. Sad, but interesting."

"I am not sad."

"You will be. You always did take things too seriously."

Life was not a game, deuce take it, Harry thought. "Madame Lescartes appears to be serious about her dressmaking business."

"Really? Then I might toddle around to her shop with my sister, see if the woman's flair for fashion can rub off. My sister can use a bit of dash, else I am liable to have her on my hands forever. A chap has to look ahead, don't you know? Neither of us is getting any younger, and there's the succession to consider, eh? Can't bring a bride home with a lady already installed there."

Harry had his sister acting as mistress of Harking Hall. He hadn't thought of displacing her with a wife or begetting an heir, any more than he'd thought of becoming the latest on-dit. Lud, he had a lot to think about besides his crops and his cows. He was not about to discuss any of his private musings, or his avoidance thereof, with Camden, though, so he said, "Your sister will not be disappointed. I have seen Madame Denise's designs. She is quite talented."

"Excellent." Camden took a step toward the cardroom with a final wave of his manicured, beringed hand. "Oh, and I saw your missing black sheep last week. Thursday, I believe it was, at Rachel Potts's place. She calls herself Rochelle Poitier these days. Jack Endicott's last mistress, don't you know. When he tossed her over she set up a salon, a bordello with pretensions. The place never became all the rage, so she lowered her sights. Now you can find blighters like your brother-in-law there."

"And you?"

Camden shrugged. "I am not married yet, either."

* * *

Hellen stepped out of the ladies' room first, her rounded face pinched in petulance. All she had to show for her grand night was another lecture, more instructions on proper behavior, and questions from the other women about her glamorous new friend. Oh, and Mr. Browne waiting outside like a faithful hound.

Browne was sweet and treated her the way Queenie said a fellow should treat a lady, but he was not exciting, not the envy of any other girls—and not rich.

The man talking to Lord Harking was another story altogether. Sporting a large diamond at his neck, dressed to catch one's eye, not fade into the crowd like every other dark-clad cull in the place, he was more handsome than Harking and Browne combined. Hellen's face unscrewed from its pucker and her dimples appeared. So did the avaricious gleam in her green eyes.

She tugged down the bodice of her pink gown again and took a deep, bosom-enhancing breath. "Here we are, then, gents, all refreshed." She stepped between Lord Harking and Mr. Browne, smiling at the stranger.

Camden smiled back, and Harry was forced to make the introduction. He looked toward the door to the women's retiring room, hoping Madame Lescartes would not come out to see how his friend was eyeing her friend. Cam was like a schoolboy with a box of bonbons. It was not a matter of which he ate first, but whether he could finish them all before anyone demanded to share.

"Miss Pettigrew, is it?" Cam bowed over her hand, holding it to his lips, then simply holding it. "And far more beautiful than your renowned mother."

Poor Browne's neckcloth must be too tight, for he was gagging.

Then Cam was asking Hellen for a dance, his purring voice asking far more.

"Ah, sorry, but we were just leaving," was all Harry could think of to say. Madame Lescartes would kill him if he let her young friend go off with a gazetted rake. Worse, she'd think he was a libertine like Lord Camden.

"Surely you can wait one more dance?" Cam was speaking to Hellen, not Harry. "Or I could see you home, my dear."

Hellen giggled. Now, that was more like it. Lord Camden was the answer to every maiden's—or every would-be mistress's—prayers. Of course Hellen was not going to accept the first gentry cove's first offer, not on her first night on the town, not even for a duke's first son. But a first dance? She tripped off, her hand still in his lordship's.

Queenie came out to the corridor in time to see the back of Hellen's flounced skirt—the flounces that she had so painstakingly stitched—swirling around the yellow-pantalooned legs of a wealthy womanizer. She knew he was rich by the flash of diamonds. She knew he was a rake by how close his head was to Hellen's, how he raised her hand to his lips, how he said something to make her laugh. And how Lord Harking's cheeks were flushed.

"I could not help it," Harry said before she could complain. "I have known Cam for ages."

"You could not refuse your friend?" she asked, her voice dripping scorn.

"I could not refuse *your* friend."

Queenie sighed. She knew Hellen had gone off voluntarily, the little fool. She knew Hellen's ambitions, but she had hoped that Mr. Browne could show her another way. Now she hoped Mr. Browne could survive the night, the poor man. His complexion was green, and his eyes appeared crossed beneath his spectacles.

"Perhaps they are serving tea somewhere," she suggested. None of them needed more of that punch.

Browne gratefully used her excuse to escape, rather than watch Hellen in the arms of a dashing, deep-pocketed, and titled gentleman, everything he was not.

"And we shall leave directly after the set is finished." Harry led the way back toward the ballroom, vowing to make sure Camden did not sweep Hellen out onto the balcony or off to a secluded nook.

"No, we shall stay," Queenie said after looking around. As the evening had worn on, some of the polite mask had worn off. Men were staggering and sweating. Women were swaying, their face paint smudged. Couples were huddled in corners, their clothing awry. Others were kissing and sharing intimate touches, right on the dance floor. Queenie was not certain, but she thought one pair was fornicating behind the draperies. Either that or a breeze had blown up in that one window.

"Are you certain?" Harry was not comfortable watching men of his class, men who ran the government or captained industries, disport themselves without any sense of dignity. The lower classes might lose themselves in drink and desire, but he expected better of his peers. Harry supposed he was a prude after all.

He could not understand Madame Lescartes's wanting to stay, not if she was as offended as her curled lip seemed to indicate . . . unless she was having second thoughts about her chosen occupation. In which case, perhaps Harry was not quite a prig. He could feel his pulse accelerating in anticipation. "Would you care to dance, then?"

"No, we shall stay here and watch, if you do not mind.

That way we can intercept Hellen when the dance is done. If the silly wigeon wishes to lead this kind of life, I cannot stop her, but I can ensure that she knows what she is choosing. Let her see for herself how cheaply the women are held, how little the men care for anything but their gratification. With your permission, my lord, we shall stay, and keep her safe for this night while we can. Then she can choose."

Harry nodded, feeling half like a knight-errant, half like the boy with his finger in the dike, trying to hold back a flood. What, was he supposed to discourage every rake in the room—which was every man except him and Browne—when Hellen smiled at them? At least he could get rid of Camden, making his hands into fists and jerking his head toward the cardroom when Cam brought Hellen back to them at the end of the dance.

Cam raised one eyebrow. "Guarding your one chick I can understand. But two?"

"This one's not fledged yet," was all Harry said.

Ten officers from the home guard could not have kept Hellen innocent or unknowing that night, which, Harry supposed, was Madame Lescartes's intention. Hellen had to see the couples having sex in the seats, others pressed against the walls. Harry knew for a fact that one man pinched her bottom, and another grabbed her breast before Harry grabbed his arm. Scores had drooled over her hand, and more than a few had planted wet kisses on her cheek before he'd planted his fist in their bellies.

Harry could swear he'd seen Madame Lescartes flash her darning needle a few times, which relieved him somewhat, knowing she could protect herself behind him.

A drunk splashed wine on Hellen's gown and another narrowly missed her hem when he cast up his accounts. They moved on to the supper room.

They saw women running down the corridor, some in tears, some in torn clothing. They saw women with bottles, and women with bruises.

When Harry saw the girls, younger than Hellen, kneeling between the men's legs at the tables, he turned, blocking the view. "Enough."

Queenie swallowed the bile in her throat. She could not eat a bite anyway. "Enough," she agreed.

Hellen was ashen, the rouge on her cheeks standing out in bright contrast, like a wide-eyed doll. Her lovely gown was ruined; her slippers were beyond repair. She would have black-and-blue marks tomorrow on places no one had ever seen, much less touched. And she was frightened of what could have happened without Lord Harking and Mr. Browne beside her.

"Enough," she agreed.

Browne had reached his limit hours ago. He grabbed Hellen's arm, pulled her from the assembly rooms, and then kissed her while they waited outside for Lord Harking's hired coach.

"Why should every other man in the room get to sample your wares?" he asked, panting. He quickly kissed her again. "There, now it is enough."

So Harry kissed Queenie, too.

CHAPTER EIGHT

He asked first. Not with words, but with his eyes and raised brows, and how slowly he lowered his head toward her lips.

Queenie said yes. Not with words, but by moving a step closer, holding her face up, closing her eyes. She told herself that she wanted to show Lord Harking her gratitude. Heaven only knew what would have happened tonight without him. Hellen could have accepted a dishonorable proposition. Worse, she could have been dragged off by some cad who would not take *no* as an answer to his offer. Queenie's darning needle could not do much against a determined drunk or debauchee. It was bad enough that both Hellen and she had been groped at and insulted, despite the valiant efforts of Lord Harking and Browne. His lordship had certainly not bargained for bodyguard duty when he asked to escort them to the ball. So Queenie was grateful to him. That was all.

No, that was not all, not even by half. After this evening Queenie desperately wanted to feel something sweet, something unsullied, something solid and real. Viscount Harking seemed to be the most decent man of her acquaintance. He truly was looking for his brother-in-law, and he had not been looking at the half-naked women at the dance. He'd hated the licentious behavior at the ball and had stayed only to please her.

Who was she fooling? Yes, she was grateful; yes, he was a true gentleman. More than anything, though, Queenie wanted to kiss Lord Harking. So she did.

Ah.

The ground did not shake—except when the horses brought the carriage closer. Her toes did not curl—but they did grow numb from the cold in her thin satin slippers. No thunderbolt pierced the night sky, or her heart; no bells chimed or heavenly choir sang.

But, oh.

His lips were warm and gentle. His lemony scent was fresh and clean. His hand on her back was strong, but not coercive. She could have pulled away anytime, if she had the moral fiber of a flea. This was where Queenie wanted to be, though, where she might always have wanted to be, without knowing it. Even if he was a lord and she was a bastard pretending to be a businesswoman, this moment was hers, and it was perfect.

Then someone coughed.

Uh-oh.

They were in the street, in public view, in a disgraceful embrace. Worse, they were near strangers, from different worlds, who would never meet after tonight. Queenie raised her hand to her mouth as if she could wipe away the warmth, the tingling, the memory of his lips.

Harry knew he should apologize, but he was not sorry, not in the least, except for the interruption. And Madame

Lescartes—deuce take it, he could not keep calling her such a mouthful—Denise had enjoyed it, too, from those tiny sighs he'd heard. Nor had Browne apologized to Hellen, not that Harry needed to take lessons in behavior from a green-as-grass schoolmaster. What he needed was a cold bath.

He must have been wanting to kiss this woman since the moment he laid eyes on her, so he was glad he'd gone and done it. Better to get such things over with, like going to the tooth drawer. Unfortunately, now he only wanted to kiss her again. And again.

Damn.

"Thank you," he said, hoping his voice was steadier than his racing heartbeat.

"Th-thank you?" Queenie's wits had definitely flown away on the wings of that brief passion. He was thanking her for a short, inexperienced, most likely schoolgirlish kiss?

"For not stabbing me with your needle."

"Oh."

Harry had not wanted to stop kissing her, of course, but they were in the street and his coach was there waiting, one of the grooms clearing his throat as he pretended to inspect the harness. Hellen and Browne were already stepping into the carriage, while another groom held the door. Harry knew he would not get another chance to be so close to Denise on the ride home, not with the others present, and yet he could not bear to see all hope gone with the end of the evening.

"Would you come to supper with me? That is, all of us? I hate for the night to end so badly."

She wiped at her mouth with her gloved hand, so Harry quickly added, "No, not the kiss, but the ball. I would like to have better memories, wouldn't you?"

Better than his kiss? Queenie did not think that was possible, but she nodded her agreement.

Hellen was worried about her soiled gown.

"We can eat at my hotel. The chef is a wizard, and the tables are lighted with candles, so no one will notice. Or you
can keep your shawl around you. Please, I would be glad of
the company."

"Well, I never did get to eat at the dance." And Hellen
had never eaten at a fine hotel.

Browne was hungry, too, with nothing to look forward to
at The Red and the Black, which was empty of both staff and
food.

So they went back to the Grand Hotel, where the desk
clerk seemed relieved that Harry was not escorting the females upstairs to his suite. This was a respectable hotel, after
all.

The maître d' in the dining room wrinkled his nose at the
sight of the two women in their daring, slightly disordered
finery. Harry's handsome gratuity restored his sense of
smell, that and Queenie addressing him in his native French.

While they waited for their order, Queenie tried to make
conversation. She did not want to speak about the ball. Or
the future. Or her past.

Hellen was no help, still lost in dismay over her dress and
her shattered dreams. Mr. Browne had little to offer in re-
porting progress at the school, and Queenie did not wish to
appear too interested in Lord Cardé or Captain Jack Endicott.

The weather was cold, they all agreed, but not surprisingly so, since spring had not yet begun. The hotel was elegantly furnished and the chandelier in the lobby was
magnificent. The wine Lord Harking selected was excellent,
and the violin music in the background added a lovely
touch.

Thankfully the soup was served, so there was no need for more inanities. When those plates were taken away, though, Queenie told the viscount, "I am sorry we did not find your brother-in-law at the ball. What shall you do next?"

Harry choked on a sip of wine. He was going to visit Rochelle Poitier's house of convenience next—that was what he was going to do—but he could not say it in front of the women. Zeus, if Denise thought he was a rogue for stealing a kiss in the street, she'd think he was a total reprobate for patronizing a brothel. "My friend Camden had, um, a few ideas where Martin might be staying."

"So you will not be leaving for the country immediately?"

"No, not yet."

They both considered the possibilities—and improbabilities—while two waiters served the next course.

Hellen, meanwhile, had recovered some of her spirit over the wine and mock turtle soup. "Your friend was very nice," she hinted. "And a fine dancer. He told a good story, too."

"Oh, Cam is all of that," Harry told her, "the best of good fellows." Then he saw the drawn look on Madame Lescartes's face. He doubted her disapproval was for the vol-au-vents of veal, so he added, "But old Cam is a confirmed rake, you know. He is never seen with the same woman more than twice." Since Harry saw his friend only a few times a year now, that was no lie. Nor was, "I have never known him to keep a mistress." Harry had no idea what Cam did or did not do with his numerous women, married, widowed or simply available. Harry preferred it that way.

Denise's face relaxed. She sent him a grateful smile, so Harry elaborated, half to win her approval and half to discourage the pretty little peagoose further. "And Cam confided in me that he was thinking of marrying and starting his nursery. He would never embarrass his bride with an, uh, outside interest." At least Harry hoped his friend would wait until the honeymoon was over before visiting bordellos and balls for the demimonde.

Hellen sighed and went back to her meal.

The Frenchwoman's black eyebrows were raised in doubt over those startling blue eyes.

"Not all men are unfaithful spouses, you know," Harry said, although he could not with any certainty name a loyal husband. He did not know why, but he very much wanted Madame Lescartes to know he was not like the rest of his gender. "I, for one, intend to honor my wedding vows."

"As do I," Browne added, somewhat muzzily, from all the wine and from gazing at Hellen, who was licking a drop of sauce off her lips. "My mum would have my guts for garters otherwise. Same as she would my father's. He's never looked at another woman in all the years they've been married."

"How . . . commendable." Queenie dabbed at her own lips with her napkin.

Harry felt a bit muzzy himself.

"And I know Captain Jack swore fealty to Miss Silver," Browne added. "They say she wouldn't have him elsewise. And I heard that Lord Carde has hardly left his lady wife's side since they were wed, and them with a babe and another on the way."

"I am happy for both couples." Queenie was not surprised Lord Carde was a faithful husband, although she'd had doubts about the captain, owner of a gaming parlor and a notorious womanizer. Still, the two men were trying to fulfil one oath by finding their sister. They would not break another vow if they held their word so dearly.

"What of you?" Harry asked, interrupting her musing on the so-far elusive Endicott brothers.

"Me? Why, I have never considered marriage, remarriage, that is, much less adultery."

"What, a beautiful woman like you not thinking of matrimony? I thought all females were born wanting a wedding band."

"They desire a husband because they have no other choices if they wish a home and family, security for their future. I have my shop."

"Can you not have both?"

"Should I support an idler with my labor? A man who approves of my career is likely a good-for-naught who has none of his own. He would have the right to my profits, the power to make decisions concerning my every transaction. I would not relinquish that control to any man."

That was the law of the land, Harry knew. Like children, women were not considered competent to manage their own affairs.

"But what about love?" Harry wanted to know. "Would that tender emotion not change your mind?"

Queenie brushed that aside like a crumb. "I am no romantic, believing all the poets' pretty verses. How could I trust words of affection from a man after he sees how successful my shop is going to be? I would be like one of the young ladies of your *ton* with a handsome dowry, never knowing if my suitor was interested in me, or in what I brought to the marriage."

Harry had never considered the woman's point in all their maneuvering to make the best match. He knew he resented being chased for his title and his lands and his bank account. "I always thought true love made that leap of faith, but I am no expert, nor a poet, either. But what if a gentleman had money of his own? Would you wed a rich man who did not need your income?"

Queenie pushed some peas around on her plate without eating. "Men of means do not usually permit their wives to work, out of pride or fear of gossip, or merely demanding that their spouse's interest be focused on them, not on running a business."

Harry knew that was also true. He doubted he would wish his wife off tending a store every day, no matter how much blunt she earned. Supporting his family was a man's job. Charitable works, keeping house, raising their children—those were suitable activities for a viscountess.

Madame Denise Lescartes was not, of course, a suitable viscountess for him. He knew that, and knew it far before Camden reminded him. What he really wanted to know, though, was if the beautiful young woman, who professed not to be in the oldest profession, would be a faithful wife. It was none of his business, of course, and would be an offensive question coming from him, a virtual stranger who shared nothing but a dance, a kiss, and now a dinner.

He really wanted to know.

She did not volunteer the information, nor any further thoughts on love, marriage, or poetry. She commented on the capon in plum sauce instead.

Since he was a gentleman, one who was not currently interested in marriage or his prospective wife's dowry, Harry had to follow her lead. "If you think that the dinner is good, wait until the sweets course. The chef here specializes in desserts flambé, although the management makes a waiter with a bucket of water follow along in case of fire, since they already had one disaster."

Hellen clapped her hands together like a child. "I cannot wait!"

Harry decided that Madame Lescartes was correct: Hellen was far too young to enter a life of sin, no matter her upbringing and expectations. A man would have to be a true cad to take her innocence, even if it was given freely. Unfortunately Harry knew that certain men relished despoiling maidens.

John George Browne did not appear to be such a one. Harry eyed him with speculation. The poor-sighted chap was moonstruck, all right, or maybe that was the wine. Too bad Harry would not be in London long enough to encourage a match between these two, easing at least one of Madame Lescartes's worries. A legitimate match, that is, he considered, sanctioned by the church and the law.

But Hellen as a schoolteacher's wife? Harry would have doubted she could read, but she read the menu, except for the French, which Denise translated for her. But she was not raised to cook and clean and care for babies, just to please men, so heaven only knew what her future could hold, her friend's best wishes aside.

Harry wondered again at Madame Lescartes's background. Was she reared to please men? He doubted it. Sometimes she did not seem to like the males of the species as a group. Was she taught to be a wife and mother? Harry thought that was questionable, considering her attitude about supporting herself. Hers had to be an unconventional upbringing to send her into trade, to make her so independent, so confident of her skills as a modiste. He could not ask about that, either, dash it, or Monsieur Lescartes.

Queenie, meanwhile, had given up trying to make conversation, letting Mr. Browne and Hellen talk about their favorite desserts while she pondered Lord Harking's words. He intended to be a faithful husband? He was most likely lying. Or thinking optimistically. He did not even have a fiancée. How could he know how he would feel a year after marriage, or two, or ten? What if his wife turned shrewish, or lost her looks, or grew fat with child? Would he still hold to his vows? Molly had said no man did. Queenie knew that at least half the men at the Cyprian's Ball were married. The other half did not look as if a gold band would change their characters and their skirt chasing. Even Mr. Browne admitted that fear would keep him to the straight and narrow, as it kept his father. What if his wife was a meek little mouse? Would he stray then?

Perhaps love was the glue that kept couples from transgression. Queenie had never experienced such a strong emotion except in those foolish poems and lurid novels, so could not begin to guess. But none of it mattered to her anyway. Browne was not going to offer for Hellen. His career would be ruined. A peer was not going to offer for a dressmaker. His standing in society would be ruined. And a girl thinking of giving her all for love would be ruined altogether.

Queenie told herself she was tired, mentally and physically, even to be thinking such thoughts. Molly had taught her that a woman did not need a man to survive, or to be content, and Queenie had planned her life around her mother's lesson. She had her business for income, her drawing for pleasure, and her dog for companionship. Wondering if Lord Harking would be faithful was absurd, after one evening. But that one kiss . . . made her think about yearnings a bank account could not satisfy, pleasures a picture could not express, and loneliness a dog could not ease.

She sent back her plate, untouched. "I will save room for the dessert," she told the concerned waiter with a smile.

Alas, they were never to see or taste one of the chef's famous, fiery creations.

A trio of men had come to dine. The maître d' seated

them at one of the few empty tables, in the corner next to where Queenie and Harry sat. The men, all older than Harry, ordered three bottles of wine with their dinners, although they had obviously already had more than enough to drink that night. Their speech was slurred, their voices loud, their cravats loosened, and their posture careless, especially that of the one who seemed to be falling asleep in his chair. Before his head landed in the basket of rolls, one of his friends propped him against the wall, laughing uproariously.

"Weren't no wallflowers at the ball," he joked. "Derwent's the only one we've got."

"Otherwise we wouldn't be here on our own," the third man added, not laughing. He was nearly bald and his coat barely buttoned across his paunch. His complexion was choleric and his voice held a belligerent note. "It ain't fair all the pretty gals were swept up before we got there. Nothing left but toothless old drabs with their udders hanging to their knees. I may be drunk, but I ain't that far gone."

His conscious friend raised his glass, spilling wine on his limp neckcloth. "Here's to being sober enough to notice. I don't need to look now, so I intend to get even more castaway. And the night's still young, Fordyce. Who knows but we might find likely women later. I got plenty of addresses from the jarvey who drove us here."

"Those'd be whores."

"What did you expect at the Cyprian's Ball, then, dukes' daughters or foreign princesses?"

"I thought there'd be a higher class of prostitute. If I wanted to bring the pox back to m'wife I could find a Covent Garden doxy." He pounded on the table. "I'm a good husband, I am."

The headwaiter came by and asked the men to lower their

voices. "This is a respectable dining room, gentlemen, not a bawdy house."

"Respectable, ha!" Fordyce jerked his thumb in the direction of Harry's table. "We saw them at the assembly rooms, didn't we, Renfrew? Couldn't mistake the black-haired dasher, now, could I? Not in that gown, I couldn't. Makes a man hard just looking."

Harry started to rise from his seat, but Queenie laid her arm on his sleeve.

"The man is a sot and a boor, but he is right," she said softly, for Harry's ears only. "We were there, Hellen and I. We should not have attended, but we did, and so must pay the price." She tried for a smile. "At least he noticed my gown."

"Shh," the man called Renfrew warned his friend, noticing Harry's frown. "You don't want to offend any lord."

"What do I care?" Fordyce snarled, tossing back another glass of wine. "*He's* got a pretty woman for the night."

"He's handy with his fives, I heard. And the wench is spoken for anyway, they say. In his pocket, more's the pity."

"T'other one's not. I saw her putting herself on display, looking for a rich protector. Batting her eyelashes at Camden, wasn't she?"

"If Camden wasn't paying her price, you can't afford the Jezebel, either."

Fordyce cursed. Or that might have been Browne.

Hellen's eyes were filling with tears. "I am not a . . . a whore or a Jezebel."

"Of course you are not, dear." Pale-faced, near to weeping herself, Queenie turned to Harry. "Could we leave, my lord? I find I have no appetite for sweets."

Harry stood. "Let us go. I apologize. I thought the hotel had higher standards."

They gathered their wraps, and Harry told the waiter to add their unfinished meal to his hotel bill.

"But your dessert is on the way," the man protested, knowing his tip would be diminished by the dark look on Lord Harking's face.

"Toss it to the swine," Harry said, indicating the drunks at the corner table.

Browne was helping Hellen with her shawl. Somehow, as he turned to follow her after Queenie and Harry, he stumbled against the other men's table. Trying to right himself, he grabbed for the tablecloth.

And stumbled again. The dishes, the glasses, and two bottles of wine all landed in the men's laps.

"So sorry," the gentle, bespectacled schoolmaster apologized. "Clumsy, don't you know." He proved it by trying to right the remaining bottle of wine but tipping it on its side instead. "So sorry," he repeated. "Bad eyes."

The sleeping man jumped up with a start, sodden, shouting, and swinging. He hit the fat man, Fordyce. Fordyce fell backward, right into the chef, on whose tray was the brandy-soaked, pear-topped cream cake that was supposed to be Harry's table's dessert. The chef started howling in French, some phrases that even Queenie had not heard. The waiter with the bucket of water, thinking the dessert, and the cook, had been set on fire, threw the water at the chef.

Hellen applauded.

Harry told the frantic waiter to add that mess to his bill, too. It was worth every shilling.

Queenie was laughing.

CHAPTER NINE

Hellen was still in raptures over Mr. John George Browne the next morning. He was clever and kind and smart and handsome, too.

Queenie thought love must be making Hellen as blind as Mr. Browne without his spectacles, but she listened without comment, getting her shop ready for its first real day of business.

"Isn't it a marvel?" Hellen asked, disarranging Queenie's careful piles of fabrics and fashion journals. "There are two *l*s in my name, and he has two first names."

Well, there were two *r*s in Harry, and Queenie had two entire identities, but she did not see anything portentous in that. And she really had to start thinking of herself more as Denise. Queenie was gone, lost as permanently as Lady Charlotte Endicott, the child killed in the carriage crash all those years ago.

For that matter, she really had to stop thinking of Lord Harking. They had had their evening, and now she had her business open for the morning. Sadly—as if never seeing the viscount again was not sad enough—while Hellen was full of Mr. Browne's charms, the shop was full of nobody.

Queenie tried to tell herself that ladies of the night seldom rose before noon, especially after a ball and the private entertaining they did afterward. If they did not come today, perhaps they would come tomorrow. Her designs in the new magazine would be published next week, so other customers, from other walks of life, might visit the shop. She had her sketches ready to show, and nearly a dozen gowns partially finished, waiting to be fitted. The side seams were loosely basted and the hems were not cut. Queenie supposed she could work on another ensemble or more designs for the magazine. She could go over her accounts to see how much more fabric she could order from the linendraper, and how long she could consider herself a saleswoman if she had no buyers.

That was entirely too dreary, so she thought about Lord Harking instead. While Hellen chattered on about young Mr. Browne, his prospects, and his parting kiss on Hellen's hand, Queenie reviewed the previous night, the same as she had done all the long, sleepless hours until morning.

During the drive home, they had all laughed at the debacle in the hotel's dining room, relieving the tension and Hellen's tears. Lord Harking had joked that he might have to beg for a room at The Red and the Black if he was evicted from his lodgings at the Grand. Browne regretted he could never dine there again. Everyone agreed that the results of Browne's "stumble" were well worth missing the chef's dessert. And no, no one was still hungry enough to seek out a coffeehouse, although Queenie thought of claiming she was thirsty, just to prolong the evening.

The viscount must have had the same notion, for he insisted on walking her dog with her when they reached the shop and her rooms above.

"But I only take Parfait in the rear yard," Queenie told him. "And your carriage is waiting."

"The man is paid to wait, and it is far too dark for you to be out alone. Even if the area is fenced, you never know who might be lurking."

Queenie did not mention what an excellent watchdog she had in Parfait. If Lord Harking chose not to recall all the barking when they approached the front door, she would not remind him, for another few minutes of his company.

"Besides," he went on, nodding toward Hellen and Mr. Browne, "our friends appear to need some privacy to make their leave-taking."

Queenie appreciated that he was of like mind to promote a match there, so she led him through the store and the workroom, shielding her candle from the drafts. The viscount took the lantern from its hook by the back wall without asking and lit it while she unlocked the rear door.

He had even paced the length of the tiny yard, making certain no evildoer hid behind the single tree—as if Parfait would not have warned her of any strange scent. Queenie smiled, but felt warmed by someone's looking after her welfare. Someone like Harry, Lord Harking, a true gentleman.

Proving that he also had perfect manners, Parfait went behind a bush, leaving Queenie and Harry alone.

"Are you warm enough?" the viscount asked, ready to shrug out of his overcoat for her.

But Queenie had taken her thick wool cape off its hook and was well protected from the cold, damp air. As usual, one could not even glimpse the stars through the low clouds or the fog or the coal dust. "I am fine, thank you, and Parfait never stays out long anyway unless we are going to the park. He likes his comfort, too."

To prove her words, the dog bounded back to her side, tongue lolling, tail wagging. "What, did you miss me, *mon cher?*" she asked in French.

"You are not truly French, are you?" Harry asked.

Protected by the night, Queenie answered honestly: "No, but Parfait is. And I did spend a lot of time in Paris. Englishwomen and fashion editors seem to think the best styles come from France, so it was expedient to let them believe." She did not mention Monsieur Lescartes, and Lord Harking did not ask about him, thank goodness. Queenie was so tired of living a lie.

In fact, she was so tired that she yawned.

Apologizing for keeping her so late, Lord Harking led her back into the building. Hellen and Browne sprang apart, and Browne went out to the coach. Hellen went upstairs, where she was spending the night.

Neither Queenie nor Harry had anything to say. The night was over. Their temporary arrangement was done. She half hoped he would kiss her again, but knew he should not, so she held her hand out.

Harry shook it, then blushed in the lantern light for acting so . . . so like a country clodpoll and not like a polished gentleman. He brought her hand to his lips, and held it. "I . . ."

She shook her head and reclaimed her hand. Whatever he was going to say, whatever offer he would make, Queenie did not want to hear it. "I, too."

"Then good night, Madame Denise Lescartes, and thank you."

"*Adieu*, Lord Harking, and *merci*."

"Good-bye."

And he was gone.

How foolish now, by the light of day, to regret that they might never meet again. Such black thoughts were for the night, alone under her covers. Queenie remembered wishing her hero soldier father would return from the wars, miraculously alive. He would love her and never go away again, she used to hope. Then she would be sad when her wishes never came true.

Silly child. She never had a father.

And she never had a future with Lord Harking, so she was better off without seeing him again. This way she could not be disappointed. Nothing could come of their acquaintance, she had told herself throughout the night when she recalled his kiss, his tender good-bye. Nothing honorable.

Except maybe friendship. Queenie had never had a male friend; her ancient tutor did not count, nor her solicitor nor her French employer. She was not sure such a thing was even possible.

But no, a final farewell was better. She feared his lordship might want more than friendship—or she might want more. Better disappointment now than despair later.

On the other hand, Queenie owed the viscount money. The dinner was by his invitation, but the ball was by their bargain. The price of admission to the dance was minimal, especially for a gentleman of his consequence, but Queenie's pride was substantial. She did not like to be beholden to anyone, especially not a man, not an aristocrat.

Taking the coins to his hotel was tantamount to offering her body. Sending them by messenger might make him think she was pursuing an acquaintance he wished to end, since he would then have to thank her. It might even insult him, since swells seldom spoke of money matters, and the amount was trifling by his standards.

While she was trying to decide what to do, if she did anything at all, Lord Harking himself opened the shop door, sending the bell fixed there to jingling, and her spirits with it.

Harry had not slept well, either. After delivering Browne to The Red and the Black, but before seeking his bed at the hotel, Harry had directed his hired coach to Rochelle Poitier's place. He reasoned that a brothel would be doing a lively business after a night of carousal. For all he knew, the woman herself would have been at the ball, seeking new business.

Here was a job he hated, but the sooner he found his brother-in-law, or his diamonds, the sooner Harry could return to his comfortable, satisfying, decent life in the country. The only problem was, that life was beginning to seem confining, staid, and dull the longer he stayed in London. He knew his life was worthwhile and respectable, but now it felt boring, and parts of him were anything but satisfied.

No, he was not about to sate his physical longings with Jack Endicott's cast-off mistress or one of her scantily clad minions. The girls looked weary, used. Some were too young, making him think of Hellen, and some were too old, making him think of his housekeeper. Neither prospect appealed.

Mademoiselle Rochelle Poitier herself was a beautiful woman, tall and lush, with red hair that made a man think of fire and heat. It made Harry think of a fox stalking a rabbit. That avaricious gleam in her eye when she saw a well-dressed gentleman step through her door and heard his title dampened whatever ardor he might have been feeling. And her French was atrocious, limited to a few *oui*s and a *mais non* or two.

The woman could not ignore his lack of interest. Her mouth set in a cold line and her eyes narrowed when he refused her favorite girls. She turned frigid when he turned down her own favors, a boon offered to only the most select of customers. Rochelle had not been rejected since Captain Jack Endicott dismissed her as his gaming den's hostess and his own mistress. She had not liked it then, and she did not like it now. She forgot her French and she forgot her ladylike manners.

"Why'd you come here, then, bucko, iffen you were going to be so fussy?"

"Actually, I am looking for a man."

She slapped him. "This is not that kind of place. I run a respectable house, I do. Take your filthy habits and go—oh, is that for me?"

Harry had reached into his pocket for his purse. He took out the velvet jeweler's box by mistake. He thought about offering the sapphire pendant to the madam in exchange for information, but she had green eyes. Mean eyes. And his cheek still stung. He reached for a coin instead.

"The man is my brother-in-law and I have a message for him, that is all. Sir John Martin? I heard he patronized your, ah, place of business."

The coin disappeared down the front of her gown. "He was here a night or two last week, but he didn't pay his shot, so I tossed him out. He said he'd be coming into money, but I never saw a farthing of it. Your brass won't cover his bill."

So Harry handed over another coin. And held out a third. "An address where he might be now?"

Rochelle stared at the coin the way a drowning man looked at a floating log, but she shook her head. "The dirty dish never said where he was going, more's the pity, else I'd go shake my blunt out of him."

Harry tossed her the coin anyway. "In case you hear from him or see him on the street. I am at the Grand Hotel, and will pay more if you help me find him."

Rochelle looked at Harry's broad shoulders and calloused hands. "That must be some message you want to give him."

"You can count on that."

Harry could not begin to count the number of lesser houses of ill repute in London. He supposed he could eliminate the most exclusive of bordellos if Martin could not pay for a stay at Rochelle Poitier's. Still, Harry would have to spend days and nights in unsafe districts, handing coins to unsavory whoremongers. At least it appeared that Martin had not sold the Harking diamonds yet if he was still in Town and still below hatches. Most likely the heirlooms were too well documented for reputable establishments, or for those under Bow Street's scrutiny. In his rounds of jewelers, Harry had learned that the gemstones would have to be taken from the settings and recut, which was doable, but only by an expert and at great expense. That maggot Martin had been too stupid to think of the difficulties. If he'd filched a silver candlestick or two from Harking Hall, no one would have noticed, any pawnshop would have given him cash, and Harry would not be fishing in fouled water.

He was not casting his line tonight. Not with the memory of Madame Lescartes's sweet, almost innocent-seeming kiss in his mind. Not with the feeling of her still in his arms. He went back to his rooms, hoping for pleasant dreams, but hardly slept enough for that. He tossed and turned, worrying not about how he was to find his brother-in-law in the sinkholes and stews of London, but how he was to see Denise again.

He knew he should not. She had stipulated one night, and made it abundantly clear that she was not interested in any illicit liaisons. Harry was not seeking an affair with a dressmaker, either. Hell, no, not when he'd spent half his life subduing his own base urges. He merely wanted to enjoy her company a bit more, that was all. If he could unravel the riddle of the woman, the who and why and how she came to be what she was, his curiosity would be satisfied, if nothing else was.

A gentleman often sent flowers to the lady he'd escorted the previous night. Harry wondered if such rules pertained to dolly-mops and their dance partners. He was not placing Denise in that category, naturally, but the Cyprian's Ball was not Almack's, and whatever else she was, Madame Lescartes was not a true lady.

But she might like flowers. She wore some in her hair last night. And he could use a bouquet as an excuse to call in person. No, then he might look too much like a suitor. A note inviting her to the park? Too chancy that she would decline. A stroll through her neighborhood, passing the shop as if by accident? Too transparent.

It would have to be flowers . . . or the sapphire necklace.

She slapped him.

Damn, weren't his cheeks red enough from the walk and the weather? Or was his face so ugly every woman thought she had to smack it? "You do not understand."

The light of welcome had died in her eyes and the sparkle had turned dull and cold when she saw the velvet box he handed her. "I understand perfectly, Lord Harking." She spoke his name as a curse, reminding both of them of the differences in their stations. "A wealthy gentleman brings an unattached, unprotected woman an expensive gift. What is there to misinterpret?"

"That I meant no insult, and that the necklace is a, ah, gift for my sister. She has few enough jewels of her own. I was hoping you would help me select a fan or a shawl or a dress length to match." He opened the box to show her the delicate sapphire pendant on a gold chain.

"Oh," was all she said.

Harry held out a posy of early violets he'd purchased from a street vendor. "These are for you, to thank you for last night. There is nothing wrong in a bouquet, is there?" He stepped back, just in case.

Queenie took the flowers and held them to her burning face, so mortified she wished they were a bush she could hide behind. "I am so sorry. The flowers are lovely, and thoughtful of you. You are too kind. Please forgive me."

"There is nothing to forgive." Lud, he was guilty as hell, and he supposed she was tired of being propositioned. He should be thankful, he supposed, that she had not stuck her needle through his nose. "Will you help me?"

"Help you?"

"Find something for my sister."

"Oh, to match the necklace. Of course. I think I have a roll of fabric that would be perfect if she likes blue. She must, or you would not have purchased sapphires, would you? Will you wait?"

"Of course. Olivia would be thrilled to have one of your gowns. She'd be the envy of the neighborhood, but unfortunately I do not have her measurements, so a dress length will have to do."

"I can include a copy of the French fashion journal with my designs in it. Perhaps her dressmaker would be able to copy one of the styles."

"The lending library at home only gets a few London ladies' magazines, late at that, so Olivia would be doubly delighted if you can spare a copy."

"That will be my pleasure, in return for your paying our admission to the ball last night."

"What, a few shillings? You underestimate your value tenfold. I am sure Olivia would put a much higher price on just one of your sketches, especially when I tell her how famous you are going to be. I insist on paying a fair price, both for the fabric and the journal."

"Since you are my very first customer, you will get a special rate," Queenie firmly insisted. Then their accounts would be even.

Harry had been too busy admiring her to notice anything else. She wore another black gown, a simpler day frock, but still elegant and still clinging to her perfect, slim figure. Blue ribbons trailed from the high waist, and another blue ribbon was threaded through her black curls. She looked as fresh and lovely as the spring violets she still held, even if the beauty mark on the side of her mouth was a bit lower than he recalled. Harry forced himself to look around the shop, the thoroughly empty shop.

She saw him frowning at the vacant space. "It is early still."

He pulled on his watch chain and consulted the timepiece. Eleven o'clock was not early, not by country standards. "Quite. London ladies pay morning calls after noon."

Queenie tried not to show her own anxiety. "Yes, well, I shall fetch the material for your sister." She took the necklace, to match colors, and thrust the violets at him. "Please find a place for these."

When she left, Harry looked around for a suitable spot for the posy. He found glasses on a counter, along with a decanter of what looked like ratafia, but no water. He wandered around, admiring the gowns hanging from hooks and hangers along the walls, and pictured Madame Lescartes in each of them. Finally he put the violets in the hand of the mannequin in the window, and bowed to her. "For my lady."

The dog sneezed.

On her way to the back workroom, where the shelves were not half as full as she wished, Queenie called up the stairs to Hellen. "Hurry and get dressed, and bring the tea tray. Lord Harking has come to purchase some fabric for his sister."

She thought her friend called down, "I doubt he even has a sister," but Queenie ignored that. Of course he had a sister. He was looking for his brother-in-law, wasn't he? In the workroom she opened the jewelry box again and could not help admiring the necklace and wondering if Olivia had blue eyes. She was a lucky sister either way, to have such a caring brother.

And Queenie was a fool for thinking he had brought the necklace for her. Her cheeks felt warm all over again, thinking of her buffle-headed blunder. Gracious, he must think her the most vain woman on earth, supposing every man was lusting after her. Well, enough were, or had been. But not Lord Harking, it seemed.

If Queenie was disappointed, she refused to dwell on it, finding just the right shade of blue watered silk to match the blue gems. Any woman would feel beautiful in a gown of that fabric. Queenie had even saved a dress length for herself, for when she had time to make a new gown, and when she had established her signature style in black.

Now she cut the fabric carefully, adding extra yardage since she had no idea if Olivia was built on the same generous proportions as her brother. She folded the cloth and wrapped it and the fashion journal in silver tissue, tied with a silver ribbon, with a black silk rosebud tucked in the bow. She put the jewel box on top and went back to the showroom, the crowded, noisy, busy showroom.

Half the women from the ladies' retiring chamber last night seemed to be in the front room of her shop, exclaiming over the unfinished gowns, looking through her sketches, fingering the fabric samples, and petting her dog.

Because they could not pet Lord Harking.

He was too busy acting as store clerk.

CHAPTER TEN

"Here she is, ladies, the finest dress designer in all of London, soon to be the most famous. Madame Denise Lescartes." Lord Harking bowed deeply in Queenie's direction.

She would have been mortified at his grandiose act, making her the center of attraction, if she were not so amazed. Not only was her shop filled with courtesans, but they were laughing and smiling, not the least irritated at the wait. Hellen was pouring ratafia, and handing round a plate of biscuits that had somehow appeared.

Lord Harking wasted no time in consulting a list in his hand. "I believe Miss Sophy Patterson is first to consult with Madame, with the raspberry-colored—what did you say that gown was made of?"

"Lutestring," Queenie and Miss Patterson both answered at once.

"Of course, lutestring, whatever that is. It sounds musical, perfect for the opera Miss Patterson is going to attend in two nights with her beau. I mentioned that such haste would be more expensive, but we all agreed the gown was worth the cost."

Queenie wondered how they could agree when Lord Harking did not even know the price of the gown. No matter, the first of her sample gowns appeared sold, but for a few alterations and hemming. How could she take Miss Patterson back for the fitting, though, when so many other sales were waiting to be made? She looked at the eager young woman, at the raspberry gown, at the dozen more demireps, then at Lord Harking.

"Go," Harry said, smiling at her. "The ladies and I shall manage. We'll send for more wine and biscuits and discuss fashions."

Miss Patterson giggled.

Queenie shook her head, but she started to lead the young woman back to the fitting room, with the raspberry gown over her arm. Two of the other women were starting to argue, however.

"I wanted that gown."

"I saw it first."

"But my gentleman likes me in pink."

"Well, I don't have a gentleman, so I need to look prettier more than you do."

Harry was laughing. "My dears, you are sounding like my sister Olivia's children. Surely Madame Denise can make up another similar gown for . . ." He consulted his list. "Margaret, who did arrive later than Miss Katherine Rigby. Shall I make an appointment for you, Maggie mine?"

Queenie stepped back toward where he was standing, with another page filled with dates and times. Softly, so the other women could not hear, she asked, "You will do this? For me?"

"But of course. Think nothing of it. I am used to children

bickering, and acting as arbitrator when one of my tenants' pigs gets into another's garden or an unmarked calf strays over a boundary. This is more fun. And I do have a small favor to ask in return."

"Anything!"

He smiled again, and Queenie could hear two females sigh at the sight. Or maybe that was one harlot and herself.

He whispered, "We shall talk about it later, after you become a great success."

"Thanks to you."

She led Miss Patterson to the back room, where the courtesan confided that her lover was paying the bill, and he was rich and generous and forty years older than she was. The perfect gentleman, Queenie agreed with a mumble, her mouth full of pins.

Miss Patterson's beau might have been a baboon, for all the attention Queenie paid her chatter. She would be able to hire seamstresses, an assistant to help take measurements, perhaps a clerk and an errand boy. She was truly going to see her dream come true.

No, she could never have dreamed of such a success, so fast. And she could never have come this far without her own perfect gentleman. She smiled at the image of Lord Harking surrounded by straw damsels, and dropped half the pins. Then she dropped the rest when she realized he might find one he fancied. He really was not *her* gentleman. Some of her excitement faded.

He was here in her shop for now, though, Queenie told herself, and she did not want anything more from him. Of course not.

By the time she came back into the front room, every one of her partially finished gowns was bespoken. Even the mannequin in the window had been divested of her frock, one of Queenie's favorites.

Someone, she hoped Hellen and not the efficient Lord Harking, had protected the mannequin's modesty with a draped length of white muslin from the stack of samples. The same someone—heavens, had Lord Harking been dressing a female figure in front of the barques of frailty and anyone who passed by?—had placed the violets in the mannequin's hand. Now the figure looked like she'd just come from bed, wrapped in a sheet, holding her lover's token. That was *not* the image Queenie wished her shop to convey, so she'd have to create something new for the window, as soon as she had the time.

The orders had to come first, of course, especially since half of them were paid for already, with bank drafts and cash carefully piled in a drawer. Lord Harking had another list of receipts and balances due, and an appointments calendar that was filled into the next week. Queenie's head was spinning, but she kept fitting and pinning and listening to her new clients. Many were no older than herself, talking about their lovers and their longings to be more beautiful, more desired, more popular, so they could demand higher prices. Which was what Queenie was doing with her gowns, so she understood. Her sympathetic ear won her as many future orders as her designs. Having a friendly aristocrat in the showroom did not hurt, either.

By three o'clock there was nothing left in the shop to sell, and Queenie was exhausted, but thrilled. She agreed when Lord Harking declared the store closed for the day. She did not agree to go to Gunter's for ices to celebrate.

"Oh, no. I have to go to the placement agencies and interview new employees. I already have far more work than

I can accomplish myself. And the new fashion journal comes out next week, so I am expecting even more orders."

"I will help," Hellen said, "if you are still willing to pay me a salary so I can give it to my mum. I am not much for sewing, but I watched Lord Harking make appointments and keep accounts. At least I knew how long a fitting would take, and how much you had planned to charge. Harry said your prices were too low, so he raised them."

So Queenie was even more ahead of her goals. "If you will be my assistant, I will pay you a fine salary, and provide your wardrobe, too. It would be perfect." And a respectable, honest living for Hellen, thank goodness.

"Too bad you cannot make Harry your manager. I've never seen the like, him taking charge that way, keeping the women from scratching each other's eyes out, or leaving."

"And sending out for biscuits was brilliant, too. I do not know how I can thank you, my lord."

"Well, you can call me Harry for a start. Everyone does. Then I may call you Denise."

She'd been calling him Harry in her head, but this gentleman was too honorable, too straightforward, for her lies. She could not give him the truth, but now loathed having an assumed name. "I think it better that we not be so familiar." It was safer, too.

"Ah, then I shall just have to call you *chérie*."

That was not safer.

Queenie quickly fetched the package for his sister from the counter. "And I shall call you my hero for this day."

He blushed, as he often did when embarrassed, Queenie realized. She found it endearing. She doubted if five other men in all of London ever turned red, except when they had too much to drink. "I truly do not know what I would have done without you."

"You would have managed, I am certain. But I am no hero, merely an organized type of chap. I can tell you to the newest chick how many hens I have, how many bales of hay and sacks of wool. I enjoy keeping records and making order out of chaos."

Since he was grinning, nibbling on the last of the biscuits, Queenie said, "I can see you do. Are you certain you do not want a job?"

"If I did not have Harking Hall to manage, I might consider your offer. I like to be useful. In fact, this afternoon was the most pleasure I have had since coming to London except . . ." He was looking at her lips, where Queenie was licking a crumb from the macaroon she had eaten.

. . . Except the kiss. So he had not forgotten it, either. She hurriedly placed the ribbon-tied package in his hands, an indication that he should leave. "Oh, but I owe you that favor. I am certain I owe you far more, but what can I do for you? If you get your sister's measurements, I shall make her a fine gown. Or trim a bonnet to match the silk. Unless she sent you to purchase corsets and stockings and nightclothes, which I can understand you might not wish to do. I would be happy to complete your errands for you."

"No, it is nothing like that. I have but one mission in London, and am hoping to succeed tonight. If not, I might consider hiring Bow Street. But the favor I am asking is for your company—and yours, too, Hellen, and Browne's if he wishes—at the opera tomorrow night. I seldom get the chance to hear fine music, so I like to indulge myself when in Town. I just do not care to go on my own."

Queenie was not sure, not sure she should go anywhere with the man she was coming to care for far more than she ought.

Harry misunderstood her hesitation. "I promise this will

not be like the Cyprian's Ball, where you were exposed to all manner of rude behavior. I shall hire a private box for us, and no one will treat either of you with disrespect, not while you are in my care. Besides, you can get a chance to show off more of your creations."

Everyone would think Queenie was his mistress. They already did, after last night. This afternoon in the shop would have confirmed the suspicions, and her customers would not have kept his presence there a secret. A peer of the realm acting as a shop clerk was just too delicious an on-dit not to share. And why else would he have done it, if not to please his inamorata?

Far more conversant with the London gossip mills, Lord Harking must know what was being said, Queenie decided. He must not care.

So Queenie decided not to care, either. She knew the truth, and that was what mattered, not what a bunch of strangers thought. If her notoriety cost her business among the haut monde, so be it. To her own surprise she liked her new customers. They treated her with respect, which *ton*ish females might not do, and they paid on time. They appreciated her skills, and they truly did need to look their best to be successful. Society's daughters had their dowries and their fathers' names to barter. They could do without one of Madame Denise's designs.

Queenie had little to lose by going to the opera with Harry, then, except for the hours she could spend sewing, and more of her heart. She was not strong enough to deny herself one more memory to cherish when he left.

She let herself touch his hand, as lightly as a feather, as briefly as a sigh. "That is the favor you wish, to take us to hear wonderful music, in the grandest theater in the city, with the grandest escorts, while finding new customers?"

"As I said, the opera is far more enjoyable when it is shared."

"I cannot speak for Mr. Browne, of course, but I would be delighted. Hellen?"

Hellen's pirouette around Parfait spoke for itself.

"Then we are pleased to accept your offer, my lord."

"No, it is my pleasure, *chérie.*"

Queenie was right about Lord Harking's notoriety. The next day's scandal sheets made much of the standoffish viscount's standing in for a store clerk. One cartoon pictured him as a ringmaster in tailcoat and top hat, long whip in hand, putting pretty girls through their paces around a dress shop. It was obviously Harking, with his broad chest and shoulders, and dark circles painted on his cheeks. He would hate that, she knew, being held to public ridicule, and wondered if he would change his mind about escorting her to the opera. She could not blame him.

She should not be going out for the evening anyway, not with so many orders to fill and gowns to complete. That same cartoon had shown the name of her shop, and brought more shoppers, who became buyers when they saw her designs. She did not cry off the engagement, however.

Instead she visited employment agencies, leaving Hellen to make appointments and excuses.

Harry visited brothels.

Queenie came away satisfied.

He came away disgusted.

She found three ideal employees.

He found no trace of Sir John Martin.

She needed only a messenger boy.

He needed a bath. And a drink.

*   *   *

Queenie made certain that the three women she hired were not snobbish. Their needlework was excellent, but she needed their characters to be generous, also. Her current clients were what they were, and their money was as good as a gentlewoman's, better at times. Queenie would have the courtesans treated with the same courtesy a countess would receive, the same respect she herself demanded.

The women were happy to have the positions. They would have sewn sequins on Satan's red suit if it paid as well. At Madame Denise's they worked with wondrous fabrics and elegant, exciting designs, and were treated like valuable assistants, not slaves. Besides, without their skills at sewing, two of the females might have found themselves in the same position as the women they sewed for: on their backs.

In less than a day most of the sample gowns were completed, new orders were cut from Queenie's patterns, and measurements were taken for more. The window mannequin was dressed in Queenie's gown from the Cyprian's Ball, turned sideways to show the nearly bare back. She held a sprig of silk forget-me-nots in her hand to replace the violets, which were in Queenie's bedroom.

The shop was truly in business now, except for a boy to deliver the finished goods and to fetch biscuits for the customers, a midday meal for the workers, and thread when they ran out. He could sweep and wash the windows, Queenie thought, and save her from a hundred other little tasks that needed doing. The personnel agency she used did not have such a creature, and none of her seamstresses knew of any.

Queenie had frequently seen a ragged boy in the neighborhood, usually near the alley a few doors down, waiting for an opportunity. She had seen him holding a gentleman's horse a few times or carrying a package. He looked to be about ten, although he acted older, and was smaller in stature. The next time she walked past, she said, "I would like to speak to you, young man."

The boy stepped back, ready to dart into the alley. "I only filched one. The nob gave me t'other, I swear."

"Filched one what?" She could not hire a thief, not when he might be collecting payment on delivery of her finished gowns. "Who gave you another one?"

"T'gentry cull what was here t'other day. He gave me a coin to go to the bakeshop for biscuits."

Ah, Harry. "Would he have known if you had eaten two?"

The boy shrugged thin shoulders. "He never said how many to get, just to spend the blunt he gave me. He weren't going to count them or nothing."

"But you can count?"

The boy looked offended. "And cipher some, too. How else could I know I ain't getting cheated?"

"Quite right. Then I suppose you are mostly honest?"

"I wouldn't of eaten any, but I was hungry."

No child should go hungry. "Would you like a position with me, then? I need a lad to fetch and carry, like the biscuits, but also to sweep and clean and make deliveries. Do you know your way around London?"

"Like the back of me hand. Born and bred here, I am."

"But there can be no stealing, not ever. If you are hungry, you ask. If you accept payment for a delivery, I will know exactly how much money should come back with you, do you understand?"

"I ain't no fool. You'd kick me out in a flash iffen you got shortchanged. And that's a hanging offense, asides. Or transportation."

"Quite right. Crime does not pay. I will. And you might make extra in tips when you deliver the packages."

"And you'd really hire me?"

"On a temporary basis, to see if we suit, to start. But only if it is all right with your parents, of course."

Now he made a rude noise. He jerked his thumb toward the alley between buildings. "Do you think I would be living there iffen I had a ma and pa?"

"Gracious, you live in the alley?"

"It's safe, and I got me a tight crate to keep warm. It's a lot better'n the orphanage or the workhouse."

No employee of hers was going to sleep in a crate outdoors, for goodness' sake. Even her dog lived better than that. "No. You shall sleep in the shop's workroom on a pallet mattress."

The boy shook his head in disgust. "You really need me, lady."

"Odd, I thought you needed me."

"I ain't the one who'd hire a pickpocket and then let him sleep in my house without knowing his intents."

"A pickpocket?"

"Only when I can't find no honest work. I told you, a bloke's got to eat. But I can make sure you ain't gulled by no one else. And no one'll break in, neither, not when March is on the job."

Queenie did not mention that no one would gain entry to the shop or the house when Parfait was there, either, but she did ask, "Do you like dogs?"

He shrugged. "Does yours like boys?"

"If they treat him well and behave properly. So do we have a deal, Master March?"

"It's just March. That's the month I got left at the orphanage."

"No first name, no pet name?"

"Never stayed anywhere's long enough. No one ever cared. I could never decide on one for m'self."

Queenie had so many, she wished she could give him one of hers. The poor boy had no home, no family, not even a name of his own. She knew exactly how he must feel. Why couldn't she give him something besides a place to sleep and a job? She offered him the name of the child she was meant to impersonate, Lady Charlotte Endicott. "How would you like to be Charles March? It is a fine name."

He swirled the name around in his mouth and his mind a few times. "How 'bout *Charlie*? Sounds more regular, like."

"Then *Charlie* it is. Are we agreed?"

The boy stood taller and proud. Having two names and an important job for a lady gave him stature. "Agreed." He spit in his hand and held it out to seal their bargain.

"Ah, you will need a bath first, and a new set of clothes, and a haircut. What say we shake on the deal afterward?"

CHAPTER ELEVEN

The woman was a marvel, Harry decided when he arrived at the shop before the visit to the opera. In just two days, Madame Denise Designs was restocked, restored, and ready again for business. New sample gowns hung on the pegs, pins and threads dangling, but available to view. Soft fabrics in rainbow hues draped the counters, and the mannequin in the window was attracting attention from every gentleman who passed by.

A neatly dressed red-haired boy leaped to hold the front door open for Harry and proudly pronounced that Madame and miss would be ready on "t'instant, gov."

Harry could only guess at how hard the woman had worked to replenish her wares. He thought about his sister, whose most strenuous effort was in giving orders to the servants, or occasionally arranging flowers after the gardener had cut them. London ladies exerted themselves at entertaining and being entertained, nothing more.

Even the working women he had been visiting slept the

days away after a hard night's labor. Madame Denise
Lescartes and her staff must never have rested.

She deserved the holiday. Lud knew Harry thought he
did, after hours spent looking for his missing relation in
repugnant places. He wanted the night at the opera, at
least, to be perfect.

Tomorrow he might have to call in Bow Street, making
the world privy to his ugly private business, but tonight, he
vowed, would be an evening of beauty: beautiful women,
beautiful music. He was not going to let anything interfere
with the pleasure of a few hours, with him away from his
search, her away from her store.

So he hired the best private box available that night,
purchased opera glasses for all, and studied the libretto of
the German work so he could appear knowledgeable. He
sent flowers; he hired the fanciest coach; he spent hours at
his toilette. He engaged a footman from his hotel to attend
the box and fetch refreshments so he did not have to leave
Madame Lescartes alone, and to see that no one entered
without Harry's permission. No rake or rogue was going to
embarrass his guest with unwanted familiarity, Harry
swore . . . or steal her away.

Harry swallowed his moral doubts and his feelings of
guilt along with a peppermint drop to freshen his breath.
He was not trying to seduce the woman, by Jove, just enjoy
her company. He was not enamored, he told himself,
merely fascinated by a type of creature he had never come
upon before, like an exotic butterfly. He could admire his
discovery, he told himself, without wanting to trap it, keep
it, own it for himself.

He straightened his cravat and told himself once more
how he respected her talent, her intelligence, her
ambition . . . and her charm.

But he was not infatuated. Of course not.

Of course his tongue would not wrap itself around a "good evening" when she entered the shop from the rear hall. His feet would not propel him closer; his fingers were too numb to reach for her hand. But, oh, portions of him strained toward her. Lud, she was the most beautiful woman he had ever seen. And she was smiling at him, Harry Harkness.

She wore black again, but this time, instead of the back of the gown gone missing, half of the front was. Breasts, snowy mountains that begged to be explored, satiny skin that screamed for caresses, rose above black velvet. What was softer, the fabric or the feel of her? And how could he find out?

Worse, how could he sit beside her without embarrassing her and himself? Unwanted familiarity? Good grief, even he was unfamiliar with such raging, roaring lust!

"Thank you for the lovely flowers," she was saying. "They are perfect."

Harry dragged his eyes from her breasts and his mind from the bedroom—or the floor, the back workroom, the carriage. No, Browne and Hellen were waiting to go, waiting for him to say something.

"Not as perfect as you are, *chérie*," he blurted, relieved he could remember a name, an endearment, any word but *please*. He noticed now that one of his costly red rosebuds was fixed in the vee of her neckline. He should have paid more.

The other rosebuds, all carefully trimmed of thorns, of course, were woven into a tiara atop her short black curls, with three plumed red feathers at the back adding the height and formality de rigueur at the opera. A black lace shawl trimmed in bands of red velvet foamed over her nearly bare shoulders. And her slippers peeking from under the flounced hem of her gown were red, making him wonder what color stockings she wore. And wonder if spending an evening at the woman's side, in public, would kill him.

Hellen was twirling in front of Browne, who appeared nearly as tongue-tied as Harry. She was dressed in white lace, like the young girl she was, with Harry's white rosebuds fixed at her waist. The contrast was poignant, the innocent maid in virginal white, the sophisticated woman of the world in black that had little to do with mourning and everything to do with nighttime. And yet Harry knew that Hellen was open to suggestion, while his *chérie* was open for store business in the morning, and nothing else. Besides, as Hellen circled, laughing and begging for compliments, a long strand of perfect pearls bounced against her rounded chest. They were a mistress's bounty, Harry thought, not a young girl's birthday gift. He hoped, for the besotted Browne's sake, that the pearls were borrowed from Hellen's mother.

Madame Lescartes wore no jewels. Harry was delighted.

"We'll sell a dozen gowns tomorrow, won't we?" Hellen was cooing.

Oh, Madame Lescartes would sell a hundred gowns after tonight, Harry thought. She might start a manufactory for gowns. But no other woman would ever look so stunning in them.

Or, he'd wager, out of them. "Shall we go?"

She bent to pet the poodle, telling the dog to stay, to look after young Charlie, and to be good. Parfait wagged his tail in agreement. Now, if only Harry could promise good behavior so easily.

But that was wrong. His wayward thoughts were wrong, reprehensible. Harry had promised a night of culture, without compromising the scruples of either of them. As soon as they were in the coach, and he had his wits abut him again—and his hat in his lap, to make sure—he reiterated his promise. "Nothing and no one shall disturb your pleasure. I have taken measures."

Still, her hand trembled slightly on his arm when he escorted her out of the coach and through the wide doors, then up the stairs to their box. Surprised yet again by the shyness mingled in her sophistication, Harry patted that hand reassuringly and said, "Do not concern yourself with the crowd tonight, *chérie*. They will stare and be stunned by your beauty, but you shall not have to do anything except listen to the music."

But Queenie had to look around, to admire the grandeur of the building itself, the gilt, the glittering chandeliers, the ornate plasterwork, before the lights were dimmed. And she had to see what the other women were wearing. While she tried to take mental notes about the colors and styles and sizes—gracious, she ought to cut her sample gowns fuller if the London ladies had such generous figures—she could not help noticing how many intense gazes were fastened on Lord Harking's box.

Half of the women, it seemed, and more of the men, were looking directly at her, through opera glasses or not. She supposed they were interested in the viscount's companion, for they could not see her gown while she was seated. She knew what they were thinking, and had vowed not to let the small minds of society destroy her enjoyment of the evening. Still, she felt the disapproval, from the nearest box where a turbaned dowager turned her shoulder, to the pursed lips and pale cheeks of several young ladies in pastel gowns across the way.

Men might have their little affairs, but the gentlewomen pretended ignorance. When a handsome bachelor, new on the town, paraded his mistress in public, the doyennes and damsels of society were doubly offended.

Lord Harking was one of theirs, the dagger glances seemed to say, meant for one of the marriageable misses. His title and fortune belonged to the beau monde, not an adventuress, not a woman in trade, not a woman of easy virtue.

Queenie had no doubt what the men were thinking. Those few without female companions blew her kisses or stood and bowed in her direction when her glance passed their boxes. Some with ladies at their sides gave her subtle winks or nods or raised eyebrows, as if their companions, wives, sisters, or lovers could not notice. One gentleman received a slap from his partner; another was rapped with a fan. The women noticed, all right, and resented.

Perhaps coming tonight would not be good for business if her prospective customers thought she was a threat either to them personally, which was absurd, or to the standards of their society. She could not leave, yet did not think she could bear the scrutiny much longer. Discomfited, she turned to Harry. He was a better view anytime.

At least the women would not think she was interested in *their* men. What female would be, sitting next to Harry? Just looking at his profile as he pointed out a duke to Hellen made Queenie smile again. He was so handsome in his evening dress, she could feel a catch in her throat, as if seeing a sudden rainbow or a rare masterpiece. When she'd come into the shop to find him standing there, even though she expected him, her breath had flown. His smile could stop her heart, she feared.

Tonight he looked even more like a London swell than the country gentleman she had first met, and Queenie regretted the change, while admiring the results. A simple landowner was far enough above her touch, but a viscount?

Harry was every inch a lord tonight, from his perfectly tied neckcloth to his silk stockings and formal satin knee breeches. His jaw was smooth from a recent shave, and his every hair was in place, for once. He was laughing kindly at Hellen's excitement, though, not at all stiff and on his uppers. And hadn't he made her those earnest promises, his brown eyes flecked with gold, foolishly but nobly swearing she would be safe from gossip and malice, as if he could protect her from the world? He was still Harry, and they were still friends. She would be happy for that. She would be happy for tonight.

Just as the orchestra started to play and the lights were lowered, Hellen touched her sleeve and said, "Look, there is Miss Patterson, in your raspberry gown."

The young woman was in a box nearby, and she gaily waved to them when Queenie turned in her direction. Queenie could not help noticing that the large ruby at Miss Patterson's throat did not quite match the color of her gown, nor did it suit the style, but Miss Patterson did not care. She seemed delighted with her bauble, and with her elderly beau beside her. Lucky Miss Patterson, who did not care about society's sneers, only her sixty-year-old swain, who beamed proudly.

Then the music began and Queenie forgot about the stares and the slurs. She even forgot about Harry's warm shoulder next to hers.

Browne softly whispered a translation of the German

for Hellen, but Queenie needed no help interpreting the plot. The beautiful sea sprite, languishing beside a shimmering waterfall of gold-and-silver tinsel, loved a fairhaired mortal, who swore to worship her until his dying day, which was bound to be all too soon. A bearded god was lusting after the nubile beauty, and his goddess wife was jealous.

No good could come from such a confluence, Queenie knew. She could already feel tears at the back of her throat, and the first act was not half over. The music soared, the arias filled her senses, and the hero's valiant, hopeless adoration touched her heart.

Then the lights came back on.

A footman brought lemonade and wine, slices of oranges and poppy seed cake. Queenie did not have to look at the audience or Lord Harking, who fretted about her silly damp eyes and quivering lip.

"You are not enjoying yourself?" he asked in concern.

"Oh, I am, immensely. It is just the, ah, smoke from the candles and the excitement. But how thoughtful of you to provide refreshment."

"I should have provided a comedy, dash it," he muttered.

In the second act, Queenie lost all patience with the sea nymph. The ninny should have held strong against the god, slapped him with a salmon or something. She should have sent him back to his wife with a shove. So what if he promised the moon? The mortal loved her, and only her. And didn't the stupid soprano realize the vengeful goddess controlled the immense fanged sea serpents that rose on strings from the stage? The poor hero was supposed to defend her from them? With nothing but his puny sword and his love as a shield?

"*Sacre bleu,* they are both imbeciles!"

"Are you quite certain you are enjoying yourself?" Harry asked again at the next intermission. "We could leave."

"What, before I see the end?"

He shook his head in confusion, but stood to permit Hellen and Browne to pass by on their way to the corridor to stretch their legs.

"Would you care to stroll in the hall, my dear, rather than sitting here so long?"

Queenie was still lost in the waterfall. Besides, all those gawking strangers would be in the corridors. Let the ladies notice Hellen's gown. Queenie would rather sit beside Harry, who was wise enough, or bewildered enough, not to make idle conversation at such an emotional moment.

The footman entered the box and cleared his throat. "Lord Camden offers his regards, and asks if he might join you and Madame Lescartes for the intermission."

Harry was about to shout *no.* Let that reprobate near his *chérie*? Never, while he held a sword. Well, it was the hero in the opera who held a sword, but Harry was ready to fend off any number of forked-tongued fribbles.

Then the footman added, "With his sister, Lady Jennifer Camden."

His sister? A gentleman did not introduce his sister to another chap's ladybird. It simply was not done. Yet here was Cam, paying a social visit to Harry's box. Which meant that Cam, at least, recognized Madame Lescartes as a lady. Or his sister wanted a new gown. Either was good for Denise's reputation, her business, her place in the world. Harry looked toward his companion, who shrugged. He nodded toward the footman and stood again to welcome his guests.

At first he worried that his companion would be disconcerted at meeting a duke's daughter, especially after he promised her a night of no awkwardness. Lady Jennifer was a formidable member of society at that, a tall, broad, hawk-nosed spinster at thirty, and seemingly satisfied that way. She was outspoken and opinionated, which also accounted for her unwed state, in Harry's mind. She had a fortune of her own and her father's and brother's consequence to protect her, so she was deemed an Original in the haut monde, not an outcast.

Then Harry worried that his seamstress would not know how to address a lady, how to converse with one of her betters, that she would embarrass all of them, and herself. The disloyalty stabbed at him. He'd put her in this situation, and he would see her through.

Harry should have known better. Madame Lescartes curtsied the precise correct degree, with respect but without deference. She held her black head proudly, the feathers swaying majestically. Her spine was as erect as that of any graduate of the most select academy for young ladies, and she conversed in better French than any of those dunderheaded daughters of the nobility. Damn, if she was not a lady at heart, Harry thought, as proud as Miss Patterson's aged protector.

"My brother highly recommends I purchase a gown of your design," Lady Jennifer told Queenie after the introductions were concluded. "And I can see why. Since he is willing to pay for the nonsense, I have agreed."

"Gold," Queenie said without thinking, after quickly noting the outdated style of her visitor's gown, with its fitted waist and muddy brown color.

Lady Jennifer raised her prominent nose and her thick eyebrows at the same time, a well-practiced method of putting inferiors in their place. "I usually have my secretary send a bank draft. Camden might be rackety, but he is good for the money."

Queenie blushed. "Forgive me, ma'am. I did not mean to imply mistrust of your finances, nor speak of monetary matters away from the shop. I meant your gown should be gold, a rich heavy fabric, brocade perhaps, or figured satin, bringing out the gold in your hair and your dignity. Like a czarina from a fable."

Lady Jennifer laughed, but she was flattered. "Me, a czarina?" She waved her gloved hand at the stage. "You have been watching too many fantasies and have let your imagination run away with you."

"No, I see the bearing of a ruler, and a woman who is far too wise to try dressing like a *jeune fille* or in the current mode of filmy fabrics. You have stature. I would make that your signature. No mere miss could match such an effect."

Lady Jennifer tipped her head a regal inch, already enjoying her role of exotic empress. "I like you, madame. You are not afraid to say what you think."

"Not when it comes to fashion."

"Or otherwise, I believe. I should like to get to know you better, with your permission. I am at home Thursday afternoons. Please call."

Now Queenie was indeed flustered. "For your fitting?"

"For tea, madame, for tea and conversation. No, do not refuse over some silly social conventions. A duke's daughter, especially one of independent means and nature, can entertain whomever she wishes, and I wish to surround myself with intelligent women with opinions."

Queenie had no wish to sit at a lady's table pretending to be what she was not, speaking of a world she did not know. This was her first opera. What could she discuss with a duke's daughter? "But I—"

"You are recently returned from France, I understand. I would seek your impressions of the political climate there. Fashion is not my métier. I shall leave that to you. But rational discourse is. I seek information, firsthand accounts of what you saw and heard and learned."

Queenie doubted the lady meant seeing the back rooms of dressmaking shops, or learning how to avoid a Frenchman's advances, or hearing French words never spoken in polite drawing rooms.

Her uncertainty must have shown, for Lady Jennifer said, "I count a novelist among my Thursday guests, and a famous world traveler, as well as a scandalously divorced baroness and a former Spanish nun. Do you speak Spanish, by any chance?"

"Un poco."

"You shall do. I will expect you then. If nothing else, the afternoon might lead to more business for your shop."

"I fear that if I have much more business, I shall have to move to bigger quarters and hire scores more workers."

"That is no bad thing. Too many women are at the mercy of men and the poverty they leave behind. The females need respectable positions if they are to make something of their own lives. We shall talk about that, too. Oh, and a few gentlemen attend my little gatherings, so do try not to look so alluring, can you, so we might have a bit of conversation instead of heavy breathing? Your own respiration might be improved, Brother, if you raised your eyes from Madame's bosom."

Harry laughed, well aware of his companion's effect on any male over the age of thirteen. Camden, that nonpareil among London notables, actually blushed. So did Queenie. "But I need time for your gown, ma'am."

Lady Jennifer looked at Harry, so proud, so pleased with himself. "I suspect you need a friend more."

A sale, a friend, the respect of someone of Harry's own class—and the opera. What more could Queenie ask of the night? She did not even notice that she was grasping Harry's hand when the third act started. She felt the tender warmth seep through her gloves, part and parcel of what he had given her this evening.

CHAPTER TWELVE

The opera ended as expected, with murder and mayhem and melodrama, and last-gasp arias that lasted long enough to wrench the hardest heart. Thunder boomed from the orchestra pit, and lightning flashed behind the painted scenery. Enough tears flowed from the audience to extinguish any fires that the wondrous effects might have ignited.

The gods won, of course. The mere mortal, no matter how fine his voice or how constant his love, never stood a chance. The worst loser, naturally, was the poor female who thought she could change her destiny, the one who gave her heart so unwisely and lost everything she held dear.

Queenie wept, and not delicately like a lady, either. She sobbed and moaned and shook with sadness.

Damn, Harry thought, he could not do anything right! He'd wanted to give her a night of joy and instead he'd brought her grief and pain, and more stares from the other operagoers.

On the other, brighter, side, now he would not have to worry about escorting Madame Lescartes back through the hordes of would-be admirers as they left the theater. Gone was the gorgeous dasher, and only a swollen-eyed, splotchy-cheeked, and sodden female remained. Unfortunately, Harry could not help noticing that her magnificent bosom was heaving, but he told himself no man could consider that a compliment. And no man wanted a watering pot as a bed warmer.

Of course Harry was not just any man. An imperfect diamond suited him far better than an untouchable cold stone. Now he wanted nothing more than to fold her in his arms, to comfort her and kiss the wetness from her cheeks, her smoky eyelashes, her damp, swanlike neck. If he happened to feel her bosom against his own chest, that was not his intent.

He could not do anything, though, not in front of half of England's elite. He merely handed over his own, larger handkerchief when the tears showed no signs of abating.

"Perhaps we should wait for the corridors to empty," he suggested when Hellen and Browne started to rise. "There will be less of a crush on the stairs. The carriage will take ages to come around anyway."

Queenie was grateful to agree, knowing that poor Harry must be mortified at the spectacle she was making. He would not want any of his friends to see her looking like a drowned kitten, nor like an ignorant, silly chit from a tiny village who mistook fantasy from fact. And she did not want him to see her as an overwrought, emotional female, either, subject to megrims and vapors and public scenes. She could only lose his friendship that way . . . the way the sea sprite had lost everything she valued most.

Besides, what if her crying had smeared the blacking she used to darken her blond eyelashes? Then Harry would know she was fake, living a lie. So Queenie hid in the shadows of the box, hid her face in the freshly laundered scent of Harry's monogrammed linen cloth, and whimpered.

Hellen and Browne were in the shadows, too, whispering rather than whimpering. Harry stood and turned his back to give them all privacy, helplessly staring over the balcony railing. He pretended to be studying the departing crowds, planning their own best exit, when something in the pit caught his attention. Something scurvy, with its paw down the neckline of an orange seller.

"Bloody hell, it's my brother-in-law," he cried, gaining the attention of anyone still in the vicinity who had not noticed the apparently brokenhearted woman and the besotted mooncalves in his box.

Queenie stopped crying, and Hellen and Browne stopped cuddling. They all came to the front of the area to look out over the pit.

"Where? Which one?"

"The bastard with the bald spot on top of his head I never noticed before, about ten rows behind the orchestra. Deuce take it, he is getting ready to leave with the orange girl. Lud only knows where he'll take her."

And then the gentleman who had spent his adulthood avoiding scandal, who disliked making a spectacle and having his manners and morals dissected, who had been known for years as a sobersides, stood at the front of his box and shouted across the entire auditorium. "Sir John Martin, you maggot, I want my diamonds!"

Every eye of every remaining operagoer was focused on Harry. Hellen gasped. The dowager still sitting in the neighboring compartment started fanning herself and clucking her teeth in cadence. She did not get up to leave, however. No one seemed to move, except Sir John Martin. He looked up at the tiers, shielding his eyes to see better. He lurched back,

obviously recognizing retribution from on high. He looked
down at the doxy at his side, then at the exit. Was Harry high
enough? That was the question. Martin decided not. He
started to run.

"Damn it, he is going to get away!"

His *chérie* was sniffling behind him, his family heirlooms were speeding toward the doors, and Harry was never
going to make it down the stairs in time. Hell and damnation, then he'd go over the balcony!

Harry started to climb up on the railing. Hellen shrieked.
Browne and Queenie both grabbed for the tails of his coat.

"You'll be killed, man!" Browne yelled.

"Do not do it, my lord! It is too dangerous." Queenie was
sobbing again. "No jewels are worth your life!"

The dowager next door swooned. So did half the misses
in pastel gowns. The other half were screeching like they'd
seen a mouse, or a madman. Gentlemen started placing bets
on Harry's making it down to the pit in one piece. The orchestra struck up a waltz, "The Leaves Fall in Autumn," and
the opera manager jumped on the stage and started calling
for calm.

"Do not panic, dear sirs and madams. All will be well."

Which meant everyone panicked, naturally. Those in the
cheap seats started rushing toward the doors, rather than get
flattened by a bellowing bedlamite who thought he could
fly. Who knew what the knock-in-the-cradle nobs would do
next? If nothing else, the pit patrons clogged the aisles, so
Martin could not reach the street.

Harry noticed that while he stripped off his gloves. Then
he looked down, far down. Perhaps swinging from railing to
railing like an ape was not the best idea, especially not in
evening pumps and a closely fitted jacket. Letting Martin
get away was worse.

"I am coming, you crook!" he yelled. He pulled out of his friends' grip and dashed for the rear of his box, shoving Hellen aside and nearly mowing down the hired footman, who was waiting for orders to send for the gentleman's carriage.

"Follow him!" Queenie demanded. "He could get hurt!"

The footman and Browne both looked at her as if dementia were contagious. The footman was trained to be helpful, not heroic. Browne was brought up to guard women in his care.

"Go!" Queenie shouted, but did not wait. She grabbed Hellen's arm and started tugging her past the slack-jawed servant and Browne.

The hallway was nearly empty, since those who had not already departed had returned to their boxes to view the spectacle—or nurse their nerves. Queenie could see Harry tearing down the corridor toward the stairs, yelling for anyone to get out of his way.

She followed, Hellen at her back, Browne and the footman finally running behind them. Everyone seemed to be shouting questions, no one having answers.

The stairs were more crowded, and more confused, as everyone there wanted to know what was happening, and where. Should they go up, go down, stay? A few of the older opera patrons were furious at having their evening pleasure destroyed by being bowled down by a bacon-witted viscount on the way home. The younger generation were all geese and gudgeons anyway. One ancient baronet was flailing his cane in the air, to the consternation of those trapped nearby. Another relic was clutching his heart, but that was because his wife was striking him there with her fan, for making her miss the most excitement of the evening. Blighted love and blithering baritones aside, this was bound to be tomorrow's choicest morsel, and she was stuck in a stairwell? She shoved past the others to chase Queenie and Hellen and their followers.

Another level down and Queenie could tell where Harry had passed by the muttering and the head shaking and the ladies leaning against their escorts in distress or because they could without being scolded by their mamas.

When they were finally on the main level, Queenie was undecided which way to turn. The hall was crowded, the auditorium still half filled. Fistfights had broken out among those who had been shoved, and shoved back. The music lovers in the pit were not of the polite world, and were not inclined to accept slights, slurs, or slaps graciously. Betting circles were established around each makeshift mill, which further hindered any outward exit.

A group of orange sellers grew angry that their wares, both fruit and sexual favors, would go unsold. Too many of their customers were running before the Watch arrived, or running to make wagers. The girls started throwing the oranges.

Queenie could not spot Harry. She simply was not tall enough. So she stood on a vacant chair.

"There he is!" She pointed toward the right, clambered down, and started off again, begging pardon, asking permission to pass—or pushing like everyone else.

Harry was leaping over benches, and sometimes those seated in them, rather than attempting the clogged aisles.

Queenie could not see the fleeing brother-in-law, but doubted he could have escaped. Harry would have stopped his mad dash if the man was gone from the building, wouldn't he? She tried to keep him in sight, but he often fell between the benches on his hands, sometimes having to fend off belligerent sots who had emptied their flasks before the second act. Sometimes he seemed to slip on rotten oranges, skidding forward. Twice he landed a punch before some thug could swing at him while swinging at anything that moved. More often he simply moved faster. Once a group of young men, students, they seemed, picked Harry up and propelled him forward over their heads, laughing uproariously. Others applauded. More females fainted.

Queenie was too intent on keeping Harry in sight to swoon. Otherwise she might have, and happily, to avoid watching him get pummeled and pushed. Her breathing was ragged; her heart was racing; her mouth was too dry to call out to the clunch before he was killed or arrested. All she knew was that Harry was alone. She had to get to him, to help him, to stand by him. Then she would murder him with her bare hands.

So Queenie followed in his wake as best she could. She lost her shawl, her rosebuds, and a bit of skin. She had lost her dignity ages ago, and her temper. Why would a black-toothed blighter think he could pinch her bottom at a time like this? She swung her reticule and now the lecher had one less rotten tooth.

Hellen had been hauled in by Browne ten rows back, Queenie thought, but she could hear her friend screaming that her pearls were broken. A group of soldiers and their soiled doves hurried back to help retrieve the baubles, and pocket a few, which left Queenie a more open space ahead.

Now that she was closer, she could see that Martin was stuck in the crowd with no way out, for the press in front of the doors was impossible to penetrate. And Harry was getting closer.

Martin looked around, frantic. No one was coming to his aid. In fact, once the crowd realized that he was the intended target of the assault, they backed away, giving Harry room.

Lord Harking launched himself through the air and landed atop the lighter, smaller, but more desperate baronet. Martin kicked, and Harry rolled off, clutching his other family jewels, to the hilarity of the watchers who were eager to be entertained, now that they were not in danger.

Harry leaped to his feet. He swayed a bit, cursed a bit, but made his large, capable hands into fists and came on toward his lying, thieving brother-in-law, blood in his eyes.

Martin had his walking stick in his hand, though. He beat Harry on the head and shoulders, while ducking and bobbing. "I can explain. I only borrowed the diamonds."

Harry landed him a facer. "And my horses." Harry hit him again. Blood spurted from Martin's nose. "I want them back, and you gone from England, do you hear me?"

But Martin had heard his nose break, and feared for every other bone in his body. This was not the easygoing Harry that Martin knew and despised, the simple farmer content with his mangel-wurzels. This was raw fury, looking as if he'd be content with nothing less than Martin's liver and lights, on his breakfast platter. Besides, Martin had nowhere to go except to prison or the gibbet.

So he twisted the knob on his walking stick and unsheathed the sword hidden in the cane. He slashed out. Harry's left sleeve was torn, and some of his skin with it.

The crowd gasped. This was no longer fun, not even a fair fight. Hands reached for Martin, and got scraped and bloodied in return. His hair was dangling in his face, drenched in the sweat pouring off his forehead. He circled the area like a cornered rat, which he was. Harry came on, his right arm wrapped in his ruined coat he'd pulled off.

"My sister will be free of your filth at last," he rasped through clenched jaws. "A widow."

Holding his protected arm in front of his face, Harry

leaped straight for Martin. Someone screamed, perhaps Queenie. The sword went flying, but so did Martin. Harry had hit him so hard, the dastard flew backward on the orange-coated floor and skidded under the legs of the closest watchers. Harry fell, too.

Hands reached to raise Harry to his feet. He turned around, tried to clear his battered head with a shake, and saw his brother-in-law scrabble along the floor, under feet, under skirts, toward the door.

Harry would have followed, but then a woman landed in his arms.

"*Chérie?*" he asked, falling back to the ground with her in his lap.

She was weeping and patting at his bleeding arm, the cuts on his head, the bruises on his cheek. "Please, Harry, please do not go after him."

He could not if he wanted to, Harry decided, for his legs were like rubber and his left arm could not even rub the precious girl's trembling back. Besides, the circle of onlookers was too close, offering aid and encouragement and congratulations, and whistles were blowing, warning that the Watch or the sheriff or the men from Bow Street were on the way.

His supporters hastened toward the now open doorways. Only a few people remained close by, one holding a trumpet, as if he were ready to defend the opera with his horn. Browne and Hellen came hurrying forward, and the footman stood up from under the bench where he had taken shelter.

Harry looked down at Madame Lescartes in his lap. He could not see her eyes, because they were pressed to his chest now. But he stroked her cheek, not noticing the streak of blood left there from his scraped knuckles. He softly kissed her forehead.

"You see? Just what I promised you. A quiet evening.

Nothing to worry about. No scandal, no insult, only a good time."

"Oh, Harry," was all she said.

He kissed her again. "But at least you said my name."

They decided to take Harry back to the dress shop.

"What, find a surgeon at this time of night when I have the finest seamstress in London at my side? You can stitch this up, can you not, my dear?"

The sleeve perhaps, but Harry's flesh? Queenie wished she were one of those women who carried smelling salts instead of a sewing needle.

"Besides, any surgeon is likely to be drunk this time of night," Harry said as they helped him into the coach.

Queenie wished she were drunk, too.

"And I doubt I would be welcome at the hotel looking like this." He did not mention his companions' states of disorder and disarray. Luckily the coach's lantern light hid the worst of it from him. "Lud, I'll be thrown out of there next, bag and baggage on the street come morning."

"You were not precisely thrown out of the opera house," Browne noted in his careful way, trying to hold his broken spectacles together with his hands. "And the manager did not say you could never come back."

"Not once I offered to pay damages. He did, however, mention that he hoped I took my speed leaving and my leisure returning." Harry shook his head, then groaned at the pain. And at the results of this night's work. "Lud, the Cyprian's Ball, the opera . . . I could be banished from London altogether with a little effort."

"I would say tonight took a great deal of effort," Queenie said, and all four passengers in the carriage sighed.

*   *   *

The dog met them at the door, not the boy, Charlie.

"Check the money drawer," Hellen said. "I'll wager the filthy urchin stole your blunt and left, in return for all your efforts and kindness." She looked around as Queenie started lighting more lamps. "I am only surprised he did not let his fellow sneak thieves come inside to rob you of everything they could, from the dry goods to the dog to your scissors."

"Oh, hush. Charlie is not a criminal." But Queenie hurried toward the back room to check anyway. The boy was fast asleep under the cutting table, on the new mattress Queenie had purchased. He looked warm and innocent and content, wrapped in soft blankets, with an empty plate beside him. Queenie envied him. She would like nothing better than to crawl into her own snug bed, where, with any luck, she would not dream about Harry facing a villain's sword.

Hellen was still complaining when Queenie went back to the showroom, to escort her sudden guests upstairs to the living quarters, where the light was better and supplies were handier.

Queenie tried to soothe her friend, ignoring how Browne and the footman had to help Harry up the narrow steps, but Hellen was simply in an understandably petulant mood. Her lovely gown was spotted with blood, her mother's pearls were in her reticule, likely two inches shorter than before, and she had been deprived of the promised dinner at the Clarendon, London's fanciest hotel. Besides, she had not understood a word of the German opera. Why had the scaly sea sprite chosen the mortal man anyway? Everyone knew the gods had all the power, all the money. The silly goose deserved to die. Too bad she had taken so long about it, too, or they might have left their seats before Harry spotted his brother-in-law.

That was another thing Hellen did not understand, which she made plain to anyone who would listen. Gentlemen were supposed to act like . . . gentlemen, not ruffians and rowdy boys. She had spent her life thinking of aristocrats as better than the common folk. If they were not, why were they so wealthy, so powerful, so arrogant?

Now Hellen's sense of the rightness in the world was destroyed, along with her gown and her pearls. No one could explain the matter to her, for no one understood any better, least of all Harry.

He apologized again, but offered no reasons to Hellen for his irrational behavior, if any such existed.

Hellen seemed satisfied with an apology, pulling Browne toward the threadbare love seat to help restring the pearls. Queenie envied the younger girl, too, not for Browne or the beads, but because Hellen could fret about such trifles, while Queenie had to face hurting Harry worse.

While she fetched towels and basins and more candles— avoiding thoughts of the job ahead—Queenie promised Hellen that her gown could be repaired.

"If we cannot get the stains out, we can dye the whole thing. Or we can embroider butterflies where the spots are. As a last resource, we can paint flowers over the marks. One of the French designers hand paints all of his gowns, so no two are ever alike. His creations cost more than a new carriage."

"Truly?"

Queenie spent a moment thinking that perhaps that was how she could earn more money without having to produce scores more designs and dresses that no one now would likely buy. Then again, she would paint dragonflies on derrieres rather than stitch up Harry's arm.

Leaving the others in the tiny upstairs sitting room,

Queenie said she needed to gather her supplies. What she needed to gather was her wits, so her hands would stop shaking. Stalling, she quickly washed her face and restored the eyelash darkener. She forgot the beauty mark.

Harry thought she looked beautiful anyway. Of course, he had finished the gin the coachman carried in his flask.

Queenie envied him, too.

CHAPTER THIRTEEN

The job was done, thank heavens. It was not Queenie's neatest seam, but neither was Harry still bleeding.

Hellen and Browne were near the fire, toasting bread and cheese that the footman had brought back for supper. Harry'd sent the man out for spirits at the same time, both to wash the wound and to restore the color to his *chérie*'s pale cheeks. If the fellow had taken a bit longer than expected, and come back with a rosier complexion himself, well, Harry could not blame him.

Hellen had stopped complaining about her necklace, especially after Harry promised to pay to have a jeweler fix the strand the right way. He also offered to replace the missing pearls with matching ones if they could be found.

Now Harry held Queenie's hand in his lightly bandaged ones as they sat at the rickety dining table in the corner of the room. Speaking for her ears only, he promised to make good on her losses, too.

Queenie snatched her hand back. It had stopped trembling long ago and now felt warm and fluttery, as if her hand were a bird that wanted to land on Harry's shoulder, his cheek, his brown wavy hair. Or give him a good peck.

"I am not your responsibility," she said, brushing at crumbs on the worn table. "My business stands or sinks on its own merits, not a wealthy patron's."

"I shall not be so wealthy when this night's tally is completed, I'll wager. But I might have cost you business. Honor demands I reimburse you for the loss."

"You cannot know that the shop will suffer. Women were impressed by my designs long before the, ah, events at the opera."

"Of course they were. Your gowns can make an old besom look beautiful. But your customers might not choose to patronize a shop whose proprietress has been involved in an unfortunate instance."

An unfortunate instance? Tonight was more like a public spectacle, which was abhorrent to polite society. A woman behaving like a common strumpet or an unmannered hoyden could not be trusted with dressing a lady properly. Why, women of substance would not expose their innocent daughters to such a dangerous influence.

Queenie could not lay all the blame at Harry's door. "I contributed, running after you that way."

"True, you should have left me lying on the ground in the filth, my lifeblood pouring out of me."

"You were hardly bleeding by then. But a lady would have stayed in her box."

"Calling for her vinaigrette," he agreed. "Thank you."

"For not being a lady?"

"For being the perfect lady. I looked up and saw you, and knew I was not going to die. I could not. Not yet."

Now she did brush his hair back, and touched his cheek.

"I am merely checking to see if you are taking a fever, my lord, spouting such nonsense."

"I thought I was Harry. Or 'Oh, Harry.' "

"I thought you were nearly dead then." Her lip started to tremble again.

"Oh, no. Please do not cry, *chérie*. That hurts worse than anything Martin could have done. I was never in danger of expiring, you know. It was the surprise of his fighting back that set me on my heels."

"How could I know he would not kill you? He had a sword and you did not." The very thought of that horrid scene made Queenie sniffle.

Harry quickly buttered another slice of bread and pushed it toward her. "Here, you will feel better with food in you," he said, speaking as a large man who was always hungry and always felt more at peace with the world with his belly filled. "And that is more on my dish—or not, I suppose— that you had no supper. I had reserved a private room at the Clarendon, too, with champagne."

Queenie sipped at her tea, from a cup that matched no other on the table. Molly's good tea service was downstairs, for the customers. "This is better."

It was.

The sitting room was small and shabby and crowded, but it was warm and filled with friends. No strangers were serving lavish courses—and superior airs along with the meal. Here shopgirls and schoolteachers and lords could mingle with no one to say them nay. Even a street urchin in his nightshirt was welcome to join the simple meal.

Charlie had woken up with the dog's barking at the footman's return. He was happy for the food, but sorry he'd missed the excitement. So Harry had to unbandage his arm and show the neat stitches.

So Charlie had to show the scars on his legs from when he ran away from the chimney sweep.

So Queenie felt ill to her stomach again and pushed the plate of bread and butter away.

Noticing, Harry sent the boy back to feeding scraps to the dog. "Not in front of a lady, my boy."

"Right, gov. Sorry, ma'am." Charlie curled next to Parfait on the hearth, futilely trying to stay awake to listen once the bread was gone, his head on the dog's soft back. Hellen and Browne were back on the worn sofa, talking quietly. Their clasped hands were hidden by her skirts, or so they believed. Queenie believed they would make a match of it, and was willing to relax her chaperonage. After tonight, she hardly counted as a proper duenna anyway.

Speaking of the night, Queenie looked directly at the man opposite her. His coat was ruined; his cravat had been used as a bandage. His hair was every which way, and his cheek sported a bruise that was already turning purple. His knuckles were wrapped and his chin was scraped. Queenie went back to studying her chipped cup, rather than smile, or throw herself into his arms.

"Now, my lord, perhaps you would be so good as to explain."

Harry held his own cup toward the sleeping boy across the room. "What, that no one wishes to be reminded of how children are treated in our world?"

"No, not that. I wish to know why a gentleman, one who has been nothing but kind and even-tempered, turns into a demon from hell at the sight of one fairly nondescript, balding baronet. Surely a necklace is not worth facing a scoundrel who would stab an unarmed man."

Harry looked away. "It is not merely a necklace. There is

a bracelet and earbobs, too. The ring was added later, but it matches."

The stare she gave him could have withered one of the rosebuds he'd sent, if they were not long gone. Hellen might think jewelry was worth any price. Queenie did not. She waited, not speaking.

Harry took a deep breath. He did owe her an explanation, especially since the gossip columns were bound to have the whole sordid story in the morning. And the afternoon and evening, until another juicy tidbit occurred.

"The set belongs to the Harking viscountcy, not to me or my sister. Surely not to Martin. But you are right—this was not about the jewels. It had more to do with what else the dastard stole from my sister."

"He was not a good husband, I take it."

"He was barely a husband, leaving her at Harking Hall to return to his London life as soon as the settlements were signed."

"I have heard that is not uncommon among your class, contracting a marriage of convenience, then leading separate lives."

"Ah, but this was no arranged match. The dirty dish turned Olivia's head with protestations of love, simply to get his hands on her dowry. Having a gullible in-law who disliked confrontation and contretemps made the bargain all the more rewarding for Martin. So I paid. So did Olivia, with her pride."

"But you mentioned a niece and nephew?"

"My sister's only joy in life. Martin did not deny himself his connubial rights when he bothered to visit Olivia in the country. He denied himself nothing, it seemed. He had women before the wedding and after. He had a wench during the wedding breakfast, for all I know. There is a child in the village I support, perhaps another one near Martin's own ramshackle estate. He gave me no proof, so I refuse to pay. His parentage is not the poor by-blow's fault, I realize, but I cannot fund every baseborn child in England."

"Of course not. But could you not do anything?"

"Olivia chose him herself. It was for her to make her marriage work, or not. At first she would hear no ill of him, saying all men had their faults. I believed I could not come between a man and his wife."

"Of course not. She would not have appreciated the truth, or having to admit she had made a poor selection for a husband. I suppose she still loved him?"

"Love?" He set his cup down with a thump that might add another chip. "How long can love last with such neglect?"

He would be surprised at how long, Queenie thought, but she kept still.

"Then Martin realized he had gone through all of Olivia's money and what little he had of his own. He beggared his estate, so there will be nothing but debts for my nephew to inherit. He no longer had to pretend an interest or an affection for my sister."

"That poor woman."

"And poor me. Martin came to me with his gambling debts, and I paid them, the more fool I was. I could not let my sister's husband wallow in debtors' prison, nor disgrace us further. At least that way I had some control over the cad's activities. In exchange for an allowance—I was not stupid enough to hand him a purse, ever—I made him stay in the country, at Harking Hall. I thought he would come to appreciate a quiet life, the pleasures of his children. I thought he could not lose as much of my blunt at the card tables, or keep as expensive a mistress."

"You were wrong?"

"I was worse than wrong. Martin turned meaner. He hated the country, and was bored without funds to support his wagering and wenching. So he harassed the servants, especially the females, until none of the local girls would work there."

"What about your sister? She was running the household, was she not? She could have said something to him."

Harry studied the dregs in his cup. "She was afraid."

"To tell you?"

"Afraid of him."

"I . . . see."

"The problem was that I did not see. Olivia tripped. A pot overturned. A painting fell off the wall while she was adjusting its angle. I did not see!"

"She did not want you to see."

"The children hid from him."

Queenie gasped. "His own children?"

"I could not pretend ignorance anymore. Yet I could not throw him out. He would have been within his rights to send Olivia and the children to his own property in Devon, where they would have starved, or worse."

"Worse?"

"If something happened to Olivia, he would have been free to marry again, a wealthier woman this time, perhaps a widow with no one to look out for her."

"Oh, no! He could not be that evil!"

"As you said, gentlemen do not pull swords on unarmed men. At any rate, I told him I wished to speak to him after the party we were holding. I intended to thrash the daylights out of him, and threaten to keep doing so unless he mended his ways. Instead he left with the family heirlooms."

"So you followed him."

"They are mine, dash it. And I could not stand Olivia's remorse and weeping. Besides, I wanted to make sure he was gone for good. I still wished to avoid a scandal, but I would have seen him transported for thievery before I saw him back under my roof. Unfortunately, I could not find the muckworm."

"Until tonight."

Harry nodded. "Until tonight. And then, deuce take it, there he was. It was the opera, you see, and your tears."

"Mine? I had nothing to do with your brother-in-law!"

"But you were crying, and I could do nothing about it. That poor fool in the opera died to no purpose, and I could do nothing about it."

"That was a piece of fiction!"

"Then why was your heart breaking for him?"

"Because he was so helpless, and the world is such a hard place," she said, rather than explain that she had cried over shattered love and hopeless dreams.

"The gods are too strong. Man is too insignificant. Love is a pipe dream. I know all that. But I know that I did not help my sister. And I knew you were crying and I could not help you, either. I had no right to comfort you or hold you, especially not in front of all those stiff-rumped swells. Then I saw Martin—and suddenly I could do something. I could fight back against injustice and evil and a world that lets a woman be hurt." He raised his voice. "I could do something!"

"You could break your foolish neck," Queenie yelled.

"But I did not."

Charlie was sound asleep, but Hellen and Browne had wandered over, disturbed by the loud talk. They had heard enough to make Harry's actions understandable, if not reasonable. They both knew about tilting at windmills, slaying dragons, or otherwise trying to beat the odds.

Browne asked, "What shall you do next, my lord? Your vermin is bound to go to earth."

Harry agreed that finding Martin would be harder now that he knew Harry was in Town looking for him. "Although I cannot imagine him thinking I would let such an affront pass, no, not even to protect my sister from the scandal. He must have guessed I would set the magistrate's office on him, if nothing else. I thought he would have sold the jewels and taken ship before I arrived in Town."

"I wonder why he did not, since being found with the stolen goods would be tantamount to a confession."

"Oh, I suppose he thought he could wriggle out of the charge on some lie or other, having the diamonds cleaned or some such. Of course once he saw me in Town, he knew that effort would be futile; I could disprove any claim he made. No, I doubt he was afraid of having the pilfered property in his possession. The delay was in trouble turning the diamonds into cash." Harry went on to explain what he had learned at the jewelers, that no reputable merchant would handle the transaction. "And a lesser gemsmith would not pay nearly the diamonds' worth. In fact, the shabbier and shadier the operation, the less blunt Martin can expect."

Queenie and Hellen exchanged glances. They both know the shabbiest, shadiest fence of all. Queenie tried to send her friend a signal, but succeeded only in drawing Harry's attention.

"Are you feeling ill again?"

"Not at all. You were correct. The bread and butter was perfect." It might have been if she'd eaten any.

Finding Harry's diamonds was a great deal more entertaining than discussing Queenie's megrims, and Hellen wanted to help. "We might know a person—" she began, only to be interrupted by Queenie.

"You and your mother?"

Hellen was not entirely featherheaded, only somewhat fluffed. "Yes, of course. We, my mother and I, might know someone who has such dealings."

"A jeweler? I visited scores of them."

"Not precisely. I would not take my necklace to him if the clasp were broken, say. But he would be perfect for finding the missing pearls."

"That were not precisely lost?"

"Exactly. Ize is known to pay a pittance, but he does not ask questions. He is a great help to people who find themselves temporarily embarrassed by a lack of funds."

"Ah, a philanthropist," Harry offered, with a dash of sarcasm.

Hellen looked at Queenie. "I thought they called Ize a fence?"

"They call him many things, most less complimentary. Ize, that is, Ezra Iscoll, would take your money and your diamonds, as well as your watch, your back teeth, and your unborn son. Or so I understand from his reputation, of course. You do not want to have anything to do with him."

"Oh, I do not think he is so bad," Hellen said. "He was pleasant enough at the Cyprian's Ball."

Harry raised an eyebrow.

"He was that small man with the protuberant eyes," Queenie offered.

"By reputation?"

Queenie ignored his dry tone. "You will do better looking elsewhere."

Browne wanted to know why Lord Harking had not gone to Bow Street. "That man who is on Lord Carde's payroll,

Geoffrey Rourke, seems a decent sort. Competent, too, or Captain Endicott would not have kept him on. Of course, if he were all that competent, he would have solved the mystery of their sister."

Queenie wanted Harry going to Bow Street as much as she wanted him talking to Ize. She wanted him talking about Lady Charlotte Endicott least of all. "You would do better asking young Charlie to speak with his friends. Street children know everything that goes on in the city, and work for far less reward money."

Browne disagreed. "His lordship wants a professional thieftaker, not false leads and rumors of sightings."

Queenie realized she did not want Harry going after his brother-in-law on his own, either, so she swallowed her words.

Harry rubbed at his sore chin. "I can do both, speak with Charlie and visit Bow Street. The reason I have not gone to Bow Street already was that I dreaded making my family business public." He laughed. "I suppose I do not have to worry about that anymore, do I?"

CHAPTER FOURTEEN

Harry did not become the laughingstock he feared.

The sporting gentlemen, at least, appreciated a good fight. The bored husbands and fathers liked anything that could enliven an evening at the opera. The scandal sheets celebrated anything that sold newspapers. They termed Harry "Viscount Vengeance," and pictured him as a warrior angel, complete with wings. Or an eagle, launching itself over the private boxes of the opera.

Harry preferred the angel, he supposed. He liked best the cartoon of a black-haired Blind Justice, with a beauty mark.

When he went to his club, after staying in his rooms at the hotel for most of the next day while his bruises turned from purple to yellow, he found himself welcomed with a camaraderie he had never known.

He was a hero now, one of their own, not the vicarish chap who made the other members feel inferior with his righteousness. Damn, if Harking was not up to every rig and row, hunting for his diamonds, a diamond on his arm.

Harry stopped denying that Madame Lescartes was his

mistress. No one would have believed him anyway, the way she leaped to his defense, or the way he leaped to hers when someone spoke her name with disrespect. He ensured that the gentlemen spoke politely about her simply by inviting anyone who considered doing otherwise to a bout of fisticuffs. No, not at Gentleman Jackson's—that was too civilized for the new Harry —but in the nearest alley. After seeing him in action at the opera, the bloodlust and the brute strength, no one took him up on the offer. Madame Lescartes? Lovely female, talented, too. Maybe they would send their womenfolk around to her shop.

Sympathy was on Harry's side anyway. Martin was known in Town, and not liked. Too many people had lost to him at cards under doubtful circumstances. Too many others had waited too long to be paid for Martin's losses. Play and pay, that was what the men admired, not cheat and chisel.

"I always knew he was a dirty dish," Lord Cholmondely pronounced.

"Bad breeding," another gentleman declared.

"Poor sport."

Unfaithful on his wife? Feh. Letting tradesmen and tenants go begging? Bah. But holding a sword to an unarmed man? For shame! Harking was doing the world a favor by ridding it of that trash.

Harry could not like being the center of gossip, nor the skewed values that made him a hero. He did not like his own behavior, either, though, so he could not censure anyone else's.

Still, now everyone he knew was on the lookout for Sir John Martin.

Unfortunately, Harry had been the last to see the scum scuttling through the crowd, Martin's nose leaving an untrackable trail of blood. Lord Harking would have to go to Bow Street.

Queenie was not shunned, either.

The morning after the opera she expected canceled orders, missed fitting appointments, and an empty store. Instead she was busier than ever. The courtesans wanted their gowns, and a glimpse of Harry. Camden's sister wanted to look like a queen. Other ladies simply wanted a good look at Lord Harking.

Harry did stop by to speak to Charlie, bringing two bouquets of violets, one for the mannequin, one for the shop's owner. Violets became another emblem of the shop, along with a black gown in the window, the black dog inside, and high prices. Queenie was too busy to talk to the viscount, and she found his presence sent the customers into a dither, to say nothing of what it did to her pulse rate and concentration. She sent him off with her errand boy, leaving the shop less efficient and far less exciting for everyone until bachelors like Lord Camden arrived with their sisters. Then she had even more unwed females passing by her shop window.

When her designs finally appeared in the new fashion journal, her success was assured. The magazine sold so many copies, the delighted publishers requested ten more drawings for the next issue, at double the price.

The store itself was inundated with customers. Women of high birth or low wanted to look as beautiful as Madame Denise herself, and as daring. Besides, the most observant women did not believe she was Harry's mistress after all, not the way she blushed and turned the subject back to flounces and furbelows. Why, they asked each other, would her prices be so high, and her workload so heavy, if she had a wealthy protector? As long as she was discreet and acted like a proper female, they would bask in her notoriety and bespeak her creations.

Other dressmakers benefited from Queenie's imaginative designs, for she could never complete that many gowns. Unemployed seamstresses benefited, too, for Queenie had to increase her staff to meet her obligations. She employed other women to do piecework in their own homes, for lack of space in the back workroom. Fortunately the women she had first hired turned out to be as skilled and experienced as they had promised, so soon Queenie designated a master cutter, a head fitter, a patternmaker.

Hellen ran the front of the shop. She had moved in with Queenie temporarily, so her mother could travel north in hopes of a visit with her gout-ridden baron. Hellen could not manage the accounts, and she frequently mistook appointments, orders, and delivery addresses, but she did pour wine and tea gracefully while Queenie herself dealt with the individual customers in their turns. Dressed like a sweet young miss, on her best behavior, Hellen reassured the matrons that Queenie could be trusted with dressing their young chicks, as well as the old hens and highfliers.

Charlie was not so sure about Hellen's place at the shop. He feared Miss Pettigrew would bring disgrace on his mistress—and cost him the best opportunity he was likely to find in his life. He had landed in clover, and now he would walk through nettles to please Madame Denise and Lord Harking.

With the best will in the world, though, and a wide acquaintance in the underworld, he could not find Sir John Martin. His friends spotted a score of bruisers with broken noses, a handful of battered bald men, and a swell selling emeralds, but none turned out to be the viscount's brother-in-law. As for the diamonds, it was assumed they were being cut up on the quiet.

Charlie could also not find half the addresses Hellen wrote out for him, for fetching supplies and making deliveries.

"Mebbe if you wasn't so busy making sheep's eyes at Mr. Browne, I wouldn't of taken so long getting back with t'biscuits." Charlie was worried that some of the gentry morts would catch Hellen and Mr. Browne doing what no lady did, at least not in the daytime, and with no ring on her finger. Then they would cancel their orders, Madame Denise would close her store, and Charlie would be back to living in the alley.

"You're a fine one to speak, off half the night doing who knows what, coming back with your clothes all filthy again."

"That was the governor's business."

"You work for Qu—my cousin."

Charlie pretended not to hear the slip. "You ain't no more Madame Denise's kin than I am. She wouldn't go lifting her skirts in no back garden."

"I did not!" Well, perhaps an inch or two. Or three. "And that is none of your business, either! You are nothing but a Paul Pry and a sneak thief. I saw you pocket that coin Lady Haversham dropped."

"She left it behind!"

"An honest boy would have returned it. So I shall tell Madame Denise."

Charlie could have countered with a threat to report Hellen's own backdoor misbehavior, but he was no squealer. Besides, he thought the mistress was too downy a bird not to know what was going on. She knew every bolt of fabric on the shelves and every matching ribbon in the drawers. She could draw like an angel. Sure and be damned she could draw her own conclusions as to why her assistant needed an escort to walk the dog, in the tiny fenced yard.

Instead of matching threat for threat, though, Charlie tossed a pearl in the air. "Then I s'pose you won't be wanting this back. Or t'others I come acrost on the governor's business."

Hellen was so happy she did not have to show her mother a shortened necklace when she returned to London that she kissed the boy.

"'Ere now, none a' that! In fact, you keep away from kissin' anything what wears trousers and I'll give you the rest. We don't want no scandal here. A respectable shop, that's what this is."

The dressmaking business was so respectable, and so successful, in fact, that Browne took over the bookkeeping. With the Ambeaux Silver School for Females at The Red and the Black not open, he had time on his hands, he told Queenie. With Hellen at the store, he had no better place to spend it.

Of course Queenie went over the accounts herself when she found time, and did all of the banking instead of trusting a near stranger—to her, at least, if not Hellen—with her income. That income was increasing despite the higher payroll and outlay for materials, and gaining momentum by the day. Soon she would be able to start repaying her debt. Her education, her sustenance, the nest egg Molly had left her that permitted her to start this very business—everything was owed to Lord Carde and his brother, Jack Endicott . . . or the man who had been paying her way at Molly's all those years.

No, she knew Phelan Sloane did not deserve her gold, for he had started the whole kidnapping and extortion scenario.

An honest man could not be blackmailed. And it seemed he had stolen the money from Lord Carde's estate anyway. Her debt was to the house of Carde, no one else.

With the Endicott family in the country, though, for who knew how long, Queenie would have to give her coins, and her information, to Bow Street. She should have already, she knew.

Now, however, there was Harry, who was stealing into her dreams and stealing her good intentions to come forth with her information. His good opinion of her suddenly mattered more than those strangers'. She had never felt so bright, so warm, so alive, as under the glow of admiration that shone in his soft brown eyes. If that light dimmed, so would her world.

On the other hand, Queenie realized she had found an ally. She even thought about telling Harry her story, or parts of it, anyway, and asking what he thought she should do.

Harry would not let her be sent to prison if worse came to worst, would he? They were friends, and he had some influence. Certainly more than hers. He would make the authorities see that she'd been a child kept ignorant of the crimes—and then too afraid to admit her part in them. But if Harry knew her circumstances, her upbringing, her uncertain heritage, perhaps he would not want to be her friend. Nor would such an honorable man take kindly to being lied to about her name, her background, her very hair color.

No, Queenie would not take the chance of confiding in Lord Harking. He did not have to know anything more than he did, she decided, unless the situation turned ugly. Then she would beg for his help finding barristers and bondsmen, and pray he forgave her.

In the meantime her information, or the tale she was prepared to tell, was for the Bow Street man and his employers only. She'd go soon, and perhaps sleep better after that, even though the guilt that had kept her awake for months was being replaced by midnight thoughts of Lord Harking. Who knew a sheltered virgin could have such warm notions? Warm? She'd had to toss the bedcovers to the floor, when she was not tangled in them.

Not all of those dreams were as deliciously intoxicating as others, though.

The night of the opera, she'd had a nightmare from ages ago, of falling and screaming for her mama. Of course she'd dreamed of falling, after seeing Harry nearly jump off the balcony, Queenie told herself. There was nothing odd in that or in an orphan crying for her mother.

She was worried about losing Harry, that was all. Losing his friendship, she told herself, which had become so important to her. Of course a friend did not think about a friend's bare skin when she stitched his arm, or how he must not wear his shirt outdoors to be so tanned, or . . .

Well, those made for better dreams, anyway. Tonight, Queenie vowed, she would think about new dress designs, rather than wonder if Lord Harking still had designs on her virtue.

First, she had to attend Lady Jennifer's afternoon salon.

When the lady had actually arrived for her fitting and to approve the fabric Queenie had selected, Queenie was a bit surprised. "I thought I would be ignored or ostracized," she told the duke's formidable daughter.

"What, because of the opera? Bosh, you simply became more interesting. Are you certain that figured gold fabric will not make me look like an upholstered armchair?"

Queenie was certain, and once the material had been gathered and draped and pinned in a semblance of the style Queenie had sketched, Lady Jennifer was convinced, too.

She was more convinced than ever that Queenie would make a fine addition to her Thursday gathering.

Queenie was too busy, too tired, too much in demand at the shop.

"Too fearful?" Lady Jennifer challenged.

Queenie went.

She dressed in a long-sleeved black gown, trimmed with pale rose-colored ribbons. For Lady Jennifer's sake, the neckline touched her collarbone. For fashion's sake, the sleeves were made of blush-colored lace, leaving her looking half bare.

Lady Jennifer's very proper butler nearly dropped Queenie's cape when he took it to reveal more than he was expecting from such a soft-spoken female who seemed almost reticent to join the company. "This way, madame."

The ducal town house appeared larger than Carde House in Grosvenor Square, from the outside. Inside, it could have rivaled Carlton House for opulence, for all Queenie knew. The artwork on the walls alone far surpassed that in any museum or gallery she had visited. She would rather have studied the masterpieces than follow the butler toward the drawing room, but that would have been a dreadful breach of manners—as opposed to giving a false name, lying about her time in Paris, and pretending to be a widow.

Lady Jennifer laughed when she saw Queenie's interpretation of a modest gown, but took her arm and led her about, making introductions. A dozen people were in attendance that afternoon, most of them female, all of them seemingly pleased to meet Queenie and compliment her on her gown and her burgeoning success. A copy of *A Lady's World* was on a piecrust table, open to one of her drawings.

The former nun wanted a gown just like Queenie wore;

the divorcée laughed and said she could never afford one, but would send her cousin.

Queenie met a lady poet and an inventor and a retired general who was penning his memoirs, when he could remember where he left his notes. To her surprise, she was introduced to the musician playing the cello in a corner of the enormous room. She had thought he was hired to entertain in the background, not a guest.

More surprisingly, she was introduced to the proper, powder-haired butler, Ames, too. He was tall and erect, of middle years, and had a friendly smile, especially for Lady Jennifer.

Queenie decided that Lady Jennifer was truly an independent female of progressive ideas. She also wondered what the lady's family thought. Lady Jennifer's ducal father was in the country nursing his rheumatics. Her brother, Camden, did not make an appearance.

"My gatherings are too tame for him," the lady admitted. "Not much opportunity for flirting, since you are one of the youngest females to be invited. I did not tell him you were attending today, on purpose. No cards or deep drinking, either."

But there was a loud argument in French near the fireplace. Three guests were debating the merits of a large, smoky seascape that stood on a nearby easel. Queenie peered at the signature, then realized she had just been introduced to the artist himself, one of the loudest defenders of the new style of painting.

"What do you think, madame?" he asked in his native tongue. "You obviously have an eye for style and color."

"I?" Queenie wanted to shout that she was nothing but a wardrobe mistress's foster child. What did she know of fine art and polite conversation? She did not even know if she was supposed to curtsy to the butler. Luckily the cellist had his bow in his hand, so she did not have to wonder about offering hers. Lady Jennifer was looking at her. So were three prospective clients of various ages who were expensively if unfashionably dressed. Queenie took a deep breath.

"I think it is wonderful," she said in French. "It reminds me of when I left France to return to England to start my business. You see the gleams of light through the fog? That was how the passage appeared, and that was how I felt. With hope, yet uncertainty. The grays, the swirls of clouds, such were my emotions leaving the familiar for the unknown. I was going to England, but as a new person, carried on the roiled waves of fate. Surely a painting that speaks so eloquently with so few words is the work of a genius."

One of the women clapped her hands. Another shouted, "Brava!" And the artist instantly gave Queenie the painting.

"Oh, no, I could never accept such a valuable gift."

"It is nothing, madame. I have, to my regrets, many others equally unsold. But if you hang it in your place of business, it is good for both of us, *non*? You get to enjoy the painting, and I get seen by your wealthy customers."

Queenie was not sure of the protocol involved. But the butler was nodding encouragement, and if such a starched-up individual thought she should accept such a generous gift, it must be *convenable*. Of course a proper servant would have stayed in the background, invisible. "I would be proud to display your artwork in my humble store."

"And accept a commission if any sold?" Lady Jennifer pressed, afraid her new friend would be taken advantage of by the talented and canny, if impecunious, artist.

"But of course, my lady," Queenie answered. "I am not that humble."

The others laughed. Queenie felt her shoulder muscles

finally relax, aided by the excellent wine being passed around by liveried footmen under the butler's watchful eye. He winked at her as he went to stand by Lady Jennifer's side, far closer than any servant she had ever seen. And Lady Jennifer let her hand brush his.

No one else seemed to notice, or perhaps they were used to such intimacies between a lady and her upper servant. Progressive indeed! And perhaps, Queenie thought, that was why the wealthy woman had never married, to her brother's consternation. Lady Jennifer must not be quite as daring and freethinking as she would pretend, if she was afraid to follow her heart out of her own class. Queenie wondered, while the others continued their discussion of the painting—her painting!—what she would do, were she of such elevated birth. Her own friends were clerks and courtesans, street urchins, seamstresses, and one viscount. Would she have the courage to keep her companions of lower birth? Or would she want to associate only with those of her own social level, who could further her ambitions? And what did Harry think?

Queenie laughed at herself, catching Lady Jennifer's observant eye. Luckily that woman could not know what Queenie was thinking, that Harry was no egalitarian. With one notable exception, he avoided doing anything to disturb his social set. He would never wed a servant, either. Or a seamstress.

Conversation had left the painting and moved on to the government's support of the arts, then the education of artists, and finally the education of women.

After Hannah Moore had been quoted several times, Queenie told the others about the Ambeaux Silver School that Captain Jack Endicott was starting, with Lord Carde's help. She mentioned that she would be assisting there if the brothers approved. If she was not teaching outright, then she could provide experienced instructors in the sewing arts, and later help by training their graduates for rewarding employment.

"A worthwhile cause indeed," one of Lady Jennifer's friends said, "especially coming from that daredevil Jack Endicott. Nothing like a reformed rake, don't you know. I am hoping to meet the woman who could make such a difference, dragging him from a gambler to an educator of women." She promised her patronage.

Another woman offered scholarships for worthy girls from unfortunate circumstances. Soon the others were nodding and adding their support. Not that the Earl of Carde could not fund a hundred such ventures, but why should he carry the entire burden? They all agreed the school offered promise as an example of what concerned citizens of every class could do to improve young lives, and thus the world.

Queenie felt she had done more to settle her debt this afternoon than she could do in a lifetime. She could not give the Endicott family peace of mind concerning their lost half sister, but she could do this for them. If they truly believed in helping girls to better themselves, she had done more than her few pounds and shillings could.

Now perhaps she could put off going to Bow Street.

Bow Street came to her.

CHAPTER FIFTEEN

Harry accompanied Browne when the man went to make his monthly report at Bow Street.

"I have to speak to Geoffrey Rourke there anyway, so I can introduce you. You said you are getting nowhere in your search for your brother-in-law."

"Ah, but Charlie March's friends are eating better."

Browne gathered up his notes. "That is something, I suppose, but is no closer to finding your diamonds any time soon."

The viscount was no longer in such a rush. Finding Martin or the diamonds, destroyed or not, meant the demise of his London visit. Likewise, if Harry handed the case to Bow Street, he had no good excuse not to return to the country, and no practical reason whatsoever to remain in Town.

Except that leaving might be like ripping his innards out.

At home he had spring planting to plan, all the new lambs and calves and foals to count, swamps to drain, cottage roofs to repair. He had an honest, competent land steward, of course, but in the country Harry would be busy from dawn to dusk or later. Once he called at Bow Street, Harry had nothing whatsoever that he had to do in the city.

At Harking Hall, scores of tenants, servants, and village businesses depended upon him. No one needed him here in London. Not even the scandal sheets needed him to sell newspapers, now that Earl Rucklesby's twin daughters had run off with twin footmen.

No, Harry's presence was not necessary, needed, or desired, it seemed. The dressmaking business was a success, and its proprietress had no time for foolish gentlemen who caused public spectacles. She would rather attend a fusty tea than go for a drive in the park with him.

Of course the tea would gain Madame Lescartes new clients, and a drive with him would only damage her reputation further. But it might bring color to her pale cheeks.

With no one to drive with, the park was merely a cold, stark, and futile effort to bring the country into Town. Harry did not even have a riding horse of his own here to exercise.

The gentlemen at his club had had enough chuckles at his expense, and the street children had earned—or not—as many of his coins as he could distribute without causing fist-fights. He had left his card—and more largesse—at every bordello he could find. Truly, he had no choice—and no reason to delay—calling at Bow Street. And then leaving Town.

He was right, Harry decided, already feeling a sour taste in his mouth. Leaving Madame Lescartes would tear him to pieces.

And he was right. He had no choice.

Geoffrey Rourke was a well-set-up man only a few years older than Harry. He had deeper lines in his face, and a few gray threads through his reddish hair. He had papers and pencils and wanted posters above his scarred wood desk, not impressing Harry with his organizational skills until he immediately found a clean sheet and started taking notes.

Harry sat in the single battered chair facing the desk while Browne stood behind his shoulder.

"With your permission, my lord?"

"Damn, you tried to cover my back at the opera, didn't you?" Harry replied. "And you know the whole sorry mess anyway. You might as well stay."

Harry took out a sketch of the diamonds and a written description of his brother-in-law, to which he had added "a broken nose and various bruises," but that was all he had to offer.

Except a reward, of course. The Bow Street men were salaried, if one considered their pay to be more than a pittance. Their living came from pursuing cases that paid a bounty for the return of stolen property or the capture of criminals. The Crown and the magistrate's office provided some of the blunt; wronged parties posted rewards for others.

Rourke must be a successful thieftaker, after all, Harry considered, noting the man's well-tailored clothing, his neatly barbered hair and manicured fingernails. Dressing like a gentleman did not come cheaply.

The man spoke in educated accents, too, when he asked what avenues Harry had already pursued.

"I have been to every halfway respectable brothel I was told he might patronize, and as many of the others as I could find. I visited polite gambling clubs and low gaming hells. I also went to scores of jewelers and pawnshops. No one has seen Sir John Martin in recent days."

"Or they are not talking to you, despite the color of your money. They might not know, or your brother-in-law might have found a crib with someone no one wants to cross. Either way, my lord, while your friends and fellow club members will speak freely, the common cardsharp or Covent Garden familiar is more likely to speak to someone he or she knows. They all know me."

"But why would they talk to someone in authority?"

"Because I have the authority to make their lives miserable otherwise. Bow Street turns a blind eye to a great deal that is illegal until law-abiding citizens are threatened. That does not mean we cannot conduct searches and make arrests when the need arises, or as we see fit in order to gather information."

Rourke's reasoning made sense to Harry, if not perfect justice. Besides, he had reached an impasse in his own search.

"So you will visit the same barrooms and bawdy houses?"

"I am sure I know of others you missed."

Rourke might have smiled; his lips twitched. Harry wondered how much those repeat visits would cost him, again, and if Rourke would enjoy them more than Harry had. The smile seemed to say he would. He reached for his purse, seeing no other way.

"It might be too late to find your jewels, however," Rourke told him as Browne shuffled his feet.

"So I understand. A friend mentioned a dealer in somewhat shadowy transactions that I might try to locate."

Rourke nodded. "No one dealing by light of day would touch the gems. What was the name this friend gave you?"

"Ize, or some variation of that."

Rourke immediately said, "You do not want to know him."

Harry resented everyone's thinking that he could not

handle one small, petty criminal. He was no effeminate lordling, by Jupiter, who could not defend himself from a toad-faced felon. Nor was he some gullible flat who would let a man take his money with getting the diamonds in return.

Of course he was already close to handing his purse to Geoffrey Rourke for expenses, with nothing in return. He frowned, not certain if the man's red waistcoat truly made a difference in his honesty. "I did not want to know a great many people I have recently met. That has not stopped me from doing what needed done."

Rourke ignored the implied insult, that he might be one of those less-than-desirable new acquaintances. Bow Street was not held in high regard by many. He was used to the slurs. "Ize might well know about your jewels, but you will not have an easy time finding him anyway, not unless he wishes to be found. He was running a lavish operation until a few years ago, with a fancy shop and all. Some of his merchandise was even legitimately come by, from your friend, perhaps, pawning the family silver or his watch. Then Ize went underground. I have not heard what cellar or alley he calls his office recently, and I have made inquiries."

Harry felt some satisfaction in saying that Ize had been at the Cyprian's Ball. He was not certain why he resented Rourke, except that the man was going to take his money, and take away his reason for staying in Town.

Rourke was more interested in Ize than he had been in Harry's brother-in-law. "A short, ill-kempt man of middle years, with eyes like a pug dog's?"

"Yes, but far less charming looking. His face was a mottled gray and his nose sprouted hair."

"That's him. Who pointed him out to you?"

"No one precisely pointed him out. It was Miss Hellen

Pettigrew who later mentioned he might know something about stolen diamonds."

Browne's shuffling footsteps behind Harry had turned into a near gallop in place. The man might be uncomfortable mentioning his sweetheart's name at Bow Street, but Harry could not lie. His cheeks always turned red when he tried to, anyway. "I believe her mother might have had dealings with him. Legitimate dealings," he hastened to add.

Rourke made a notation on a fresh sheet of paper. "That would be Valerie Pettigrew? And you say her daughter was at the Cyprian's Ball?"

"Miss Pettigrew is not following in her mother's footsteps," Browne nearly shouted, although Rourke had not questioned her reason for being at the notorious mistress mart. He had not needed to, in words.

"Mr. Browne is correct," Harry said in a lower tone, but one more befitting a peer whose word was his bond, and whose fists were the size of plow horse hooves, only harder. "Miss Pettigrew is gainfully and respectably employed as an assistant to the owner of a prosperous dressmaking establishment. She is a particular friend of mine." Which meant he would not hear of the little twit being labeled a light-skirts.

Rourke looked between his two visitors, obviously wondering what a doxy did to deserve such defense from two such disparate men. "I daresay any number of women in London know Ize or his ilk. Females are always punting on tick, pawning their jewelry with or without their husbands' knowledge. Perhaps Mrs. Pettigrew might know of the man's current place of business."

"She might, but she is traveling north to visit, ah, relatives. She left three days ago and is not expected to return for a month."

"Too bad. I do not suppose Miss Pettigrew—"

"No!" two voices shouted at once. If Ize was too dangerous for Harry, he was certainly too dangerous for Hellen.

"What is your interest in the man, anyway?" Harry asked, wanting to get back to his own situation.

Rourke looked at Browne. "It has to do with your affair."

"I told you, I am not having an—oh, the Lady Charlotte Endicott business. You think a pawnbroker might be involved?"

Rourke shrugged. "A man was seen a few times in Manchester with Molly Godfrey, who called herself Molly Dennis." For Lord Harking's sake, Rourke explained the interest in the child Molly had raised. "A small, shifty, pop-eyed man. There must be hundreds of such across the breadth of England, and Ize denied knowing any such woman or child or place. We could find no other ties between them. Of course he would not tell the truth if his life depended on it, but I had no cause to arrest him, where we might have interrogated the gallows bait with a bit more . . ."

"Enthusiasm?" Harry supplied. "As if his life did, indeed, depend on speaking the truth?"

"Precisely. Although we did keep an eye on him. When we lost all traces of the young woman known as Queenie Dennis, we also lost track of Ize, which was odd. We do not like coincidences in this line of work, Lord Harking. That is why I am interested in the man. So I shall certainly make an effort to find him and ask about your diamonds."

"I can ask Miss Pettigrew if she can suggest an address."

"Thank you."

They next discussed a sum commensurate with the diamonds' worth, and the worth of getting rid of Sir John Martin. Harry offered a higher bounty if the man was transported after a speedy trial. "I do not wish my poor sister distressed more than she needs be."

Rourke sympathized. "It's always best all around if scum like that meets a sorry end at the hands of one of his fellow crooks. Saves the Crown a trial and a cell. Saves the family the public notoriety, or a hanging."

Harry did not wish to think he was paying for Martin's murder, although that was what Rourke's words seemed to imply, a misfortune in prison or some such. "I just want him brought to justice and gone."

If Rourke understood, he did not acknowledge Harry's concerns. He straightened the sketch of the diamonds and the description of Martin, then set his pencil down and stood. "I shall see what I can do." He gestured toward the other Robin Redbreasts scattered around the busy office. "With the promised reward, you will have a lot of eyes looking for your quarry. We'll find him if he is still in Town."

Harry stood up to make way for Browne to give his report to the Runner. The schoolmaster stayed him. "This will not take long, my lord. Almost nothing of note has happened at the club—that is, the school—concerning the search for Lady Charlotte."

"Not much here, either," the Runner said in disgust. "But let us hear what you have to say."

Browne consulted his notes.

There were two blond, blue-eyed Lotties who came for the reward, down from the scores of pretenders who used to come to The Red and the Black to try their luck, but not at the gaming tables. One of the would-be heiresses had not bothered coming to Bow Street with Browne's note. The other had not lasted five minutes before Rourke recognized her as one of Mother Carey's chickens.

One enterprising female declared she was Queenie Dennis, the newest name on the reward posters, but she had no idea where Queenie and her mother had lived near

Manchester. A peddler did know the town, and could describe the girl and Molly, but he had not seen them in five years. An old actor who knew Molly Godfrey from her days at the theater thought he had seen her in London a fortnight ago. Since Mr. Browne knew the woman to be dead, and the actor to be out of work, he'd sent him off with two coins, instead of the one he gave the others.

Browne cleared his throat, debating loyalties with his own conscience. Just as he did not like Hellen's name being bandied about at Bow Street, he did not wish to mention her friend and employer. He was a law-abiding citizen, with a citizen's distrust of a policing force.

With an apologetic glance toward Lord Harking, he concluded with the last informant or claimant to appear at The Red and the Black. "It is undoubtedly nothing, but a young French widow asked to speak to Captain Endicott on a personal matter."

Harry studied his fingernails.

"Not to apply for a job as dealer?" Rourke asked.

"Why, no. She did say something about a teaching position once I explained about the school."

"So she did not actually come to apply for a job in the casino or the school?"

Browne cleared his throat again. "No. As I said, she told me it was a personal matter. I gave her your address."

"She never came here. How young?"

"Early twenties, I would guess."

"Was she a beauty?"

"Definitely."

"Most likely she was one of Endicott's old amours, then, trying to get money out of him."

Harry knew he did not like the man.

Rourke set his notes aside without writing. Harry and

Browne both released the breaths they had been holding. But then Rourke showed why he had Lord Carde's confidence: He was a bulldog for details. "I thought you explained the club was to be a school for working females, not a finishing academy for young ladies. Why would your widow think charity girls needed French lessons?"

Browne sighed. He'd known this was going to be hard. He also knew who paid his salary. "She suggested giving sewing instructions. The woman is a dressmaker."

If Rourke had dog ears, they would have perked up. "This is not the same dressmaker who so suddenly and so gainfully employs Miss Hellen Pettigrew, is it?"

Browne had to nod. Then he had to readjust his spectacles.

"Now, there is a coincidence to fair send chills up a man's spine: Ize, Miss Pettigrew, and a pretty seamstress who came looking for Jack Endicott, all on the same morning, all connected somehow. Meanwhile the world knows Endicott is searching for a female whose mother was a seamstress, who may have known Ize, who had to have had a friend in London. Molly Godfrey came to town to withdraw money from her bank. We know that, but we never found where she stayed, or who watched the little girl. Hm, I wonder when Mrs. Pettigrew will return to London."

"I have no idea. She did not say."

"No matter. A pretty French dressmaker ought to be easy enough to find. You did get her name, did you not?"

Browne pretended to consult his notes. "Madame Denise Lescartes. Perhaps you have heard of her?"

Everyone in London who could read or listen to gossip had heard of her. And her supposed protector. Rourke looked at Lord Harking again. Harry could feel his blasted cheeks grow warm.

"I met her at the club when I called to see Jack Endicott to ask his help finding my brother-in-law. We were schoolmates."

"Lucky," Rourke said.

Harry did not think he meant going to classes with Jack. "I think so. The lady is charming." He emphasized the *lady*.

Rourke was not intimidated. "And yet not quite a lady, if she was seeking employment, or Endicott."

"Nonsense," Harry told him. "You are grasping at straws because your case is at an impasse. Madame Lescartes has short, curly black hair. Lady Charlotte was supposed to have straight blond hair."

"As does that Queenie woman we are looking for now," Browne put in, lest Rourke accuse him of letting the object of their search slip through his fingers.

Rourke brushed both assertions aside. "Hair can be dyed, cut, and curled. Does your friend have blue eyes?" he asked Lord Harking. "That is the one thing that cannot be altered."

Harry did not answer fast enough. Browne gulped. "Yes. But hers are much prettier than those in the portrait of the child's mother, the previous Lady Carde, or her cousin, the new Mrs. Endicott."

"I have met Mrs. Endicott, too, and her eyes are surpassing fine, so I would be interested in seeing the Frenchwoman's."

Not if Harry could help it.

Rourke went on: "No one was quite certain what shade of blue little Lottie's glimmers would turn out to be."

"Yes, well, Madame has a birthmark near her mouth," Browne triumphantly added.

Harry did not mention that the enchanting mole was often migratory. He stood to leave. "This is a waste of time, time which would be better spent solving my problem, rather

than a decades-old disappearance. Madame Lescartes has
nothing to do with your inquiry. If she did, she would certainly have come forth as soon as she returned from France."

"Returned? She is not French, then?"

Harry could have bitten off his tongue, and then wondered why. His *chérie* was an honest woman with nothing to
hide. He was positive of that, almost. She did not need his
defense. She was a private woman, that was all, he told himself, who did not like speaking about her past.

He himself did not like Rourke and did not wish her sub-
jected to the man's curiosity. "I cannot say where she was
born," he finally answered. She had never said, or anything
about her childhood. "But she married a Frenchman." At
least Harry thought she had. "And she studied with a French
fashion designer." Now he felt on firmer ground. "Her name
appears with his in a ladies' journal, to prove it."

"The young woman we are looking for, Queenie Dennis,
who may or may not be Lord Carde's half sister, Lady Charlotte Endicott, could have been anywhere these past months
while we searched high and low."

"Absurd," Harry declared, ready to dismiss the damned
detective from his own inquiry. "There are too many contra-
dictions."

"There are too many coincidences," Rourke claimed.

"But . . . but Madame Lescartes cannot be Queenie Dennis," Browne said.

"She cannot?" both Rourke and Harry asked.

Browne shook his head. "All the reports from everyone
who ever met the young woman say that Miss Dennis is
quiet and shy."

Rourke nodded. "Timid as a church mouse."

Browne lowered his voice and leaned toward the Runner

as if telling a confidence. "Madame Lescartes was the young woman with Lord Harking at the opera."

The one who wore half a dress, who defended herself from the mob in the pit with her reticule and her fists and a darning needle, who by all accounts was a brilliant, brazen Amazon in support of her lover?

No, that was not Queenie Dennis. Rourke sighed, defeated.

CHAPTER SIXTEEN

Rourke reached for his topcoat. "I still want to speak to her."

Harry and Browne looked at each other, but it was Harry who asked, "Why?"

"To see what she wanted from Captain Endicott. I do not like loose ends any more than I like coincidences."

"But Browne told you she said it was a personal matter."

Rourke shrugged as he put on his coat, which was as well tailored as Harry's own. "I act for the family."

"Dealing with a man's former mistress is not a family affair," Harry insisted, almost choking on the words that labeled the woman he l—*liked* so much a prostitute. "You will embarrass her."

"You can't embarrass a whore."

Now Harry almost choked the Runner. "Denise, that is, Madame Lescartes, is not a whore."

"Then she wanted something else from the captain other than his money or his affections. I cannot be satisfied until I know why she came to his establishment."

Harry did not give a damn if the detective was satisfied or not. He knew that Madame Lescartes would not wish to speak with Rourke—hell, Harry did not wish to speak with Rourke—and that was enough for him to try to protect her from the Runner. She never spoke of herself to Harry and they were friends, so she would hate answering a stranger's questions. She said the past made her sorrowful, and so Harry stopped asking. Rourke would not care if she cried.

Another reason Harry wanted to keep Rourke away was that he knew the fiercely independent female, all brave and brazen on the outside, was a coward at heart. She had a mole that moved, and a backbone that bent in the wind.

Harry recalled her hand fluttering on his sleeve at the Cyprian's Ball, her quavering voice, her ashen complexion when one of the choice spirits asked her to dance. She had put starch in her spine and soldiered on, but at a high cost, he knew. No one else knew, because she was that valiant an actress . . . for a church mouse.

Harry did not understand any of it. *Chérie* could not be the Endicott heiress, of course, or she would not be struggling to make a living. She would be knocking at the Earl of Carde's door, not dressing old biddies and birds of paradise. If she were the Queenie Dennis woman, she could have collected the reward.

What he knew, in his heart if not in his head, was that Madame Denise Lescartes, mysterious past and inconsistent beauty mark aside, was a good woman. She was no harlot, he would swear to that—and her kiss was too inexperienced for a paid paramour. She was good to her employees and caring of the less fortunate, like a lady. This was no opportunist, no adventuress, no underhanded conniver running a rig.

"No," Harry said. "You cannot see her."

Rourke stopped in his tracks and eyed Harry with disbelief. "I suppose the woman no longer seeks Mr. Endicott because she found herself a new protector, but to say I cannot see her? You are going to impede an officer of the law to keep your ladybird from answering a few questions?"

Harry could not decide whom he loathed more: his brother-in-law or the man he'd just hired to find him. Rourke made Madame Lescartes seem cheap, dirty. Harry took satisfaction in saying, "No, you cannot see her today because she is spending the afternoon with Lady Jennifer Camden. Daughter of the Duke of Camfield, you know."

Rourke knew. And he knew that the likes of Queenie Dennis would never be invited to tea at a duke's house. A notorious courtesan might be, since Lady Jennifer was known to be eccentric in her choice of guests, but a common chit from the country with no countenance or connections? Doubtful. Rourke owed his employers a thorough report, however. "I'll wait at the shop for her return, then."

"That will not do, either. You will destroy her new business and embarrass her customers, some of whom have husbands who vote to fund this very office, or not."

"Then when?" Rourke asked, showing his impatience. "After you speak with her, and warn her of my coming? I wonder what it is you fear, my lord, that you would hinder my investigation?"

"I worry that you will treat the woman with less respect than she deserves."

Rourke pushed past Harry. "And your family and friends, my lord, ought to worry that you treat your . . . dressmaker . . . with more. I am going to speak with the woman, with your approval or not."

Harry knew he could not stop the man short of a fistfight, which Harry would lose, surrounded as they were by

•

Rourke's fellow Runners. Browne and his spectacles were not much help. And violence was beneath Harry's dignity, and likely illegal besides.

"Then I am coming, too," he said. If Rourke wanted to think Harry was a jealous lover, so be it. He was not leaving a gentle female to face this hardened inquisitor alone, especially one who dressed well and spoke well and might be considered well-favored by some.

No one was in the shop except Charlie and Hellen, arguing over the last slice of lemon cake. As soon as the boy saw the Runner, along with Browne and Lord Harking, get out of a hackney carriage, he ran.

"I'll be gettin' more biscuits, then, gov," he called over his shoulder from halfway down the street. He might just travel to Richmond to fetch the sweets; that's how long Charlie intended to stay away.

The light that shone in Hellen's eyes when she saw Browne faded a bit when she saw Lord Harking come into the shop behind him. Now she and Browne could not steal a moment's privacy before Queenie came back. The light died altogether when she saw the red-vested Runner. She did pour him a cup of tea, though, and offered him one of the gilt chairs placed around the shop's front room, as if her knees were not knocking together beneath her skirts.

"How nice to see you gentlemen," she started to chatter. "It has been a boring afternoon, with Madame gone. The customers want to meet with her in person," she explained, although no one asked, "and did not want my opinions about colors or fabrics or styles, which I thought a shame, since I am supposed to be Madame's assistant, although I have no training, of course. They all left when I told them she would not be back until late. So while I could make appointments and see that measurements were taken and fittings were accomplished, I did not have much to do."

Except eat the cake.

Rourke eyed the empty plate and said, "I would like to ask you a few questions, Miss Pettigrew, if you do not mind."

"Oh, I know all about the new designs. Do you want a gown for your wife?"

"I am not married, thank you. I want to know if you or your mother are acquainted with a fellow by the name of Ezra Iscoll, commonly known as Ize."

She looked at Lord Harking, instead of the Runner. "Oh, did you speak with Mr. Ize about your diamonds?"

Rourke answered before Harry could. "I will speak to the man on Lord Harking's behalf, once I find him. Do you know where he lives?"

Hellen knew Ize would kill her and her mother if she peached on him to the law, and yet everyone had seen her talking to the toad at the Cyprian's Ball. "No, I only see him now and again, like at the assembly we all attended. He used to have the most cunning shop, though. Mother and her friends often gathered there to see his latest, ah, finds."

"And sell their baubles to him?"

Now Hellen looked at Mr. Browne, refusing to deny her mother's profession or her own background. "Is there anything wrong with that?" she asked the Runner. "Trinkets are nice, but a full purse and a full belly mean more."

Rourke sipped at his tea. Mr. Browne and his lordship looked uncomfortable. Hellen knew she was. Especially when the Runner asked, "Do you know of a Lady Charlotte Endicott?"

Hellen feigned a laugh. She held up her own cup and said, "Of course. Her ladyship and I take tea all the time."

Rourke frowned, but Browne smiled, so Hellen went on. "Goodness, sir, if I knew aught of the lady, I would be beating down your door for the reward money. There cannot be a soul in Town what doesn't know about the missing lady."

"What about Miss Queenie Dennis?"

It was a good thing Hellen had set her cup down, else she would have dropped it. She had sworn to Queenie not to give her away. Her friend had been so good to Hellen, giving her this job, giving her the chance to show John George Browne that she was a decent woman.

And Queenie feared for her very life.

"Her name is on all the posters, too, isn't it?" Hellen asked, pasting a smile on her face.

"Everyone knows it is. But I wonder if you and your mother know the woman more personally," Rourke prodded.

Hellen tried for another laugh. "Information about that female is worth a fortune, too, according to your reward notices. Do you think my mother would be traveling north in this cold weather, trying to pry a dowry for me out of my father so's I don't have to make a living on my back, if she had that kind of news to sell?"

Browne was grinning. "Is she? A dowry, you say?"

Lord Harking smiled. "You'd better watch yourself, Browne. Your bachelor days are numbered, it appears."

Rourke was the only one not amused at Hellen's improved prospects. There were still too many coincidences for his peace of mind. "Very well, then perhaps you can tell me how you met Madame Lescartes. How long ago and where?"

Hellen knew she was not needle-witted enough to make up a convincing story, and then remember it long enough to tell Queenie. She also knew John George was looking at her with love in his eyes. He could not marry a whore's bastard, but a baron's illegitimate daughter with a dowry and a respectable position, now, that was a more suitable match for a schoolmaster. Mr. Browne's innkeeper parents would approve—if she was not in jail for lying to the Bow Street Runner.

So Hellen did the only thing she could think of: She spilled her tea in her lap.

She jumped up, screaming. "Oh, no! Madame Lescartes will strangle me! Worse, she will dismiss me!" She started crying, while Browne leaped to fetch napkins and Lord Harking reached for his handkerchief.

"She would not—"

"I have ruined another of her pretty gowns!" Hellen sobbed, ignoring their assistance and reassurance as she ran from the room, holding her sodden gown away from her. "I will lose my position and be out on the streets if I cannot remove the stain!"

The men heard her feet pounding down the hall, then up the stairs to the living quarters.

"Should I follow?" Browne wondered.

"Can you remove tea stains?"

Browne poured them more of the brew instead, and Rourke added a bit of spirits from the flask in his pocket to each of their cups.

"Drinking while on duty?" Harry asked, one brow raised.

"A woman's tears go above and beyond the call of duty, and sure as hell require more than tea."

They all raised their cups to that.

"Just look at us now," Queenie told her dog, who had been lavishly petted and amply fed in her hostess's kitchens.

"Being driven in a duke's own carriage, with a crest on the door, no less."

Parfait could barely wag his tail, he was so full of the French chef's delicacies.

"And being driven home," Queenie went on as if the dog understood, "to our own profitable business. Who would have thought we could come so far?"

Surely not the dog, who went back to looking out the window.

And surely not Molly, even though she had not thought the village children good enough for her little girl. Queenie thought Molly would be horrified that she was socializing with the unworthy aristocracy. Molly never trusted any strangers, and some of Lady Jennifer's guests were strange indeed.

Then again, Molly trusted men least of all. She would be appalled that Queenie was thinking of when she could tell Lord Harking about her visit, her easy acceptance, the plans for the school. Sharing her exciting news with Harry would make the day that much better, in a way Molly would never understand. Queenie barely understood it herself, since she had never wanted to share her thoughts with anyone.

Harry was different. He was strong and capable, yet kind and gentle. He was silly and serious and he would surely break her heart, but he was—

Waiting for her at the shop.

As the carriage turned down her street Queenie could see the glow of the lamps that were lit against the early dusk. Her lamps. Her shop. Her success. "Wake up, Parfait. We are nearly home."

Then, as the coach drew to a stop, she could see an unmistakable, broad-shouldered figure outlined behind the mannequin in the store's window. Her friend. Her admirer. Her Harry.

Her heart was not shattered yet, so it warmed at the thought of spending the evening in his company. Queenie nearly tripped over the dog in her hurry to get out of the carriage when the groom let down the steps.

But Harry was not alone. Browne was there, looking pale and rattled and swaying on his feet. If Queenie did not know that there was nothing in the shop stronger than Madeira, she would think he was drunk. Another man had also stood when she hurried through the doorway. Parfait was stifflegged, sniffing him suspiciously, a low growl rumbling in the poodle's throat.

A moan was rising in Queenie's. The man was wearing the red waistcoat of Bow Street.

Harry made the introductions and Mr. Geoffrey Rourke murmured the appropriate words. So did Queenie, she hoped, after calling the dog to her side. Then she said, "I see you took Mr. Browne's advice and consulted an expert at capturing criminals, my lord."

"Yes, but Rourke has a few questions he would like to put to you, my dear. Do you mind?"

"Of course not, but . . . where is Hellen? And Charlie?"

"Charlie went out to fetch more refreshments," Harry said, his lips quirked in a half smile. "An hour ago. I doubt he will return any time soon. Are you hungry? I could find another lad to—"

"Oh, no. I ate enough at Lady Jennifer's to last until tomorrow morning. She has the most remarkable French chef. But what of Hellen? Surely she did not go with Charlie, leaving the shop unattended."

"No, but she had an unfortunate accident with her gown

and is abovestairs making reparations. It is past time for customers to be calling anyway."

"Miss Pettigrew was distraught that you might dismiss her over the ruined gown," Browne added in worried tones.

As if Hellen could ever believe Queenie would cast her out over a stupid thing like a scrap of muslin. Queenie shook her head at her friend's supposed foolishness. Hellen was upstairs, brilliant girl that she was, out of the Runner's reach. "In that case I had better go reassure her."

"Surely that can wait until I am finished with my questions, ma'am," the Runner said, almost as an order.

Queenie lowered her eyes modestly. "But I need to make a few repairs myself," she said, delicately implying a call of nature. "I won't be but a minute."

Rourke bowed slightly.

Queenie turned to go, hoping her feet could still obey her head's command to move. If she fainted, would he leave? If she fled out the back door, could she climb over the fence? Maybe Hellen had fashioned a rope ladder out of the bedsheets and Queenie could climb down the side of the building and hire a hansom cab to drive her to the antipodes. Or she could hide in Charlie's alley.

Then, when she feared she might actually swoon, right at the Runner's feet, Harry took her arm and turned her toward the back, to the stairs.

"I will make sure the back door is locked while you are gone," he said, "now that your seamstresses have gone for the night."

Once they were in the hall, though, out of sight and hearing of the Runner, he took both of her frigid hands in his and rubbed them between his own warm ones.

He leaned closer and softly kissed her trembling lips, in case Rourke had come out and was watching the supposed lovers. He whispered, "I am here. No one will hurt you. But whatever you do, *chérie,* do not let him see your fear."

Queenie raised her chin, squared her shoulders, and cleared her throat. She took a deep breath, pressed a quick kiss of her own on Harry's mouth, and asked, "Who says I am frightened?"

"That's my girl."

CHAPTER SEVENTEEN

Hellen started babbling the instant Queenie reached the sitting room of their apartment.

"I did not know what to say, what you were going to say. What if Mama comes back and says something altogether different? And you know I'll never remember half of it anyway. I am sorry about the gown, but that was all I could think of."

Queenie was taking off her hat and gloves. "The gown does not matter."

"But John George does, and he will hate me when he finds out we have been pulling the wool over everyone's eyes."

"No, Mr. Browne will not hate you. He loves you. And he will love you more for being a loyal friend. The whole affair was my doing, not yours, anyway. And your mama cannot return any time soon because of the distance, and because it will take more than a day to convince your father to provide you with a dowry. But he will, I just know it. Even if only to

get your mother out of his neighborhood before his wife dis-
covers her presence."

"Mama said the same thing."

"When she finally returns"—the later the better, for Valerie Pettigrew could not be trusted to keep quiet about her
friend Molly forever—"your John George will be so pleased
and relieved that you are not a poor shopgirl that he will
sweep you off to the altar before you can say 'Jack Rabbit.'
You will live happily ever after and have three bespectacled
babies. You can name one after me."

"What, *Queenie?*" Hellen was horrified. Her children
would be Mary and Jane and John. Or George.

"You are right. You can think of me, instead."

"But where will you be? In prison?"

"I hope not. I have a story that ought to satisfy Rourke for
now. It will take him a while to discover the lies amid the
truth. I'll be trying to think what to do until he does. Perhaps
I can sell the business and make enough money to live on
somewhere else." With yet another name, with another career, but without Harry.

"But I like the shop! And you are such a success."

Queenie splashed water on her face, hoping the tears
would also rinse off. "I like the shop, too." While she repaired her dark brows and lashes—and the beauty mark—
Hellen came over and handed her a fresh handkerchief.

"Harry will help."

"Yes, he said so. But I do not think even Lord Harking
can fix this. And he will hate having to try. His brother-in-
law's actions were sordid enough, and you know how he
tried to keep that quiet and private."

"Until he shouted it across the opera house."

Both young women had to smile at the memory. Then

Hellen asked, "I will not have to go back downstairs, will I?"

"No, I shall tell them you took a drop of laudanum to settle your nerves." Queenie looked longingly at the bottle. "Get into bed, in case Rourke insists on looking. If he is as diligent as he appears, he might ask."

Hellen was already in her robe, with the stained gown soaking in a tub of water. "But I will stay awake until you come back. You have to tell me what you told him, so I will know what to say in case he comes again tomorrow. He wanted to know how long I have known you and where we met."

"Why, you have merely to say that you never heard of Madame Denise Lescartes until I returned from France last month."

"Heaven knows that is the truth!"

"And we met, I suppose, in the park while I was starting to set up shop. You admired my dog, and we started talking. You were, ah, visiting the stationer's on the corner and kindly helped me word my calling card. The clerk there will recall seeing us together. Remember how he spilled an entire tray of quill pens when we walked in?"

"And how his wife boxed his ears!"

"Exactly. Then we discovered that we both had an interest in visiting The Red and the Black. Mr. Browne already knows that you considered becoming a dealer there, but that I hired you instead, as soon as I saw that I could afford an assistant."

Hellen clapped her hands. "Which is true! And our meeting in the park when you came home from France. How clever you are, to think of telling the truth. I would have made up some faradiddle that no one could believe."

Queenie quickly combed through her curls with her fingers, leaving off her bonnet. Her head already ached enough without that weight. She left off her gloves, also, rather than find a fresh pair. She was in her own home, after all, and she was a businesswoman, not a fine lady. "There, I suppose I am as ready as I will ever be."

"You are as beautiful as ever, anyway. Perhaps if you flirt with Mr. Rourke, he might forget about his questions?"

"Hellen! I am no Siren, to steal a man's wits. And I think it would take more than a pretty face and fluttering eyelashes to distract Mr. Rourke from his duties."

Now Hellen's eyes filled with tears. "But what if he does not believe you? What if he asks a question you have no answer for? You cannot very well spill tea on your gown, for I already used that excuse. And tears. You know how men turn to pudding when a woman cries. But I doubt Rourke can be gulled twice in one night."

"Well, I can always swoon, I suppose. But no, I can do what I always planned to do eventually, which is talk to Lady Charlotte's family. If Rourke does not swallow my tale, I can refuse to speak to him or his fellows until I have seen the earl or his brother. Rourke will not take a chance of my contracting jail fever or such, not when I might have the information he needs, so I will get to visit the Endicotts one way or the other. I will throw myself on Lord Carde's mercy."

"What about Harry?"

"Oh, I doubt such an upstanding gentleman like Lord Harking will have any mercy once he finds out how I have lied."

"But he loves you! I swear he does."

"I think he might, a little. But so what? He would never marry a shopkeeper, a female in trade. Nor would he wed an orphan from who knows what origin, whose adopted family was involved in dreadful crimes."

"But John George wants to marry me—he said so even before he knew about a possible dowry—and he knows what my mother is, and that my father is not her husband. If a man loves you enough . . ."

"Your Mr. Browne is a kind and intelligent gentleman, who is not afraid of society's censure. But he is not a viscount."

On that sad truth, one of the few truths that would pass her lips that hour, Queenie went back downstairs.

The men had finished their tea, as an excuse to finish the contents of Rourke's flask. Harry was hoping Rourke would relax his vigilance; Rourke was hoping the liquor would loosen Harking's and Browne's tongues.

"She is even prettier than I expected," Rourke said, looking for a reaction.

He got a grin from Browne. "The prettiest girl in all of England. Can you believe a regular dasher like her is willing to settle for an ordinary chap like me?"

"I meant Madame Lescartes, although Miss Pettigrew is a lovely young woman and you are a lucky man."

"Oh. Madame. Takes your breath away, doesn't she? I almost forgot my own name when she walked into the school."

Rourke looked around the shop. "It is hard to believe a woman could be so beautiful and talented besides. And ambitious. A woman would have to be ambitious to open a fancy shop, wouldn't you say, my lord?"

Harry's smile faded. "There is nothing wrong with ambition."

"Not unless it leads a body to step beyond the pale. With

a lord on the line, who knows what a female might do, or try
to hide?"

"This lord is not on any line, and Madame Lescartes is
not a schemer. You will see." And if he did not, Harry would
make him. There was no building full of law officers behind
Rourke now, and there would be no insulting Harry's *chérie*
or intimidating her or implicating her in some long-ago
crime. Not while Harry was in Town.

Somewhere between hiring the Runner and having
Rourke show an interest in Denise, Harry had decided to
stay on in London. That way, he told himself, he could take
the diamonds home with him if they were recovered. He
could testify against his brother-in-law if, heaven forfend,
the ugliness came to a trial. And he could stand by his friend.

Friend? Who was he fooling? He could no more leave
Madame Lescartes than he could stop breathing, and that
was no friendly feeling. Hell, he was half tortured by the
thought of her upstairs in that cozy sitting room, perhaps
changing her clothes, brushing her shiny curls, going to
sleep there later. Oh, how he wanted to share her bed. His
bed. Any bed. A chair.

He did not need the alcohol to heat his blood. The sight
of her coming home, so obviously eager to see him, had
rekindled a fire that was barely banked since he had met her.
And his blood and his body were not the only parts of him
burning. He ached to protect her, shield her from worry,
make her laugh, and erase those shadows that lurked behind
her blue, blue eyes. She was a friend the way his wrist and
his hand were friends: attached, inseparable, one no good
without the other.

Damn, what was he going to do about it?

For a start, he was going to pull the only empty chair in
the shop closer to his own. Then he was going to listen.

*   *   *

Queenie took the last chair in her showroom, drawn close to Harry's, thank goodness, and sat with her hands folded in her lap, the picture of unconcern. Harry nodded his approval.

"Would anyone like more tea? No? Very well, then, Mr. Rourke. What would you like to know?"

"Perhaps we should go somewhere more private?"

"I would invite you to the sitting room above, but Miss Pettigrew is close to sleep. Would you prefer to sit around the cutting table?" He'd likely prefer the guillotine, she thought.

Rourke scowled at Harry and Browne, who had made no signs of leaving. "I meant apart from the gentlemen."

Queenie raised her chin a notch. And her eyebrow, the way she had seen Lady Jennifer do. "Why? I have nothing to hide from anyone. Nor have I anything to say that my friends cannot hear." She raised her hand to her mouth to cover a delicate yawn. "Perhaps you might get on with your queries, then. I find I am *très* weary, also."

"My pardon, ma'am."

Queenie thought his apology might be a shade sarcastic, but she dipped her head regally in acceptance. Harry hid a smile behind his hand, as if he, too, were covering a yawn. She was magnificent, and he had worried for nothing; his *chérie* would take her fences flying, throwing her heart over the hurdle.

"How long have you known Miss Pettigrew?" was the Runner's first question.

"Long enough to know that she is kindhearted and sweet-natured and will make some man—Mr. Browne—an excellent wife."

Browne was back to grinning.

"And before you can ask, Parfait and I met Miss Petti-grew in the park when I returned from Paris." Queenie bent down to pet the poodle, who had taken a guard position in front of her feet. "A dog is a great socializer—*n'est-ce pas?*—and an easy topic of conversation between strangers. Neither Hellen nor myself are of circumstances to stand on ceremony, needing a proper introduction by a mutual ac-quaintance or a maid in tow every moment. While speaking, we found we had mutual interests and similar errands to ac-complish. With Hellen's knowledge of London, which I lacked, she was invaluable in helping set up my shop."

"Ize?"

Queenie blinked. "Well, I suppose Hellen has a good eye for colors, but I prefer to make those decisions on my—"

"Ezra Iscoll, the fence. Do you know him?"

"I choose not to know persons of his profession and rep-utation. I understand Hellen's mother has made use of his services in the past, but I would rather deal with the devil himself." She smiled and touched her bare neck. "Besides, as you can see, I have no jewelry to sell. I disposed of every-thing of value in France to finance my apprenticeship with Monsieur Guatheme, and then to secure my passage to En-gland. I even sold my wedding ring."

"I take it Monsieur Lescartes has passed on, then?"

Now Queenie looked at the Runner as if wondering how such a stupid person had attained such a post. "Would I be here alone in London otherwise? Establishing my own busi-ness? Wearing mourning? Going to the opera with Lord Harking? *Non, non, non,* and especially *non.*"

Harry could not like the *especially,* but the Runner did not like looking stupid. "Of course not. My apologies. Was your loss recent?"

He was not being polite, Queenie decided. He was trying

to get more damning facts out of her. Before he could ask for dates and places that would be too easy to disprove, Queenie gave him more hogwash.

"As recent as yesterday, it seems sometimes." She dabbed at her eyes with the handkerchief Hellen had pressed on her. "He died too soon, poor Lescartes, before he had time to reclaim his family's vineyards."

"What of your family?"

Again, Queenie spun the tale she had made up of whole cloth. "Le Blanc was their name." *Blanc* meant "white," or "empty," and was a common French last name. It would take Rourke ages to trace, if it were at all possible, with so many records lost in that war-torn country. "They were from Paris originally, but when my father was conscripted to the army, my mother fled to England, as so many others tried to do. We traveled anywhere she could find work as a seamstress."

"You went back to find your father, to reclaim his property, perhaps?"

"He was killed in his first battle. And no, there was no wealth or lands. They would not have come to *ma mère* anyway. You see, they never married."

Ah, Harry thought, so that was why she held her cards so close to her superb chest: She was a bastard. No woman wanted to admit such an obstacle to making a good marriage or making a successful career. And no wonder she and Hellen Pettigrew had become friends, with so much in common. He could see the Runner making those same conclusions.

Before Rourke could ask for more details, Queenie went on: "We went back to France after the war because *ma mère* missed her homeland. She was ill with the wasting disease and wanted to die on French soil. I buried here there." Queenie had no trouble summoning real tears while she thought of Molly's last days. She sniffled once or twice, then said, "I had few acquaintances in France, having lived abroad so long, but few in England to return to, either. There was little money left after the doctor's bills, and I could not earn enough on a seamstress's salary to live. Then I met Monsieur Lescartes, an answer to my prayers."

"Who lived . . . ?"

"Too short a life, although he was not a young man even then. Oh, you mean where. His vineyard was in the south of France, but he was in Paris, trying to raise enough money to restore the fields and the buildings. He was a clever man who taught me much about finances and investments, and not waiting. He waited, and never got to see his efforts, or his vines, bear fruit. A heart seizure, they said. The money went to his family, of course, for the grapes. He had grown sons from his first marriage, which is why he could take a baseborn wife with no dowry."

Harry felt better knowing Lescartes was already an old man when he wedded his beautiful young second wife. How much could Denise have loved a man old enough to be her father? Lud, he had not suffered his heart attack while making love to her, had he? Harry almost missed her next words, as the thoughts flashed through his mind.

"I stayed with his sons and their wives for a time, but I had no place there. I had no reason to wait, either, and every reason to make something of myself after seeing how fleeting life could be. I decided to go back to England to seek my fortune because the English were hungry for French fashions." Queenie was relieved to be able to tell the truth for a change. "First I went to Paris to seek more experience, credentials, and references in my chosen vocation. It was hard for a woman in London—or in France, for that matter—to rise above seamstress or dressmaker. I wished not merely to sew, not only to have a shop of my own, but to design beautiful clothes. I found a position under Monsieur Guatheme."

How far under? Harry wondered, now that he was not half as jealous of Monsieur Lescartes. Even he had heard of the couturier's vast sexual appetites. A young widow, one as beautiful as this one, would have been a choice morsel landing on the Frenchman's plate.

"When I felt that I had learned all I could, I came to London. Again, life is too short to waste in wondering what if. One has to say, what now? Voilà, here we are."

Rourke had been scribbling notes in his occurrence book. He looked up. "I will not bother to ask if you know Lady Charlotte Endicott. But what about Queenie Dennis?"

"Ah, that is what I wished to discuss with Captain Jack Endicott, which is why you are here, *non?*"

The Runner nodded. "There were too many coincidences and connections."

"I understand, and now you will have to, also. You see, I heard rumors when I left my husband's family. There was talk in Paris of a beautiful blond English girl, a seamstress. When I applied to various dress designers, I was asked if I knew this Queenie Dennis from my days in England, for she had no references when she sought a position, although she sewed a neat hem and spoke adequate French. A quiet girl, she also had no friends, it seemed. I do not know if she found a job. I meant to seek her out when I was more settled at Guatheme's, because I spoke her language and could possibly help her, but then I heard she had consumption. A few months after that, I heard she had died."

Rourke sucked in a deep breath.

Browne groaned. "Captain Endicott will be so disappointed."

Rourke said, "I am disappointed you did not come to me

with this information, ma'am. I could have had someone in France weeks ago."

"But the rumor was mere repeated gossip and hearsay. I believed I should tell her brothers myself, in case this Dennis woman was indeed Lady Charlotte. And I thought they could wait a month or two until they came to London, after they had waited all those years." She waved her hand in an arc that encompassed the store and the large gentleman who sat beside her. "And I did not need to come to you."

"Need?"

"For the reward. I needed money to establish myself when I first saw your posters. But now I have the store."

She also had Lord Harking, Rourke thought bitterly as he closed his book, who would stand by his *chérie* amour against a more . . . intense interrogation at Bow Street, damn him.

"And my dressmaking and fashion designing are making profits. I am a success."

CHAPTER EIGHTEEN

"**D**o not be so sure, *chérie*," Harry said after Rourke left. He hated to destroy her obvious sense of relief, but he had to. With a jerk of his head he had indicated that Browne should also leave. Since he could not see Hellen that night, the younger man took the hint and walked out after the Runner.

"What do you mean?"

"About being a success. Your skills as a modiste are not in question. Your skills at lying, at hoodwinking an officer of the law, are less certain. I do not think Rourke believed half of what you told him. And why should he, when he could drive an oxcart through the holes in your story? He will be back."

"But not for a while." That was all she had wanted, time.

He raised her right hand and brought it to his mouth for a polite salute. His other hand touched her soft black curls; then he turned her hand over. "It was a good thing the officer did not see your fingers without their gloves."

They were dark from dye.

Queenie stepped back and put her hands behind her. "That was from Hellen's gown. You know, the one that had blood on it from the night at the opera. Your blood. Now that I think of it, we should check the wound to make sure it has not turned putrid."

"Here? Now?" He started to remove his jacket.

That would be more dangerous than letting the conversation continue. Harry without his shirt, in the lamplit shop? Queenie could touch him, and look at his muscles and marvel at the hair on his chest, the way she could not do when they'd simply cut his shirtsleeve off. And if the wound was healing, which it must be, since Harry did not seem to be in any pain, then Queenie could throw herself into his arms.

She was so relieved at having the Runner gone she would have kissed Harry there and then, shirt or not. He'd given her confidence with his smile, with his very presence. She felt relief, gratitude, and, oh, an ache just to be in Harry's embrace! And he would kiss her back. In all her heart, she knew that. They would both want more, and heaven knew where that would lead.

No, the devil knew precisely where that would lead, and Queenie was not going to take that path, not even with Harry, not even with her whole body wishing to press itself against him, to be surrounded by him, to be filled by him. She was no harlot. "On second thought, someone at the hotel can help you, or you can see a surgeon if it looks red or swollen."

He looked disappointed, but did not unfasten another button on his coat.

"As for Hellen's gown, we could not get the stains out, so we tried to dye it."

"Ah," was all he said.

No matter what Harry believed, Queenie thought she had

told enough of the truth to keep the Runner from pouncing. The business about Lescartes and the Le Blancs would take a long time to check. She had time now, time to decide to flee yet again, or meet with the Earl of Carde, who could protect her from Ize by prosecuting him. No one else had been so affected by the snake's sins, and no one else had the wealth, power, connections —and cause—to get rid of the viper before he struck.

Yet there was a poison seeping through Queenie's heart already. "You do not believe me?"

"I do not know what to believe. Do you know that when I lie my cheeks turn rosy? They always have, to my despair. My tutor merely had to ask a question and he could tell whether I was guilty or not. I learned to tell the truth early, for it was useless to try otherwise, and I seldom play cards for high stakes for the same reason. But you give yourself away by folding your hands in your lap."

"*Ma mère* taught me a lady always sat thus."

"But not to keep her hands from trembling, and not holding them so tightly that the knuckles turned white."

"I was anxious about speaking to Mr. Rourke, that was all. He does not appear a very comfortable gentleman."

"No, which is why he is so good at what he does. Like a bulldog that never lets go, no matter what."

"He might not let go, but he has not found your brother-in-law."

"After one conversation? I should think not."

"Or the missing lady, or the other girl. He has not located that woman, Queenie, after how many years? And she was living her whole life right here in England, they say."

"I do not believe he was on the case since the beginning. He is far too young. But he was the one who unraveled some of the connection between that female and the earl's half sis-

ter once new information came to light. He will not stop
until he has found her, or proof of her death, you know. That
is what the earl is paying him for."

Queenie bit her lip. She knew. But she had given the bulldog enough to chew on. He would have to send messengers
to France, at least. Letters would take weeks. Tracking down
the rumors Queenie had planted would take longer.

When she did not reply, Harry softly touched the lip she
was nibbling. "You can trust me, you know."

Queenie looked up into his eyes, that soft brown a
woman could sink into like a fur wrap, and be warmed and
cherished. She might trust him, but she could not trust her
own feelings. She lowered her eyes so she would not see the
tender concern in his. "Can I, my lord? When you do not
trust me?"

"I trust you. I simply do not understand you."

She tried for a laugh. "I believe men have been saying
that about women since Adam and Eve."

He did not laugh back. "With cause. But I can help with
whatever is troubling you now. I can see that you might not
wish to confide in Rourke. He is a stranger, and has his own
goals and purposes and loyalties. But I have nothing but
your interests at heart. Surely you know we are friends?"

"Friends, my lord? A shopkeeper and a viscount?"

Harry nodded. "A man and a woman. Friends. And that is
Harry, chérie."

"Not *Denise* or *Madame Lescartes*?"

"They do not suit. But we do. You came to my aid at the
opera. I would come to your aid now."

"Then believe me," she nearly begged. "Do not ask me
for more than I can give. Believe what I told Rourke. Much
of it was true. Much of the rest is impossible to confirm or
deny."

"But why?"

"You see, if you trusted me, you would not ask."

"But I want to—"

She touched his lips to stop his talk. "No, not even to help. I am not yours to protect, my fine and noble friend. And they are not all my secrets. You have to accept that."

"You are protecting others who might be guilty of something?"

"I am protecting myself and others from danger the best way I know how. If that is a crime, then yes, I am guilty, too. But know this, and believe it above all else: I never intended to hurt anyone. I never knew that anyone *was* hurt until I was full grown. Now I am trying to make amends in the only way I can, in my own time. I am not a criminal."

"I never thought you were, my dear. I never, ever thought that. But if someone is threatening you, I could—"

"You could be killed. These are people who carry knives the way you carry handkerchiefs and fob watches."

Harry did not mention the pistol he had tucked in his boot since encountering his dastardly brother-in-law. "I am not afraid."

"You should be. They hire assassins to do their dirty work. You might be the strongest, bravest man I know"— she patted the blush that instantly came to Harry's cheeks— "but you would not prevail against a group of thugs paid to waylay you in an alley or on your way back to your hotel. I will not chance it. This is not your battle, and you are too important to me."

Harry took her hand and kissed it, the fingers, then the palm. "But you are important to me, too. I think I love you, *chérie*."

He only thought so? Queenie was certain. Her heart ached when she said, "Friends, Harry. That is all we can be."

"No. I could take you away where you would be safe. I could find a cottage for you near my home where no one needed to know who you were, ever. Another name. A different look. I always fancied redheads."

What, become yet another person who had no past but lies? Queenie could not do it, not even to be with Harry. Not that way.

"A red-haired woman tucked away on your estate? What would people think but that I was your mistress? That would be a hundred times worse for me." She looked around at the shop. "I would have no life, no work, no income but what you provided. I would have no friends, no companions, but you. I would not even be welcome at church or the nearby shops, a fallen woman to be avoided. Perhaps most importantly, I would have no way to make amends for the past, which I am sworn to do. I would have no respect for myself. Soon, you would not, either."

"I am sorry if I offended. I had not thought that we would be lovers, only of keeping you safe."

She laughed. "Now your cheeks are flaming red with such a whopper of a lie. Silly, you have thought of little else. Do you think I do not notice where your eyes stray? How often you try to stop your hand from reaching out to me, and how often you fail? I am not a green girl, my lord. Paris cures that innocence and ignorance, especially for a woman on her own. And," she hastily added, purposely keeping her hands at her sides, unclenched, "I have been married."

He raised one eyebrow.

Queenie went on before he could ask about Lescartes, how old he was, how long they had been wedded, why she'd married him. "I admit I feel the attraction between us, too, as I have never felt for a man who would look at me that way. But no, life in a cozy love nest is not for me. Nor for the children I would hope to bear."

"I had not thought of children." He did now, and knew he would cherish any blue-eyed babes this woman bore.

"Men seldom do. But a woman must. I would not have a daughter like Hellen, with so few choices but to follow her mother's footsteps."

"You have guided her down another path."

"As best I am able. But what paths could an illegitimate son take? Oh, I know honorable men pay to educate their by-blows, find them posts or buy their colors. But they are forever bastards. No child of mine shall be, no matter what else I have to do. Besides, children need a father as well as a mother. I know, for I never had one. My mother did her best, and raised me with scruples I shall never sacrifice, no matter how desperate things get. Please, for the sake of our friendship, do not ask me again, for selfless reasons or for satisfying the urges we both feel."

They both knew that Harry had nothing else that he could offer, no wedding ring, no title, no home and family. No forever.

"Dinner?" he asked, grasping at straws. "You cannot still be full from the refreshments at Lady Jennifer's. And we never had our meal after the opera."

Eat? After facing Rourke, hearing that Harry thought he loved her, and telling him she would not be his mistress? The man must be insane. She knew he was, for still liking her, still wanting to spend time with her, knowing she was hiding her past. Then again, he was so large he must always need sustenance.

"No, thank you. I am not hungry, and I would not leave Hellen here alone, asleep. I shall wait for Charlie to return and send him for a meat pie for our supper. I have much to think about."

"Will you think about me, *chérie*?"

"Too much, I fear."

Harry gathered his hat and his gloves, but he could not leave, not that he had been invited to stay. He'd never told a woman he loved her—or thought he loved her. It was not enough, he knew, but he had no other words. He was no practiced flirt, no silver-tongued rake. He was a simple man who did not even believe in keeping a mistress, in stirring scandal, in letting lust rule his life. But he could not go home.

"It is not just wanting, you know." He had to make sure she understood.

"I do know that. You are a good man, Lord Harking."

But not good enough to leave. "You are a good woman, Madame Lescartes. I do believe that, with every fiber of my being." He tapped his chest. "I know it, here."

"Thank you."

If she was a virtuous woman, and he a principled gentleman, he had to get out of the shop, out of her life, before he caused her more woe. He managed one step. Somehow, it was one step closer to her, not to the door.

"I . . . I do want you. I would be a fool to deny that." If not for his coat, she could see the evidence of his desire all too clearly. "But more, I do want to keep you safe and see your business a success. And I want to see you smiling. You have a smile the angels could envy."

He touched her lips, and the corners turned up.

"You see? One smile and it's as if the sun came out."

"Harry, you mustn't."

"I know. What I must do is go back to my dreary hotel, alone, eat my supper, alone, and worry all through the night that you are in trouble, alone. How can I do that, *chérie*? Tell me and I will go."

"You can do it by knowing that I have handled worse problems, and I shall handle this one, by myself. Do not worry, for then I would fret for your sake. Good night, my good friend."

He said good night. And then he leaned closer.

The dog growled.

"Hush, silly. It is only Harry and nothing is going to happen."

The dog was wiser than both of them. He gave up and went into the rear room.

Queenie could have backed away. She knew that Harry would never coerce her or force her to do anything she did not wish. Oh, how she wished. She was a healthy young woman, just coming into awareness of her own passions, and she was curious. More, she was as drawn to her gallant companion as he seemed to be to her, and not merely as a physical attraction. She wanted to be held by him, enfolded in his strength, making him a part of her that could never, would never, go away. Harry was the best, the finest thing that had ever happened to her. How could she let him walk out of her door without knowing how much she cared for him? What if he never came back?

"One kiss," she said.

"One kiss," he echoed fervently, as an answer to his prayer. "Then I can leave."

It was not one kiss, of course. It never was.

The first one did not have their noses angled right, and the second did not have their lips touching perfectly. But, ah, the third. That was one kiss, one kiss for the ages.

Harry meant it to last till dawn, at least. Queenie meant it to last a lifetime.

She pressed herself closer, and his arms came around her back while hers reached for his neck and his hair and his shoulders, anything that she could touch.

He could touch the fabric of her high-necked gown, and it was not enough. There was lace, not skin; material, not warm, womanly flesh. He groaned.

Queenie wriggled closer. He groaned again. Now he felt her breasts pressed against his chest, her soft belly against his hardness. She fitted perfectly, if he bent his head. She was perfect altogether, responsive and eager, making little mews in her throat that echoed in his brain, in his gut.

Queenie felt a tingle that began in her lips and turned to a throb lower, where she had not known she could feel a response. Then his tongue parted her lips and she stopped wondering at the new feelings and wondered if her legs would hold her up. She need not have worried, for Harry was lifting her, carrying her to one of the chairs, to his lap. She stopped thinking altogether when his hand reached for her breast.

One kiss? One maelstrom, rather, one earthquake, one whirlpool swirling their attraction and affection and admiration into another world, another level, where wits went begging and hearts begged for more.

One kiss.

One of his hands reached down to raise her skirts.

One bark from the dog.

One small boy cleared his throat. "I brung the biscuits, ma'am."

Harry proved what a fine gentleman he was by not strangling Charlie, kicking the dog, or flinging the female over his shoulder and carrying her out the door. He raised her to her feet instead, got unsteadily to his own, and adjusted his neckcloth, which had somehow come unknotted.

Queenie swayed, breathing as if she had run from Land's End to Lincolnshire. "I was, ah, checking his lordship's shoulder. His wound appears to be healing well."

Charlie did not bother acknowledging the lie. He opened the bakery sack and pulled out a biscuit for the dog. He stared at the two adults, one more red-faced than the other, but only because Madame Lescartes had more chafes from Lord Harking's whiskers.

"I suppose I should be going, then," Harry said, ashamed, embarrassed, wanting to apologize, but to the lady or the boy, he did not know. He did not regret the kiss. Hell, he regretted more not locking the doors. But it was wrong and the only way he could make it less wrong was by leaving.

This time he made it to the exit, prodded by the glare of an ancient ten-year-old's disappointed eyes. Afraid of what he would see in his *chérie*'s blue eyes, he bowed, said he would call on the morrow, and finally left. He did not even kick at the first lamppost he passed. The second one, though, felt all of his fury and frustration and total befuddlement.

He limped all the way back to his hotel.

CHAPTER NINETEEN

"**Y**ou told me I had to tell the truth, always."

Queenie looked into Charlie's accusing eyes and felt tears come to her own. The boy had so little, and now she had stolen his trust, too. "Sometimes the truth is not so obvious as all that. Sometimes, it is hard for even an adult to know what is true or false."

"You said you wouldn't be the governor's light-o'-love."

That was not light. It was a conflagration. If not for the boy and the dog, Queenie knew she might have followed the flame right to the shop's front floor, or Harry's hotel. And enjoyed it, for as long as the affair lasted or until she burned to cinders. She could already taste the cinders in her mouth, thinking of what the boy might have seen or heard.

"You should not have eavesdropped," she said. Heaven knew that was a minor breach compared to her own transgressions, but Queenie had to tell Charlie something. She was supposed to be his mentor, his teacher. Oh, dear.

"I wanted to know what that Robin Redbreast wanted."

She sank into one of the chairs. "You heard that, too?"

"I clumb over the back fence and sneaked in the back door. You lied to the Runner, asides."

"I—" she began.

"You said you met Miss Pittipat in the park."

"Miss Pettigrew."

"But she calls you cousin sometimes."

"We are not cousins. I swear that. It is a pet name, only." Like *chérie*, unless she truly was Lord Harking's sweetheart. Queenie was having trouble concentrating on Charlie and not her own concerns. But he *was* her responsibility, too. She combed her fingers through her disordered curls, hoping for a more dignified look, despite her swollen lips. "Do you understand?"

"I ken Miss Pittipat says it when she forgets and starts to say somethin' like *queer,* or *question.*"

"That is *Pettigrew,* for heaven's sake. She is the one who barely recalls her name, not you, so you cannot be surprised when she misspeaks."

Charlie scuffed his new shoes on the floor, looking down, not talking.

"You think she means to call me something like *Queenie,* then?"

He nodded. "The mort they are all looking for."

Queenie sighed. "You want the truth?"

"You said it was a command."

"A commandment, Charlie, from the Bible." She leaned her aching head back against the chair rail. "Very well. But I cannot tell you everything, for that would put you in harm's way, too."

Charlie had lived his entire life at the edge of danger. Knowledge made a chap safer. "Better to know who's lookin' over your shoulder than to find his knife in your belly."

Queenie shuddered at the image, but went on. "There is no longer such a person as Queenie Dennis, the woman they seek. There never was, really. She was made up years ago, like a fairy story. I tried to erase her, to cause less pain for that family looking for her. Some of the other people searching for her do not mean her well. Or me, for knowing about her. They are evil, Charlie, desperate to keep themselves from the hangman's noose, so Queenie Dennis is far better off dead and buried in France."

"I wouldn't let no one hurt you. Me and Parfait can look out for you, 'stead of Lord Harking."

"Thank you, but it is too dangerous for all of us. I would be horrified if harm came to you, or Parfait, because of me. Soon I will tell the truth to the right people, when they come to London. They will protect us all, I hope."

"But you ain't sure?"

She shook her head, not willing to tell the child one more lie. "Meantime, I am an orphan, just like you."

"For true this time?"

"That is what they told me."

Charlie took a biscuit from the sack and held it out to Queenie, which she took to mean she was partly forgiven. She accepted it, despite her dry mouth and tear-choked throat. Parfait came and put his muzzle in her lap, so she shared, taking comfort in the big dog's warmth and uncritical affection, especially when he had a treat. While he ate, she stroked his curly head, ignoring the crumbs on her skirt.

Charlie pulled out another biscuit, one with a raspberry center. "They told me I was born under a cabbage leaf."

"How is a child to know?" Queenie asked, more of herself than the boy. "And how is a grown woman supposed to know what is right?"

"You had a mum to teach you," Charlie said, wiping

crumbs away from his mouth with his sleeve, leaving a red streak across his lips and his shirt. "I never did."

"Yes, I was fortunate. I had a woman who called herself my mother. She taught me needlework, so I have a living. She taught me manners, so I can deal with my customers. She hired tutors and instructors so that I could advance in the world, knowing as much as my poor brain could hold. But she lied, too."

"Go on with you. She never."

"She did. And now I do not know who I am anymore."

"You ain't no light-skirts."

"No. I am not that. And I swear to you I shall not be."

"That's all right and tight then, 'cause we can keep the shop 'stead of hidin' out in a cottage in some woods."

Queenie was touched that Charlie would go with her wherever she went. On the other hand, she now had to plan to take him with her wherever she went, except to prison. Perhaps Lord Harking would take in the boy, find him a place on his estate. "What about Mr. Rourke, the Runner?" she asked.

Charlie made a rude noise. Queenie was going to have to do something about his manners soon, and those of Parfait, who was nosing about for more food.

Indignant, Charlie asked, "What, you think I would peach on you to Bow Street, after you took me in and all?"

"He would pay you handsomely for what you said about Miss Pettigrew."

"You pays me enough. Money ain't everything, you know."

She stood up and brushed out her skirts. Then she pulled Charlie close and hugged his thin shoulders, ignoring the raspberry stains that would get on her gown. "I do know. And you have repaid me tenfold."

*   *   *

The day had been a vampire, sucking the life from Queenie. She was exhausted, despite the hour being far earlier than her usual bedtime. She should have stayed up sewing or sketching or going over her accounts in preparation for a busy day at the shop tomorrow, especially after missing so much work today. Instead she was simply too drained by the day's events: the hectic morning at the store, then Lady Jennifer's gathering, Hellen's hysteria, Rourke's interrogation, and Charlie's accusations.

And Harry, always Harry, Lord Harking, a man she thought even misanthropic Molly might come to adore. He was softhearted and gentle, and hard where it mattered. In his principles, of course. So what was she going to do about him, besides get her heart broken?

If it wasn't too late.

It was too late to worry about it tonight. She would have the rest of her life for that, anyway.

Queenie wanted nothing more than to collapse onto her bed, in her clothes if she could not manage to undo the tapes and ties and fastenings of her gown without a struggle. Then again, if the gown came apart as easily as that, poor Charlie might have been shocked worse.

The only good thing Queenie saw about being so tired was that maybe she would fall asleep without endlessly reliving a single one of the day's nightmares, and stay asleep without any of her usual nightmares, either. Whenever she was sorely troubled, she had come to learn, her dreams had her falling, tumbling downward, crying out for help that did not arrive. Perhaps tonight she would be too tired to care if she fell, landing shattered at the bottom of whatever crevice beckoned. Oblivion might be welcome if no one came to her aid.

Lord Harking would come if she called out to him. Oh, he would come like a knight on a white charger, a hero from a storybook, stalwart, ready to take on any dragon for his damsel in distress. How many cavaliers got cooked in their armor by the fire-breathing fiend?

In her weariness, Queenie wondered if he could hear her in her dreams, if true soul mates knew each other's hopes and fears, as the poets declared. She was being foolish, of course. Harry merely wanted to keep her safe, at his side. He wanted her, period, which might have been a fine dream, a lovely fairy tale, or a new nightmare in her life.

She hoped she might at least be able to rest without recalling Harry's kiss, which would have kept her awake, tossing in her blankets for something she could not name and could not have.

Despite her fatigue, she managed to undo her clothes. She washed quickly and changed into her nightgown. Her short curls needed nothing more than a quick brushing and a glance in the mirror at the roots, which were still dark, thank goodness. She crawled under her covers, more than ready for this day to end.

Parfait whined.

She sighed and patted the mattress beside her. "Very well, you can come onto the bed."

But the dog was not making those mournful cries. Likely Parfait was still below with Charlie, having biscuits for supper, proving what a poor provider Queenie was, on top of her other sins. No, the sniffs and sighs Queenie could hear all too well were coming from the second, smaller bedroom, Hellen's chamber.

"Hellen, are you still awake? Are you well?" Queenie called, desperately not wanting to get up again.

"Nooo," came back through the thin walls.

No, she was asleep, or no, she was ill? Maybe Hellen was simply having a nightmare of her own. Queenie waited, but the whimpers grew louder.

Either way, Queenie had to drag herself up to find out. She pulled a blanket around her shoulders rather than finding her robe, and went barefoot to the hall, shielding her candle.

Hellen had not taken the laudanum, had not been asleep, and had not recovered from Officer Rourke's visit. Now she was splotch-faced and sobbing, huddled in her bed like a sack of rags left out in the rain.

"Everything is ruined," she wailed when Queenie trailed into her room.

"No, I think I satisfied Officer Rourke for now." Queenie set down the candle and carefully explained again what she had told the Runner about their meeting in the park, hoping Hellen could remember it. She also made up a story about why Hellen called her cousin on occasion, in case anyone else had heard or noticed. "We became close friends, that is all. And *Madame Lescartes* is too formal, while *Denise* is too familiar for an employee. Besides, we can say your mother feels better letting people believe we are related, rather than your going into trade working for a stranger."

"Mama will kill me for not telling her it's you."

"But Ize might kill her if he thought she'd go to Bow Street."

Hellen sniffled and blew her nose into the handkerchief Queenie had thought to bring, Hellen's own being sodden already.

"But that's not all."

Queenie had not thought it was. They had been over this ground often enough that even Hellen understood the peril.

"Can we not discuss the rest in the morning? It has been a trying day for me, also."

"No matter," Hellen wailed. "Nothing will be different in the morning! He won't marry me then, either."

Queenie sank onto the side of Hellen's mattress, shoving her over. "John George? Mr. Browne?"

"Who else, silly?"

Queenie's mind was too tired to make sense of Hellen's anguish. "What, was he going to marry you tonight?"

"He wanted to, I know it. No, I do not mean get a special license or run off to Gretna Green this very evening, but he was going to ask, for certain. He invited me to have dinner with his parents at their inn in the country Sunday after church."

"Excellent. You see, that must mean his intentions are honorable. You have nothing to worry about."

"He is an honorable man. His intentions were never anything else. But now he will never come up to scratch."

"Of course he will. He loves you. I have never seen a man so smitten." Queenie patted Hellen's hand in reassurance. There, now she could go back to bed.

Hellen wailed when Queenie stood up and reached for the candle. "No, he will not marry me. He will not be permitted to."

"Nonsense. His parents will be glad to have such a beautiful, well-mannered daughter-in-law, the perfect wife for a schoolmaster. You will charm the parents and patrons and make the students feel welcome. You can help the girls learn about fashions, if they are to be trained as ladies' maids. Mr. Browne's parents are sure to give their blessings."

"They are not the problem!"

If not anxious about meeting her prospective in-laws, Hellen must be in a fidge over money. Mr. Browne would never be as wealthy as a titled gentleman—or as casual in his affairs, thank goodness.

Queenie tried to sound encouraging. "You know your mother went to fetch back a dowry, and the baron has never refused her anything." Except a wedding license, of course. "Mr. Browne seemed pleased by that, happy that he can support you in the manner you deserve until he advances in his career. And I shall provide your trousseau, so he will not have to pay for your bride clothes, either. You are a bargain, my dear, one he will be eager to snap up."

Hellen kept whining. "But that was when I was a baron's daughter, even from the wrong side of the blanket. I was never a liar and a cheat!"

Queenie was ready to throw her blanket over Hellen's head and smother the impossible chit. "What, have you been seeing other men?"

That stopped the whimpers, at least. "Of course not. But John George is bound to find out when that awful Runner uncovers the truth."

Ah, the truth. There was that, again. Queenie pulled the cover closer around her own shoulders. "If Mr. Browne was willing to accept you as your mother's daughter"—and a bastard, besides, although Queenie did not say the last aloud—"what makes you think he will change his mind over a few mistruths and misdirections?"

"Because the people we are lying to are his employers, you goose! They paid for his very education and gave him a position of authority at the new academy. Without their notice, he would be back in the country helping his father and brother with their acres, or minding that dilapidated inn. He owes Lord Carde his loyalty, and Captain Jack, too, who started the school."

"They do not have to know—" Queenie started.

"If I told John George the truth, the way a proper wife should, he would have to tell them. And if I do not tell him, and they find out, he will lose his position."

"I do not see why he should be dismissed. Why would they blame him for what he could not possibly know?"

"And you are supposed to be so smart! Well, you are not, Queenie, not in the ways of the world. The earl and his brother won't want one of your friends associated with their school, one who did not come forward when they asked. They would never trust me, or John George, no matter what they decide about you."

"I intend to—"

"But not until you have to. And then it might be too late."

"Fustian. A man owes his wife loyalty, too. Everyone understands that. And if the Endicotts are so harsh and cruel and condemning"—she shuddered, even in her blanket, thinking of her own confrontation with the noble family—"then your Mr. Browne will be better off in another position."

"But Lord Carde was his benefactor! How will John George find a decent post without references from the earl? You know that will be impossible."

"Difficult, not impossible. But you shall have your dowry to live on until he finds a school that suits."

"That money was meant to find us a tiny house of our own here in London, for when we have a family, away from the students and the school. Besides, John George would be too proud to live on his wife's fortune, not that the dowry will amount to much anyway, knowing the baron."

Queenie sighed. "Then you can live at his parents' inn until he finds something else. I know he is close to his family. They will adore you and you will like them."

Hellen wailed. "They are farmers and tap keepers. You

know how I like the city and pretty gowns and parties. How will I live in a deserted inn set amid turnips and cabbages and cows? I have hardly been out of London in my life."

"If you love him . . ."

"But he won't love me any longer if I cost him his dreams."

"Of course he will. Mr. Browne is not the inconstant type. That is one of the things you said you admired about him, how steady and straightforward he is."

"But what if I do not love him enough to live with his old mother and dwindle into a dowdy rustic drab?"

"Then perhaps you should not marry the man no matter what, if you have such doubts."

Hellen started crying again.

So did Queenie.

Men did not cry, of course. They kicked and cursed and drank themselves into oblivion.

Nothing worked for Harry, especially not his numb toes.

He sat in his empty hotel room with a bottle in his hand, his feet in a tub of cold water, all out of swearwords. The place was elegantly appointed, and as cold and empty as he felt. He wanted his own books, his comfortable worn chair, his faded robe, his Stubbs paintings on the wall. Instead he had polished wood, gleaming mirrors, velvet hangings, and still lifes of fruit that scores of strangers had gazed at.

Harry wanted to go home.

He wanted Madame Denise Lescartes, whoever, whatever, she was.

He could not have either tonight, only another swallow of brandy.

A few minutes later, he went back to cursing.

Damn, he was a man of honor, above all else. He had devoted most of his life to upholding that honor because he cared. He believed in it and in himself. He knew what he owed his title, his lands, his ancestors, and his heirs.

His father had dragged the family name through the gutters, and Harry had sworn to wash away the stains. His mother had been a harlot, and Harry had promised himself to wed a female above reproach.

All his life he had acted as he believed he ought, making up for those who came before. He was a dutiful, respectful man, correct to a fault, some might say, but Harry had chosen that path for himself, and trodden it with satisfaction.

Now he was not satisfied, not by half. He would not be satisfied if he lowered his burning loins into that cold water at his feet. He might never be satisfied again. His bed was empty, true, but so were his arms . . . and his endless future.

And for what? The good opinion of people whose regard mattered not a whit? Who were no better than they ought to be, and often a great deal worse? Why did he have to uphold higher standards than everyone else—and what about his own happiness?

He supposed he could eventually find a decent woman to wed, one who would be suitable as his viscountess, accepted in his country circles, welcome to polite society when they visited London. She would be faithful and fecund, filling his nursery, performing her duty as he was performing his.

Oh, hell.

That is what it would be. Hell.

Men did not cry. Except on the inside.

CHAPTER TWENTY

John George Browne did not rescind his invitation to Hellen to take Sunday dinner with his parents. He wanted them to see what a fine young woman she was, no matter her background. There might be questions ahead, Queenie thought, but he seemed absolutely certain now.

Instead, he extended the invite to include the others. His mother loved cooking and having company at the inn, the more the merrier, Mr. Browne swore, and his brothers would like to meet Lord Harking, to discuss his farming methods. His sisters and sisters-in-law, he was positive, would be in raptures at meeting Madame Lescartes, the fashionable dressmaker.

Queenie hesitated about accepting, but not for long. Hellen needed her support, and Queenie needed a day away from the shop. Since Rourke's visit, she had been furiously finishing gowns, sketching new designs to sell to the fashion journal, taking orders. She was filling her coffers as fast as she could, in case she had to flee London or hire a barrister.

Sunday was the day of rest anyway. Queenie could think of no better way to spend it than in the country, away from London, away from her daytime chores and her nighttime worries. She could find no finer escape . . . except spending the day with Harry.

Lord Harking accepted, so Queenie accepted. The viscount had not spoken of leaving for his own home, and Queenie did not ask. He had stopped at the store every day, bringing bouquets and bonbons, taking tea with the customers, but never taking liberties. Part of Queenie was disappointed, but the other part celebrated his unquestioning, undemanding affection. One more day in his company, safely among others, would be a treasured memory in years to come. Like her coins, it would be there to see her through whatever tomorrow brought.

Queenie had one more reason for making the trip past Richmond: She wanted to see the Brownes' inn's resident patient for herself. Phelan Sloane had set so many lives on end, surely he would have horns and a red tail and a forked tongue. That was what Queenie told herself, anyway, that she was simply curious.

Sunday dawned bright, thank goodness, but cool. Harry arrived driving a rented curricle with gold wheels, pulled by a pair of highbred bays. He took a thrilled Charlie up behind the driving seat as his tiger, while the groom from the livery stable held the horses' heads.

A closed coach followed. Queenie headed for that.

"What," Harry asked, stepping down, "you would rather sit inside on such a glorious morning? But I wanted to show off my prowess, like the coxcomb I am. I can't dance like the London chaps, can't recite verses to your eyebrow or serenade you worth a tinker's damn. But I can drive to an inch. I swear not to overturn us, *chérie*."

Queenie eyed the light curricle with dismay, the restless horses with horror. "No, I do not like spirited horses or fast equipages. This one looks fragile, besides."

"Nonsense, I inspected every spoke and spring myself, and tried out the bays' paces. They are such sweet goers, I am thinking of purchasing them. Besides, you would not want to ride with Miss Pettigrew and Browne and ruin their pleasure in a little bit of privacy, would you?"

Parfait was already in the hired carriage, acting as sole chaperone. Instead of paying attention to his charges, though, he had his head out the window, nose sniffing the air. Hellen and Browne would not welcome Queenie.

"Do you know, I think I am not feeling at all the thing? Perhaps I should stay behind, resting quietly at home."

"Craven, the formidable Madame Lescartes who traveled to France and back and forged her own fate? I do not believe it." Without a by-your-leave, Harry lifted her right off her feet and up to the—far too high—bench. He was strong enough to manage her weight without effort, and mean enough, she thought, not to notice her trembling.

"Cold?" he asked, the dastard, tucking a lap robe over her knees and repositioning the hot bricks at her feet. Then the groom jumped back, Harry flicked the whip over the horses' ears, Charlie whooped, and they were off.

Trying to maintain her balance and her breakfast, Queenie kept her eyes closed, both hands clenched around the seat rail beside her. They did not collide with another vehicle, though, crash into a building, or collapse into splinters as they left London proper.

Eventually, Queenie had to open her eyes, just to see how far they had come and how much longer the torture would last. The horses were keeping a steady pace, the curricle was hardly swaying, and Harry was laughing. Now she knew he was touched in the upper works.

Without looking at the horses or the scenery or the ground rushing past, she stared at him, shaking her head. He was obviously glad to be out of the stifling confines of the city, with its crowds and congestion. He wore no hat, letting the breeze ruffle his brown waves. His muscular thigh, pressed so closely against Queenie's on the narrow driving bench, was encased in buckskin, like that of the country gentleman he was. If his lordship was not the finest whip in the country—and how could Queenie tell?—he might be the happiest. He talked to the horses, joked with Charlie, called out to riders passing the other way. She could see he was reveling in the horses, delighting in the speed and his own skill. His cheeks were rosy and his lips never lost their smile, not even when a flock of sheep blocked the road.

From the following carriage, Parfait barked at the herding dog trying to gather the stragglers. Queenie almost offered to get down and help—not that she had any intention of stepping foot in the curricle again—but Harry reached for her hand, prying it from the rail and bringing it to his lips.

"Isn't this glorious?"

She could only look into his laughing brown eyes. "Yes, glorious."

As they moved on, thankfully a bit slower now that the horses were not so fresh, Queenie felt her cares slip away in the light of his enjoyment of the day, the drive, and her company. Other than the cold chill in the air, Queenie had nothing to think about now except the countryside, the coming dinner, and her companion. The day would have been perfect, despite the horses, except for one cloud on her horizon.

"I do not see why you had to invite Mr. Rourke to accompany us."

The Runner had called at the shop the previous day to check the spellings of some of the names Queenie had given him, of other dressmakers where she had, in fact, applied for positions, where she had laid rumor trails about another English seamstress. He or his messengers would be kept busy, and would be convinced that Madame Denise Lescartes spoke the truth as she knew it. She had been careful again to say that the whole story was nothing but hearsay. They would find that true, too.

Hellen had blushingly claimed that she was too busy to answer any more questions, since she was in a swivet getting ready to meet her possible new family, the Brownes, at their inn. She had to decide on the proper gown and the suitable hairstyle to make the right impression, didn't she? And did Mr. Rourke think it mannerly for her to bring a gift?

The Runner thought he would ask the peagoose his questions another time. Meanwhile, Rourke hinted that he usually checked on Mr. Phelan Sloane once a month, in case the unfortunate fellow remembered anything more about the coach tragedy so long ago, or wanted to cleanse his soul with another confession. Mostly, Rourke told the others, part of his job was making certain Phelan Sloane could cause no further trouble, scandal, or upset for Lord Carde and his countess, Sloane's sister. The Runner looked straight at Queenie and said, "I always do my job."

That was when Harry invited him to come along in the hired coach, with Browne's permission. The journey was tiring, time-consuming, and expensive without a gentleman's carriage, so Rourke promptly accepted. At least he had the courtesy to sit up with the driver, so Hellen's day was not ruined.

Queenie's nearly was. She looked back to see the investigator watching their rig, almost as if they were going to try to outrun him and escape. She shivered. "He could have visited the Brownes another day."

"But I wanted him to see we had nothing to fear."

Harry's "we" warmed Queenie as no blanket or hot brick could.

She vowed to put the Runner from her mind. He had his reasons for coming to the inn; Queenie had her own. They were not the same.

She expected the Brownes' establishment to be run-down and ramshackle, from Hellen's description. After all, the reason Lord Carde placed Phelan Sloane here was that the inn had practically been abandoned as a coaching stop when the new toll road took a different route. The Brownes needed an income aside from their farming acres, and the instigator of the crimes needed a secure sanctuary.

Sloane might be slime, a slug, and more than half insane, but he was still Lord Carde's brother-in-law. The earl made sure his beloved wife's brother lived like a gentleman. He might not be free to drive to the village, borrow a horse, or stroll past the front gate anywhere unaccompanied, John George explained, but Mr. Sloane's surroundings were genteel, a far cry from what he would find at a lunatic asylum, or a jail.

In fact, with the earl's assistance, the Browne family had refurbished their inn into a kind of convalescent hospital, the profitable kind. They had no medicinal waters, no hot baths, no scores of hovering physicians. They did have healthy fresh air, good plain cooking, and enough eyes to make sure none of their "guests" wandered off. Whereas the distance from London and Richmond had caused the inn to fail, cer-

tain members of society were delighted to place their embarrassing relations so far out of sight.

Browne warned them to bow to Lady Fishkill's decades-
dead husband, present only in the old lady's mind's eye, and
to avert their glances when Lord Rothmore raised his nightshirt. As for Mr. Bushnell, well, he was usually locked in his
room when company came.

"Nervous?" Harry asked when the inn came into sight
over a slight rise in the road. Queenie was clasping the hand
rail again.

Not about the lunatics, she was not.

The inn was freshly painted, prosperous looking, with
sheep grazing in the distance past fields almost ready for
spring planting. She relaxed as much as she was able, finding comfort in the peaceful, bucolic scene. "What a lovely
place. It is no wonder people come here to . . . recuperate. I
had not realized how much I missed the countryside."

Harry sorely knew how much he missed his own estate,
although drives like this almost made up for not riding his
own fields. He had never realized that the woman beside
him, so elegant and polished, might enjoy rural life. He
knew better than to ask which area of the country, or of
France, she recalled so fondly. She would only prevaricate
or avoid the question as she always did when her background was mentioned, saying her family traveled a great
deal or some such, her mother seeking employment.

So he did not ask. Better to be ignorant than lied to, he
had decided one long, sleepless night. She would trust him
with the truth when she was able, he had also decided, re-
solving to wait as patiently as he could. He had slowly restored his family reputation, his fortune, and his fields. He
would restore the woman's faith in mankind, see if he did
not. And he would not go home until he did, simply because

he would spend every waking minute worrying about her, wondering if she was safe, or was entertaining another man who was less worthy of her.

Home would not be home, Harry told himself, with Madame Lescartes left alone in London. So that was what he had decided to do about the conundrum of his *chérie:* win her confidence. As a friend. Nothing else was possible, but he would have that, by Jupiter.

Their welcome at the inn was loud and noisy, and obviously well-meant. All of the Brownes gathered to meet the guests and make them feel at home, but especially their successful young scholar's chosen lady.

John George was a favorite of his sisters and brothers, nieces and nephews. They were all prepared to love whatever female he brought into the family. They were not Hellen's usual kind of acquaintance, but she thrived on their acceptance, and on John George's pleasure in introducing her. Queenie was relieved to see that her friend made a fine impression; the Brownes, in turn, impressed Queenie.

They were kind and accepting, with no hint of censure about Hellen's parents, or Charlie's. Queenie's street urchin was congratulated on his job as tiger, and hurried off with two older boys to tend to "his" horses before dinner.

Of course they were tolerant, Queenie thought. People who took murderers and maniacs into their home had to be more forgiving than most, and what was the stain of bastardy compared to that fat man in the corner who was wearing a bedsheet like a toga?

She would never recall all the names and faces, but they were obviously a close-knit family, with infants being passed from shoulder to shoulder, toddlers asking for horsey rides from whatever adult was handiest. Everyone helped serve the delicious meal at long plank tables in the inn's common room, even the strapping Browne sons carrying heavy platters piled high with food. Everyone looked out for the deaf old auntie, the invalid in the bath chair who needed to be spoon-fed, and the thin woman who refused to eat anything on her plate that was not white.

There were toasts to the guests, and Harry made a lovely salute to the hosts on behalf of the visitors. There were glasses raised to Hellen and John George, which might have become ribald had Mrs. Browne not cleared her throat. "Not in front of the children. And we shall not embarrass our John George's dear Miss Pettigrew."

As if Hellen could be put to the blush by a racy remark, after knowing her mother and her mother's friends. Queenie liked Mrs. Browne the better for the thought, and liked how Hellen would fit in with this lively, laughing group.

She, herself, would not. She moved the food around her plate; she sipped at her wine; she smiled at the gentle jokes. She answered questions passed her way across the table, as vaguely as possible.

She might have been eating rocks and drinking rat poison, in a den of scorpions.

Never in her entire life, not with Molly and not since— unless one counted the orphanage she could not recall, where she assumed they had crowded communal meals— had Queenie been part of a large family gathering. Unlike at the opera or the Cyprian's Ball, everyone here knew everyone else, or was related.

Harry fitted in, talking of farming concerns to the brothers and Mr. Browne, eating as if he had not had a meal in days, to Mrs. Browne's joy. Hellen was the center of attraction and glorying in it. Charlie was almost too excited to eat, elated at the plans to show him his very first piglets and chicks, alive and loose, that was. Parfait was stationed beneath the thin lady's chair, eating green beans and orange carrots and red meat.

Even Rourke seemed at home, from all the times he had visited.

Queenie was the outsider. She had no family, none of the sense of belonging the Brownes and their resident guests shared, no easy camaraderie with strangers. She was jealous of the warmth and caring she had never known and might never—but she was also in a near panic, the same as when she had to sit beside Harry on the high seat of his curricle, behind the prancing horses.

There were so many people laughing and talking at once, so many people who had lives without secrets, that Queenie turned cold again, despite the tiny beads of perspiration forming on her forehead. She was nothing but the pale, shy little girl she once was, cowering if she had to leave her house, hiding behind Molly and her books. How could she be comfortable now, when half her life had been spent listening to—and believing—Molly's lectures about never speaking to strangers, never telling anything about her personal life, never trusting anyone?

They wanted to know about her, these nice, decent people, and she could barely speak the lies. If not for Harry sitting beside her, she would have fled. She would walk back to London if she had to, to her own little nest above the shop, where she could hide until she had to be Madame Denise Lescartes again.

She could not ruin the others' enjoyment, though, and she could not disappoint Harry. He thought she was brave, which was perhaps the biggest lie she was living.

She trusted Harry, Queenie kept telling herself. She might not trust him with all of her secrets, for his own protection, but she knew he would not let her drown in this sea of strangers.

He kept looking at her and smiling. He touched her hand once, passing a platter. He frowned in concern at how her knuckles were white on the fork and knife she used to cut her meal into little, barely eaten pieces. She took another swallow and smiled back, for him. Under cover of the table he patted her thigh, which almost succeeded in taking her mind off the others.

Besides, she had to smile and laugh and look happy. Rourke was watching her.

The Runner appeared to be concentrating on his meal and the woman sitting beside him, one of the Browne cousins, Queenie thought. Yet his eyes kept coming back to her, not Harry beside her, or the man he had come to see. Rourke's gaze was piercing, looking behind the modest gown she had donned for the Brownes, beyond her use of less face paint. Queenie feared he could see right to her quaking knees, her trembling toes, the sawdust in her throat, and the butterflies in her stomach. He knew she was a fake.

She laughed and flirted with the bearded patriarch, Mr. Joseph Jacob Browne, at her other side.

He blushed. Harry dropped his fork. Rourke looked away.   •

She was a good fake, at least.

CHAPTER TWENTY-ONE

One person at the tables did not bother pretending to be enjoying himself. A slender, middle-aged man spoke to no one but the woman at his side, John George's sister Mary Jane. He ate and he drank, but he did not laugh and he did not seem to be aware of the cheerful conversations around him. Queenie had not met him before dinner, but his identity was obvious, even from the distance between his place and hers, across the large room. He was dressed finer than any of the other men, including Harry, who was talking to the woman on his other side, a very obviously enceinte Browne relation.

The thin man had light-colored, receding hair, amid the sandy-haired Brownes. She could not tell the color of his eyes from here, nor if they had a madman's glitter to them. From her seat, the man did not seem demonic, only aloof and somewhat arrogant. "Phelan Sloane."

John George's father heard the name she had not meant to utter aloud. He looked toward where she was gazing.

"Aye, that's our Mr. Sloane. You might have heard he is

some kind of ogre. Everyone has, no matter that the earl tried to keep that ugliness quiet. But he does fine here. Polite, soft-spoken, never gave us a bit of trouble until now."

Sloane did not appear to be in a rant or a rage. Queenie doubted they would let him sit to dinner with the family if he was wont to throw food . . . or carving knives. "Now?"

"It's our Mary Jane." Joseph Browne raised his glass of ale toward his youngest daughter, who was leaning closer to Sloane, as if they were alone in the room. "Our gal is good for him, no matter what my wife says."

"She does not think Mary Jane should be assisting him?"

Mr. Browne's brow was furrowed as he watched Mary Jane and Sloane. "Mrs. Browne is afraid."

"He is dangerous, then?" Queenie could not decide if she should call for her dog, Charlie, Hellen, or Harry. All of them, to get them to safety, she decided. The man who would hire a highwayman to waylay a coach was capable of anything. She was halfway out of her chair when the elder Mr. Browne guffawed.

"Not that kind of dangerous, not anymore. And not with the soothing tisanes my wife brews him or the careful eye my boys keep on him. He's more a threat to our girl's reputation than anything," he confided in Queenie. He might have spoken of family matters because Queenie was a woman of the world and he wanted her opinion, or because the entire family, and the neighborhood, were already giving their own opinions. The older man might simply have been afraid Queenie would throw out lures to him if he did not make conversation with the dashing Frenchwoman. "He only wants Mary Jane on his walks, only wants Mary Jane to read to him at night when he can't sleep and has bad dreams. "

"So Mrs. Browne does not think he will hurt Mary Jane."

"Nary a bit. She's afraid of what the neighbors will say, them together so much, away from the others. I stopped asking where they go on their walks, I did. Better that way. But the boys don't like it much. Their little sister, you know."

Queenie had never known a brother's protectiveness. "What does Mary Jane think?"

"Oh, she comes back from the strolls smiling. She always did say he was better'n the cream what rises on the fresh milk, only a touch confused. She gave up being Lady Carde's maid to tend him, don't you know, and she was a fancy London abigail afore that. Turned down the blacksmith's boy, too, onct she came home."

"Perhaps she feels sorry for Sloane?" Queenie could not, knowing what he had done, but she was not a forgiving soul, and her life had been too deeply affected by the man's actions to forget.

"Mebbe. Mebbe. Still, there's no saying but that our girl does keep Mr. Sloane on an even keel. The doctors the earl sends all agree to that. We had to dose him with laudanum the time she went off to visit my sister in Bath. And he frets if she goes into the village on calls with my wife."

"How fortunate he is to have her to look after him."

Mr. Browne nodded his head in agreement. He leaned closer. "I mean to speak to Lord Carde about that very thing when he comes next to visit. No reason they cannot get hitched, I say. Fix my gal's reputation, a ring would."

"But is he . . . that is, would such a marriage be quite legal if the groom is not in his right head?"

"Who is going to care if it makes the both of them happy? Asides, he's as sane as you or me and the Earl of

Carde combined most of the time. And it's not as if we'd be asking any settlements or such over what the earl already pays to keep Mr. Sloane with us. All we'd want is that scrap of paper that makes our Mary Jane a wife, not a nursemaid what takes care of a gentleman's needs, if you get my drift." He took another swallow of his ale. "Not that a gal of mine is fast, don't you know, but people will talk."

Queenie well knew all about gossip and rumor and scandal. She was presumed to be Harry's fancy piece, after all. She doubted Mr. Browne would be speaking of such matters otherwise, and unless he had swallowed more than his share of the potent brew. Queenie felt uncomfortable again, but Harry was debating children's names with the pregnant woman. She was going to need a name for her infant any instant, it seemed, so Queenie could not interrupt.

Mr. Browne was still watching his daughter and Phelan Sloane, a worried look still on his bearded face, despite the ale. "If the earl gives his blessings, we'll all be happier, I swear. My wife, my girl, and Mr. Sloane, too."

Queenie knew too much about the man's past to trust him with anything sharper than a butter knife, or more valuable than a hairpin, much less a beloved daughter. "You truly do not worry for your daughter's safety?"

Mr. Browne passed her a slice of apple he had peeled. "He loves her."

"He loved the former countess, too, they say. Loved her to death." The woman's coach had fallen off the road, killing her and her servants, all because Phelan Sloane had hired a thug to stop it. Everyone knew that, so Queenie was not speaking out of turn.

"He never meant to hurt the woman, though. She was his own cousin."

"She was also married to the previous Lord Carde.

Sloane might have felt that the earl should not have her if he, himself, could not."

Browne shook his head. "No. I never could believe that, not and have the man under my roof, no matter how much Lord Carde pays me. Asides, if he'd set out to do Lady Carde harm, he wouldn't be so torn up he'd try to kill himself, would he?"

Queenie had not heard that, about any suicide attempts. The Endicotts must have closed ranks to keep it from the on-dit columns. "I do not know what is in the mind of one such as he."

"No one does, ma'am. No one does. He did tell us that he only wanted the lady to stay with him a bit longer, that was all. And that's another reason he and our Mary Jane should get buckled. If he's married to the girl, he won't worry that she'll find another beau. One less worry for his troubled mind, don't you know."

Mary Jane did seem attentive to the gentleman, leaning close to him, passing him this choice cut of meat, that favorite dish. The former ladies' maid did not have to stay here, not with her references and experience, so she must like the man, Queenie reasoned. Maybe she really did want to marry him, even knowing what he had done. "Love is strange."

Mr. Browne brought his glass to his lips again. "I'll drink to that."

After the meal the tables were pushed back. Most of the invalids—"We call them infirm," Mr. Browne told Queenie—were taken up to their rooms or outside for some air. Some of the younger men went into the taproom for a game of darts, and many of the children went off to show Charlie and Parfait the farm animals. John George and Hellen were going to visit the vicar, while Harry went with Mr. Browne to look at a prize ram. Harry looked toward Queenie, as if seeking her permission to leave her alone, but both he and the older man seemed eager to step through fields of manure, so Queenie said she would be fine in the house. So would her new half boots.

The women cleaned up.

Queenie would have helped, but Mrs. Browne refused. "You are company, ma'am. And work hard enough, John George tells us. You sit."

Queenie did for a while, listening to the soon-to-be mother waver between *Jason Henry* and *Julian Robert, Joyce Ann* and *Elizabeth Jo,* while a pair of moppets played with their dolls nearby. Queenie decided to sew up some clothes for the toys when she got back to Town, and a gown for the new infant, as a thank-you for the hospitality shown to her. The children ran off to another game, and the breeding Mrs. Browne—Queenie never did catch her first name, or names—fell asleep.

For all practical purposes, she was left alone, except for Mr. Phelan Sloane, sitting in the corner where Mary Jane Browne had left him. He kept watching the door to the kitchens, one hand twitching slightly.

Up close she could see that his hair was darker than that of the woman in the portrait at The Red and the Black and the colored reward notices, and very straight where it was not gone altogether. His complexion was pale, his physique thin and narrow, like the murdered countess's. His eyes were blue like hers, but a faded, watered blue, not the vibrant blue Lady Carde was said to have passed on to her daughter.

His eyes were nothing like Queenie's own, either.

She curtsied in front of him. He nodded politely, but looked past her.

"Sir," she said softly, lest she wake the sleeping woman, and because this was why she had come. If she still harbored the least infinitesimal doubt, the last niggling suspicion, now was the chance to put it to rest. "Mr. Sloane, do you know me?"

He shook his head and went back to watching for Mary Jane's return.

Queenie could not say she was disappointed. How could he recognize a female he had never met? And how could he connect a grown woman with curly black hair to his dead cousin's missing blond child?

And yet.

And yet he would be kin to Lady Charlotte Endicott. He was a blood relative, along with the half-sibling Endicott brothers and Charlotte's other cousin, Sloane's sister, Eleanor, who was now the current Countess of Carde. Surely some chord would resonate between them?

If not that, which Queenie did not believe anyway, even before Ize told her otherwise, Phelan Sloane had paid blood money for Queenie's life. He'd stolen from Lord Carde so that Molly Dennis's fosterling might be fed and housed and clothed and educated . . . and used for more blackmail. Yet Phelan Sloane did not know her at all.

No chime of discovery rang in Queenie's mind, either. She did not know this man. He was not any generous benefactor, not a relation, but neither was he evil incarnate. He was pitiful, in fact, waiting for the innkeepers' daughter like Parfait waited for a walk or a bone. Queenie realized she had been chasing smoke and fog, hoping someone could point to her, name her, give her back her identity. All she had captured was a handful of nothing.

She went outdoors, breathing in fresh country air, looking into the distance and looking into her own heart. She saw sheep, and no surprises.

Mrs. Browne came out to join Queenie in the front of the inn where a circle of chairs had been placed to catch the sun on clear days. The matriarch had taken off her apron and tidied her hair under a clean lace cap. She apologized for leaving their guest alone.

"No, I should apologize for not insisting on helping. I do know my way around a kitchen."

Mrs. Browne laughed. "One more pair of hands and it would have taken twice as long to clean up."

Queenie had to agree, knowing that sometimes she could accomplish as much in one hour as two of her helpers could in three.

After that, the two women spoke of the inn and Mrs. Browne's large and growing family and how females were treated in the world of men. Queenie found the older woman to be wise and witty, not the country drudge Hellen had described, who knew nothing but cabbages and cows and chores.

The Brownes were a well-read family, with two sons university educated. They traveled occasionally to London for the theater and the opera—not on the night of Harry's debacle, thank goodness—and read the city newspapers. Queenie thought Lady Jennifer might enjoy having a farmer's wife as her guest.

Then, as she knew it would, the conversation turned to their mutual acquaintance, Hellen Pettigrew. Mrs. Browne approved, thank goodness, seeing Hellen's good qualities instead of just her background. Hellen was sweet and sunny and adored John George, which mattered far more to his mother than any fancy pedigree. If the matriarch had not noticed that Hellen had not half the brains as young Mr.

Browne, well, Queenie was not going to inform her. Besides, John George did not have half Hellen's good looks.
Now Mrs. Browne could expect more grandchildren who
were bright and beautiful.

"Speaking of what a babe is born with," the older
woman declared, "I say you cannot blame a child for its
parents. But you can surely blame the parents for the child,
illegitimacy aside. Mrs. Pettigrew seems to have done a
fine job rearing her chick, and on her own for the most
part."

"She is an excellent woman."

"Oh, I did not know you had met her. I thought your as-
sociation with the young miss was too recent."

Drat. Stupid mistakes like that were just what would
bring Rourke down on Queenie's head. She had to keep her
stories straight and forget about trying not to deceive decent
folk. "I have heard Mrs. Pettigrew is a good person, that is,
from Hellen and others. As you say, one can tell much of a
mother by the quality of her offspring. You are to be congratulated on yours."

Mrs. Browne was so pleased, she forgot about finding
discrepancies in Queenie's conversation, like the lack of a
French accent now that the young woman was speaking in
private.

"What of you?" Mrs. Browne asked. "Your first husband
did not provide you with any children, but do you hope for
babies of your own?"

"I would only hope for children if the circumstances
were right for them," Queenie said, at which Mrs. Browne
nodded approvingly. She might accept a baron's by-blow as
a daughter-in-law; she did not want to turn her respectable
inn into a home for wayward women and their illegitimate
offspring.

"For now, I have young Charlie. I am the closest thing he has to a parent, and I find the responsibility daunting."

"That is good. If you thought you knew what you were doing, you would be doing it wrong. He seems a likely lad, so all you have to do is love him and encourage him, teach him the right way to go on, and see that he has opportunities."

"That's all?" Queenie laughed. "I thought teaching him manners was going to be my hardest job."

"But he is nearly grown, not a sweet baby to hold and cuddle."

Queenie did not wish to speak of her empty arms. "I am content with my dog," she said, wishing Parfait were at her side instead of off exploring.

Mrs. Browne clucked her tongue in disapproval. "Here we only keep the ones that earn their living. Sheepherders and such. And they stay outdoors."

"Oh, but Parfait works just as hard. He is the emblem of my store, you see, a walking advertisement, especially with his stately manner. And he is an excellent watchdog."

"The creature does not look like any dog I've ever seen, with that fancy haircut."

"He is as hungry as any hound, and good company."

"As is Lord Harking?"

Ah, there was something of the bloodhound in Mrs. Browne, too. "His lordship is an excellent companion. And a fine whip," she added.

"He seems fond of you."

Queenie knew what Mrs. Browne really wanted to know: if Queenie and the viscount truly were lovers. She might turn a blind eye to her daughter's taking long walks with a windmills-in-the-attic gentleman, but she could not be as accepting of a gentleman and his kept mistress at her table. She was open-minded, but the vicar might come back with Hellen and John George, for tea and cake. One simply did not entertain a man of the cloth and a member of the muslin company at the same time.

Queenie shielded her eyes so she could look in the distance, and avoid answering. She wished Parfait were here, or Harry back from watching a ram service his ladies. Mrs. Browne thought that was acceptable, but not a couple trying to obey their principles instead of the blood pounding in their veins.

None of which was the woman's business, but Mrs. Browne had been too kind to insult. Queenie relieved her fears. "Lord Harking shall be returning to his country estate shortly. I shall have my dog and my shop and young Charlie."

"Ah." The older woman understood what Queenie left unspoken. "That is better in the long run, you'll see. Although I am sorry for you now, and will feel sorrier when he leaves. He is a fine man, Lord Harking. But he is a lord."

"Precisely."

Mrs. Browne pushed herself up to go inside to see about tea. "They'll all be hungry again soon enough. Especially the vicar, if I know his housekeeper. The others will be back from their chores and games and rambles, acting as if we had not eaten in a week."

Queenie offered to help and this time her offer was accepted. She followed Mrs. Browne through the common room, where Mary Jane and Phelan Sloane were quietly reading aloud, to the huge, immaculate kitchen. Mrs. Browne handed her an apron and said, "It is better for John George and Miss Pettigrew, you know."

The kitchen? Another meal? "Meeting with the vicar?

But nothing is to be settled until Hellen's mother returns, I thought."

"No, your lordship's leaving will be better for the young people. I am sorry, but the plain truth is their wedding has enough to overcome without the bride keeping fast company. Lord Carde and Captain Endicott—no matter what devilment they raised in their youth—won't like it."

They would not like Queenie, either.

CHAPTER TWENTY-TWO

"**D**id you enjoy yourself?"

Sloane, strangers, Rourke—and two rides in a rickety rig? Queenie bit her lip. Harry had obviously had a pleasant time, smiling and patting babies and kissing Mrs. Browne's cheek when she packed a hamper of food for them to take home. He'd promised to come again, and Queenie thought he meant it.

She slightly loosened her hold on the curricle's side rail. "Yes, everyone was lovely. And I thought they liked Hellen very well. It was good for her to see that her betrothed's family are not all clodpolls and cabbageheads, too."

"Mr. Browne knows as much about farming as any man I know."

"Yes, but the Browne women know something of fashion and theater and novels, besides cooking and cleaning and childbearing, which is important to Hellen. She will not be gaining a mere husband, but an entire family."

"Isn't that always the way?"

Only if the husband—or wife—had a family. "Especially so in this case, when the Brownes are so close. No woman would wish to come between her husband and his loved ones."

Thinking of the impossibility of her ever winning a loving family's approval as a prospective bride was almost more distressing than the speed of the horses. Almost. Queenie studied the road ahead so that she could warn Harry if a rabbit darted in front of the carriage, or if a sharp turn loomed in the distance. He was watching her too closely and too often for her comfort.

"You seemed interested in that queer chap, Sloane." Harry tried to keep the jealousy out of his voice, but he had twice caught her looking at the madman over the rim of her teacup, and again when they were leaving. Sloane paid her no attention, which piqued some beautiful women, Harry knew. He did not believe Madame Lescartes could be so vain that she needed the adoration of every man in the room, but hell, she usually got it. Every male at the inn, from pimple-faced adolescent to old Mr. Browne himself, had been moonstruck by her. Everyone, that was, but John George, of course, who was used to her startling beauty, and Phelan Sloane. Even the women were won over by her inner beauty, as she knelt to take measurements for doll clothes, pressed a coin for luck into the enceinte woman's hands, and tucked a blanket around the deaf old auntie before they left. Sloane had not noticed.

Harry let the horses pick their own pace. "Mr. Browne is hoping Sloane will marry the youngest daughter, the one who hardly left the man's side."

"Yes, he mentioned that to me. Mary Jane is devoted to the gentleman, so I see no reason why Lord Carde should forbid the match. Still, the entire time there, I could not help thinking of Phelan Sloane's sad story, how he loved so deeply the first time."

"So deeply that he destroyed his own beloved." Harry had no sympathy for the man and less interest in him, especially now, knowing that his companion's concern was merely romantic claptrap. "He was a fool."

So was Harry, for still dreaming of a little cottage tucked in the woods somewhere, where only love resided, no doubts, no danger. He and his woman, and to the devil with the rest of the world. He could love her and make love to her and not care what anyone thought. It was all he could do right now not to turn the horses down a narrow side path, to find a clearing out of sight of the road, to lift her down against his aching body, to ask her—nay, to beg her—to let him love her. He could take the blanket from the carriage, the wine Mr. Browne had packed, and all the yearning that he had tried to ignore. Ignore? Deuce take it, he had been trying to dampen his desires in wine, drown them in cold water, defy them by willpower alone, to no avail.

He wanted this woman, none other, and for far more than a tumble in the grass. In the cold. With the others in the following coach wondering what had happened to them.

To say nothing of Charlie, riding behind them.

So Harry kept the horses and his urges to the straight path, and dreamed of that cottage. There he could worship a goddess, pay homage to a princess, cherish the most precious jewel a man could hope to hold this side of heaven.

. . . And he would destroy the woman as certainly as Phelan Sloane had killed the object of his unholy affections.

With all her gifts, all her talents and beauty, both inward and outward, Madame Denise Lescartes had to be free to live her own life, in her own fashion. He could not trample her scruples.

And she would not let him.

"Do keep your eyes on the road, my lord.

"I think you should slow down for that turn.

"Is the horse on the right limping?

"No, you may not come inside. It grows late and I have to be at work in the shop early in the morning. Besides, I worry where your good-nights would lead."

To a better night if he had his way, but Harry was neither surprised nor disappointed. So his love was a nag as well as a principled prude. No matter, the regret in her voice as she turned down his offer of a late supper when they reached her street made up for that. She wanted his kisses as much as he burned to give them, which did nothing to put out the fire, of course.

"I think you should go home, Harry," she said as she took out her key.

"Well, yes. I have to return the horses to the livery stable, and cannot leave Charlie to hold them for long, even if they are tired."

"No, I mean home to Harking Hall. I saw you in the country today. You belong there, with your crops and your cattle. They need you."

"I have estate managers and competent tenants. And messengers to convey my wishes or any problems that might arise. Nothing will suffer without my presence."

"What about your sister and her children?"

"She has her friends in the neighborhood to commiserate with her on her husband's defection, and the children have nannies and tutors. I would be de trop, I swear. And it is not as if I am planning on being gone forever."

"But there is nothing for you here in London." Especially without the promise of forever.

She was closing the door, literally and figuratively, but

Harry was not ready to go. "I cannot leave while you are living your life in terror."

He had noticed how she waited for the other carriage to come before she left the roadway, looking over her shoulder and up and down the street. She had let the dog sniff around the shop before she entered the darkened building; then she had lit every candle and lamp in the place. Harry did not know if her hands were shaking from fear or from clutching the side rail so long, but he hated the idea that she was afraid, and hated more that he could not protect her. "If I can do nothing else, share nothing else with you, I would stand beside you as long as you need a friend in London."

"I do not deserve your loyalty."

He kissed her hand, while Hellen and John George Browne disappeared into the back room, to check the rear door. They would be a while.

"You have it, and anything else I have to give."

"You are so good, Harry, but you must not stay on my account. I told you—"

"How soon?" He did not release her hand, but rubbed his thumb across her palm, sending shivers through both of them. "You said you would act soon to bring an end to the danger and indecision. How soon?"

Part of the difficulty was him. If Harry stayed in Town, Queenie did not know how long she could resist him. The more time she spent with Harry, the more she loved him, and the more she wanted to throw herself at him, to beg him to take her away—yes, even in the curricle!—and forget about everything, in his arms. He was the worst danger she had yet faced, and the sweetest. Why, she did not even have the fortitude to take back her hand because his touch felt so good. She could trust him—except with all her secrets, which would shatter his affection anyway. She could not trust herself.

That was not the danger he was speaking of, though.

"I am tired of not knowing my future, too. This limbo of uncertainty is beyond unnerving. I thought I could wait until the people I need to speak with returned to London, but now I am thinking that I should travel to them." Then she would know if she was free to make her own life or not, however barren it would be without Harry.

"I will take you." That was a statement, not a question.

Yes, Queenie decided. That was fitting. She could enjoy her last days with Harry, seeing the love in his eyes, and then tell the truth once and for all, to everyone. Lord Carde could decide to prosecute her or not after he found Ize, and Harry could go home, without regrets. He would not even want her as his mistress after hearing all the lies unraveled. He would be happier for that. She would not look at him, she decided, when she confessed her role in the mess and her silence afterward. That way she did not have to see the love die. "Very well. I will go with you. But not in the curricle."

She spent half that night composing a letter to the earl, asking if she might come for an interview concerning his search. She was not about to travel north—no, not even for the sake of time with Harry—to find Lord Carde on his way to London, or gone to another of his properties.

She wrote another letter to the earl's brother, Captain Jack Endicott, asking if he could be at Carde Hall at the same date. She did not think she'd have the courage to recite her tale twice. In addition, she wanted to make certain that Browne's employer knew that John George had no knowledge of her background, and that Hellen was not involved in his family's losses.

She rewrote the letters three times, half deciding that she could tell the whole tale on paper and not have to make the journey at all. No, she was a coward, but how much worse to wait here in London for the magistrate to pound on her door or the constables to come cart her away. Or Ize to realize she had turned him in.

Besides, she wanted that time with Harry. A closed carriage, at least several nights on the road, meals in private rooms ... separate bedchambers, naturally. Goodnight kisses? Queenie remembered Harry's kisses, and had to use one of the discarded letters to fan herself. What if they had adjoining bedrooms?

She was no whore, selling her body. She was no mistress, letting a man pay her bills. She was no light-skirts, free with her favors.

She was no shriveled old maid, either. What was she saving herself for? She would never marry, never have a family. Even if she was free to go her own way, Queenie knew, she could never love another man, not after knowing Harry. Shouldn't she have a few days of pleasure to savor for the rest of her life?

Queenie knew there were ways to prevent children. Perhaps Hellen knew of them; if not, Hellen's mother's friends had to. Their livelihoods depended on not looking like that woman at the inn, breeding another little Browne.

It would be wrong. It would be delightful.

Molly would be spinning in her grave. Molly never loved a man, not that Queenie knew of.

Queenie's own beliefs rejected the notion of her giving herself to Harry. Her own body rejoiced.

Maybe she should think about sending her confession in a letter after all, and avoid temptation.

She did not send her letters, not any of them.

*   *   *

Queenie and Charlie were up early a few days later, cleaning the shop before opening. Queenie might not be able to sweep all her cares and concerns away, but she could get rid of a week's worth of London's soot, grime, and dirt from the front of her premises. She was washing the window, since she was taller, while Charlie swept the walkway and polished the brass railing. No one was about except servants and deliverymen, so Queenie was wearing a faded old gown and a kerchief over her hair for the messy job. She had thought about not bothering with the face paints or the fake beauty mark, but servants often noticed more than their masters, and gossiped just as much. Thank goodness she had taken the time.

"'Ere boy, outta my way," a familiar voice rasped. A small man pushed roughly past Charlie on his way toward the front door. He was dressed in a stained coat and a limp-brimmed hat with long, oily hair sticking out the bottom. Hair also stuck out of his nose, and his eyes stuck out of their sockets.

Queenie could pick up her bucket and leave, pretending to be a maid. Or she could throw it at Ize. Neither was a good idea.

She unwrapped her kerchief from her head so he could see her black curls, but she kept wiping at the window, her face turned from him.

Parfait was growling, which was also not a good idea, as the cur—the two-legged one—appeared ready to kick out at her dog. Queenie called the poodle to her side, in French.

Bending down to hold Parfait by the collar, her all-too-distinctive blue eyes averted, Queenie said, "Pardon, monsieur, but the store, she is closed. You must—*qu'est-ce que c'est?*—come back later."

"What, do I look like I've come shopping?" He cackled, licking at his thick lips. "I'm come to see Hellen Pettigrew. They said at her house she's been staying here."

Queenie forced a shrill laugh. "Mademoiselle Hellen never rises this early in the morning," she said, in French.

"Huh?"

Queenie repeated herself in English, and added, "Her friends would know that."

"I heard she was a shopgirl now, not lollygagging like a gentry mort."

"Que?" Queenie said. "That is, huh?"

"She's working, ain't she?" He looked at the building, the apartment above. "Less'n you're working another lay." He cackled again at the double meaning. "I heard as how the fancy culls was hanging around."

Queenie looked up also, but not at Ize. "Monsieur, I do not know your *anglais* so well. But my shop is everything *comme il faut*, proper. I do not think Mademoiselle Hellen is wishing to see you, *non*?"

"She'll see me. I heard she was looking for some pearls."

"Oui, but no longer."

"They wasn't wee, 'cause I've seen those pearls. As big as my littlest fingernail, they was." He held up his hand, showing the smallest finger with dirt under the nail. "And they better be as long as they was afore her mother gets back. I know Valerie Pettigrew, and she has her baubles counted to the bead."

"No, monsieur, you do not take my meaning. Mademoiselle has her pearls returned, so your visit is unnecessary, no? You will be leaving now, I think."

Charlie was standing in front of the door, no deterrent to Ize, but the dog was growling again, and the woman's hold on its collar did not appear that strong.

"I was wanting to ask her about something else, too. Mayhap you know what a Bow Street man's been doing hanging around here. He's been to Valerie Pettigrew's, too, the neighbor says, and he's been asking around Town for me." Ize had had to move, again.

Queenie gave her best Gallic shrug. "But how can I know, when I do not know your name?"

"I thought everyone knew me. Ize, they call me."

"Ah, because of your—"

"No. Because my name is Ezra Iscoll," the small man angrily insisted.

"Yes, I have heard your name."

Ize instantly reached for the knife in his boot. "And? What does the Redbreast want?" he asked, pretending to clean his nails.

Queenie thought he must seldom use the knife for that job, judging from the results. She shuddered to think what else he used the sharp blade for. She petted the dog, so Ize would not see her hands tremble. Trying to keep her voice steady, and disinterested, she said, "He wants to know about *mon cher* Harking's diamonds."

"Ah. That's all right, then. I heard about them, too."

"Yes? There is a reward."

"Didn't hear that." He stopped picking at his nails, as if he could not do that and think at the same time.

"You are a jeweler, *non*?"

"In a manner of speaking. I might know something about them diamonds, though."

"Then you should speak to Monsieur Rourke, or Viscount Harking. If you tell me your address—"

He looked at her sharply. Queenie knew she had made a mistake, and quickly added, "But you know where this Bow

Street is, *certainement. Mon ami* Harking stays at the Grand Hotel."

"Enemy, is he? I thought you was lovers."

"And *moi,* I think I have heard enough." Queenie started to let go of the dog's collar after telling Parfait to stay, in French. She knew the dog would not move; Ize did not.

He took a step back, away from the shop. "Here, now, no insult. A pretty gal could do a lot worse." He started to walk away, but turned back.

"You sure that's all the Runner wanted? Hellen and her mother didn't mention nothing else to him?"

"Mademoiselle's mother is away from home."

"The girl, then? She always did have more hair than wit. She didn't talk to the Runner, did she?"

"What should mademoiselle know about the *vicomte*'s jewels?"

"Nothing. And you tell her to keep it that way."

"*Je ne comprends pas.* I do not understand."

"But the wigeon will." Ize tossed his knife from hand to hand. "You tell the gal that she better not have any conversations about me with no Runners, you hear? And especially nothing about a mutual friend we might have."

Queenie did her best to look confused. She shrugged again.

"A kind of royal friend. And if I get wind she said something, or thought about that reward money . . ." He made the universal gesture of sliding his hand across his throat, only this time he had a knife in it. "Understand?"

Queenie understood. She swallowed hard and nodded. "But what about the reward money? It is for the diamonds, no? And for Sir John Martin?"

"I might know a thing or two about both of them. I got to think on that. But you tell the peagoose, you hear?"

Queenie heard her heart beating so loudly she was glad a carriage drove by then, hiding the sound. She nodded again.

He put his knife back in his boot and scuttled down the street.

White-faced, Charlie came to stand beside Queenie and the dog. Queenie put her arm around the boy, for both of their comfort.

She had to send those letters. Now.

CHAPTER TWENTY-THREE

First she was going to send a spy, if possible.

"Charlie, do you think you could follow that man, without him knowing?"

"A'course I could, ma'am." He pulled a wool cap out of his waistband and put it on to cover his red hair; then he wiped the polishing rag over his cheeks to dirty them. "No one notices a street sweep or a beggar boy. And he's too ugly to lose in a crowd. I'll follow him to hell an' back, I swear!"

"Stop short of that, Charlie. I would not want you in danger. But go." She pressed some coins from her pocket into his hand. "Find out where he lives if you can. Or where he does business, or has his coffee. Then hurry back." She handed over more coins. "Take a hackney so you are here sooner. And remember that he is as crafty as he is mean. Do not let him see you."

Charlie set off at a run.

Queenie stood in the street looking after him, hoping she had done the right thing. Charlie was a child of the city who knew his way around the streets, and around the pickpockets, press-gangs, and predators. He would be fine.

No one would be safe while Ize was free, though.

If Queenie knew where he was, she could send Rourke a message when she was on her way out of London. That had to be soon, before Hellen's mother returned, before Ize grew impatient. Harry might not want to leave, not right when his diamonds might be recovered, but Queenie decided she could not take the chance.

Harry would not be happy to give up their privacy on the drive north—neither was Queenie, to be honest with herself—but she would take Hellen and Charlie with them, so Ize could not take revenge if he escaped capture. They were all safer that way, and her virtue, too. If Harry chose not to go with her, well, she knew they had to say farewell sooner or later. That emptiness was already eating at her insides.

She would not cry, Queenie vowed. Let him see the pretty woman he admired, not one with black streaks down her face from the paints she used to darken her lashes and brows. Let him not see that he was taking part of her with him when he went home.

If he did not go north with her, Harry would be gone before she returned to London. He might never hear her explanation, not that it would change anything. He would always be a viscount and she would never be a lady.

Neither would she come back to the city while Ize was free. Sooner or later he would look at her eyes, or she would forget the French accent, or Hellen would call her by her name.

He would kill her. Queenie had no doubt of that. He had to, to silence her.

So she and Hellen would start packing as soon as Charlie came back, without bothering to send the letters to the earl and his brother. She would get to Carde Hall in Northampshire before the post. If the earl was not there . . . she would face that later.

"Just let him not hurt Charlie meantime," she told the dog, picking up the cleaning supplies to bring inside.

"Who is going to hurt Charlie?" asked a voice that warmed Queenie, from her toes that tingled, to the lips he'd kissed, to the heart he had stolen.

She had not seen Harry come, yet here he was, his rented curricle and the bay horses being walked down the street by a groom from the livery stable. Harry's hair was still damp from his morning wash, and his jaw was freshly shaved. Surely there was no handsomer man in all of England, Queenie thought, clutching the bucket so she would not clutch his broad shoulders right in the street.

He looked tired, she noticed, as if he had not slept well. Queenie wanted to caress his skin, to soothe him. How could she bring him ease when she was about to lie to him again, though, then leave him?

"No one, I hope. But Ize if he catches him."

"Eyes? Oh, Ize, the fence. He was here, then?"

Diable, she should not have spoken! "He was looking for Hellen," she quickly said. "About her pearls. I got rid of him, but thought to send Charlie to find where he lives."

"Capital! I'll send a messenger to Rourke to come here and wait for the lad to get back. We'll get there and nab the dastard before he has a chance to leave again."

"No!" Then Ize would guess who had sent the Runner. Queenie needed more time to leave the city. "That is, no, it is the Runner's business, not yours."

"But he might know about my diamonds, too."

"You cannot know that. There is no proof that Ize stole

anything or dealt with Sir John Martin at all. You cannot have him arrested on such flimsy charges."

Harry's forehead was furrowed. "You don't want me to see him put in prison? You were the one who told me the man was dangerous. And now you are worried he might hurt Charlie."

"I—oh, I do not know if I should have sent the boy or not. I am upset, merely."

Harry brushed a speck of dirt off her cheek. "Rourke will want to know where the knave is hiding. He has merely to interview Ize, not arrest him."

"But then he will know I told Rourke."

"Gammon. Why would he think that? And what does it matter?"

"It matters that he is a villain, and he will want revenge. Harry, I want to leave London today. Will you still go with me?"

"Before we hear what happens with Ize? You have waited this long. A day or two will not matter."

"Yes, it will. You do not understand. I have to leave, and take Hellen and Charlie with me."

"Silly. I won't let anyone hurt you. Don't you know that by now?" He started back toward his vehicle, to send the groom to Bow Street.

Queenie set down the bucket and ran after him, tugging on his arm. "You do not know Ize."

He turned. "Do you?"

If Queenie had the bucket in her hand she would have tossed it at him, slop water and all. Why did he have to pick today to be suspicious? "Too well, after this morning."

"Then he has to be dealt with, especially if he threatened you. Running away solves nothing. Don't you know that?"

She wanted to shout that running away kept her alive,

and kept him out of harm's way. Running away to Lord
Carde was an act that took more bravery than she possessed,
but it was the only way now. "If I leave London, I can get
help to get rid of Ize once and for all."

"I am not enough? I know you do not trust Rourke, but I
thought you had more confidence in me than that."

Queenie had nothing to say that would not offend him
worse.

Harry turned his back on her and gave the groom a message for the Bow Street man, then watched him drive away.

Queenie was frantic. Maybe Charlie would not find Ize's
lodgings, only a coffeehouse or a grogshop. Maybe Ize lived
in a rathole Charlie was smart enough not to enter. Maybe
Ize took a hackney Charlie could not follow. And maybe
Harry could forgive her for seeking another man's protection because he had a higher title and deeper pockets.

"It is part of a debt I owe," was all she could say to his
back.

He finally turned. "Which you also do not trust me with.
I know I swore to wait, but you make it deuced difficult,
woman. And if you are in danger, I shall not stand aside and
let you be hurt by anyone. I shall not! Do you understand?"

Parfait started growling at the anger in his voice. Then
the dog started to sniff at the basket Harry had taken from
the curricle before sending the groom off.

Queenie called the dog away. "I do not understand myself. How can I understand you?" Out of frustration and fear,
she lashed out: "And I thought you promised to stay away
from the shop."

She got nothing done with him around, and all her cabbage-
headed customers giggled and simpered over him until she
felt ill. Besides, if he kept stealing kisses in the back room,

she would never go into the front room, and to the devil with her business.

"The shop is not open," he said reasonably. "And I wanted to ask you two questions. Will you—"

Queenie kicked out at the bucket, sloshing some of the dirty water onto her shoes, which made her angrier. "*Sacre bleu,* you promised not to look for any more answers. I told you I would tell you the whole sorry story as soon as I could."

"Those were not the questions. I have been up all night thinking about them, about you." It had been a deuced uncomfortable night, too. Now Harry was resolved, and as ready as he would ever be. "Would you—"

Parfait nudged again at the basket in Harry's hand.

"Blast." Harry raised the basket higher.

"What is in there, anyway?"

"Just some liver, and kippers and meat pasties. A few lamb chops and a bit of eggs and ham. And bread and cheese. I thought you might like to share breakfast with me." Forever. "But not the dog. I brought him a steak bone."

How could he think about eating at a time like this? For that matter, how could he eat all that at one meal? Queenie had nibbled on a sweet roll along with her morning chocolate, and that was enough. If it would keep Harry from more questions, though, she would fight Parfait for the bone. She picked up the bucket again. "Come inside, then. I am done here. Hellen will be awake and hungry."

"Hellen? But if she is there, how can I ask you to ma—"

Queenie was already inside.

"Do not say anything about anything," Queenie ordered when she helped Hellen with the fastenings of her gown.

"How can I not answer if Mr. Rourke asks me questions?"

"Eat. Keep your mouth busy so you cannot talk."

"But I ate the sweet roll you left for me."

"Hellen, if you do not wish to be speaking to the magistrate tomorrow, do not speak to Rourke today. As soon as he leaves we can start packing, so we will be done with his prying."

"Packing? Where are we going?"

"North. That is all you have to know, so you cannot let anything slip out."

"But I cannot leave London now. You know Mama is coming back any day, so we will know about the money from the baron. Besides, John George cannot leave his post."

John George was not invited, but Queenie supposed he would have to come, since she was going to speak to his employers. That carriage was growing less and less private.

"And what about the shop?" Hellen wanted to know. "You cannot just leave it, after you worked so hard to make it a success."

Making things right with the house of Carde was far more important. That was the reason she had gone into business in the first place. "We will talk about it later."

"But you told me not to talk."

Rourke came and ate Harry's food. Luckily Harry had brought enough for a small army, or several hungry men and growing boys. Hellen cowardly declared a headache and took a filled plate upstairs. Queenie took a slice of bread.

Rourke seemed impressed that Queenie had the presence of mind to send Charlie after Ize. Just like a good citizen.

Queenie shredded the bread. Then she went to wait by the

window, so she could watch the street for Charlie's return. She moved the CLOSED sign to the other side of the window, where she had not left a big streak in her distress.

She let in her seamstresses and fitters, telling them the store would open late today, if at all. On their way to the workroom they all batted their eyelashes fast enough to chill Harry's eggs with the draft.

"Ladies, we have orders to fill," Queenie said, wondering if they could keep the store running when she left. If Hellen stayed behind . . . no, she needed Hellen to satisfy the conventions. Alone, Hellen and Browne just might satisfy their baser urges. Alone, Queenie would look like a fallen woman, under Harry's protection. Lord Carde might not agree to see her, not with his wife and children nearby to be contaminated with her presence. Hellen was no proper chaperone, but she was Browne's betrothed, and she was all Queenie had.

And Hellen might not be safe in London, staying at the shop. Queenie recalled that suspicious fire at Captain Jack Endicott's gambling club, right after she had tried to make inquiries there before she fled for France. She decided to hire a guard to watch the store while she was gone, to protect her investment and her seamstresses. They had enough orders and new patterns to complete to stay busy. The store would suffer, but the women would suffer worse if she merely left the CLOSED sign out. They needed their wages the same as Queenie needed the income and the goodwill of her customers.

She also needed to go to the bank before leaving. Queenie tallied sums in her head: how much to leave for running the store, how much to pay a guard, how much to take for travel costs. She would not let Harry pay her way, if he came.

The rest of her bank account would go with her for the family looking for their half sister, Lady Charlotte. Lord knew, the Earl of Carde did not need Queenie's paltry sum and her promise of part of whatever she earned in the future. He had a fortune, fields, and investments, enough to support his family, his brother's family, the Browne family at their inn, charity schools, and heaven knew what else. Giving him the money, though, was Queenie's act of good faith, her proof that she never meant any harm.

The Endicotts were born to wealth. The money would mean little to them. It meant everything to Queenie, because that was all she had and she had worked so hard for every shilling.

Money was the only thing she had to give. She could not give them back their kin. She could not repay what Phelan Sloane had paid in blackmail. She could never even hope to restore what Lord Carde and his brother had spent in the search.

Her shop and her dog were all she had. And the dog was begging for scraps from Lord Harking.

She would miss Harry far more than the money. Whether or not he came with her to Cardington, the earl's seat, he was nearly gone already. The lies and the mistrust would send him away long before the nature of her birth did. Not for the first time, Queenie damned whatever fate had tied her life to a dead child's.

Harry was finished with his meal, and finished with being angry at his beloved. She could not help holding her own counsel, not if creatures like Ize were what she knew of men. Nor had Harry acted entirely honorably, stealing kisses and caresses whenever he could. She had never slapped him or pushed him away, so he knew his attentions were not repulsive. His passion was definitely returned, judging from how his own clothing was often disordered and his own carefully combed hair was looking like a gale had passed through the shop's tiny rear yard after he led her out there.

It had, a storm of desire and devotion, and a dedication to making his woman happy. She would be happy, he vowed. And she would be his.

Of course she did not know that his intentions were honorable. How could she, when he had not known himself until yesterday when he finally realized that he could not live his life without her in it? But how the deuce was he to ask her, with Rourke in the room? He had no pretty speeches prepared, not even a bouquet of flowers. What kind of fool brought breakfast instead of a betrothal ring? Damn!

And there was this mess with Ize, and her wanting to fly away on some secret mission Harry could not comprehend.

He did not have to understand. He would take care of the inconvenient Ize; then he would take care of whatever mare's nest awaited at the end of her journey. And then he would care for her for the rest of their lives.

He came over to her near the window and put his arm around her, not caring what Rourke saw. He stroked her taut neck, hoping to lessen her tension. "Charlie will be fine. In the meantime, I need to know what name to put—"

"There he is!"

On the special license.

CHAPTER TWENTY-FOUR

"I followed him, ma'am, just like you said. And I waited outside this old place—it looked like a rooming house—to see if he came out again."

"He didn't see you, did he?" Queenie asked, handing the boy a piece of cheese and a slice of ham on bread as soon as he jumped down from a decrepit hackney carriage pulled by a swaybacked old nag. She knew better than to hug him in front of the men.

"A'course he didn't see me. No one notices grubby brats. I would of been back sooner, but no jarveys take their coaches down those streets." Charlie swallowed the sandwich nearly whole. After all, he had not eaten in almost two hours. "So I started to walk home, but afore I could get to the corner, I spotted a gentry cove headed toward Ize's house, so I ducked in an alley and watched him go in." Charlie turned toward Lord Harking now. "I watched 'cause he was better dressed'n any other cull on the street, but his beak was broke, all swollen sideways and purple. And he had a bald spot. Do you think it might be your brother-in-law what stole the diamonds, gov?"

"It might just be, Charlie. You did well."

The boy beamed with pride. "I started to run then, to tell you, and headed toward a wider road, but no one would take up a poor-looking fare, and I didn't want to flash my brass, not in that neighborhood. Afore I could go too many streets away I finally spotted Old Jim and Millie—Millie's the horse—what I knew from before. Jim sometimes gave me a ha'penny to watch the mare when he needed a break. They brung me home."

So Queenie handed Old Jim a sandwich, too. Millie looked older than her driver, if that were possible. She was drinking out of a leather nose bag, her sides heaving with the effort.

"Did you get the street name and number of the house?" Rourke wanted to know.

Charlie spoke to Harry, not the Runner. "I was watching Ize too careful-like to see street signs, if there was any, and there was no numbers on the houses. But I can show you where it is, all right."

Queenie shook her head. "No. You cannot go back. Ize will recognize you."

Charlie was already clambering up onto Harry's curricle. Harry took her hand, kissed it briefly, and let it go in the shortest time ever, and not because it smelled of ham and cheese. "Do not worry. I will bring the lad back safe and sound."

"There is no reason for either of you to go! It is too dangerous, dealing with criminals and cutthroats. You know your brother-in-law tried to stab you once already. Please, my lord, do not go! This is a matter for Bow Street and the courts, not a country gentleman and a child!"

Both the country gentleman—who took her comment to mean incompetent bumpkin—and the child—who took her comment to mean bumbling baby—frowned at her. So did Rourke as he climbed up to sit next to Harry on the bench. The groom from the livery stable and Charlie shared the narrow tiger's stand behind the seat.

"We will be back soon," Harry promised as he gave the horses the office to start. "In time for luncheon."

Queenie was left in the street amid swirling dust. The man she loved and the boy she had practically adopted were driving away, perhaps into peril. They did not even realize how treacherous Ize could be—or how many secrets he knew. Thickheaded Harry was even thinking of his stomach instead of his safety! Luncheon? She'd give him a piece of her mind and let him chew on that, the clunch.

There was not another blessed thing Queenie could do about his leaving except curse, in two languages.

. . . Or she could hire Old Jim and Millie, who looked to be settled in front of her store for a nap. Queenie looked at the ancient mare. Then she looked at the curricle, careening around the corner. "Can you follow them?"

Old Jim scratched his head. "Not at that speed, we can't. But I knows where they're going, so it don't make no nevermind. Asides, Millie and me, we know shorter ways to get there."

Stay behind packing? Wait for word of whatever mayhem ensued? Or trust her life to a tired old horse, an antique coach, and an ancient driver? Two of the things she feared most in the world were facing Queenie now: a rickety, unreliable carriage, and a rabid, rapacious Ize.

She feared losing Harry worse.

"Hellen, mind the shop!"

*   *   *

At last! Harry was finally getting somewhere. He was doing something about his missing heirloom, and doing something about rescuing Madame Denise Lescartes from whatever demons plagued her. Then she would trust him. Then she would marry him.

She had to. Even if she did not love him, the woman was too smart to turn down such a golden opportunity. Not that Harry wanted to be wedded for his title, money, or what influence he had. But she loved him—he knew she did—even if she did sometimes think he was a flea-brained farmer, which he sometimes was. She'd expressed her love in words. Better, she'd expressed it in those sweet little sighs she made when he kissed her, in how she pressed her soft body against his hard one. And in how she desperately did not want him to rush into danger. She would marry him.

Nothing else mattered, not what his sister would say, or the gossip columns, or his neighbors. Life was good. Life was simple, just the way it was meant to be. There would be no more riddles, no more regrets . . . as soon as he got rid of his brother-in-law and the bastard who threatened his bride.

He flicked the whip over the horses' heads to quicken the pace.

"If Ize lives at this place or does business there, he'll keep until later," Rourke said, holding on to his hat. "Or I can take a handful of Runners and get him tomorrow. He'll tell us where your in-law is, if we have to shake it out of him."

"We will finish this today. Now. The two of us."

Rourke tried to stay upright as the vehicle turned a corner on two wheels. "You know, my lord, this is a matter of the law now. You reported those diamonds stolen, a crime committed. You wouldn't be thinking of taking justice into your own hands, now, would you?"

If Lord Harking did not have the reins in his hands, he'd have his pistol. "Of course not."

"I have a solemn duty to remind you that dueling is illegal."

"And I need to remind you who is paying your salary for this case. Furthermore, dueling is for gentlemen. Sir John Martin is no longer one. That pop-eyed poltroon Ize never was."

Rourke did not seem reassured. "I am in charge, is that understood? No one makes a move without me. Right?" He cautiously turned to look behind him, to include Charlie and the hired groom.

The groom yelled back, "Right, sir. I have a wife and children. I ain't no hero. My job is staying outside with the horses. If we live long enough to get there."

They did reach the dark, narrow, littered street Charlie directed them to, not quite in the rookeries, but not far distant. He pointed out a soot-begrimed house that was even shabbier than its neighbors, some of the windows boarded over, a beggar with a gin bottle in his hands sleeping beside the doorstep.

Harry pulled ahead, out of sight of the remaining windows, and stopped. "We'll go back on foot," he said, already forgetting that Rourke was supposed to be in command.

The Runner did get down first while Harry was transferring the ribbons to the groom. Rourke was too relieved to be on firm ground to argue, and he agreed when the viscount took the words out of his mouth and ordered Charlie to stay behind.

"Do you know what Madame Lescartes would do to me if anything happened to you, my boy?" Harry asked when the lad would have protested being left with the horses.

Charlie grinned. "She'd likely baste your ballocks to your backside."

"Precisely. So you keep your eyes open and whistle if there's anything untoward in the street."

"Right, gov. Iffen I see Ize or your kin come out, I'll follow him."

If Charlie saw either of those loose screws walk out of the building, Harry would be lying unconscious somewhere. "We do not know if they are still inside."

They were, and arguing loudly enough on the third-floor landing to be heard from the ground floor entryway. One of the rooming house renters saw the Runner with his club in his hand and jumped out an unboarded ground floor window, landing on the sleeping sot. Two other boarders pushed past Harry in a hurry. Some doors on the upper levels slammed shut, locks turning; others creaked open so the rooms' occupants could peer out at the commotion in the upper hall. One of the men there did not seem to notice or care, as he kept up his loud carping.

Harry headed for the stairs. "It's Martin, all right. I recognize his whining."

Rourke tapped the viscount's shoulder, then put his finger over his lips and stepped to the side of the stairwell, indicating they should stay out of sight, listening. "We'll learn more this way. Maybe get a confession."

Harry wanted his diamonds, not a discussion, but he bided his time, now that he knew Martin was there. He nodded and left his pistol in his boot.

Then he wished he had it in his hand when someone came through the door behind him. Someone who smelled of lilacs.

He pulled her roughly toward the space behind the stairs, among brooms and mops and buckets. "What the devil are you doing here?" he demanded in the harshest whisper he could manage.

"I heard shouting and saw people running out the door and leaping out of windows. I thought you might be in trouble."

"So you came to my rescue? With a darning needle? Devil take it, woman, I am supposed to be the one who slays the dragons! Why can you never act like an ordinary female?"

"Should I swoon or weep?"

"You should stay home and sew!"

"Sh," Rourke ordered, glaring at both of them. "Unless you want to announce our presence."

Harry tried to push her outside, but someone else was coming in. Charlie.

"Damn it! I told you to stay with the horses!"

"I work for Madame Denise. I came to see she was safe."

"She'd be perfectly safe at home, or outside, where you can watch her to your heart's content."

The noises from above were stopped, as if the arguers had heard something and were listening. Harry scowled at Charlie, but he pulled both the boy and the woman into the shelter of the stairwell, out of view of the upper landing. "And don't be knocking anything over."

The shouting resumed. "What do you mean you don't have any money for me?" Martin was ranting. "You've had the necklace for over a week now! Deuce take it, are you trying to leave Town with my blunt?"

"Shut your trap. The neighbors can hear you."

So could Rourke and Harry and the others. Harry thought the Runner had enough evidence to arrest at least one of the maggots. He jerked his thumb up the stairs, but Rourke shook his head no.

"I do not care who hears! And everyone in this neighborhood knows your shifty, shady business anyway. How do you think I found you, with you moving so much? I had to use my last coins to buy the information. Now I need the brass, I say. You told me a few days, for your stonecutter to pry the diamonds out and reface them so no one could suspect where they came from. I paid for passage out of England at the end of the week—and I need the ready to start a new life! I can't stay in Town much longer, damn it, not with that buffle-headed Harking issuing rewards and hiring Runners to look for me."

"And me. So what do you do? You chance leading them straight to me. So who is the bigger fool? I told you I'd send word when I had the blunt, damn it. Now, get out of here."

"Not without my money or my diamonds, damn your cheating soul."

"You call me a cheat, you bastard? You're the one who tried to pass off paste jewels!"

"Paste? Those are the Harking diamonds! They are famous! Otherwise I could have sold them at the high-toned jewelers."

"And I say they are glass! Here, let me show you."

The listeners below could not see what Ize was doing, but they heard something drop to the bare wooden floor, like a pebble. Then they heard Ize strike it with something, likely the handle of his knife. The stone shattered. "You see? Diamonds don't shatter like that, now, do they?"

Martin was not that easy a pigeon to pluck. "How do I know that was one of the Harking diamonds?"

"Listen, you muckworm, you came to me. I took the sparklers in good faith and gave you a down payment, for when my cutter could make the stones salable. I say they are fake. You're lucky I don't carve your liver out, 'stead of asking for my brass back. Here, take the bloody necklace and get out."

The listeners below could hear a heavy chain—lighter by the missing stones—drop to the floor.

Three pairs of eyes behind the stairs looked at Harry.

Charlie's mouth was hanging open, and the Bow Street Runner was shaking his head in disbelief.

Queenie rasped out the question they all wanted to ask: "You knew? You have been turning the town upside down for fake diamonds?"

Red flags flew in Harry's cheeks. "They were mine," was all he said. And hers, was what he hoped. To hell with waiting, was what he decided. He left the shadowed cover and stepped over to the bottom of the stairs. "He's lying, Martin. They weren't all glass."

Ize cursed. So did Martin. So did Rourke.

Harry went on: "It seems my profligate father pried out a few of the stones to pay his gaming debts. I think my mother used one or two to finance her flight. I pawned one myself, to make a better dowry for my sister, which you wasted within a year. I've been purchasing the real ones back when I can, or replacements for the missing stones whenever I had the blunt. I'd say more than half were real by now."

"You dastard!" Martin saw the Runner and knew he was finished. But he was not going to go by himself. He twisted the handle of his cane and pulled out his hidden sword. "You were going to give me nothing, you frog-faced rotter? You were going to let me believe they were all imitations? Not on your life!"

Martin tried to end that lying, cheating, ugly life right there. He lunged forward with his sword aimed at Ize's heart.

The target was too small. He missed, but not by much,

piercing Ize in the chest. When he pulled his sword back and out, Ize kicked him, sending Martin flying against the stair railing. The rotted, termite-ridden railing.

The wood shattered. Martin kept going, right through the splintering wood and over the edge. He screamed.

Queenie screamed as his body landed at her feet.

Ize clutched at his chest, where blood was dripping down. He looked over, careful to keep away from the edge. He got a good look at Harry and the Runner beside him. "Bloody hell."

"That's precisely where you are going. Come down, Ize. You are under arrest in the name of the Crown. We have heard enough to know that you were well aware the necklace was stolen. If you give back the real stones, you might not hang." Rourke could not see the blood pouring over Ize's fingers, which made the subject of his punishment moot.

"Unless they charge him with the murder of a baronet, dirty dish that Sir John Martin was," Harry added, holding Queenie so that her head was averted from his broken brother-in-law.

"Is he dead?"

Rourke did not have to bother kneeling down to check for a pulse. "I never saw a live man with his neck at that angle. You are right, my lord. There's always barristers willing to plead self-defense, I suppose, but it looks like murder to me."

"You ain't going to hang me," Ize shouted down, knowing he was not going to live long enough for a hempen necklace. He'd seen enough knife stabs in his time—hell, he'd inflicted enough—to recognize a fatal wound.

"You could jump out the window, I suppose. Take your chances on not ending in a heap like Martin."

The nearest window had a board nailed over it.

Ize still had his knife, and he had nothing to lose. He was already losing his balance and his eyesight along with his claret. "Come and get me."

"I'll go up," Lord Harking said.

"No, Harry! Let him be."

Something in the woman's voice sounded familiar to Ize, but all he saw through a red haze was the top of the head of the dark-haired French seamstress, Harking's mistress, the witch who'd likely had that brat follow him home.

"All right, you win. I am coming down."

He did, slowly, staggering, one hand up in the air, the other over the wound in his chest. When he reached the bottom steps, he lowered his hand, so a knife dropped out of his sleeve. He rushed down the last steps and pushed past Rourke, who was reaching in his pocket for his manacles. Now Rourke had a gash across his hand.

Ize would have slashed out at Harry next, but Queenie threw a broom at his head, then a mop.

Then Harry had his pistol in his hand, where he stood in front of the door. Ize was not leaving that way.

Charlie had picked up the Runner's fallen club and was guarding the hall toward the back door that led to an alley.

Queenie was in the middle, too far to pick up a dustpan or a bucket. Ize snarled at her. "You bitch! You brought them here!" He leaped forward with his last strength, knocking her down, his knife at her throat.

Charlie swung the club at his back. Harry brought the butt of his pistol down on the man's head. He kicked the knife across the hall for Rourke to pick up in his uninjured hand.

Ize did not move, and Queenie was frantically pushing him off her, trying to roll out from under his dead—or nearly so—weight. Harry quickly pulled him up and turned him over. They all saw the sword wound and the blood for the first time.

Rourke took his time wrapping his handkerchief around his hand. Charlie cast up his accounts in a bucket. Queenie stopped sobbing, knelt at the dying dastard's side, and started praying.

Ize looked up, into the bluest eyes this side of heaven, which he was never going to see. He opened his pop eyes as wide as he could, to see those eyes one last time, and their distinctive dark rims.

Blood came out of his mouth, along with his last word. "Queenie?"

CHAPTER TWENTY-FIVE

Rourke finished knotting the cloth around his hand. "What did he say?"

Harry pulled Queenie away. "Nothing."

"Well, he said enough before. We'll track down the rest of your diamonds, real or fake, now. A few might have been cut and sold."

"No matter. I find I no longer care as much. The setting is recovered. Maybe in the future I will finish replacing the stones. Maybe not. Too many people have died over them to give me any pleasure in owning the damned things."

Rourke agreed, setting out to call for the Watch and the constable and more Runners to complete the case. They'd all want to talk to Lord Harking and Madame Lescartes later, take their depositions, decide about disposal of the bodies, etc., but they were free to go now. Seeing how the lady was trembling and as white as the lord's linen neck-cloth, Rourke told them to leave before the crime scene became overrun. He might be able to keep their names from the newspapers for a while that way. A heavy purse changed hands, and gratitude.

Harry led Queenie to the old carriage, where they would have a bit of privacy, not the curricle. Charlie climbed up to ride with Old Jim, although he could have walked as fast as old Millie, who had earned her retirement this day.

Harry did not bother asking; he simply picked Queenie up and placed her on the worn and torn seat, stepped up, and pulled her onto his lap, his arms wrapped around her so she could not be bounced around by the rough passage of the rickety wheels. He stroked her back until the trembling stopped, telling her what a brave girl she had been, and how proud he was of her, and if she ever walked into danger like that again he would beat her with a broom or a bucket himself, or whatever was handy.

Queenie had to smile, cocooned in safety, knowing Harry would never hurt her, and Ize could never hurt her again, ever. She needed a moment to reflect on the changes in her life. Now she was free of Ize's threats, free to go to Lord Carde without fearing for her friends' safety or her own life. Her shop was safe from arson, as were the women who worked there. Ize's death was ugly, and she would pray for his soul, but his life had been ugly, too.

Then Harry said, "Is that the name I should put on the special license, Queenie? What was it, *Queenie Dennis*? The girl they think might be Lady Charlotte Endicott?"

He could feel her stiffen in his arms as she pulled away to sit across from him. She did not look at his face, but rubbed at a spot of blood on her glove. "They say Queenie Dennis was blond-haired, the same as the missing child. Ize saw my blue eyes and got confused. His guilty conscience made him see more than was there. Perhaps he wished forgiveness for his sins." She shrugged. "He was delirious, hallucin— What special license?"

"The one I would purchase as soon as you agree to marry me, when I have a name to give the archbishop's secretary."

"M-marry?"

"That was the question I have been trying to ask you. I don't know how. I suppose I should go down on my knee, but the floor of this carriage is less than appealing. I think Old Jim's last passenger was a chicken grower. I should bring flowers, I know, but I was in such a hurry this morning, and hungry. I am always hungry when I am anxious."

"You are always hungry," Queenie managed to murmur, through her amazement.

He ignored that. "I wanted to give you the Harking diamonds as an engagement present—but if one of the stones is cut, I can have that made up into a ring, so you will still have all the centuries of my name behind it. That is what I want to give you, a new name, one that you can keep forever. My name."

"Lady Harking?" she asked in disbelief. "You are truly asking me to be your viscountess? Not your mistress?"

"That, too, but both. Only both. I would wed a woman who seduces me with her smile and her scent and, yes, her secrets, but this is not about lust, not only passion. I will have a virtuous wife, if it kills me to step back from you. I want you, sweetheart, as the mistress of my heart, mistress of my home. My wife." He liked saying that so much he repeated it. "My wife."

"But you cannot. You will hate the scandal."

"I would hate more living the rest of my life without the only woman who can complete my life."

"You do not know—"

"It does not matter, I tell you."

"You trust me that much?"

"I love you that much." He reached for her hands, bring-ing them to his lips, and whispered, "I know I love you, *chérie*, whoever you are, and I do not want to live without you, no, not for another day. I thought long and hard, and I know this is the only way for me to be happy, and for you, I hope."

Queenie was back across the carriage and in his arms, kissing him with all the love she had felt for so long. But she would not marry him.

"What?" He was out of breath, and out of patience. "You cannot go around kissing gentlemen like that, madam, if you are not prepared to make honest husbands of them. I tell you now, I shall not accept carte blanche, no, not even for the delights of sharing your bed. We share a name or nothing."

"I want to marry you, Harry, more than you will ever know. I dreamed of such a thing, but never thought it was possible. We are from such different worlds."

"We will make our own world. You'll see. I shall spend my life making you happy." He put another inch of distance between them, so he could see her better. "What, are you crying? Deuce take it, that's a fine start, isn't it?" He handed over his handkerchief.

"You have made me happy enough to weep, my dearest Harry, simply by loving me. Your asking me to wed is be-yond my hopes and prayers. But I cannot accept, not until you know my past."

"The devil take the past. I have spent too much time worrying over what went before, trying to atone for my par-ents' sins, my brother-in-law's crimes. It is the future that matters, our future together."

"That is what I have been trying to tell you. I cannot know what the future will bring once I reveal my past."

"That is what I have been trying to tell you, that I do not care. I will love you no matter what. I know who you are now, and what you have done to make yourself into a magnificent success, and a loving, generous, good-hearted woman. That is enough. I trust you, and you trust me, I think."

"But I am not a fit wife for a viscount."

"You are the only wife this viscount wants. I do not want a mistress kept hidden away, nor one whose children I cannot acknowledge as my heirs. I want you, *chérie,* and I have since the day I first saw you. If you are worried that I will become a possessive, demanding sort, stealing your independence, do not be. You will not need the income, but you can keep the shop, if you want. I will buy us a town house in London, take my seat in Parliament, and spend as much time in the city as you need. All I ask is that you come to the country with me first, and as often as you will. You will love Harking Hall, I know. And you can set up a shop in the nearby village. The local ladies will be delighted. And I shall build you a studio so you can draw and design to your heart's content. I would never try to harness your talent or your dreams, only your love. I could not bear to see you in danger, at the mercy of the rakes and reprobates in Town. Where you go, I go."

Which called for more kisses, and a few more tears. Harry had to borrow back his handkerchief. Queenie had to wipe her eyes with her gloves, leaving black streaks on them from her lash darkener. Her throat was too clogged with emotion, but she shook her head no. "I cannot."

"You can!" Harry insisted. "I want to protect you and

give you the protection of my name. The only thing I would
ask you to give up in return is Lescartes's name."

"He never existed."

"Even better. Now I can stop being jealous of him."

"Silly Harry. I have never loved another man."

"I am silly for you. Say yes, sweetheart, and make me
the happiest of men."

"Your asking has made me the happiest of women. I
never thought it possible, to wed where my heart leads. And
I could not marry without that. But, Harry, it is not that
easy. What if I am a criminal?"

"Are you?"

"Not in my eyes. But the law . . ."

"Then you need me more. Our marriage puts the power
of the peerage at your back. And my money in your pocket.
I have acquaintances in high places who will help. Believe
me, the courts are far less eager to take on the wife of a viscount than some questionable French dressmaker with a
shadowy past."

Queenie knew that to be true. "But for your sake, you
need a wife who is acceptable in your circles."

"I need you."

"Yet you speak of taking your seat in Parliament. With
an orphan as a bride? You shall be a laughingstock. That is
right, Harry—I am an orphan, taken from an institution,
with no name, no family. Nothing. There are no baptismal
records of any Queenie Dennis, no school records or com-
munions, nothing to say that she ever existed. And I will
never know who I truly am."

"Darling, people already think you are my mistress, a
foreigner, and in trade. I cannot imagine your being an orphan any harder for them to accept as my wife. And I do not
care if they do. I never was fond of the so-called polite

world, where the manners are mean and swinish. And Camden's sister will stand your friend, so we shall not be entirely shunned if it comes to that, which I doubt. A woman takes her place in society from her husband's standing, not the other way. So we shall not be invited to Almack's? It is not half as entertaining as the Cyprian's Ball. The women are not dressed as well, either, and the refreshments are stale."

"Your family will care."

"What, that I do not attend Almack's? Perhaps my sister can go, once her mourning period is over, and find herself a decent husband. If my sister cares for me at all, she will be delighted I found happiness. And she will love you for that. Meanwhile, I think Olivia can be encouraged to relocate to Sir John Martin's estate, which belongs to her son now. He should be raised there, knowing his lands and people. I know the place is heavily mortgaged. We can use some of the real diamonds to bring it back to self-supporting profitability. I can hire a trustworthy steward, and she can set herself up as the lady of the manor, without the disgrace Martin brought to her at Harking Hall. That way she will not feel that she is taking second place to the new Lady Harking, after running the estate so long."

"I know nothing of being chatelaine to a country estate."

"You learned how to be a designer of dresses. You can learn to manage our house. Besides, there is a competent staff."

"You have thought of everything."

"I have thought of nothing but you."

He tried to prove it with his kisses, his caresses. If his words could not convince her of his love, perhaps his passion could. She returned his kisses; she let her hands go exploring the same as his. His cravat was undone. Her bonnet was tossed to the muck of the carriage floor. Her skirts were raised. So was Harry's standard, at full mast.

But he did have standards. He would not take his bride in a filthy carriage, in the middle of London, without a wedding.

"Say yes, sweetings, before I die," he gasped.

Queenie took a moment to catch her own breath, and raise the bodice of her gown. "I cannot until I speak with Lord Carde."

He dropped his hands, which were lowering that neckline so he could touch the rose-petal velvet of her breasts. "The deuce, you say. The earl is to decide my happiness?"

"He is to decide my fate. Until then I cannot know what I have to give you, a nameless orphan or a wanted criminal. I did commit crimes of omission by not telling what I knew, so I am guilty of deceiving that family, at the very least. But know this, my dearest, that I want to marry you more than I want anything in this world. I think I love you more than my own honor—but not more than yours."

"Tell me, then. Let me decide."

"Not yet. Will you come with me, though? Listen to what I have to say, what they have to say? They deserve the truth after all these years, truth that I have helped keep from them."

"I will never leave your side again."

"Oh, Harry."

So Harry banged on the carriage roof and told Old Jim to take his time returning to the shop.

Old Jim cackled through toothless lips. What, did the jobbernowl think Millie was hurrying?

Harry had to leave her, of course, to make arrangements to have Martin's body shipped to the baronet's own run-down estate. Harry did not want that bastard befouling the Harking crypt, not did he want to attend the ceremony. So he hired a hearse and a mourner to go with it, and said good riddance.

He wrote letters to his sister, made frequent appearances at Bow Street, and made payments to jewelers to buy back his own gems.

He used some of the cut stones to pay off the reward. Part went to Rourke, but another portion belonged to Charlie, who agreed that having a real education paid for was a handsome enough windfall, as long as he did not have to leave Madame Denise. So Harry swore he could go wherever they did, until he decided to attend university.

Harry now had the ring, with one of the Harking diamonds in a new shape and setting. He brought flowers every day. He bribed the archbishop's secretary to issue a totally reprehensible and exorbitantly expensive special license with the bride's name to be inserted later. He was ready.

Queenie was ready, too. She had promoted her head fitter to store manager. She had completed stacks of sketches with her special customers in mind. She had stacks more for the fashion journal, and a much larger stack of coins to hire on new workers, and to take with her. She did not want to close the store, putting so many out of work. Nor did she want to disappoint Lady Jennifer and her plans to help expand it into a training school when Jack Endicott finally opened the Ambeaux Silver academy for needy girls. And Queenie could not forsake her dream, in case Harry changed his mind.

Charlie was going because Harry had promised. Parfait was going because he always went where Queenie went.

Hellen was not going. Her mother had scribbled a note

that she was due back soon, "victory-us." Valerie Pettigrew wanted to meet this John George Browne and his family before she handed over her only daughter and the hard-won dowry. Hellen agreed to stay on at the shop while Queenie was gone, but then she would move home to prepare for her wedding. Then she would move to the school, to help her new husband get ready for his students . . . if Jack Endicott forgave what Hellen perceived as their disloyalty.

Rourke was nearly ready to go, not that he was invited. The two deaths at the rooming house were accepted as a falling-out among thieves. A fencing operation was shut down; jewels were recovered; a commendation went into his file and a tidy sum into his bank account. The Runner's hand was healed enough. His bulldoggedness was not. Whatever this journey to Carde Hall entailed, he was certain it had something to do with the missing heiress and the reward for her return. This was his case; he was going.

A letter was sent to Carde Hall in Cardington. A coach was hired. Bags were packed. Farewells were made to the store customers and Lady Jennifer.

Lady Jennifer Camden was not informed of the reason for the visit out of Town, but she still had advice for her friend. "You do know that traveling alone with Lord Harking without a maid or a chaperone will create difficulties, don't you? You will not be accepted at decent inns, and you will be treated as dirt at the ones that do give you rooms. And think on this: Whatever your mission, you will make a poor impression on Lord Carde and his family. No matter the gentlemen's reputations, they will protect their wives from any so-called contamination by fallen women. Carde's wife is known to be a quiet woman with country values, not a London dasher. Jack's bride is a strict schoolmarmish type. She was a teacher, you know. They will not listen to you as Harking's mistress, if they permit you through the door at all. And they will not readily believe a woman who is considered no better than she has to be. I better go along."

"You would come to Northampshire?"

"London grows tiresome anyway, until the start of the true Season. And perhaps I can get a glimpse of spring in the countryside. But you need not worry about making arrangements for me. I never travel without Ames, my butler."

Queenie never traveled without her dog, but she did not think it was the same.

Neither did Harry's friend Camden. He came along, too, because his sister's majordomo was becoming altogether too major in her life, in his opinion. Also, there were two Endicott brothers at Carde Hall. Harry should have a friend at his side, whatever the situation.

Before they could depart, Hellen's mother returned. If they were going to the earl, she was going, too. Didn't she know Queenie and Molly better than anyone else? If they were handing out reward money, she had information to give, so she informed Madame Lescartes. And Hellen and her John George had to go along, she insisted, lest they be blamed for not speaking up—or getting up to monkey business on their own. Her girl was going to be married, with a ring and all, and nothing was going to stop Mrs. Pettigrew from protecting her baby's reputation.

They were going to be a bloody caravan, Harry swore. He'd been hoping to use the travel time to good effect, showing his betrothed—he would not consider her anything less—how comfortable they could be together, away from the world and its wearisome rules. He was going to make her love him and his lovemaking more, so she would never say no. Hell, he'd been planning on telling the innkeepers they were man and wife. Now the best he could hope for was private rooms. Damned if he would room with Camden. Or Rourke, or Charlie. Or Lady Jennifer's blasted butler.

They would have adjoining rooms, at least, if he had anything to say about it.

CHAPTER TWENTY-SIX

The first night Harry did have a private room, a tiny cubbyhole under the eaves of the mediocre inn where they stayed. The ladies were sharing the two best suites, two floors below.

Camden spent the night in the taproom, or wherever one—or perhaps two, knowing Camden—of the buxom serving wenches slept. Rourke bunked with young Charlie in the stables. Harry should have found another bed, too, not that he was interested in a quick tumble, but for all the rest he got. The thin mattress in his attic room was too hard, too narrow, and too short, so his feet stuck over the bottom, in the cold, because there was no fire there.

Worse, Browne in the next room snored loudly enough to make the thin walls shake. Harry wondered if he should warn Hellen, but thought she might already know, the little hoyden. The sooner those two were married, the better.

For that matter, the sooner he was married to his darling, the better, too, and not just because his accommodations would improve. His temper would improve, and his outlook and his health, for surely he was suffering. No man was meant to be deprived of his senses and his sanity this way. Why, the barmaids did not even appear pretty to him, despite their inviting smiles and revealing blouses. He wanted one woman, and one woman only.

So he tossed and turned, wondering what secret she kept, what power the Earl of Carde could have, and when she would realize that none of it meant a ha'penny's worth of difference to him. He dissected every possibility, every hint he'd had, wondering what he could do to convince the woman who held his heart to give hers into his keeping.

He did not wonder where the butler slept. Some things were simply better left unexamined.

The next day, Harry hired a horse. He rode ahead of the carriages and made his own arrangements at the inn where they had chosen to spend the night, on Lady Jennifer's omniscient butler's recommendation. Money changed hands, a great deal of money. Explaining to the innkeeper and his romantically inclined wife that his friends were coming to help celebrate his betrothal, Harry ordered a festive dinner, flowing wine, and connecting bedrooms for himself and his bride-to-be.

The innkeeper winked, his wife giggled, Harry blushed like a schoolboy, but his plan worked.

The dinner was lavish and well cooked. The wine was excellent, and the mixed company was surprisingly convivial, especially after the third or fourth bottle had been opened.

No one mentioned the betrothal, thank goodness, but the innkeeper kept grinning and refilling glasses, without noticing how reserved the supposed newly affianced woman was. Harry thought his *chérie* looked anxious, her lips pinched, her knuckles white on her fork, which moved the food around on her plate instead of coming to her lips. He

encouraged Camden to tell his amusing anecdotes, and
Browne to describe for Mrs. Pettigrew his plans for the
school. Hellen chatted about her trousseau, and Lady Jennifer discussed her latest charity project.

When Mrs. Pettigrew started yawning, Lady Jennifer
started looking around for her butler, and Hellen started
doing something under the table that made Browne go seven
shades of scarlet, Harry suggested the ladies retire, so they
could get an early start the following morning. Instead of
staying with the gentlemen over port and cigars, Harry excused himself, saying he needed a good night's rest, also.

Instead he escorted the reason for this whole journey to
her room—her private room, next to his.

"Please do not be so worried, my dear. We are all here for
you. I am right next door."

Queenie stood on tiptoe in the corridor outside her room
and kissed his cheek. "You are truly the best friend I could
ever hope for, going to all this trouble for me. I know this
trek is not what you wanted. Indeed, I know that I have not
given you the answers you wanted, yet you are still patient
and still caring. This would be so much easier if I did not
love you so much, knowing I could lose everything."

"Have you not learned yet that I am a hard fellow to lose?
Thickheaded and stubborn, that's me. I am not leaving you."

This time she kissed his lips, in a brief, sweet joining that
tasted of wine. She stepped back and through her opened
door. "I wish . . ."

She did not finish.

"Go to sleep, *chérie*. Nothing shall bother you."

Except him. Even as Harry watched her door close and the
lock click into place, he had every intention of waiting for the
others to go to bed, and then coming back through the connecting door to give more reassurance and encouragement.

He did not intend to try to seduce her—unless she wished it, of course—but he fully intended to prove how compatible they were, how happy they could make each other by making the world wait outside those doors. He was patient and stubborn, but he was willing to take any advantage he could.

In his own spacious, well-appointed room, Harry undressed and washed. He did not own a nightshirt, but debated between a fresh shirt and breeches, and his robe. He chose the robe. Slippers or bare feet? Lud, he was as nervous as a debutante.

He forced himself to read an article in an agricultural magazine to pass the time for the inn to settle. Then he waited another two hours. Well, he waited another twenty minutes, but it felt like two hours.

Damnation, he should have saved the money he spent for the dinner and the private rooms.

He scratched on the connecting door. *"Chérie?"* he whispered.

There was no response, so he whispered a bit louder. Nothing.

So he turned the knob and opened the door, only to find his hopes shattered. His beloved and would-be bedmate was fast asleep in the center of an enormous, billowy, all-too-tempting mattress. The dog, curled at the foot of the bed on a soft blanket, raised his head, then, recognizing Harry, went back to sleep.

Harry stood for a moment, watching her in the glow of the low-burning fire and a lamp left on the nightstand. He breathed in the floral scent of her soap, aching to join her on the bed and knowing he was too much the gentleman, damn it. He was not enough of a gentleman to leave quite yet, though.

She looked so young in her sleep, with her black curls all

tousled and her face free of paint and rouge. Surprisingly, the dashing, sophisticated woman who dressed in silks and satins, in daring, revealing, seductive styles, wore a plain white flannel gown to bed. Harry could not see as much as a scrap of lace or an embroidered rosebud on the virginal night rail, over the bedcovers. The loose gown was buttoned to the chin, with sleeves down to her wrists, so she had never been more covered, or more appealingly innocent. The viscount realized he did not even know precisely how old she was, not that it mattered.

He wanted to shout out his frustration—and not just his body's yearning. There was so much he did not know. But there would be no answers tonight, and no release, either. She needed her sleep, to face whatever ordeal awaited.

Walking back to his own room felt like walking through a field of ice. Damn, he should have worn his slippers. No, the inn was warm. His soul was cold.

Oh, how he wanted to hold her—just hold her. Well, maybe not just. What would he do if she never agreed to marry him? Lud, the thought was too dismal to contemplate, yet he feared it would keep him awake all night, again.

Damn and blast, he was not interested in finding a game of cards in the public room, or a wench or a bottle. So he read another boring article about crop rotation, then got into his bed. At least the mattress was the right size, even if it was cold and lonely and as empty as his arms. Once he found a comfortable position, he would sleep well tonight, Harry thought, knowing she was safe and close.

Safe? She was being murdered in her sleep, judging from the cries that woke him an hour later.

Harry leaped out of bed, grabbed his robe and his pistol, and raced through the connecting door.

The fire still burned, the lamp was still lit, and his

beloved still slept. He looked around, not finding any intruder or threat. The dog had not stirred, making Harry wonder if he was the one having nightmares, but then she cried out again.

"Mama! Help me!"

Harry went closer to the bed, bringing the lamp nearer. Now he could see that her face was knotted in a grimace, bathed in sweat.

"Sweetings," he whispered, not wanting to startle her. "Wake up. You are dreaming."

"No!" she yelled, threatening to wake up the entire inn.

Lud, they'd have twenty people in here next, thinking he was the one attacking her. Realizing he would not make a convincing impression of innocence, Harry fastened the tie of his robe. "Denise, wake up."

She tossed her head, sending tears down her cheeks.

"Queenie?"

Her eyes opened. She looked up at Harry, unafraid of him, thank goodness, but sobbed, "No one came to help me! No one came. I was falling and falling, and then I was all alone and no one came."

"I came, sweetheart," he said, gathering her into his arms while she cried against his nearly bare chest. "I came."

She clung to him, wracked with terror still at the old nightmare, but taking comfort from his strength until she could stop crying and let him go.

Embarrassed, she said, "Oh, I am so sorry I disturbed your rest. But thank you for coming. I shall be all right now."

"I am not leaving." Harry went around lighting every candle he could find, refilling the lamp, adding more coals to the fire, all to chase away the shadows. "Never again will I leave you to be afraid like that."

Queenie blew her nose on a handkerchief beside her bed. "It was just a silly dream I have when I am tired or worried. Perhaps I merely had too much wine at dinner."

"Tell me."

She did not pretend to misunderstand, and for once she thought she might feel better for sharing the oft-relived horror. Maybe it would finally go away if Harry shared the burden on his broad shoulders. She touched the silk of his robe as he sat beside her on the bed. "Oh, I am in a carriage that gets out of control and topples. I understand that falling is a common nightmare. That and being left alone and helpless." She trembled one last time and he pulled her closer.

"But you were a child in the nightmare, calling for your mother. Yet you said you were an orphan."

"Even orphans had mothers, once. I cannot recall mine. Perhaps I lost her in a carriage accident."

"Lady Charlotte was in a coach that fell, with her mother."

Queenie shook her head. "There are many carriage accidents, which is why I am so fearful of them, I suppose. But I am not that woman, Harry, as much as you might wish me to be, for then I might be a proper wife for Viscount Harking."

"But you are Queenie Dennis? The woman they are looking for?"

She was not ready. "Queenie was blond-haired, as the lost child was. But, yes, information about Queenie Dennis is why I am going to Lord Carde, and why you will not wish to be connected to one such as I."

"Dash it, woman, stop telling me what I will wish or not. I love you, whoever you are."

"I am . . . I am Madame Denise Lescartes, a slightly scandalous, partly French dressmaker."

Angry, Harry pulled away. How could she keep putting him off this way, feeding him rubbish and roundaboutation? When the devil was she going to trust him?

He tucked the covers around her and stood to leave. Otherwise he would be too tempted to shake her, or kiss her, reddened nose and all. She would sleep soundly, he thought. He would not, listening.

She raised one hand, palm out. "And I do love you, Harry. Please do not go."

"Do not . . . ?"

"Do not leave me alone tonight."

"Sweetheart, you do not know what you are asking. I do not know if I could stay in this room much longer without climbing under those covers beside you. You infuriate me, yet you fire my blood past bearing, until I doubt my own control."

In answer, she pulled the covers aside, making room.

Harry groaned. She wanted comforting. He wanted . . . everything. "I cannot promise—"

"I am not asking for your promise. Only your love tonight."

To lie with her so she could fall asleep? He made one last attempt to save her from her own innocence. "But I am only a man."

"The only man I have ever wanted. And will ever want."

He was lost. She was lost. How could he refuse? He smiled. "Well, my feet are cold."

She smiled back, with a look that was anything but innocent. "Mine are as warm as toast."

So were her lips when they met his, as warm as melted honey, as warm as nectar in the sun. Harry's lips were burning, along with the rest of him.

"Can you feel my heart?" he asked as her hands stroked

that organ, and traveled lower under his robe. He quickly
stopped her hesitant exploring lest he too quickly explode.
"It is hammering, thundering, pounding for you, the woman
who holds it in her hand." And soon he might be blessed to
feel her hold that other organ in her soft, tender hand, but not
yet. "But are you certain?"

"As certain as my poor muddled brain is about anything.
No matter what happens tomorrow or the next day, I want
tonight. Harry, please."

His fingers had unbuttoned the collar of her gown, and
were now reaching for her breasts, cupping them, fondling
them, stirring the nipples into peaks while he murmured into
her opened mouth. "So beautiful, so soft. So responsive to
my touch."

"So hurry."

"Oh, no, not tonight. I have waited too long to rush." Still
stroking her tender skin, he asked, "Do you not realize that
I have been dreaming of this night since the day I first saw
you? Now I intend to savor every inch, every second."

She was tugging at his robe, so he shrugged out of it,
tossing it to the floor. The dog growled when it hit him.

Queenie laughed, then started to raise the hem of her bed-
gown.

Harry almost choked on the words, but he had to ask one
more time, "Are you certain? There is no taking this back,
no second chance if you have regrets tomorrow. I could wait
until we are married, you know. It might kill me, but I can
wait, as I intended. Well, half intended."

She tucked her hem back down. "We are talking of lovemaking, my lord, not marriage."

"Are we?" Harry smoothed the line between her eyebrows. "You do understand that if you give yourself to me
tonight, you are mine forever? I am no despoiler of maidens.

Uh, you are a maiden, are you not? Not that it matters, of course."

She nodded, and he smiled. "I lied. It matters. I am thrilled to be the first, and the last and the only. But make no mistake: I am not a rake taking his pleasure and leaving without a backward look. I am not leaving!"

"Oh, Harry, do not pull at me now. Let us have tonight and think about the future later."

"But we might make a child. I have to know that my son or daughter will bear my name."

"I would not wish to bring a bastard into the world any more than you would. Yes, if I conceive, I will marry you."

"Then I shall keep you in this bed until we make triplets! But you shall marry me anyway," he said, lifting the nightgown over her head. This time the dog barely grumbled when the soft flannel landed nearby. "Because you will not want to miss what we will share tonight. You will see, I swear, and then you will want me in your bed forever." He grinned, very much the rake he denied being.

Queenie smiled back. "Conceited clunch. Are you so positive I shall enjoy your lovemaking?"

Now he frowned. "Perhaps not the first time, from what I understand, but I shall try my hardest."

She could already feel his hardest against her thigh. "Show me."

And he commenced to do so, worshipping her body with his hands, his tongue, his sighs, and his warm breaths, the entire time murmuring words of love that were almost more arousing than anything else. Almost. Soon Queenie could not differentiate any of the sensations; she was one pool of desire, one liquid fire from her head to her toes and all kinds of new places between.

Harry started at her eyebrows and admired every inch of her as he started his loving journey.

He paused at her ears, delighting in the shivers he felt quiver through her. "Do you mind the light?"

"No, I love to see your face." Queenie could feel the flush spreading from her chest to her cheeks. "And the rest of you. I never realized a man was built so differently, with such firm muscles."

She had not seen firm yet, he thought.

"And your hair, here, so different from mine." She was caressing his bare chest, wondering at his muscles, feeling the cords at his ribs, then discovering that she could make his nipples harden, too.

By then Harry had worked—pleasured—his way past her chin and was feathering kisses and tiny nips of his teeth up and down her neck, before devoting himself entirely to her beautiful breasts.

Queenie was nearly writhing in her rising passion. She knew there was more, and she wanted it, now. She was hot and moist and wanting, needing to be filled with him and his love.

"Harry!"

"Soon, my love. Soon." He was licking at her belly, tickling the sensitive skin around her navel. The anticipation of his southerly journey was making them both gasp and groan in the pain of pleasure.

Blowing warm breaths on her bare skin, Harry let his fingers graze the curls between her thighs. Queenie tried to wrap her legs around his, pulling him closer, but he was not ready. He was ready, all right, but not finished introducing her, and himself, to these first delights.

She cried out, so he had to still her cries with another

long, tongue-tangling kiss, which only made her more impatient. "I thought you wanted to make a baby!"

"Sh, my love. The waiting is the best part. Well, maybe not the best part. But I need to make sure you are ready."

"I am ready, you gudgeon. I have waited all my life for you. Do you think I am not ready now?"

He laughed and went back to worshipping at the altar of her body. He stroked her inner thigh, then a bit higher, and she whimpered.

He lowered himself for a more intimate kiss. First, he had to admire what heaven had blessed him with. So perfect, so soft. So . . . fair?

"Bloody hell, you *are* a blonde!"

CHAPTER TWENTY-SEVEN

"Now." Harry was back on the floor, back in his robe, having dislodged the dog from his nest atop it. He threw Queenie her nightgown. "Tell me now. Do not say I have to wait, either. I am dying for you, woman. Surely you can see that." A blind man could see the evidence under his wrap. "I have earned the right to know the truth."

"But I do not know if I have the truth!"

"Then tell me what you do know."

So she did, because he was Harry and he was right, and because he loved her and would not make love to her until she explained. And because she needed him, and finally trusted him, and his love.

She told him about Molly and Queenie, and not remembering anything before that time except the awful man who was never supposed to be mentioned or he would hurt them all. He was Molly's brother, but he could wreak chaos on all of them, although she never saw him again. He was the bogeyman, the evil one whose name was not to be spoken.

Harry was back on the bed, propped on pillows beside Queenie. He clasped her hand. "You were just a child."

"He made threats. I tried to forget. I suppose I had to forget or I could not have survived the fear."

Harry repeated, "You were a little tot. How could you do anything else? But what about the carriage accident?"

"I do not know if it was real or just what he told me then to frighten me worse. Or else he told me so I would believe I was the lost girl, because he intended to ransom me to Lord Carde, the previous earl, who died so soon after his wife. I simply cannot recall the actual happening, so I never truly believed it occurred."

"You might have been injured. That is common, I understand, for a wounded person to lose all memory of the immediate past. Go on."

"The ransom plan failed, most likely because of the earl's death and Dennis Godfrey's own grievous wound. It seemed Dennis Godfrey and Ize devised a new blackmail scheme before Godfrey's death. I did not know any of that for years, and am guessing at some of it now. Molly claimed a dead soldier as husband, as my father, whose supposed annuity was our support. Why should I have questioned my own mother? Molly never told me anything more. She never wanted me to ask questions about her past or my father, so I did not."

"She kept you isolated and apart—that is what all the reports said—so you had no reason to doubt anything she said, or hear any chance gossip. Why would you keep asking if you never thought anything was amiss? Children adapt. They make the best of things and ignore what they cannot understand."

Queenie nodded. In hindsight, that was what she had done. "Ize said she never took me to the Endicotts, as her

brother had first planned, because they would have immediately known I was an imposter and tossed me out. She loved
me. That is one thing I truly believe."

"Of course she did. No one would part with you." He
kissed the top of her head. "I will not. But they never found
that other girl."

Queenie shrugged. "She was small. Thrown in a ditch,
who knows?"

"They took dogs out, I understand, and dragged the
water. They searched for days and never found a trace. But
go on. How did you find out you were not Molly's own
daughter, if you forgot your earlier past?"

Queenie explained how Ize came calling after Molly
died. He wanted his share of what they had been collecting
all along, for his helping Dennis Godfrey with the crimes
and for keeping Godfrey hidden until he could get away.
"But Molly's brother did not get on his ship, and I wonder
now if Ize killed him. We will never know."

"But Ize threatened you," Harry guessed from her re-
newed shudders.

"And Hellen and Mrs. Pettigrew, because we had stayed
with them. He nearly destroyed Captain Jack's gambling
club, to stop me from making inquiries. Then he told me the
truth about the extortion. They had taken a blond-haired,
blue-eyed child from an orphanage, he said, to fool the earl
into leaving the ransom money—and then to fool Phelan
Sloane to keep paying to hide his own crimes and ease his
guilty conscience. That was better than trying to get the
earl's young heirs to pay for a child they would not recognize. You see, as long as Phelan Sloane paid, they never had
to show a little girl who was not the right one. Any poor orphan that Molly raised was good enough. A lock of hair, a
miniature from an artist at the village fair . . . Sloane was

content to send the money, even if he had to steal it from those he had so badly hurt. That was why I wanted the shop to be such a success, in order to repay someone. I wanted to tell them, the two brothers, but I was afraid what Ize would do."

Now Harry did shake her, albeit gently. "For an intelligent woman, you are an incredible fool, my dear."

Queenie took umbrage and stiffened her spine. "I am not. I made myself into a premier dress designer, a successful businesswoman, and almost your lover."

"We will discuss the *almost* later. But you believed Ize."

"He was there. He knew the truth."

"He told you what he wanted you to believe. He was a liar, a possible murderer. A more dishonest man would be hard to find, except his friend Dennis Godfrey. At best Ize was a dealer in stolen goods, a thorough criminal. Darling, he could have hung if you identified him. That was likely why they never tried to return you to your family, because you knew too much, even if you could not remember it all. Of course he told you a Banbury tale about an orphanage. And of course he threatened you, the dastard. He should be glad he is already dead or I would tear him limb from limb for that alone. But you? You believed anything Ize would say?"

Queenie started weeping again. "I was so alone, so afraid. He said I could hang, too, because I had profited from the crimes."

"But you were a mere child. You led a sheltered life, never knowing anything of the world or its evils. You could not remember the horrors—what infant could? Even now, you do not know if the images are real or simply nightmares. No one could blame you, *chérie*. I swear to that."

She kept crying.

"Hush, sweetings, I did not mean to make you feel guilty. Foolish, yes, but how could you know at the time? You did the best thing, running away from him, the smartest, bravest thing you could do. You were never at fault, not ever, and you must not blame yourself, only the villains."

"I let them keep looking, even after I knew they would not find Lady Charlotte."

"You stayed alive to tell them now. Soon, with me at your side. They will have to untangle all the lies and find the truth, if it is even possible after all these years, and then we will all know. Then you will be free to be whatever, whoever, you want. As long as that person is my wife."

"And you truly do not care?"

"I care that my feet are growing cold again."

Sometime later—the candles had burned out—Harry heard a cough and a discreet scratch at the door.

"Madame Lescartes?"

It was Lady Jennifer's blasted butler, who had set himself to see to the party's comfort, damn his powdered wig. Harry supposed he must have seen the lamplight under the door, or heard the bed frame creaking while he was creeping back from seeing to his twice-mistress's comfort.

"Is everything satisfactory?" the maggoty majordomo whispered.

Queenie tried not to chuckle. "Oh, yes, everything is entirely satisfactory now. Good night."

And it was.

If the Earl of Carde was surprised at the horde of strangers descending on his doorstep, his stoic mien did not express it. Alex was too intrigued by the letter he had received requesting an interview, and the message from his man at Bow Street, Rourke.

He admitted the crowd to his home, quickly moving his spectacled glance over Lady Jennifer, who was too old. Mrs. Pettigrew was definitely too old, and far too common. Miss Hellen Pettigrew was too young, and Madame Denise Lescartes was too dark-haired.

Disappointed, the earl ushered them all into the Gold Parlor, where his wife, brother, and new sister-in-law were all anxiously waiting.

After greetings and introductions, at which Alex's countess apologized for not rising from her position on the couch due to the vast expanse of the unborn infant she was carrying, Lady Jennifer graciously excused herself and her brother.

"I think there are too many people for a frank discussion of whatever the issue might be. Cam and I shall stroll your lovely grounds, with your permission, my lord? I believe my butler has already escorted Madame Lescartes's poodle and her young servant to visit the gazebo we noticed on the drive through the grounds."

Jack Endicott opened the door for them, saying, "A poodle? Just do not let my ward, Harriet, see the dog, or she will want one like it."

Alex bowed, relieved to be spared some of the awkwardness, and invited the others to be seated.

Mrs. Pettigrew found a wide upholstered seat conveniently next to a table with a dish of bonbons. Hellen and John George Browne quickly took their place on a sofa, as close to each other as they could respectably sit, while Mr. Rourke stood by the window instead of placing himself among the company.

Lady Carde, née Eleanor Sloane, cousin to both the

murdered countess and the missing woman, stared intently at Queenie, especially at her eyes, then apologized for her impolite scrutiny. She invited her to take the seat nearest her couch, and Harry stood behind Queenie's chair, his hand firmly, obviously, uncompromisingly on her shoulder.

"Perhaps we should have a more private talk?" the countess suggested.

Queenie cleared her throat to stop the quaver in her voice. "No, these are my friends. Or they are part and parcel of what I have to say."

"Perhaps a glass of wine, then?" Jack Endicott offered, smiling at her. Queenie could see where the former hero had his reputation as a rake and a rogue, but he touched his pretty wife's cheek as he passed to the side table where bottles and glasses were laid out.

"Thank you, that would be lovely."

An even more awkward silence grew as everyone sipped their drinks, waiting. At last Harry squeezed Queenie's shoulder and asked if he should begin.

She raised her chin. "No, it is my story to tell."

"That's my brave girl."

She set her glass aside, took a deep breath, and said, "I am Queenie Dennis."

Mrs. Pettigrew peered at her over the rim of her glass. "Damn me for a fool, so you are!"

"But Queenie Dennis was always described as fair-haired, like our sister," Lord Carde said.

Hellen, her mother, and Harry all chorused, "She is a blonde." Only Harry blushed when he realized what he said and how he knew.

Jack looked at his old friend consideringly. Before he could ask any questions, Queenie untied the small black scrap of lace and ribbons she wore as a head covering. She leaned forward so the others could see the pale roots near her scalp.

She swallowed, because her throat was so dry, but she managed to say, "I am blond. I am Queenie Dennis, and I might be your sister. I do not know. I have no memory of my infancy. I was hoping seeing Carde Hall might bring insight." She shrugged. "Your home is beautiful, my lord, my lady, but it is not familiar to me."

Alex leaned forward. "But?"

"But I have nightmares about a carriage accident and being alone." Now her words came faster, as if she wanted them all out at once, to get this over with. Somehow Ize and Harry's diamonds and France got tangled in her tale. She knew they would have to sort it all out later, but she just wanted to tell them, now. "He told me I was an orphan, and guilty of crimes. I was so afraid, I did not know what to do. I swear I did not know about the extortion or Mr. Sloane's part in it."

She turned to Lady Carde. "I beg your pardon, my lady, for I know he is your brother, and he paid for my life and my home and my education, but I cannot forgive him. I did go visit him at Mr. Browne's family's inn, to see if some recognition existed between us . . ." Again, she shrugged. "There was none. He seems content, and I suppose I am glad for him."

"Thank you," Eleanor said, reaching for her husband's hand. "But you are not sure if you are, indeed, my cousin and Alex's half sister?"

"I do not know the truth. I never wanted to claim a reward, or anything like that. You must believe me that is not why I came. I wanted to repay you for the money and the sorrow if I could."

Now Jack's wife, the former governess Allison Silver,

spoke up. "I remember you from the interview room at The Red and the Black. You wore a veil and a lovely bonnet."

"I came twice, wanting to look at the portraits, wanting to ask questions. But then there was the fire, because of me and my curiosity. I could not cause you and your family more harm, so I ran away, like a coward."

"Not a coward," Harry insisted. "A young woman with no one to turn to."

Alex took off his glasses to wipe them, as if he felt guilty that he had not been there. Jack cursed, because it was his club and his attempt to find the information.

Queenie went on: "I thought I could make a new life with a new name. I would be safe, and I could find a way to earn money to give back to you."

Alex waved his hand at the luxurious room, with its treasures in every nook and hanging on every wall. "We do not need your money, my dear. And none of this was your doing. I would not have taken a farthing of yours."

"You see?" Harry asked. "I told you Ace would be fair. You had nothing to worry about."

Lady Carde leaned forward, or as far as her burgeoning belly would allow. "Nothing except who she is."

"It does not matter to me," Harry insisted.

"But it does to us," Jack's wife declared. She turned to her husband. "You have to ask her the questions. You know, the ones you prepared for all the imposters who came for the reward."

So Jack bowed and asked, "What was your pony's name?"

"I never had a pony. I have never ridden a horse in my life, and never intend to get on one of those large, terrifying animals."

"I suppose that is natural, after the accident," Jack said,

"but Lottie never had one, either. The new pony was waiting for her here, as a gift when she returned from the visit north."

Hellen was squeezing Mr. Browne's hand so hard he gasped. Mrs. Pettigrew kept stuffing bonbons in her mouth.

Jack's next question was Queenie's doll's name.

Queenie laughed. "Why, Dolly, like most other little girls', I think. I do remember how beautiful she was, so regal looking before her clothes fell into tatters and her porcelain face got chipped. I always thought she should have been called Queenie, instead of me."

"But she was. The doll was a gift from the queen herself. You were named Charlotte after her."

Queenie shook her head no. Eleanor, Lady Carde, started weeping.

Jack almost whispered his last question: "What were your brothers' names?"

"Oh, everyone knows you are Alexander and Jonathan, or Ace and Jack." She turned toward Jack's wife. "You even told me, at the gaming club, thinking I was trying for the reward."

Valerie Pettigrew started to ask about the reward, but her new son-in-law-to-be passed her a dish of comfits to shut her up.

Alex asked, "But you do not remember your brothers, for yourself?"

Queenie shook her head sadly, for these handsome men would have been the perfect siblings, ones to make any girl feel proud and protected. "When I heard the question I thought I might have recalled an Andy or Endy from another time. Perhaps the orphanage. And there must have been a score of Johns and Jacks there."

"But I was Viscount Endicott before I succeeded to my

father's dignities. Only Jack and my schoolmates called me
Alex or Ace. Nanny only referred to me as Endicott."

Without thought, Queenie said, "Nanny Molnar was in
the coach."

"Damn, I barely remembered Nanny's last name," Jack
said.

Rourke spoke up for the first time. "The name would
have been in the original crime records."

Everyone except Queenie glared at him.

She admitted, "I did read the old newspaper articles, once
I knew of the connection. I might have seen it there."

"But a poor orphan would not have had a nanny. Or been
in a smashed coach at the same time as our Lottie."

"Or had a pretty doll."

"And no pony."

Now there were more tears, and Eleanor opened her arms
for Queenie to come for an embrace. "My little cousin."

Queenie stayed back. "I am not sure."

"I am," Eleanor insisted, and no one was about to argue
with a woman about to give birth. "Alex, Jack, take her up
to the nursery and see if she recalls anything there to restore
her memory. That would be where little Lottie spent most of
her time, so nothing here could be as familiar."

Only Queenie and the Endicott brothers went upstairs.
And Harry, of course.

They were introduced to a small white dog and a dark-
haired toddler with the earl's commanding nose. Queenie
hoped little Viscount Endicott grew into his aquiline exten-
sion as well as his father had, bearing it with dignity and authority. Jack Endicott would have had the same large feature
except that his nose was crooked, obviously broken, adding
to his raffish appearance. Queenie touched her own small,

straight nose and sighed. Then she looked around. "No, nothing is familiar to me."

Alex shook his head. "My wife gets odd notions. The nursery has been repainted, naturally, and all the fragile girlish toys put in storage, out of harm's way of my rambunctious son."

But not the dollhouse. Queenie looked up to the window shelf and went straight to the closed cabinet with its peaked roof. Without hesitation she turned the latch and opened the door. She reached in and took out a palm-sized dining table. "You broke it, Jack, using it for a fort for your soldiers, but Endy fixed it before I could go crying to Papa."

One of the table legs was amateurishly glued.

Alex had to wipe his glasses again, but Jack said, "Welcome home, Sister."

CHAPTER TWENTY-EIGHT

There were so many tears, so many explanations to the others, so many toasts and hugs and more tears, that Lady Jennifer and Camden came back and had to join the celebration. Charlie and Parfait, who now wore one of Harriet's bonnets, got to sip the champagne, too. An old hound sadly eyed the empty bonbon dish.

Queenie had to make certain that no one blamed Hellen or, worse, Mr. Browne before she could relax. They were both instantly forgiven. Jack declared he would purchase a house near the school for the newlyweds. He and Alex would have bought them a castle; they were so happy. Their vow to their father had been fulfilled, and they had their sister home. They were never going to let her out of their sight again, they both swore, not even to attend her friend's wedding at the Browne family inn if they could help it.

"But what about our wedding?" Harry wanted to know.

"It will be here of course," Nell ordered, "for I cannot travel."

Alex frowned. "Not so fast. No one has asked my permission."

Jack added, "And I am inclined to darken your daylights, Harking, for taking liberties with my little sister."

Alex was holding his son, letting the child play with his fobs. He took his watch out of the boy's mouth before saying, "With respect, Harking, I am not entirely certain you are worthy of Lady Charlotte Endicott. Your prospects have never been altogether prepossessing, and your family reputation less so. Whereas you used to be known as a sober, serious chap, the word from Town and all the on-dit columns is that you have been acting the jackass, to put it simply. Our sister is a considerable heiress, you know. I would have to speak to the solicitors to find the extent of her fortune from her mother, but the sum has been invested and multiplied many times over. Lottie also owns the Ambeaux estate near Hull from her grandparents, which I have seen brought back to profitability. And then there is the reward money."

Rourke had another glass of wine, knowing he would not be able to afford such an expensive vintage again, for he had done nothing to restore the missing heiress.

Hellen and Browne were too exalted over their promised home to care about the money, and Mrs. Pettigrew conceded she had no chance at it.

"Unless you think you are entitled to the money, Harking?"

"Of course not. Queenie, Madame Lescartes, brought herself home."

Queenie was appalled. "You think I would accept money from you, after all I said? Give it to the new school, or an orphanage if you must, where the children need every groat. I will have none of it."

The brothers exchanged a silent, satisfied communication.

Not only was their little sister beautiful and bright, but she was good-hearted and full of pride, a true Endicott. Then Alex excused himself, passing his son to the boy's uncle, Jack.

Lady Carde described the property at Hull while they waited, while Harry and Jack glared at each other over the toddler's head.

The earl returned shortly bearing a small chest. He opened it and tipped the contents into Queenie's lap. Rings, necklaces, broaches, pearls, diamonds, and rubies sparkled against her black skirts.

"These were your mother's, Lizbeth's. My Nell received all of the entailed pieces, of course, and Jack's bride chose what she wanted from our mother's personal collection. So this is part of your fortune, too. When you are presented at court, you will have every eligible gentleman in Town at your feet, and not merely for your wealth and family connection, but for your beauty, also. So there is no need to rush into any hasty alliance. Furthermore, we just found you. I could not bear to lose you so soon."

"Oh, Alex," the earl's fond wife chided, "stop being so stuffy. Anyone can see they are in love."

Alex raised his eyebrows in question to Queenie. Jack made a rude noise.

Queenie was overwhelmed and overwrought from the events of the day, to say nothing of exhausted from the previous night. She looked from one brother to the other, the earl, who was so assured, confident of his authority and power, and Jack, so dashing and brave. Then she looked at their wives, beautiful although bloated Cousin Eleanor, and charming Allison, the former schoolteacher, who had made her feel less of an interloper among the aristocrats. She stared around the room, seeing a family, a loving home filled with children and dogs. They were her kin, after all these years. Her heart swelled with a sense of belonging that she had never known. They wanted to give her riches and houses and the protection of their illustrious name, a place in society, advantages she had never imagined. They truly wanted her.

But she was not the child needing rescuing, nor the shy, uncertain young female needing guidance. She was an independent woman with a mind of her own. She twisted the ribbons on her gown while they all waited; then she sat up straighter and spoke in firm tones, so they would understand. "I am sorry, my lord, that is, Brother Alex, Brother Jack, my ladies, but I cannot let anyone decide my fate for me. Never again. I am overcome at your generosity and good intentions on my behalf, but I do not need jewels or country estates or vast bank accounts. And I think I would die of fright to be presented at court. You see, I, and only I, can decide what I want."

"Which is?"

She turned to look behind her at Harry, standing so stiffly, so stoically, at her back. His dear face was tinged with color as everyone stared at him, but he stepped to the front of her chair and, ignoring the entire avid audience, dropped to his knees.

"My dear, your brother is correct. I am not worthy of Lady Charlotte Endicott. I have no fortune or vast property, no standing in polite society, and a somewhat tarnished reputation." He reached into his pocket and took out a diamond ring. "And this is the only jewel I can offer you, along with all my love, forever and ever."

"You loved me and trusted me before anyone."

"Without question, but with all my heart."

She held her hand out, for him to place the ring on her

finger. "And I love you, Harry Harkness. Without question. And I shall try to be the perfect wife for you. If I do not know how to be perfect, I shall be the best I can be, with all my heart."

Alex wanted them to wait three weeks for the wedding, to call the banns properly, to quiet the inevitable gossip. Eleanor wanted to wait for after her baby's birth, so she could invite the entire countryside and half of London to the combined nuptials and reunion. Jack thought they should wait a year, to be certain of their commitment. Harry wished to use his special license the next morning, or the carriage that evening, to flee to Gretna Green. Everyone ignored him.

Queenie decided on two weeks. It was her wedding, after all, and she was not going to let anyone tell her how to go on, or else she would be merely the little sister, the awkward bride, the willow bending to a husband's will. Besides, she needed the time to sew the perfect wedding gown.

"Blue like your eyes?" Harry asked. "Or pink as your lips? Creamy as your skin? Anything but black will do, I suppose, but I much prefer you this way."

"This way" was dressed in his embrace and little else.

They had been given rooms at opposite ends of Carde Hall, thanks to reformed rakes and protective brothers, but they had found the gazebo and a grotto, shaded, secluded paths, and even an empty cottage on the grounds, so all was not lost for the two weeks. In fact, much was found, now that all of the doubts were laid to rest.

All but one.

"I do not know how to address you, my love," Harry complained. "Your old friends call you Queenie. Your new family insists on 'Lottie,' while the strangers who have been parading through the drawing room use 'Lady Charlotte.'

Charlie refuses to refer to you as anything but 'Madame Denise.' And your bacon-brained brother Jack swears he will run me through with his sword if I say *'chérie'* one more time. He says it is disrespectful and beneath your dignity."

Since Queenie was beneath him at the time, she could only laugh at his concern.

"Truly, sweetings, what name do you prefer?"

"Why, *Lady Harking,* of course."

And so she became, and swore before her family and friends and heaven itself to be until her last breath.

But to Harry she would always be a combination of the sophisticated Madame Lescartes, the spirited *chérie* who had given herself to him in love, the Lottie who could finally laugh, and the true lady she was now. Most of all, though, and forever after, she was Queenie, the queen of his heart.

BARBARA METZGER

Ace of Hearts

Book One of the House of Cards Trilogy

Never did Alexander "Ace" Endicott,
the Earl of Carde, imagine himself to be
thrice-betrothed against his will by the
doings of three desperate debutantes.
So he escapes London for his property in
the country, where he follows through
with his father's last wish—to find his
long-lost step-sister.

But the search takes a detour, leading him
to Nell, and forcing him to wonder if two
mismatched lovers can make a royal pair.

0-451-21626-1

Available wherever books are sold or at
penguin.com

S028/Metzger

From Award-winning Author

BARBARA METZGER

Jack of Clubs

Book Two of the House of Cards Trilogy

Years ago, Captain Jack Endicott's
half-sister vanished after a carriage
accident. He now sets out to honor his
father's dying wish and find her.
Jack plans to open a lavish gaming parlor
and hire only beautiful ladies to deal cards,
possibly finding his sister. All he needs
is a little luck.

Instead he finds prim schoolteacher
Allie Silver, who needs a guardian for one
of her most precocious pupils. With such
an unlikely duo, all bets are off in
a wild game of romance.

0-451-21805-1

Available wherever books are sold or at
penguin.com